Early Stories

Other Books by Alexander Theroux

FICTION

Three Wogs
Darconville's Cat
An Adultery
Laura Warholic; or, The Sexual Intellectual

FABLES

The Schinocephalic Waif
The Great Wheadle Tragedy
Master Snickup's Cloak

POETRY

The Lollipop Trollops and Other Poems
Collected Poems

NONFICTION

The Primary Colors
The Secondary Colors
The Enigma of Al Capp
The Strange Case of Edward Gorey
Estonia: A Ramble Through the Periphery
The Grammar of Rock: Art and Artlessness in 20th Century Pop Lyrics
Einstein's Beets: An Examination of Food Phobias

Alexander Theroux

§

Early Stories

TOUGH POETS PRESS
ARLINGTON, MASSACHUSETTS

Some of these stories have previously
appeared, in modified form, in the
*New York Times, The Boston Globe Magazine,
Esquire, London Magazine,* and *Antæus.*

Cover photo by Donald Stuart.

ISBN 978-0-578-91844-0

Tough Poets Press
Arlington, Massachusetts 02476
U.S.A.

www.toughpoets.com

For
Sarah
"Non sine sole iris"
and our
beautiful children
Shenandoah, and Shiloh
with
all my love

Thus far, with rough and all-unable pen,
our bending author hath pursued the story . . .
Shakespeare, *Henry V*

Contents

A Woman with Sauce 9

Fark Pooks 27

An English Railroad 45

The American Tourist Home 83

Summer Bellerophon; or,

    The Agonies of James Querpox 99

A Wordstress in Williamsburg 151

Scugnizzo's Pasta Co. 169

The Copernicus Affair 189

Watergraphs 213

Blackrobe 229

Genius 257

Chosen Locksley Swims the Tiber 303

A Woman with Sauce

Mrs. Capitalupo might have been my mother-in-law. It was a fate I was spared, as to how touches directly upon the discovery I made of a certain secret of hers which in the course of things nevertheless lost me the fair maiden I rightly should have won. Discovery, secret, fair maiden: I realize these are the phrases of fairy tale, but fairy tales also have to do with ogres, haven't they?

And she lived with her husband, a fish-cutter, and one daughter—a son had moved away to California years ago—in one of those congested working-class cities on the outskirts of greater Boston where in the steam heat of summer neighbors shouted, children raced noisy tricycles here and about, and Italian music blared from various windows. I remember thinking upon my first visit, perhaps because of all that, how favored I was in having at last prevailed upon Angela to allow me the chance to meet her parents. Her inexplicable reluctance to do so had, for some time, frankly become inconsistent with the deeper feelings and larger but as yet unspoken intentions we had begun to hold for each other.

She was blonde and vulnerable—only nineteen—and

always wore three black rings, which habitually she twisted, looking up at any question of mine, any comment, with a gentle but
wistful smile that more often than not substituted for rather than
accompanied the few words, despite my encouragement to the
contrary, she ever spoke. Her mountain-blue eyes seemed always
to look upon submerged dreams. She had fears I could never
quite figure out. She reminded me of a lost child.

I first met Angela in Kenmore Square where nearby,
going through a bit of a bad patch myself—loneliness—I was on a
year visa doing post-graduate work at Boston University. She was
walking desolately along a sidewalk. A dog had just snapped at
her. This gave us conversation of a sort—my talk, her sad smiles.
She kindly agreed to have a cup of coffee with me. And I continued to see her. We needed each other, I suppose, but how many
afternoons, walking down quiet streets, under the tall slumbering trees, along the length of sycamore-shaded waters of the
Charles, had she to be prodded to speak of herself? I attributed
this, until I knew better, less to my being English than to the
fifteen-year age difference between us, a fact that, while I was
aware of it, never unsettled me really until that moment we
found ourselves walking up a back way to the second floor flat of
her house where awkwardly—but finally—I was introduced to her
parents.

There are certain images we are never able to suppress. I
shall never forget the first glimpse I had of her mother, a woman
in big pig-pink hair-papers and an old drabbet-like housecoat
caught unawares but suddenly hunching up and inward in
defensive embarrassment—a "Little Me" pose impossible for her
fatness—at the exact moment she was gulping down a gigantic
forkful of spaghetti. A potful of it sat on the stove from which I

was helped out a bowl the size of my surprise but impossible to finish. Sharing it, I imagine, made me an accomplice, for Angela's mother with what seemed a scratch of annoyance kept urging me on, in vain, with short forward jerks of her chin. "Don't he like it?" asked Mrs. Capitalupo of Angela—never directly addressing me would become a pattern there—and looking slightly wounded.

"It's delicious."

"He likes it?"

"Very much," I said. "And the sauce is lovely."

"It's my own," she said to Angela, "it probably needs salt." It didn't.

"Do you add something extra for flavor?" I asked. She answered nothing. I repeated my question. "Special ingredients?"

"I don't know." She shrugged, looking off at a faraway wall, saying, "A little of this, a little of that."

§

Whenever I visited Angela, as I did over the next few months, she and I sat talking in her bedroom where we were more or less confined; her mother had commandeered the rest of the flat for herself, maintaining strict cubicular boundaries and keeping the furniture of the living and dining rooms shrouded in ghostly sheets all year round for the visitors, who were non-existent, and guests—I never qualified—who might want to enjoy the brothel-red drapes, the hiccuping cuckoo clock, and that tasteful ceramic figurine of two cross-eyed Roman boys holding up a gilt lamp-with-fringed-shade, and there was literally hell to pay if anyone dared trench upon the closed sanctity of those fusty rooms, which twice, unwittingly, I did only to meet with the subtle if indirect reproval the second time that all that week she'd been finding dog hairs on the sofa.

These rooms were hers—they described her—in fact she used them infrequently herself, except when in one of her moods she characteristically moped in and huffily plumped herself down in an overstuffed chair, eating big dishes of peach ice cream and listening lugubriously to the old 78 rpm records she loved of out-of-date 1950s crooners with fruity voices and names like Al Martino and Don Cornell and, I don't know, Tony Cadenza, that sort of thing.

It was not long before I came to see Mrs. Capitalupo for what she was, a cross between Lucrezia Borgia and a case of smallpox. She never acknowledged me again whenever I appeared. She insisted that, while her husband asked me to call him Frank, I call her Mrs. Capitalupo, her name of course but a title by possession she felt in the mastery better served. And while she boasted to know everything, she was in point of fact an irreconcilable illiterate who would have had difficulty reading anything other than the movie magazines and gruesome tabloids with full-page headlines she devoured. She once pointedly told Angela in my presence never to trust anyone not in the family. She said the opposite another time. She talked more absolute rot than I have ever heard in my life. I always wondered if she herself ever believed what she said. Her mouth was huge. Every time I saw it I thought of an invasion barge or the gulping maw of a whale fish, wide and flat, filter-feeding anything in sight.

There was a large photograph of herself that she kept hanging in the hallway, one of those darling malcolored 1940s facial arrangements with the subject finger-to-cheek. I wished for darts.

During my visits Frank was either at work or on the front porch watching television. He seemed always to have an air of disgruntled amusement about him as though he were enjoying a sad private joke of some sort, the understanding perhaps, impossible to divulge, of having caught the irony of exactly what marriage was and yet still stayed with it. His wife always avoided me. She stayed either in the kitchen noisily renewing friendship with her pots and pans or kept to her bedroom from the confines of which, usually around noon, often came a fake broken-wing lameness of voice calling "Angela, what time is it?" or "Get me a aspirin" or "Oh, you're still here"—meaning, of course, guess who? It became her habit, I soon found out, a matter of pride after our initial encounter, to have to wait for me to leave in order to eat, which she did constantly, stowing away double orders and smacking her lips for more. She ate the mutton, as they say in London, and dreamt of the wool. I fought an image of her, upon my every departure, falling desperately upon a vast tableful of puddings and pies. I became, even if temporarily, her calorie counter.

Mrs. Capitalupo was fat. It was proof of her selfishness, however, not her hunger. There was such a moon-desperate fullness to her face recessing her eyes that her nose and mouth looked like accidental inequalities on a large swarthy sphere. She hadn't the trace of a waist—the effect was that of an enormous beetle—and had been on a diet for virtually ten or fifteen years, which she ever sought to broadcast after dispatching countless plates of pasta by ostentatiously sipping diet-free drinks. She suffered from heartburn—*agita*, as she called it—using the word as a medical explanation for her personal excess. She farted a lot. She wore ankle nylons and powdered her feet. She had years ago tried several jobs she had failed at, selling cosmetics, office-filing, and the like, but was now bored utterly and spent her days when not shopping in that cheerless, unlit box-set of a kitchen flipping through things like linoleum catalogs and complaining about her arthritis and making interminable food lists.

"Let's see," she'd say holding a pencil and dropping her head with a breath like a groan, "we need, what, bread, potatoes, pie crust, gravy mix, lunch meat, Cheez-Its, bacon, um, oregano, a bag of apples. You like them macaroons"—no one had said a word—"and I want a cream pie." Mrs. Capitalupo was what might be described as a giddy shopper and in the process, spending a lot of money trying to cheer herself up, became the ultimate consumer. She bought diet candy, exotic soaps, charcoal water taps, Froot Loops, electric brooms, cheese wheels, bun-warmers, fish sticks, striped toothpastes, Mary Kaye hand lotion, cod balls, turkeys-with-thermometers, and bottles of Sal Hepatica which she kept with a spoon on her bedstand to feed the pyromaniacal double who arose howling every night to be quenched. She loved kitchen gadgets and had the glutton's interest in buying *culinaire:* wafflers, egg-separators, and flan pans, each of which she would use often only once in hysterical bouts of cooking, meals she ate which somehow gave no pleasure but only left her body as an almost autoimmune system that didn't recognize itself. And yet of itself it was distinctly aware. The sole source of her busyness was her own well-being, her serenity only as recent as her last meal, her satisfaction only as relevant as the next.

She frankly wasn't old—about fifty-five or fifty-six—but she acted it, humping around with the face of hypochondria in bushy slippers and dusted feet and making everyone get up and out of the way as inspiredly she acted upon one of those rare but inexplicable fits of energy during which, maniacally, she began vacuuming or pot-walloping dishes or straying about the flat trying to sophisticate the furniture. She bulled about and threw things and grizzled. She was always angry when she was hungry, and she was hungry all the time.

Inconsistent, intemperate, and ill-tempered, she browbeat her husband with questions, the worst form of nagging. Frank of course found his life with her a continuous struggle. His marriage took the form of regret; he never thought of one without the other. Tired, afflicted, and disturbed, he simply opted out. He ate alone, kept to himself, and because he had to get up at five a.m. for work slept alone, which in his mind became a blessing to be filed under the Law of Unintended Consequences. The two of them fought all the time. They would argue about nothing, just to keep their hand in. I would drive over to the house and, knowing better than to inquire, in fact not needing to—Angela only shook her head sadly—instantly smell trouble by the sulfurous silence that prevailed in those rooms. But silence was the exception. Mrs. Capitalupo saw to that, who, whining and shouting, was a fly who always had an appointment in somebody's ointment. Noise was the country of which she was sole ambassador, except of course when she was having one of her black dogs—cloudy, malignant depressions—which were real sulks, and then it was either off to the bedroom or behind a door banged shut upon the Regal Privy from which always came the sound of a loud furious flush. She spent more time in the biffy than the float-ball.

Angela was virtually a prisoner there. It broke my heart.

It was bad for her. And it had a bad effect on our—I was going to write relationship. What I suppose we had between us was an alliance, against a common enemy. This became the source of unspoken unity in a way. But whenever I pleaded with her to assert herself, she froze, quietly weeping at the hopelessness of the situation and oddly placing me in the position of bully myself. She was so kind and lovely and desperate to be happy. Happy people laugh a lot, so she would laugh whenever she could—and often when she should not. She deserved so much more than she was given. I could often see complaint building in her soft, blue eyes, however, as time passed. She seemed always arranged in an attitude of contrition. Her diffidence often literally immobilized her. She once told me her mother always made her feel bad about herself. She had hated school and had no education, no job, and almost no money, the combination of which gave her mother further leverage in making Angela her slave, a dogsbody to wash up after dinner, someone to follow about everywhere, bleating disapproval. Anything her mother disliked or disapproved of she met with a great bulge-headed, belly-bumping refusal, which was reinforced by a spate of lies and anti-logic and contradiction.

I came to see that Angela had a terrible separation anxiety—a dreadful fear of a life independent of this woman who for so long had forced her into a state of woeful dependence by robbing her of any chance for a life of her own which the poor child nevertheless chose to interpret as a condition of her parents' incapacities requiring of her the role of self-appointed agent to keep the family together. It was a tragic error. She couldn't have been more wrong.

The only good word Mrs. Capitalupo ever had was for this one son of hers who had gone away and about whom, citing his absolute genius in playing the accordion when he was a boy, she talked incessantly. "When he done 'Lady of Spain,'" she constantly repeated, "they come up to hear from the downstairs *apaament.*" This was pure revisionism, of course; she had sorely bullied him—which is why he had left—as she bullied everyone, especially Angela, pushing and pulling and ordering her about like the big malicious dyke she so perfectly resembled. A bully because she was a coward, she kept her daughter in servitude and her husband in thrall as a way of serving notice to the fears of loneliness she herself faced for all she was. She robbed her husband of whatever position he took, that is whenever he took one. Once he had complained of a hospital fee attendant upon his wife's curiously still unverifiable case of arthritis and was immediately met with a firestorm of remonstrance. "They ain't failures, Frank! Them doctors earn more than you," she howled, "they should know more. Look at them hands of yours! Cracked! Red! Fishpoisons! But you know *eeevything,* right? Right?" She slammed shut her ironing board. "Boning out cod!"

And she robbed Angela of confidence, as well. She diminished her. One Mother's Day, for instance, Angela had boxed and wrapped a vase as a gift which early that morning she set out on the table; that evening she found it back in her room, refused— she hadn't spent enough money. Gratitude there was expensive. And it was the same with the gold locket Angela had given her for her birthday when her mother picked it up, revolved it in her chubby fingers, paused, and then squawked, "It don't open though?" It did not open, and Angela was crushed. She grew sadly silent, which seemed saucy to her mother who, accusing her of ingratitude, stood up and marched into the bog, flushing the toilet, and then went vanishing—*svanirando!*—into that cloister of spite and refusal she called her bedroom to slam the door and stay for days. No one is more stubborn than a stupid person. What I put up with from her mother, nevertheless, curiously told me how much I cared for in Angela. And yet, ironically, I seemed to countenance what I had to ignore. In matters of love it is easier to stifle a feeling than to lose a habit. I wanted Angela for all I felt she needed of me in the society of ghosts that haunted her. But as the poor thing had no defenses against her mother, I knew she would never be mine. There seemed sadly a mutual acceptance of it. We had nothing in common except love. It was hopeless.

§

It wouldn't be quite the truth, now, to say that Mrs. Capitalupo had no weak spots—or, better, no weak spots that weren't soft. She had one. It had to do with her spaghetti sauce. Compliments on that subject alone softened her, her face upon any word of flattery or approbation on that score congealing upon the instant into an expression of the most fatuous piety. She constantly protested it wasn't tasty enough, or rich enough, or zesty enough, expecting only to hear—and repeatedly—it was. And she grew smugger with each apology. Oddly enough, she could not cook very well, but she made a real dog-and-pony show with her sauce, which came in a variety of ways, Bolognese, Amatriciana, Salsa Smeraldo. She always made her sauce from scratch and had seen the practice of that ideal die out, with malicious glee, I might add, for it gave her one distinction. Now, if it is generally accepted that professional chefs are generous with recipes, it is also commonly understood that housewives are famously not—not at all. In this particular case, however, it became comic. I particularly remember one intricate *salsa alla funghi* that Mrs. Capitalupo served—I saw the mushrooms—and recall offhandedly asking her how she made it, several times. It was extraordinary. She spoke vaguely, never mentioning ingredients, of pinches and dashes. That was it. But pinches and dashes of exactly what?

"Basil?"

She said nothing.

"A bit of rosemary?"

She folded her hands and gave me a kind of in-the-pocket smile. Frank grabbed the newspaper and left for the porch.

"I taste a spice of some kind." I lilted my voice playfully. "Pesto? Ground something?"

Her face pulled. I should have let the matter drop, but I felt game. It was harmless.

"Wine? Garlic? Pignoli nuts?"

Try as she might, Angela could not repress a smile. On the instant however Mrs. Capitalupo looked immediately vexed and glared at her from across the room as a blush swept up her daughter's face; she lowered her eyes. There was a long pause. I couldn't believe it!

I realized for the first time Mrs. Capitalupo took herself to be in possession of a deep dark secret, a bit of huggery-muggery all her own and remedially concealed from anyone who by finding it out could only compete with her. She didn't want me to marry Angela, that was hardly a secret. But no one was going to get the leg up on her with this secret ingredient. I honestly couldn't decide whether it was disgusting or comical the way she sat back at the end of each such meal over the next few weeks, a huge mustachioed godforgone shaking out her housecoat and nailing me with a kind of fat-witted satisfaction that tacitly told me that, although I ate her sauce, I would learn absolutely nothing about it. Serving her sauce was actually her way of keeping it from you. And what seemed to be generosity was in fact only parsimony, a kind of avarice. It was an indictment, the offering that blames, the kindness that accuses. That was when our relationship, Mrs. Capitalupo's and mine, really began. Whereas at first I had resolved to avoid rather than taunt her stupidity, I decided now I would either learn her secret or burst. It became a contest.

§

I prodded Angela, of course, who had surely been told this secret. But she was one of those high-principled and literal people in whom guilt not to say loyalty held irrational sway—with no courage she was petrified of her mother's wrath—and she wouldn't betray a trust, no matter how foolish or trivial. There were of course cookbooks. Over the weeks I farmed through more than a few at the BU library and fumbled up the stock preparations and combinations available to anyone who can read, choices of cheese, minces and measurements, and was almost able to taste the recipes I read—but always, always without the full and final satisfaction of knowing with certainty the one special ingredient, passed to her mother from her mother whose own mother used it a century ago in the little town of Avelino, which Angela, twisting her rings, eventually dared suggest was missing from the poor lists I had begun repeatedly, and tediously, reviewing on our long walks and after the movies and over the telephone.

Meanwhile, Mrs. Capitalupo had grown suspicious. Not that I gave a toss. My simplest inquiries about anything became the occasion of her mistrust, and whenever I was around she put the monkey up. She began listening for footsteps. She pulled tricks even. For example, expressing a need to go shopping, she once for no particular reason mentioned that she needed some ribbon, a chafing dish, and—much too loudly—Gorgonzola cheese; I looked up alert, only to see her peering around the corner at me like a great buttered seal. And several times she left out the sugar bullet specifically to tease me, I'm certain of it. But, really, that was a hint? The little touch of *agro dolce?* My reading hadn't been in vain. No, Mrs. Potato Head, nothing new there, sorry. Neither was the cheese. Nor the cold *rifatto* I saw her slicing up that one time I inadvertently blundered into the kitchen when violently she sprang up like Minerva holding forth her bread-board like a shield in front of her, her lips unable to close as if that putty-ball nose, white in surprise, were pulling the top one open and suppressing the command her terrible humid eyes nevertheless wordlessly burnt into Angela: *get him out!*

I thought once that I came close. About that time, I had to pick her up shopping one night but could not manage to find her in that local mall to which habitually, operatically, she set out, all perfumed and rouged, with her big handbag for hours of recreational shopping. She looked even homelier dressed up: the monkey in the tuxedo. Mrs. Capitalupo, as I say, liked at times to go out. She bowled sometimes. She adored "functions." But recreational shopping for her was tops. Anyway, the next half-hour or so Angela and I traipsed through all the supermarkets she favored and which in American, rich coincidence, all have names like movie monsters—Caldor, Osco, Zayre, Super Giant, Foodmaster, etc.—and just after we split up to make it easier I found her. I followed Mrs. Capitalupo at a suitable distance like a comic stage detective and went scuttling into pet food, past sundries (whatever they are), and around a corner. I could see her price-comparising jars of olive oil, shaking bags of crisps, rolling pears around in her testing paws like a hungry agouti a Brazil nut.

And then she spotted me: it happened in aisle three where she was swiftly redepositing on the shelf several cans of tomato paste and pointlessly disclaiming ownership out of sheer perversity the filled pushcart by her elbow that I quickly, madly, studied and from which mock-innocently I lifted up to examine some ribbon, a knob of Gorgonzola, and a chafing dish. "Them ain't mine," she said, her eyes narrowing like flints, her high voice nasal and having something in it like the quality of string on a tightly tied package when plucked, "them are someone's else's"—and, shaking her head, she went wabbling away down the aisle. That was the extent of it. And so what finally did I discover? Nothing. The ashes of emptiness. *Jamais de la vie.*

§

Well, that's not strictly true. Over the next fortnight I made some headway on my list first by concentrating on what I had and breaking the preparation down now to fats and then to vegetables, which gave me a profitable return in what I sought of moistenings and flavorings, and then by using a sort of backdoor approach, absence being a kind of presence, I began logically to deduce what was missing by what at her table, in her cabinets, and on her counter I realized I never saw—which gave me carrots and shallots and garlic and the chicken fat I had like a dimwit overlooked. The button mushrooms I easily wangled one night out of Angela who had a particular laugh that always meant yes.

And only a dunce couldn't discern the taste of a bouquet garni. A formula thus emerged. I thought the addition, never mind the taste, of tomato paste slightly shabby and unprofessional, but the final tally looked formidable:

> 1 lb. beef
> 1 large onion (shallots?)
> stick celery
> bay leaves
> 8 fl. oz. (1 cup) milk
> 8 fl. oz. (1 cup) red Chianti
> 1½ oz. tomato paste
> 3 oz. butter
> 1 or 2 carrots
> ¼ lb. button mushrooms
> 8 fl. oz. water or clear soup
> 1 tbsp. basil
> ¼ cup chicken fat
> 2 cans tomato sauce
> bouquet garni to taste
> a bit of flour
> a bit of sugar

Something yet was missing. I knew it, I knew it, I incontrovertibly knew it as much from inner conviction as from the sweetness of Angela's wistful face and those soft eyes as blue as indigo when she would glance, furtively, quickly, at my gat-toothed column of ingredients with a silent lack of encouragement. But she wouldn't betray her mother. I both pitied her and loved her for it: of what it pointed to in the future I had stopped thinking. It was something I knew I could do nothing about, and I was discouraged enough. I was not looking for a "tried and true" recipe, remember, not simply a sufficient *sugo* to accompany spaghetti. I was seeking the secret to it! But after a while blunting my talents on invisible difficulties and shaping them around mysteries that never yielded lost its novelty. Nothing would answer. It was a washout. I gave up.

§

The Christmas holidays came and went, with the Capitalupos eating meals of such five-square proportions—great lashings of pasta, popovers, bowls of tortellini, pizzelli, and whatnot—that when it was over there wasn't a sardine left to lie down on a canapé, and so depressed, so disgusted at everything and everyone around her, was Mrs. Capitalupo for putting on weight that she dropped the housework, filed into her bedroom, and petulantly refused to come out. A strange peacefulness prevailed in consequence. And the woman snored away the days. She rolled over this way one week, on another that. Her sudden reappearance, sometimes as late as February, always resembled the dehibernation of a scowling a scowling grizzly, ravenous, and blinking cantankerously through a riddle of daylight. My visits became less and less frequent, and yet one late winter afternoon my stopping by to see Angela—we were having coffee in the kitchen—happened to coincide with the famous moment next to which, I swear, the raising of Lazarus was an egg over easy. The bed-castors groaned! The floor thumped! There was the sound of shuffling slippers!

I looked up astonished to see a great pop-faced olio, bigger than Boston, squinting and staggering forward in that moth-eaten housecoat one step at a time and looking more melancholy than a woodpecker in a petrified forest!

Mrs. Capitalupo was bloated and had even lost the uniform sense of a head. She grew immediately cross, throwing dishes and hurling insults, and lit into Angela who sat there trying weakly to smile at me but utterly humiliated and cowering under the torrent of abuse which so overwhelmed me in its sudden brutality that I was not prepared for what followed. I gasped. I gasped, I tell you, unbelieving as Mrs. Capitalupo lumbered toward the refrigerator, yanked it open, and took out a Tupperware bowl of spaghetti sauce. I was listening within me to the whisper of a revelation, one not yet formed, as I watched her crowd forward into the table with eyes small and piglike and begin spooning up the stuff with such ravenous lack of appeasement that the snuffling plosives it sent through her nose made it sound, I promise, like she was beginning to inflate. The whisper within me grew loud, louder.

And then the penny dropped.

I realized that I had looked everywhere but right in front of me. Noting merely details I had missed the whole—do we gain in repose what we've lost in intensity?—for I suddenly saw what for so long I hadn't accepted, the understanding that a certain length of time is as necessary to discover a truth as it is for a portraitist to capture his subject. And instantly I knew I had my sauce when I saw I had my subject. It was simplicity itself. I had found the secret ingredient.

But I had lost something else, and I knew it, for over that same length of time came another understanding, that while we feel in one world we undeniably think and name in another and between the two set up dreams that in the division can only dim, a sad truth to have to admit. It was even sadder to realize as I watched that poor girl shrinking into herself, growing smaller and smaller, that what was taken away was perhaps never even given, was never allowed, was stolen. Curiously, when love is lost we suddenly seek less to know our pain than to show the most appropriate image of it to the person who caused it. But of course it was not Angela who caused anything. I sat there watching Mrs. Capitalupo in the full and constant image she showed me, swilling her sauce, and in seeing the way she had abandoned that child in so deliberately owning her saw also die that dawn whose blushes her young face so briefly reflected, finding in its stead only a lost and tragic life left for her in the profound darkness that remained.

Like desire, regret seeks not understanding but satisfaction. Without being asked I helped myself to a bowl of spaghetti sauce, savored the taste, and again made my usual wide inquiries as to what was missing. I dissembled. Was it breadcrumbs? Some special kind of stock maybe? Red mullet? How about peppers? But there came no answer, none at all. Mrs. Capitalupo, folding her hands, fixed me with a hateful smile and continued simply regarding me in a cold silence warming to self-satisfaction that finally had too much smugness in it for me not to try—the pause was delicious—one more word.

I said, "Pork."

There must have been a world of meaning there for before I knew it Mrs. Capitalupo flew into the bathroom and slammed the door ringing shut, whence came the sound of a loud flushing toilet which was always the sign that reigned most supremely in her kingdom of disapproval. And yet disapproval this time was final. I never saw Angela again.

Fark Pooks

"Bassport?"

I handed it over.

"Wisa here, too?"

"Wisa? Oh, visa." I nodded.

"Hotel Rossiya, biggest hotel in world, is charmed you to be here, sir," smiled the roly-poly clerk, her henna-colored hair twisted high and sprayed stiffly into a high cone. God help me, I believe she was flirting with me. She and a group of other ladies with applepandowdy faces were stamping papers, stapling cards, riffling through pages. "Make yourself certain to come back to Intourist desk in tomorrow's *mornink*. Do this sharp. But, as you see, you are now unobligated here. It is suggested you, therefore, to soap, wash out banlon, zleep in bed with brovided billow. Is bossible next day to see Kremlin; to wisit Bolshaya; to takes Kodak picture, please, and wisit no end of chumming chops for burchases." She knocked twice smartly on the nipple of the desk bell, winked. "Haste, how you say, is waking maste, yes?"

My booking had been made in advance; why had she kept my passport? Kremlinologists, not that I knew any, were the devil for warnings.

"May I have my passport back, please?"

She clucked. "This also in tomorrow's mornink."

"May I also inquire about the restaurant?"

"Restaurant for foots?"

"Yes, you see. I want, well," I confided diffidently, "foods."

"No," she shrugged, "to eat is out."

"A ham and cheese, possibly?"

"Blease?"

"A sandwich."

"Semfish? What is this?"

I laughed. "Well, kind of a—" As a visual aid, I made a small rectangle with my two thumbs and two forefingers.

"Nah," she wagged her head exasperatedly and took me in with her fisheye, "bassport is for tomorrow's mornink!"—and banging the bell with the flat of her hand walked briskly away.

I am a minister of God. Those under the umbrella of the Gospels do not just stamp their foot and howl when things go wrong. Petulance? I have never been one for grizzling, fusses, hidebound stubbornness, spats. Well, I *would* be a minister reconciled with compliance, wouldn't I? I'm not, frankly, a digger of psychological mole-runs. My field is Hope Theology. Righto, I was doing a book. So, socks up, I thought. I seriously doubt that you'd have found the incarcerated Dietrich Bonhoeffer whining for a ham-and-cheese sandwich in a moment of exceptional *crise*, and from that, unlike too many of us in the prelatical world, I could take a lesson. Let's leave that kind of thing for the papists, I say. Hope teaches us one important lesson—you won't laugh?—to hope. I'm as high as the sky on the Fourth of July for it!

I have a heart of glass. And my congregation, a small Baptist community in Ardmore, Oklahoma, must have seen clearly through it, believe me, when only last fall a select handful of ladies from our "Mother Crusaders" announced to me with irradiated countenances that they had all chipped in on a ticket for me: to Russia! My stuttering *why* they in turn counteracted with I can't say bad arguments, concluding all of them with the idea that I would return and deliver several slide-lectures on the subject of evil. You know how women are when they have their hearts set on something? "Greet the unseen with a cheer," our treasurer, Miss Bots, would always say, quoting, she would declare with a giggle, Chauncey Alcott. Actually, it was Mr. Browning. I would know that, I guess. One does not forget a *poet* who shamelessly snatches some unworldly, innocent, and insufficiently unprepared girl right from under her poor father's nose. I can't say I approve of that sort of thing. It argues the breakdown of authority. To say nothing, with all due respect to our treasurer, of disrespect. And how about sexual license? There's a subject. I could go on about that, believe me. But don't ask.

"Me Ignat," the porter said, freely identifying himself as he puffed up the dark, carpeted stairs before me with my suitcases, a camera, and my shaving bag. He drank, I could tell.

"Why, I'm *very* pleased to meet you, Ignat."

"I carry you pags."

"I notice. Thank you very much, Ignat. Be careful of my camera, won't you? And my book," I added. It was a difficult-to-find copy of A. S. Rounce's *Unhappy Bull's-eyes and Philosophical Arrows*. I aped his language: "You, um, am liking pook, yes?"

"I *loves* pooks," said Ignat with a goofy smile and stretching his arms wide. "These much."

He dropped my book, which split the spine. Goodbye to that. Impervious to his blunder, he grinned, pointed to his chest, and said, "*Novy sovetsky chelovek* Yes, people?" I stopped, fumbled up my *Collins Pocket Russian Dictionary*, and looked up the words: the new Soviet Man!

There was a Mongol cast to his face. Was he Buryat, Chuvash, Karakalpak? Some Bolshevik minority?

Ignat seemed charming! He looked like the photograph of the man from Yakut in the rose-jam cannery I had seen in the old *National Geographic* that I had read some months before when I was boning up on my trip—a somatotonic, thick-fingered Russian Bolshevik with bubblelike cheeks and imperfectly belted trousers, coal-black at the pocket-line, whose movements, nice as he was, to me indicated a bit of the staggers. Heavy drinking and atheism is a combination for neither spiritual nor mental health, as I have said many if not a million times up front. He kept jumping by me, grunting, like a running passenger at my side. Bleating!

His facial features were heavy and massive, although the man was runty and hunched to a degree, with crow's feet creases around his eyes. He was as blunt-nosed as a tile fish and to me quite obviously haled from a brachycephalic race, with an index of eighty-three, one of those broad-headed peoples that emerged from Asia after the Cro-Magnons. I excused myself to visit the bathroom. When I got back, within minutes, I found Ignat asleep with a fat roll in his hand—a moist sandwich—snoring like a contented grizzly bear after a salmon lunch. He woke up quickly only to devour it like a bread thief swallowing the evidence.

We walked together, no further word said, up to the fifth floor of the hotel where he silently took the key from an attendant there (each floor, I saw, had a seated attendant) and proceeded to unlock my room, shove in my bags, snap on the light, throw back the curtains—when, I want to tell you, I saw a view of Red Square that left me breathless. I was church-sponsored and for that doubtless should have controlled my zeal. But I tell you it was as pretty as *Rice, North Carolina!* Moscow! I had always thought it a word that shrieked out as an anagram. But now the ruby stars on several of the Kremlin towers were just beginning to glow in the early dusk, and oh boy. My earlier ambitions for some first day thru-the-lens metering were scotched, however. Never mind, I thought, scarf up. There was much to do.

Rice, North Carolina, where my Mom grew up. Mom's people, as well. Later, we moved on to Ardmore. Green corn. Choctaw beer. Barbecue beef. No beer for us, of course. I loved Bob Wills, Oklahoma boy.

"Here, you want to be *careful* with that!" He had just flung onto the light stand my Baby Minolta as if it were a wad of goat cheese. I carefully lifted it up and gently shook it. "You can jimmy these simply by looking at them. Don't be miffed at me, but look through my end of the telescope, won't you? You see, these cameras are made with highly resistant metals, true, but the lenses are machined to microscopic tolerances. The milled synchro-selector ring in this can pop off faster than a button, believe me, I've seen it happen." Had I been short with him? I do hope not, I added his name as a bumper. "OK, what was it, Ignat?"

Ignat pushed his mouth into a purselike contraction.

"Ho Kay, Sam. Goot."

"Fine," I said, "first-rate."

Dumb as a felt boot, I thought.

He kept standing there. I felt like a fool until I realized why. I held out a handful of some coins. He took one (the largest).

"*Blagadaryoo vas,*" he bowed grandly, smiling.
But he kept waiting. Long pauses ensued.
One barrel short of a stave—or, even worse, vice versa.
"Vhiskey. Philip de Morris, Chester Peel. Jogulats with
sweet kenty," he grinned, holding out his beefy right hand
gnarled into a cup. "Dollars? To have dollars? Am having dollars?"

I had to give him his due. He ran through nearly every
modal auxiliary and, in fine, an almost perfect conjugation in
a feeble attempt at clarity. His due, don't get the wrong impression, was respect—not money. I closed my eyes, shook my head. I
wanted to be polite, civil, supple, but had no intention whatsoever through mistaken largesse of spending my senior years in
fetters in a Bolshevik pokey in Siberia singing out the "*Interna-
tionale*" with searchlights in my eyes, newspaper underwear, and
icicles hanging from my nose, no sirree, bob. When they heard
of my trip, most of them back at the deanery, auditors essentially
provincial and knowing precious little of Metaphysical Hope,
assured me that once in the Soviet Union I would disappear like
the *neiges d'antan.* Thanks, but no thanks. That I had even the
slightest proclivity for trafficking in the "black market," that I
was even vaguely interested in engaging in Trotskyite "drops,"
that I had any intention in unbalancing our Federal Reserve System, do not believe. On the other hand, believe I did in the fel-
lowship of man, you see, which included—even if at the cost of
reinforcing my belief in a personal devil—this Ignat. I am not a
graduate from the Moody Bible Institute for nothing,

"Muffilyn Murrow," suddenly blurted the porter, grinning. I looked up, let me tell you.

Ignat then made a gesture I blushingly hasten to add I

recognized, one, tragically, universal, and not at all uncommon, if the truth be told, in the slums of New Guinea where I toiled in outreach ministerial work, just after ordination. With a booming laugh he slammed the door and waddled away.

§

The long flight had taken its toll after an hour or so. Food could wait. I brushed my teeth, got into my peejays, and, after a prayer to my Maker touching on what St. Paul had to say of heathens (my Bible, which had not been allowed into the country, was confiscated at customs) I happily retired. Well, not quite true. I did try to make a quick call to the Intourist office about maps. Whereas the tone of a telephone dial in the United States is a blend of an F and an A, with frequencies of 350 and 440 hertz, it is a strange single tone at 425 hertz in Europe, which is between an A-flat and an A, sounding something like a mosquito whine—irksome reverberation to me in my jet-lagged state—so I hung up the telephone, I admit it, quite petulantly. In any case, I was almost fully asleep when—*whooosh!*—I heard the sound of something suddenly slipped, *shoved*, under the crack of my door. I sat up in bewilderment. In the close dark I crept step by step over the sticky linoleum, bent down, looked, and picked up what were several magazines. I clicked on the light and—hold onto yourselves!—read these titles: *Rent-a-Bitch! D-Cups Galore! Peckertracks! Bite My Bum!*

§

My morning in Moscow I spent, after a questionable

breakfast of kefir with sugar and almond cookies, battered per-
ilously from one place to another in a checker-striped Pobeda
taxi seeing the Kremlin, the Tretyakov Gallery, the Dynamo Sta-
dium, the Novodevichy convent, and so on. It was a grim, semi-
rainy, overcast day with something like a Communist quality. I
shot halfheartedly through inadequately thought-out f-stops (for
which I knew I would kick myself later) and took random notes
for the eventual slide show I would give when I got back home.
I was almost up the stick with worry thinking about those pornographic (and illegal) magazines. I had wrapped them all in
stiff Russian toilet paper, for want of anything better, and buried
them, tentatively, under my mattress. Call that sufficient, and you
know nothing of maids—especially the Russian type, ferocious
as regards one's property, and, as I had been told at my synod a
thousand times, matters I think wisely left unmentioned.

Wide, wide streets rolled out before me. People queued
at bus stops. Trucks loaded with cabbages roared by. Women in
babushkas swept the gutters with bundles of twigs tied with rags.
I stopped at a tiny shop, squeezed in by a wall, and ate strawberries with a glass of champagne. Later, thirsty, I bought a bottle
of Borjomi, a carbonated mineral water which frankly smelled of
sulphur, but I drank it. I wandered about the streets, narrow ones,
and old walkways with fire escapes. A lot of white brick buildings.
I hate white brick. There were newer buildings, abstract, austere,
and gloomy, like all that constructivist art over at that museum
in Oklahoma City, all aiming to reflect modern industrial society
and urban space. The movement rejected decorative stylization
in favor of the industrial assemblage of materials. Constructiv-
ists were in favor of art for art sake, I believe. The weather was
cold but had none of the nose-freshening air of Lawton or Wich-

ita Falls or even Ardmore, no way, no sir.

I was staring into the face of Communism first hand. It is a homely one. All of these people who hated business and ran down capitalism? They could well have taken a page out of that example-setting novel, *The Man Nobody Knows*, written by Bruce Barton, a great American, and published in 1924—I heartily recommend it—in which he portrays Jesus of Nazareth, not as a simpering soft-faced yam-in-the-mouth, feminine-type wimp playing with his hair, not at all, but, a no-nonsense boot-strapping powerhouse, a live wire, virile, with muscles, a sharp enterprising go-getter and vigorous self-starter ready to head-up a corporation, a high-flying eager beaver out on the hustings, no wasted words, a business achiever, in short, a comer!

"I must be about my father's *business*," declared Jesus. Note that! "*Work* is worship," states Barton, in making a magnificent point. If Jesus were our contemporary, Barton writes, "He would be a national advertiser today!" And he is so right. You want a model for youth, all of you parents out there? Consider Jesus Christ as employer, tycoon, trader, and merchant! God bless the U.S.A.!

Anyway, I wandered about. There were many onion-shaped domes. There is something cute about them, bulbous, like fat little faces. I bought a *pelmeni* from a vendor, who gypped me, I believe, when I held out my hand full of coins. I wanted to see the Tretyakov Gallery but, trying to unfold my cat's-step circular to check the bus timetable, dropped it over a bridge—I might have been woozy from the champagne—and almost got walloped by a swerving taxi. I walked around Gorky Park some. I photographed the Ostankino TV Tower, looked at sweaters on expensive Stoleshnikov Pereuloa—a pedestrian street—and sat down in Pushkin Square to rest my feet.

That afternoon in the hotel, after a thick Georgian stew of lamb, herbs, and vegetables—a *chanakh*, said to be Stalin's favorite meal, I don't know—which came with a stack of thick dark bread, radishes, pickles, and a side dish of watery borscht, I ambled about, bought some Communist pins, chose a scarf for Miss Bots, our treasurer, who I knew had a round-number birthday coming up, and a ushanka-fur hat with ear flaps. I walked along the Moscow River and took some photos of the "Worker and Kolhoz Woman," a sculpture about eighty feet tall in stainless steel of two figures with a sickle and hammer raised over their heads.

I purchased from a street vendor a bag of sugary *pastila* that I could feel ruining my teeth on the spot. I found I had a lot more leisure-time on my hands, so wandered aimlessly around the incoherent aisles of the huge, sprawling overrated GUM mega-department store. "*Nichevo v magazinakh*," I said to a uniformed man posted at a door, after consulting my Collins. There is nothing in the stores! "*Pustiye prilavki!*" I snapped. Empty counters!

A constant worry occurred to me, that Ignat might be a spy. Why else would he be sleeping on a trunk—a *sunduk*—in my hallway? Imposture. Mark Twain's favorite subject. To say nothing of Shakespeare's. Duping. Spies have popped up all through history. Queen Elizabeth I had them, ferreting out the papist clergy. What about the theory that she was a man? A thousand acts of hers prove it. Her imperial ideology. The defeat of the Armada. Sending out explorers in fleets. Enriching her kingdom. Writing sophisticated letters to the King of Spain.

I concluded about three-ish that I had seen enough. The

ticket (a box seat) I had booked for the Bolshoi would be waiting for me, or so hoped, and the crowds in the Moscow streets
and communoid suburbs monotonously started to repeat their
surprises and, I must say, began to pall: peasants in quilted jackets with boots covered in dry manure; pig-tailed Komsomolkas
(prettier, I thought, in the *National Geographic* Ektachromes);
stout women in white overalls on the streets flogging chocolate
logs filled with pink ice cream; and satchel-jowled howbeits in
gull-gray galoshes and 1950 Borsalinos standing around eating
pirozhkis—the word I approximate, thanks to my grunting cabdriver—and wiping their fingers on their coats.

You can find this in America? You wish. Not in the Heart-
land, anyway.

It is just what atheism must look like, I thought. I mean,
Russians *believe* in atheism, don't they?

§

"Judas Priest!" I howled rushing into my hotel room and
quickly locking the door. On the bed in a tidy little pile—there for
all the world to see—sat another three or four filthy magazines,
of the very same stamp. I saw this time that they were printed in
the state of New Jersey. I flashed through the pages almost with
my eyes totally a-goggle, I tell you, and, witless from fright: *Twat-
let! Boob Goddesses! Mattress Lunch!* and *Whip Me, Whip Me, Rubber
Woman!*

Correct. I immediately telephoned downstairs. Well,
that's not quite true. With the natural and, I think, inevitable
misgivings of any American tourist, but thinking no less of man
qua man, I thought better of—well, I hate the word squealing. It's

so common. Clearing the situation up, say? So, I telephoned room service and tried to explain what was going on, all in vain. Seconds later, Ignat himself unlocked (!) the door and confidently entered smiling, rolling before him on a very wobbly dented aluminum dolly my lunch. He looked like a marine slug, shiny and fat. I noticed some gimp meat on a plate, a pile of orange potatoes, and lots of black bread.

"*Shto novava!*"

"Yes, swell. Now, listen, I—"

He grandly held up his hand for silence. He pointed lasciviously toward the bed.

"Muffilyn Murrow, um, naked gorls," he wheezed with laughter, "breast of tit, please?" And, swiping geometries, he created in the proximate air the identifiable torso of a woman's figure. He bowed unctuously.

"You mean, *you*—?"

How does one convey to a near-illiterate pagan the shades and motives of outrage, while at the same time trying to lesson him, with a view to his Being Saved, in the precariousness of his crow-coloured soul? Try it sometime, friend. Now look, I had for sometime known well enough to avoid in Russia any discussion of the Sino-Soviet rip, so-called "scientific resurrectionism," and the recent decamp of Svetlana, Joseph Stalin's only daughter. And I suppose I could have spoken, without redress, about many more less innocuous things. But exactly what were they, huh? The four-fold rotation of crops? Seed-drilling? Balneological spas in Tashkent? Hell's bells, I would (excuse me)! I couldn't set a pin's fee on all that, so, true to type—ministers minister, don't they?—I untugged the trashy magazines from under my mattress and, without a moment's hesitation, exasperatedly confronted him with all of them.

Characteristically (it was becoming rather clear), Ignat happily snatched the top one from the stack—its cover, a photo of an overly lipsticked woman in hip-length boots beckoning a crouched man with an arched whip—and proudly rattled the thing in his salacious hands, uttering only one word: "*Fark!*"

There were years of crowded passion in the word.

"No, *no*. This just won't *do!*" I shouted at him. "I'm clerical! This is . . . vice, filth, *pornography*." I ran the gamut of negative nouns. Was there to be nothing but mind-pretzeling problems with this guy? And, again, he was coming at me out of some kind of enthusiasm, with an array of grunts, bleats, snorts, wheezes, and rattles, like a hunter calling deer during the rut,

"Is goot?" he grinned, plugging a finger into the well of his other fist and dandling it around in circles.

"Is *bad!*"

"Bat?" he squinted. "Fad? Vat?"

It was hopeless.

"Gif you for me Yuicy Vroots gum? Pallboint ben"—he made a scribbling gesture. "Joggelot? Panana shplitz? Salami meets? Nepseck?"

What the deuce was he waiting for? I mean, the guy had a head harder than Kittery bluestone. Quartzite!

He didn't budge.

How stood there, emboldened, unmoving, a wizened nut, trying to shake me down like a virile old ferret.

"*Chto delat?*"

I looked it up. It meant: what is to be done?

"*Nothing* is to be done, good sir," I squawked.

He jiggled his fingers. "To take dollars?"

Now wait just one sweet minute! "No, no, Ignat, uh-uh, I need," I heard myself yelling, braying in fact, "I *need* money for my trip. Dollars, me, I, I—"

"To take dollars." He bit his lip. Ignat grew darker. I stood firm. "Ab-solutely not."

"*To take dollars!*" He pointed to his hand. "Money, this, go put! Make enter dollars you! Unnerstan'?"

Good God, had he gone Asiatic? I thought he was going to throttle me! I was sure of it! But, as I have often said in dicey business, to strive, to seek, to find, and not to yield. We were poised like dancers, waiting for music to strike up. I took the initiative.

"I shall call the police, *your* police, Mr. Ignat, and I . . . I want to be perfectly open with you, as sure as I'm standing here, I promise, you will be waking up to rock-breaking in Siberia, tomorrow!" I repeated my words, very effective in the high sermon, by the way. "Siberia! Tomorrow!"

Well, what he could sift of my English I couldn't then say, but he suddenly became pliable, acquiescent, radiant even—and smiled, nodding.

"*Da*, sumorrow! *Mir! Drouchba!*"

"Listen, do you understand?"

"Yum, yup," he said, bowing. "*chto budet to budet—Что будет то будет!* Vhat, um, vill hoppen, vill hoppen!"

At that same instant, he professionally slid from the top tray of his dolly onto my room table several filled plates—cucumbers in sour cream, cold turkey in walnut sauce, warm Georgian bread—spun around thrice gleefully (managing, simultaneously, to squat down and kick his heels in an imperfectly executed *gopack* or *hopak* movement, for I had seen the movie, *Ninotchka*), whistled several birdy notes, and, just before he ducked from the room, deftly slipped from under some towels in the lower tray some obscure matter that he proceeded to pitch bouncing onto my bed like the morning edition, headlined, I saw, cupping my mouth frightfully: *Hair Brushers! Nina Does Seattle! Goomba Gal!* and *Hot Leatherette!*

Talk about complete *bouleversement!*

I was going out of my skull.

§

I got to the Bolshoi Theater that evening, begulphed. And I stayed that way. My cabdriver, a furtive little rat-faced man in a mousy old furazhka, had charged me double, and then, from a woefully located seat at the top (loge, third tier, right side), in spite of the beautiful if overwrought red and yellow gold décor of the historic theater, I watched with a crick in my neck an indifferent first-half performance of Delibes' *Sylvia*—made no more interesting, certainly, by the Polish *uhlans* and steppe peasants in their shirtsleeves in box, pit, and gallery munching baloney sandwiches and burping vodka. What was so badly nagging at me? Then I realized. It was the dirty books being shuffled into my room! What if by some hideous of compensating replevin this perfect fool, by some perverted trick, grossly to try to obtain compensation for his resulting losses and legally seek to recover his personal property—pornography!—by claiming that they were taken wrongfully and unlawfully from him?

I began to feel the borscht, radishes, pickles, and mineral water backing on me, squeezing my innards, giving me heartburn. It bespeaks ill in a minister, I am aware, to sound so displeased—displeasure, I will not deny, poignantly antithetical to Hope—but, take my side of the rope, how would you feel, manage, pep up, if you were sitting in the dead bloody center of Moscow, Russia, with a forced load of contraband under your hotel mattress and it growing in heaps by the minute! It stabbed my vitals. I was up a tree.

The interval bell rang. "Psssht!"

Could I have heard—?

"*Psssht!*"

There is a kind of shock one undergoes that stuns. Imagine mine, then, when through the blue curtain of my box in the close darkness like Pantalone enbundled stepped of all people—Ignat!

I went white. "What the sam hill—?"

He shoved his nose onto a slapped-together pile he held with the snout of a hematophagous animal, then looked up smiling.

And he went right to the point.

"More fark pook," he cacked from a mouth like a forcing bag exuding whip, and energetically dropped on my then indignantly rising lap several more illicit—illicit? illegal!—magazines, only the title of top one of which could I bring myself to read: *Unstrap Me Now, Hotsy!*

Desperate, I flung it from me like a plague rat, crouching down and covering it up with my foot.

"Why," I wailed in a whisper, "have you come here? Why have you come here with—*these?*" I ground my foot into them.

"Not to put," he winked, "how you say, all eggs in one chicken, eh?"

§

There is an expression in the Russian language, which was explained to me in what, it turned out, was the only conversation that I ever fully understood there. It is *pokachál golovói*—the untranslatable shaking of the head by a Russian to express dismay, surprise, disapproval. The policeman who explained it to me was, in point of fact, not only the one who expressed it but, indeed, the very one who caught me by weak flashlight trying frantically in the middle of my last night in his benighted country to shove down a disposal drain in a side-street off the damp Moskva Quay forty-seven pornographic magazines and a novel of the boulevard genre, Ignat's last gift, bestowed to me in a shoving crowd in the GUM department store and which was—the final insult—the replacement, I assume, for my personal wallet containing $243.25 and 31 rubles which disappeared at the same time.

Why go into the trial? It was celebrated.

What do all the peasant tunics, wooden cupolas, and birch trees mean to me now? I was dismissed from the country by train and searched, researched, and besmirched by four obviously forewarned soldiers at the Brest border. They smirked knowingly at me the entire time, I might add. *The Daily Ardmoreite* had a brief editorial on me I heard. I never saw it myself, working, as I've been for some time, with outreach in New Guinea once again and where, at least I can report, I finished last year the book I long ago started on Hope Theology. Look for it.

There is a chapter on Russia in it, by the way. I even mentioned our treasurer. To her disadvantage, if I remember correctly.

An English Railroad

A tavern chair is the throne of human felicity.

—Dr. Samuel Johnson

"Tryps."

"No, actually, just this one in London, for the summer."

"I'm afraid you've misunderstood me, old potato."

"Mis—?"

"—understood, that's right. It's my surname, in point of fact. Tryps, Major (ret.)," he announced extending his hand and shaking mine vigorously while, with a nod, sliding his glass toward the bartender. "Welsh originally, they say, going back to the days of King Lud and all that. Helluva name for a king, don't you agree? Lud? Stops you in your tracks, wot? I would ruddy well put a sack over it if I saw one coming at me, eh? Anyway, them's the facts. What are you drinking?"

"I'm sorry I confused your name." I was, very.

"Happens all the time," he said and lifted up his refilled glass to the light. "Down the disc-signal, up steam, compression, at fly—*chugg, chugg, chugg*." Glugging it down he bit his lower lip, wheezed like a bagpipe, and came out with a long vocally extended *aahhhh.*

"Name your poison."

"Pardon me?"

"Drink."

"Oh yes, thank you. *Mmmmm*, do they have—" I squinted at the squads of fat bottles lining the shelf, "no, you know, I don't see it."

"Out with it, old man. Come on."

I thought of some favorites of mine. *A Gin Daisy. A Fuzzy Comfort. A Rocky Green Dragon. A Double Derby.*

"Well, actually, I was going to say, I'm partial to Dusenberry Snap cordials. So is my wife."

"You say?"

"It's a liqueur."

Within less than an hour, it turned out, I had bought him several drinks, not that it mattered, even a bit. The bartender, it had not escaped me, had taken for the first drink several of the wet coins I had initially mounted on the bar and just left stand there. Anyway, I kept paying. I'm no piker, don't get me wrong. Hunched over his drink, Tryps would simply stare off smiling, drawing and redrawing a finger down the dexter side of his mustache, possibly fancying himself to be Ronald Colman. He had one of those ruddy English faces, rouged with hard weather, deep Dubonnet-red cheeks and a bit of a damson nose, as if it had been abraded by a stiff wind. On the other hand, he was blustery, cheerful, bright, chirping, and almost too alive, manic.

There was a raddled aspect to his manly features, his eyes shining, but the bags beneath were growing heavy. I knew his type: adventurous, congenial, swashbuckling, a trove of old yarns, yet a personality still so held in by duty of a sort that the rigid, self-contained focus he showed when speaking was strictly on himself, his favorite auditor.

"What is an Englishman?" asked Mark Twain in an 1883 notebook entry I read somewhere, and answered, "A person who does things because they have been done before." This seemed to fit Major Tryps like a glove.

I believe I had the dope on him and his like. An Englishman irons his newspaper, keeps up with cricket averages, eats thick-cut Oxford marmalade on toast, loves a cup of perfect English tea, queues up for everything, prefers tweed jackets in houndstooth check and a woolen tie, favors the man-to-manly address of surnames only, revels in the silence of a private club (all male), sports an umbrella with a wooden Murano handle, refuses to pronounce foreign words or those taken over from another language, enjoys the taste of Worcestershire sauce, Marmite, and Indian spices, and listens to the BBC World Service every evening at seven. Oh, I was ready for him.

I could picture him, if you want the truth, walking across an English flower-filled meadow with a brace of pheasants and a shotgun flung over his forearm. Tryps was wearing a hacking jacket, loose and worn at the elbow. He was vigorous, with plenty of English starch, and had the scarlet, cauliflorian face, age fifty or so, that showed him to be, or so it seemed to me, an English actor: white teeth, china-blue eyes, brandy glass chin, bucking with charm and goodwill, and, how to put it, waves of *experienced* hair. His clothes were dapper. Flat green herringbone tweeds. I thought his nose was puffy with rhinitis but decided after a closer look that it was just frank, strong, hawkish. My wife smiled at him on the way to the powder room. What do they call it in England? Powder room, anyway.

My wife, by the way, had suggested that, when traveling, we meet people like this and on the recommendation of some good friends of ours from Richmond—a repetend, theirs, complete with lovely maps, directions, do's and don'ts, *tot quots*, and gastronomic underscorings—we found our way, *wended* our way, to the English pub Ye Olde Cheshire Cheese, rebuilt—get this—in 1667. Dr. Johnson's favorite alehouse, yup. It was everything we expected, and more: old wood, smoked windows, a creaking wooden staircase, old chairs, and the devilishly superb smell of roast beef, Yorkshire pudding, and brown ale.

Chessboard punctilio you can have. The angular English pub with its totemistic fraternities, while straitjacketing others, gives me the kind of lift I can't quite explain, save, from the few unforgettable conversations I've had in some of them, experiencing the rather obvious conviction of having learned something. The pub over there is an anti-staling agent. It's a mighty catholicon. There's a word for you. I'm a wide reader, forgive me. Do I wear my learning on my sleeve? What I'm trying to say is, you don't get bored. I like to think of myself as something of a world traveler.

The ratty dark American bar bespeaks a sense of the exitless, of the subterranean, of despair. It gives one a feeling best described as, what—*ennuyant?* I can't even approach telling you how gloomy my local bar is back in the States. And how about the desperate little ersatzes and inadequates you find standing at the bar next to you? Grim? You don't know the half of it, believe me. Murk, shadow, shade. That's what elbow-benders actually go there for. Isolation is the code of the American bar room. Seclusion. Detachment. *Stay away!* Just bump into someone by mistake, merely brush his arm, and he'll go for your throat.

Anyway, as soon as we had entered the Cheshire Cheese, my wife headed for the little girl's; well, we had crossed through that park near Queen Elizabeth's palace, Buckingham Palace, that's right—and there is a park nearby, I think, with swans and ducks paddling in the water, of course, in the park, near the palace—well, anyway, we were bushed, and she had to freshen up. You know how women are. That was how we met Mr. Tryps, sorry, Major Tryps; he had raised his glass in that friendly and pleasantly common gesture so recognizably England's, I thought. My wife, by the way, suggested we meet people like this and on the recommendation of some good friends of ours from—oh, I have explained all that. The pub was very quirky, dark and dingy inside. I loved the fireplace and crackling fire, all of it cozy and comfy.

"The little woman," I laughed, flicking my head toward the ladies' room. "You know how women are."

"American chap, eh?"

"Righto," I laughed.

"Chicago? Arizona? Phoophadoophia?"

"New York City."

"My idea of squalor. Here's how." He knocked back a gulp. "Would I go there? Not for Cadwallader and all his goats." He wheezed.

"I want to tell you something right now," he stated, closing his eyes with a deprecatory shake of his head and rolling the stem of his cognac glass between thumb and forefinger. "We're your common garden-variety drinkers in England, mostly. Your beers. Your gins. Your odd ciders, eh? I like a bone-dry cider myself. A rough unintimidating scrumpy with a gentle alcoholic burn on the palate, see, with an acid, some funk, and a wood kick, resolving into a long dry finish, if you get my drift. Sour enough to make a grackle scream. A barnyard taste—peaty, see?—with a smoking kiss to it. A tannic hint. Kingston Black. Somerset Pomona. Bulmer's Woodpecker Cider was my go-to pull when I was a young rascal growing up." He winked. "Real *zoider*, see?" He wheezed over the private joke, laughing hard, and began coughing, hard, spattering out spittle. "'Pull a bird tonight,' goes the ad. 'Get out of your tree!'"

He snorted and grew suddenly sober.

"A wealthy great-grandparent of mine gave his son, my father's father from the Lancashire Tryps, a gift of a pipe of Port to put away until he was 21—700 bottles—but I never saw it. Rogues drank it away."

He asked for a shot of vodka.

"Where are you staying, then?"

"St. Ermin's. The two of us. Very accommodating."

"Oh, I know, the spy hotel, over on Caxton St., old Carlton Gardens. Once a secret spook base during the Big Blow, don't you know. MI6."

"My wife finds the sheets too shiny, the pillows bolsters, and wallpaper a bit, well, hysterical, but we're happy."

"Capital!—first chop!"

He knocked back his shot.

I offered to get him another drink. He ordered a martini.

"Thank you, my friend." He raised his glass. "To traveling, the best education there is. In these isles, the train's the way to go."

"But we're not taking any trains."

"Are you taking the celebrated 'Statesman' land cruise for the special circular tour, a majestic route, of the famous Settle to

Carlisle railway? Get a glimpse of lovely Garsdale? Appleby? The touted Ribblehead viaduct with your heart in your mouth? Or are you maybe heading out to see Cheddar Gorge? Oh, a lovely take-in. There is no direct connection, mind you—what you do, you see, is board the train to Bristol Temple Meads, and then it's a short hop by cab to the caves. Nothing to it. Mind the goats! Buy yourselves a Cave Aged Cheddar, a traditional cloth-matured, handmade farmhouse cheese. You won't go wrong. I love a Double Cottenham, a Blue Wensleydale, a red Cheshire a 'blue vinney' from Dorset—hard yet crumbly, go figure. But ever try an ale-washed Renegade Monk? Cornish Yarg prepared with wild garlic? Lymeswold with an edible white rind? On a stormy night, I would kill for a cup of hot tea, water biscuits, and a nutty wedge of hard creamy Duddleswell."

He finished his martini and gulped the olive.

"I miss the 'Cheltenham Flyer'. Made the fastest railway run in the world, I'll rub-a-dub. Staff like family. Silver service, piping hot, crested plates. Background sound of rattling cutlery and tinkling glasses, as the train sped through the countryside A shaft of midday sun that lit the white tablecloth and glittered on the cutlery. Stewards all attentive to one's needs and right at hand. They were efficient, smiling, kept pads, wrote it all down, wet the pencil tip. Blacks who can write nowadays are as rare as snow leopards. It was 'Morning, sir, a little more Dundee cake?' or 'May I adjust the foot rest, madam?' or 'Would you like the new *Strand* magazine, sir?' They saw to all the luggage, provided foot warmers, hot towels, cigars. They wore white gloves but were not permitted to sport a boutonniere, wear satin-faced coats, wear patent-leather shoes, or use cologne. No 'alarums & excursions,' as the stage direction goes, uh, if you get my drift. White passengers only. No Bank Holiday rail chaos. Britain's dining cars have died a sad death."

He sighed. "When first introduced on the East Coast line in 1879, their kitchens cooked over burning coals, everything from hot buttered kippers for morning commuters to roast lamb and salmon hollandaise on Christmas Day, not just meagre railway sandwiches with sawdust filling or a punnet of cress and a fried egg insolently looking up at you. When British Rail wound down in 1997, there were still 250 dining cars. They were quickly deemed unprofitable and the last continual service ran on the 19.33 from London Kings Cross to Leeds in May 2011."

Tryps had almost too much energy. He swirled in his chair. He *bounced.* "What can I order to drink in my dreams, you say?" he inquired with the kind of crazy vitality that animated him on every subject. "A Blue Lagoon? A Seco Herrerano distilled three times from sugar cane? A Romanian apricot palinka? A Shah Hawaash that the abo's drink in the purlieus of subfusc Somalia? A cocktail I used to drink back in Rangoon called a Pegu, a concoction of gin, lime, orange curaçao, and bitters? Right. I would start off with a Pimm's at the club. Then, a 'short-one,' well-laced with absinthe. Oh yes, we were devils. After that lovely potted shrimp and cold-smoked cheese, a good red or white wine to wash it down, and, what, maybe some port or a nip of kümmel. Drink is life's *joy,*" He laughed.

"I used to keep on hand a bottle of Calvados—Domaine Du Coquerel, Pomme D'Eve, oh yes, the very best—with which to brush my teeth!" Leaning forward, he whispered to the bartender, "I will take another martini. And, look here, do just let the gin and Vermouth cross Piccadilly together, barely touching."

He took me in to his confidence.

"A fruit-filled Pimm's Cup, with a taste of jollity thrown in? Not for me, my good man. Aye, and none of your punches, fizzes, spritzers, or floats." He had a way of stretching out a word by adding a sort of extra chord to it. "Nor can I abide even the bloody scent of mulled claret. *Steaming wine?* Come off it! Nobody will find yours truly with an umbrella in his drink."

He nodded to a nearby booth, whispered.

"Chap over there, Mr. Jowls in the pinstripes? He is drinking a cider. Swirl bubbles. You can see the little blighters swirling up the glass—practically hear them pop. Give you a headache, they will."

He turned to me, lifting his drink.

"I won't touch your modern poofter versions of cider coming down the line today. No carbonated or microfiltered yamp for me, jack. With a floral nose to it? *Quince* flavors? Not on your nelly. No apple-skin 'hints,' no, sir, and not a bubblegum green-apple aroma either. No Christmas 'spice notes.' Might as well be drinking Sanatogen or your kind of cheap guinea prosecco or teeth-killing fino with almonds concoction, some kind of aromatized wine vermouth piss."

He lowered his voice to lean in softly to whisper, "*Fucking Lucozade!* Leave that to the fags and rent boys." He swiveled with his back halfway to the bar and leaned back. "See that questionable bloke behind us, the variegated jacket with his nose deep into an ice perry?" He nudged me with an elbow. "Light in the loafers, twenty to one. A fruitcake. Mutton dressed as lamb. Friend of Dorothy. Thinks he is in a tearoom." He woofed air. "Give him a pink gin. A barrister, no doubt, probably, over from the Royal Courts." He drank. "Of Justice." He drank. "Lawyers."

He winked at me. "Siphon and Hoover, Attorneys. Get me?"

He hiccuped. "Oh yes, people once in a way will give you no end of palaver about booze. Alcohol experts, right? Growlers. Giggle water. Hair of the dog. Moo juice. Road soda. Half-rack. It is all bean water, old man."

He reached freely to select one of my cigarettes. "I'll take any of the 'O, Be Joyful,' my American friend, and be as contented as any wee lad lapping a stick of rock. Agreeable rattle all that, yes, but pay it no mind. No reason for it, you see, not at all." He nudged me. "Horse's mouth?"

He placed his hand over my arm.

"Horse's mouth," I smiled.

"Quite so, quite so."

"You know, the last time—"

"Besides, they wouldn't know what you were talking about—with these liqueurs and all—in parts of the world where I've kipped, come to that: Port Said, Gib, Mushkaf, Baroda, Sibi, Aden, Quetta . . ."

He was ticking these places off on his fingers.

"Boy."

"I could go on."

"I'll bet. Boy. I'll bet."

He finished his martini and ordered a sherry on the rocks.

"Well now, you see, point is"—he winked—"*don't* bet, huh? You would lose." He watched me with his wide, popping eyes, his shoulders heaving with dry noiseless laughs. "See? Because you would lose, old fruit." He did not so much laugh as, well, *chuff*, a chest heave with a dry chuckle.

In the meantime, Tryps told me how to eat cockles, what

a "dibbly-dobbly" in cricket meant, the top season to visit the Hebrides, why the Queen hated seafood, where best to sit at the grand opera, the chief argument for the superiority of nature over artifice (munching a Red Prince apple) and who murdered Lord Lucan. All of it seemed a great blooming confusion, I adjusted my cuffs, I kept nodding as I rotated my glass, listening with inclined head, hoping not to appear rude.

Smiling, I remarked on the low ceiling.

"Low ceiling, aye. Two-level toilets. Been a pub here since 1538. Made of stone." Tryps stomped the floor. "Sawdust." He raised his sherry glass and toasted, "A friend's eye is a good mirror! To the Queen!" and took a haust of his drink. "Oh, sorry—and to your good Mrs.!" He took another sip, "And while we are at it, to the whole bloody Commonwealth—to Scotland and her thistle, to Wales and her leek, to Canada and her maple leaf, to South Africa and her protea, to India and Ceylon and their lotus, to ruddy ol' Pakistan and their wheat, to Australia and her wattle, and, last but not least, to New Zealand and her fern!"

"You love history," I said.

"History is England's glory!"

He gulped down his glass and began laughing.

"Where are the snows of yesteryear, right? The old days! Whiskery old blacksmiths with their corduroy trousers tied beneath their knees with pieces of string, holding huge gentle horses? Peat-cutters in the shaggy bogs with their paring irons and slanes neatly cutting out turf brick as clean-cut as a mother's pie? Chair bodgers working up traditional country chairs by turning wood on a sturdy pole lathe? Old village cobblers with their tight mouths full of penny nails—and I am talking about dedicated boyos, my friend—toiling away like beavers on their lasts, spinning fudge wheels, paring soles with peg hammers and lasting pincers, sewing awl hafts, working boot stretchers, heel shaving? Buck-toothed farmers in smocks and floppy, shapeless hats, a cider costrel in one hand, a wench in the other, faces glaring red? Old fisherfolk smoking pipes weave-meshing with great doodle needles and patching fyke nets and gill nets, trammel nets and seines? Weavers working spindles? Hook the notch on top into a fluffy ball of good raw wool, give the stick a turn, whoops, the weighted end gives the spindle momentum, I want to tell you!"

"Walking through the city, I—"

"When was the last time you saw a millstone dressed, shaped, faced and segmented, I mean the real thing, harp-shaped pattern—siliceous rock called burrstone, an open-textured, porous, a fine-grained sandstone—or glimpsed a true-by-God wheelwright shaping a wagon wheel from scratch, stopper clasped, with dowels, felloes, spokes, and tongues? Can you cooper a barrel? Tinker a watering can? Build up a wall with West Country granite or Yorkshire grit?"

"In Connecticut I once saw—"

"What about ice cutters? Factory lectors, who read aloud to the humpers? Log drivers? Lamplighters? Knocker-uppers, devoted old folk who woke people up for work in the era prior to the invention of the alarm clock? Weavers at their frame looms, plying good English yarn, threading the huddle holes their crochet hooks, calculating the warp and then tying it to the fabric beam as if making a part of heaven and all done with the battening love of a gentle parent?

All were content with their lot in life. It was the land they loved, Britannia, the lovely mealy land. Albion. A golden meadow.

Mists rising from the stooks. Gleaners humbly gathering stray wheat-ears. A cricket pitch ringed by soft, gentle hills whose rising sides provided sheltering purity from the outside world, an enchanted crucible enclosing the national game—and, mind you, no aluminum bats, white balls, and funny-looking clothes back then—where hearty gentlemen at sport played to the accompaniment of birdsong and humming bees, with only the plick-plock of the bat against the ball echoing in the English air!"

"I can just picture the beauty of—"

"Stout-hearted farmers, bold yeoman, uncomplaining small holders, and well-tanned villeins out there in the wheat-scented fields growing Ambassador courgettes and deep-red Wodan beetroot and those inimitable Savoy cabbages with looser, crinkly leaves like a gorgeous woman's tresses! Titled lovelies at the races at lunchtime in May, perched on shooting sticks, eating sandwiches out of baskets, a kaleidoscope of delicate hairstreaks fluttering above them!"

"When we arrived here, my wife and I intended to set off for Nailsworth and Minchinhampton but at the Ring Road in Cirencester—"

I stopped in mid-sentence. He wasn't listening.

Major Tryps sat staring into the glass he slowly rotated in an almost Buddhistic state of glassy alcoholic contemplation. It was back again to another reverie. I checked my watch, frustratedly humming.

"It was Albion then. Land of the Rose. *Great* Britain," he said. "A Great House with its rolling parkland, hothouses, orangeries, and stables, elegant deer, serene lakes, immemorial oaks, rose gardens amid lawns, terraces, sheltered walks, meandering long footpaths, and endless vistas from curated landscapes by blue-paved fountain-basins, where, for visitors, servants in lofty vestibules stood at attention, stiff and proud in plush and powder, when a mere touch on an embroidered bell-rope brought instant and obsequious service, when platoons of grooms—"

"We are hoping to see such a park—"

"The very *air* was Saxon then, soft-faced people in out-lying farms, buxom dairymaids, a cow's sweet face peering through the window, gardens asprout, the good old days when bills were paid once a year, for such was the custom of the gentry, youngsters outside playing at squails or garden croquet, a time when you could go out hiking, pack-laden, across unknown country, bubbling streams throwing back the sunlit sky from their bosoms, wind ruffling the heather and bilberry underneath—"

"I can see—"

"—watching horses cropping rich grass in the fruitful meadows, white oxen standing in the shade harnessed to the great wagons that bear home the freshly-mown, newly-cut, golden bright hay, maybe see a dashing fox-hunting party streaming past hedgerows all a-flower in Spring, rook-racked, river-rounded, over heather and grasslands, valley and coombe, ruddy huntsmen out on the stubbles and the heath with their brave lurchers coursing the hare, which has always held an irresistible appeal to sporting young sparks with their blood up, and, oh, by high noon, sharpened by a lack of lunch, coming home to a meal of grouse or guinea hen with chestnut sauce or a hot goose swimming in an appetizing half-stew-half-sauce, garnished with good carrots, floury potatoes, and a bottle of reasonable burgundy—"

"Just exactly what I—"

"—then an hour sitting in your study with a cognac, south-facing through great bow windows, to a meadow, and of course no Jews or hairy Bolsheviks back then squatting with their families there in Golders Green or over in Stamford Hill or other subdistricts of Stoke Newington, nope, not by a long shot. Where are the days, huh? Do you realize what it was like back then?"

"Peaceful, I'd say, and probably—"

"Let me tell you. Sitting in an old stuffed armchair beside the hearth, your feet on the iron fender, a hearty pot of gunfire tea steaming on the hob, you drawing on a pipeful of Arango's Balkan Supreme. Ah! A tiny village set in the crook of a hill, its church tower sounding matins with sweet chimes, waking up in the morning for a cup or two of hot tea, a breakfast of sausages, and a plate of fried, golden brown boxty to dip in applesauce, then what, a lovely afternoon of shooting snipe or fishing for chub off a scent-filled water-meadow, the chirr of the grasshopper, the curkle of the quail, a few port-boy clouds in the sky, scudding free, a pleasing plash off the weir by the broad-leaved wood, night wind in the high tops of the beeches, and where are you all he while? There you are, feeling fitter than King Cole with a merry old soul, warmly perched by a bright log fire at night sipping a glass of Warre's Otima 10-Year Old Tawny, your faithful beagle slumbering by your feet, you and yours known by all of your neighbors, 'Howdy-do, sir,' comfortable among the hoar-ancient squirearchy? Ah yes, yes, yes."

He ordered another sherry.

"England once had *structure!* It is an order that is lost, my friend. The hayward at his hedge, the reeve taking orders from the thane, the loyal old pinder tugging stray pigs back in to the croft. *They knew their places!* The trustful lord in his demesne got respect. Villeins and bondsmen, servile and happy, tugging their forelocks and doffing their hats to the passersby? You can't buy that, you cannot buy that today."

Tryps seemed very much in his element. A bar stool was a perfect perch for such a bravura anecdotalist, someone able to find an audience right at his very elbow. He bent wedge-nosed into his fists to pay his reverie the full respect of a proper silence, then sat up abruptly with a loud *whoosh.*

"Now it's all human bumph, Pakis, babus and pishabs, greasy bean-eating Eyeties in business selling sandwiches, towelheads, Frogs—'surrender monkeys' we called them back in 1944—uphill gardeners, Lord and Lady Canustandthem, Maltese pimps, oiks, snotlaps, towel-headed Sikhs ready to bite your arms off, and of course the Irish bog-trotters, all mad as a bag of ferrets."

"But when you stop to think of—"

"No, it's all arse over tip, nowadays. No day dawning without a major event in it and all to the bad. Terrorists. Irish incendiaries. Pipe bombs. Open-air shootings. It's a bodge job just to wake up of a morning and poke your nose out the window, I won't take a bus, how do ya do."

"I imagine—"

"I grew up when hard toil was met with cheerful acknowledgment, when common people put in a right day's work and didn't think manual labor was a Mexican, when food, never mind housing, didn't cost you a ruddy bomb, when people had a 'good morning' for you, when rules bloody mattered, my man, *ordinance!* and you could set your bloody watch by the accuracy of the train schedules, ancient history we're talking, back when folks knew the difference between Arthur and Martha and assumed when they went to the loo or for a washup, they wouldn't be finding some chutney ferrets or pillow biters doing god-knows-what to each other with a bog roll!"

"Manual labor, Mexican, O, that's good. How do you put it over here, jolly good? On the other hand—"

"Men on the old railroads didn't futz about back then. Tough as beavers, they were, worked dawn to dusk without let or hindrance. Gondola rail cars. Open top hoppers. The Severn Valley Railway. The old Romney, Hythe & Dymchurch Railway, 'the smallest public railway in the world,' Tilbury and Southend, the Kyle of Lochalsh Line, what do you want to know? Flat car bridges. Boxcars. I've seen them all. They had to be in tip-top shape and ready to fly. Hard-muscled fireman on the old locomotives shoveling coal into the firebox?"

He grunted. "The ashpan mounted underneath and below the grates, catching and collecting hot embers, ashes, you see, oh, ashes and other solid combustion waste cascading through the grates to be then shaken to clean the dead ash from the bottom of the fire. Of course, the old wood-burners had fixed grates that could not be shaken. Nope. Wood ash, residue really, fly ash—used traditionally by gardeners as a good source of potash, don't you know—generally powder, you see, which will fall through the grates with no more agitation required than the vibrations of your locomotive steaming down the track." He burped. "The oil burner nozzle is usually mounted in the front of the firebox, protected by a hood of firebrick, and aimed at the firebrick wall below the firebox door. Dampers control air flow to the oil fire."

He raised his glass of sherry.

"Long live Gibraltar, long live the monkeys!" he brightly toasted, his eyes moist with glee. He slugged back his drink, and I bought him another, a gin and tonic, half of which he dispatched on the instant. He wheezed, wiping his mustache, pressed his heart, and leaning over at me on one elbow took me in with his blurred smile and swimming eyes.

I could see that he was one of those brass bound, copper-lined, iron-fitted, eat-and-drink-any-amount-anytime-anywhere British types, all chin, that, hard and round and durable as an oak cask, was as fully unbudgeable. "The Rock. 'Cradle of History.' Sits on its haunches just like the Trafalgar lions. Check it out. The official language there? English, not Spanish. Wouldn't set you wrong."

Suddenly, he grew serious. He locked his hands together under his chin and stared into his approving face reflected in the wall-mirror set off by shiny brasses across the bar. He smacked his lips and turned to me. Then he turned back. He smacked his lips again and turned back again to me. He deliberated another moment, with gravitas. Out of the blue, he asked, "What do you know about trains?"

I confessed: very little. But he was talking. "A train, say it out loud. A train. It could be defined as an iron handshake across barriers otherwise insurmountable, I tell you, in-sur-bloody-mountable, Mr.—"

"Well, actually, my name is—"

"Look at it this way—"

He stifled a rising burp with his clenched fist, puffing his cheeks out, wheezed a few times, then continued.

"A boy I was, a lad of a thin six stone, but always in the grip of trains, a right pain in the collar, they say, to be sure, to all the local harriets and herberts, but ask me what I loved as a nipper, and I'd have jumped up to twice full, cap-in-hand, with a hearty, 'Trains, sir!' Trains, sir, take it or-leave it."

"It was your hobby?"

"I *cherished* my Bradshaw, friend. Hobby? Love at first sight. Thumbed through the pages with fervor when I was nothing but a little joey. I was Clever Bill." He looked at me. "You know, Clever Bill Davis, the storybook soldier? Fairy tale? Saga? No? Oh, great train fable—wee Mary's pet toy, British footguard, bearskin hat, carries cymbals? Outruns the young child who has been invited to stay with her aunt in Dover, you see. Well, anyway, I owned a rare Bradshaw Railway Manual Shareholder's Guide and Official Directory for 1874 in full dark plum Morocco. Timetables! Railway guide listings? Oh, the endless hours of delight that it gave me! It was a benefaction to me one Christmas from my uncle, my mother's older brother, W.O.D. Dobbins."

Tryps finished his gin-and-tonic and ordered another. "Phileas Fogg carries a Bradshaw. So did Sherlock Holmes, who greatly relied upon it for travel. Why, Count Dracula swotted up on an English Bradshaw to help in the plan for his voyage to England!"

"I have never heard—"

"Let me add here, my friend, that I would sooner by far read a Bradshaw's Guide than a Dickens novel. I saw the 'Flying Scotchman' out of Doncaster; the narrow-gauge 'Gowrie'; the inimitable 'Invicta' driving from Canterbury and Whitstable; GER's 'Petrolea'; and then the old 'Edward Blount,' fitted up with patent hot-air apparatus, chugging out fit as a ninepin, not unlike the legendary 'White Star,' yes, that's right, a boat train with six-wheeler engines, of which four belonged to a leading bogie the first—the *first*, mind you—in the country, they say."

He was up on his stool now, accelerating with boyish eagerness, his Punch-like smile widening. He waggled his long fingers, his hand opening and closing like an ill-regulated wax-work.

"The Royal Train? Swanning around the world as once I did, I never did take the Royal Train, 'The Britannia'—strictly speaking, it is called the 'Overnight Train to Scotland,' whenever it appears on the engagement card, secret thing and all that, can't be too careful—old steamer, luxury, the best food ever, no 'Boots Meal Deals' for yobbos, trust me, no bangers or bacon buttys, no Ruby Murray, nothing in the way life is lived in Surbiton or the Balls Pond Road, let me tell *you*, and up to the minute? Damned right! Strict as God. Royal timetables, mind you, are quite precisely calculated and locked on to elaborate preparations on both ends of the track."

He sat back.

"Travel? My surname actually denotes a traveler, don't you know. Old name, oh yes, goes way back, found in Debrett or Burke's, whatever. A Tryps crossed the Channel with King Alfred, an intrepid Tryps was with Admiral Sir John Jellicoe at Jutland, and a cousin of mine flew Spitfires and Hawker Hurricanes with the RAF over Caithness and Wick during the Battle of Britain. You'll also find a Tryps once raced auto cars at Brookland, but who's counting?"

Tryps nipped at his gin-and-tonic. "I did once meet the Duke of Edinburgh. Visited our school. My old headmaster, G.F.W. Bibbs, was a close friend. Tall bloke, the Prince. 13 stone or so. Physically fit. Royal Navy. Frightfully good value. Had a fling or two, they say, Russian ballerina. Nudge, nudge. Despises the press, finds the lot ruddy gormless and rude, which they are. A penniless Greek prince, born skint, but mainly German, you know, pushed his own personality uphill."

"Really?"

"The 'D of E'? Oh yes, indeed—a German surname right out of the Old Teutonic manual—the guttural Holstein-Sonder-burg-Glucksburg. Rhinelanders! Yet born in Greece, how do you do! Had three sisters with Nazi links by marriage. Had to renounce his German titles when marrying and to adopt the sur-name Mountbatten, an Anglicised version of Battenberg, Oh, it all went down poorly. He was enraged all his life that a very upset Churchill insisted the Royal Family would continue to be called Windsor! Philip squawked at the time, quote, 'I am nothing but a bloody amoeba—the only man in the country not allowed to give his name to his own children.' Never forgave Winston. Chap said whatever came to mind. Never gave a toss. Remarked to the president of Nigeria, who was dressed in traditional robes, 'You look like you're ready for bed!'"

Tryps, with triple snorts, hooted in laughter.

"Not a demonstrative father. Favors his daughter, Anne, not Charlie 'Wide Ears.' But then the chap has lots on his plate, doesn't he? Never drinks tea. Won't touch it. Popinjay. Refuses to shake hands. Arthritic wrist. Tipples." Another sip. "Known as 'P.P.,' among his intimates, they say. Calls his wife 'Cabbage.'"

"You don't mean—?"

"Aye, you heard it here. Not Elizabeth or Liz or Lizbeth or Betty, but actually addresses the Queen of England as 'Cab-bage'!"

Tryps tapped a finger to his temple.

"They're an odd bunch. Well, it's all about in-breed-ing, isn't it? Handicaps the brain. Kinship? Look at the Czars. Kaiser Bill. All of the Windsors are mean as cat's piss, they say. The Queen gave the Royal laundress a bag of clothespins one

Christmas. Charles squeezes his toothpaste tube with a silver instrument called a mangle so as to eke out the last bit—insists the tubes be recycled! A sign in the Buckingham Palace loos and lavatories reads 'Don't pull for a pee.'"

He folded his arms, leaned back, blew air.

"My room even as a toddler was, was, was *filled* with magazines," he rattled on, fevered with enthusiasm. *"British Railways Illustrated. Model Rail. Crossties and Classics. Barrow Hill. Rail Professional.* I was given a book of train plans—scheme, photos, routes. timetables, fares, what-not—by an uncle of mine. Cannot tell you the fancies it brought me. I valued it as much as the first umbrella given me by my father when I gained my majority, an expensive solid stick from James Smith & Sons. Price sticker Everest high, Malacca cane crook. Cotton flag. Loft on the uplift. *Purchase*, how do you do. My father! They called him 'a good cricket umpire.' No higher praise can be had. I was the lad up front in his compact maroon Sunbeam-Talbot, 1936, munching a banjo bar or a jamboree bag or Harrogate toffees and happy as billy-be-duckets. Loved the old iron horses, he did. Short lives they had. Steam railway was my favorite."

He slipped out another one of my cigarettes.

"During WW Two, all I *had* was my magazines, didn't I? Nightly heard the bombs. Oh, frightful." He shook his head. "Bloody Huns. Germans. Thank King William Three for that. A Dutchman. Billy of Orange. Childless, a poofter, they say—went in big for strapping young gallants, or so goes the report. So? Nothing at all, other than the fact that, with the Protestant succession imminently threatened, this bloke went and solved the problem by placing all of his distant German relatives in line for the throne, all of those lumbering, slumbering Hanoverians.

Heinies. The Boche. Right here on English sod, elbows out, farting into the silk cushions."

He raised a toast, "To the mole that raised the hill that caused King William to fall from his horse and die!" In one great gulp he downed his remaining gin-and-tonic. "You've not heard that? Oh aye, William of Orange's horse, Sorrel, stumbled over a bump or hump, molehill they say—" Tryps began to cough—"over in the park at Hampton Court on 20 February 1702, catapulting him into eternity." Gasping, he stabbed out the smoke and yet, while wheezing and gasping, began pointing to the cigarette stub.

"Coffin nails," he said, winking at me. "Dad didn't want me to smoke. Why? Simple, because *he himself* did, the slippery old dog. So did J.C.F. Marychurch, a business partner of his who reeked of Rothmans which he puffed like a grampus, hypocrites both, the buggers," he laughed, wheezing, again mentioning a name that was a forest of initials which the English seemed to rely on with vainglorious pomp.

"No, no, my father wouldn't look at a fag. A good solid John Brumfit Bulldog was his pipe. Smoked coarse-cut shag. Liked the way it packed and burned. Good draw." He ordered another drink—this time a cognac, but he ordered nothing for me. "I do believe he also owned a Butz Choquin churchwarden. The real thing, mind you. Kept it on the mantelpiece for a giraffe. Said he wouldn't touch a Falcon Coolway—American import, Hollywood blokes smoked 'em, well, you would know. Oh yes, mad for a good smoke he was. Had a pipe rack. The whole bit. Tools. Pipe knives, reamers, you name it. I swear that every last one of the railway magazines of those that he kindly gave me reeked of Kendall Gold Mixed Black Cherry!"

He knocked back half his cognac.

"Ah," he inhaled, patted his stomach and pointed to his glass. "Cognac. Nothing like it. Keeps you right as a ribstone pippin." He tapped the counter. "But aye, we've all got bad habits, truth to tell."

"Back in America—"

"Right, right. You Yanks included, our cousins," he proclaimed, wheezing. "We Brits can never figure you out. You lot put *cold milk* in your tea. Employ teabags with strings. What gives, huh?" He heard the sound of chimes coming from St. Paul's. "Listen? No bells in U.S. cities, right? A pity, that. You blokes also sidle up to tip everyone, don't you, chat up perfect strangers, blow your noses in public, laugh too loudly, drink your coffee on the run, and boldly ask people what they do for a living. Why, you Americans tick every box! Oh, we've heard it all. Open gifts in front of the giver, pay sales taxes—why?—and always write the damn date out of order, what else, and, oh yes, bog-standard, refer only to yourselves as Americans when half your bloody continent is—well, I mean, is *South America* chopped liver? Your paper currency is all the same color."

"You mean green?"

"Right."

"That is odd?"

"Won't wash."

"I have never heard—"

He finished his cognac. "Mmmm, but I was talking about the rails."

"Steam railways," I said. "In old New York—"

"Steam railways? Before I was twenty, I knew every fire brick and rocking grate lever, every cylinder cock and valve rod, every link lifter and cab bracket that ever fit out any thriving iron horse you could name. Dammit, I could take down a locomotive myself in no less time than your finest engine-wright, blow on each piece for luck, and have it back together before the moon could snap her silver garters: driving wheels, iron tank, toiler, crank axle, smoke box, fishplates, cylinders, discs, footplate, points and crossings, spikes, screws, tar framing, trailing ponies, and turret-head borings, to a one, mister, and how do you like them apples?"

I checked my watch—and paid for another drink. "My wife is—"

"In the loo, she'll be out, not to worry," he interrupted and pounded out his cigarette stub. "See, I knew my Annis' *Ready Reference for Enginemen* back and forth, didn't I? Knew my fuels, too. Chapter and verse, son. From the pump governor to the automatic slack adjuster to the Kunkle Pop Valve. How many in his pub could explain the Kunkenheimer Injector, 99 model?"

"She's exhausted, poor thing. We've been sight-seeing and—"

"Ah, the joys of a being a nipper. I remember taking a holiday train through Pappelwick up to Wetwang, a two-pound bar of Cadbury's motoring chocolate on my nine-year-old lap. It was very heaven." He chuckled. "Sweets. My downfall. What, popping a Milk Tray hazelnut swirl or a truffle charm from a clutched box of them? An orange sensation or coffee crescent from Black Magic? Nothing beats it, my good man. Nothing on God's green earth." He quoted, "'Who knows the secret of the Black Magic box?'" He chuckled. "Slogan, you see. Kept them in me gob like a baby's dummy. My Mum wrapped them in clingfilm for me."

"And if—"

He was now slurping his cognac.

"My old dad, bless the man, was a supreme authority on the London and Southampton Railway. It's our arteries, boy. Remember that, he told me. Don't forget it, he said. Sew the button on. By 19-and-23, its mail line extended from Waterloo in London via Woking, Basingstoke, and Winchester to Southampton, Bournemouth, Poole, and Weymouth." Tryps took a long deep pull on his cognac. "It also operated a main line from Waterloo via Guildford to Portsmouth (the 'Portsmouth Direct line'), and another via Salisbury and Exeter to Plymouth running parallel to, but south of, the GWR main line."

He was breathing in my face. "That route, my friend, dubbed by quipsters as the 'Withered Arm,' extended into Devon and Cornwall, serving many of the south and southwest seaside resorts and was known as the 'Atlantic Coast Express.' The LSWR also had a busy suburban network in southwest London. The Somerset and Dorset Joint Railway was jointly owned with the Midland Railway. My dad, the rogue, claimed that he also knew the Taff Vale railway, which originated with a line from Merthyr Tydfil to Cardiff. Let me tell you about the Taff line: difficult, man, a bit of a dicey go, it was, as was evidenced by gradients back then of 1 in 40 at a half-dozen different places; but at Blaenclydach there is a half-mile ascent of 1 in 13 on a mineral line."

"Doesn't Freud speak of trains, generally, as sexual—"

"Heavy six-coupled trailing radial tank engines are used in this famous incline, but there must be reckoned the passenger stock, numbering upwards of three hundred vehicles humping along, three hundred? well, that would be a good estimate, I daresay, yes, I would definitely say so. Three special locomotives"—and here out of nowhere he produced a photo, which he held protectively above the palette of a sticky beer ring on the bar in front of him—

"are employed upon this incline." Proudly, he snapped at his photograph with the back of his middle finger and said, "Have a shufti. No handsomer a piece of machinery on the face of Mother Earth. The cylinders are 17½ by 26 inches, the wheels 5 feet 3 inches in diameter. The firebox and roof slope backwards so that the water is level over the top of the firebox. They are fitted with two clever drawbars for attaching the wire rope in such a manner that the rope is kept below the axles of the wagons. In addition to the ordinary equipment, there are cast-iron 'sleigh' brakes to act upon the rails. Now, the dome, you see, is on the firebox and the regulator—"

He finished the cognac. I bought him another.

"Now I remember," I enthusiastically jumped in, "Yup, yup, I once saw *Jubbulpore Gauge* with, um—"

Tryps paused, drew back, and his face grew sour. "But what the deuce—"

"It's a movie, about trains."

"*Indian* trains? I can tell you something about Indian trains, old chap, and some of the trips over there, oh yes."

"Your family lived in India?"

"Come again?"

"The Tryps in India. They are your relations?"

"*Trips*, hang it all, man—travel, runnings out, firing up the Ghat inclines, hauling out tender over the sun-scorched-blazing wog trackplate, coaled, watered, and fire cleaned." He paused. "Inja, man. Jambudvipa. Hindustan." He quoted, "'Where there is rock to the left, and rock to the right, and low lean thorn between / And ye may hear a breech-bolt snick where never a man is seen.'"

"Pardon me?"

"Kipling."

"Sorry."

"Happens all the time," he said and knocked back, at the cost of god-knows-what, the third cognac I'd bought him. He bounced energetically at me with wet crazy eyes, now beginning to cross, redden, swim.

"Take your Poona race specials shooting down from Bombay. I've run it under a filthy sun on coupled wheels, 6-feet 6-inch diameter, 66 tons and a pip of a fire carriage with 10 tons of fuel sloshing in the tender that it makes me go all weak, and fast? I'll rub-a-dub fast, old boy, give as good an account of herself as a flippin' rocket, done herself proud. Stories? You want stories?"

He swerved to look at me. "Well, I once rode the 'Rajputana Ripper' right through the dog days, with neither snipe of food nor spit of water, and, oooh, she was a tough little towser, her bogies pivoting like bent spoons, and, with its gases sparking up, it put the fear of the good God into the sweepers and native princes alike watching her racing along like billybeduckets with cannonade, batman, and tassels flying. It was a sticky patch there for a while, out there with your red man, your nigger, your darkie, don't dare think not, with dicky plate, laid any which way; dreadfully chipped tunnels, blacker than jet? Throw in, of course, your wog signalmen and what-have-you. But we came through. The beggars needed it, I won't lie—gave the poor devils insight into the agency of the rail, you see. A first-rate look. They were sods to convince, coolie minds, you know, johnny crapos, swipes, Pakis, and chee-chees, truth to tell, but, well, we did it. Granted, it was touch and go, but, as they say, where there's a will—"

"There's a way, yes," I nodded, "but my wife has been in the—"

"See? Take away the white man and all your fuzzies and golliwogs over there would still be using the straight air brake without a clue! True, the plain automatic air brake was a great improvement over the straight air brake. In a flash emergency the system still applied the brakes to the last cars in a train later than to the first cars. To remedy that condition, George Westinghouse, one of your people, mind you, invented the quick action triple brake valve in 1887, testing the system on the CB&West Burlington Hill (Iowa) in 1887, which automatically vented air locally from the brake pipe on each car, you see, and so applied the brakes more quickly. South Africa?"

"But in the United States—"

"The old Blue Trains from Jo'burg to Cape Town? Know them? *Do I know them?* I'll say I do. I have ridden the blighters many's the time, oh yes, many is thee time, you hear?" he loudly proclaimed, wheezing, a quick hand to the mouth stifling a belch. "Now we're going back here, you understand, oh yes, returning to the days of the 'Union Limited' and the 'Union Express,' remember, which was started back in oh, 1923 thereabouts. They

went for luxury features back then—dining saloons added in
1933, air-conditioned carriages in '39."

He ordered a whiskey. "Hot? Try the Karoo. I saw a couple of blueguns—boogles—wandering around Letaba in Lim-
popo Province, just South of Tzaneen, near dead as nails from
calenture. Heat stroke. Delirium. I want to tell you—grim. Tropi-
cal-weight suits that were crisp in W1 crumble like blotting paper
in the habitat they were supposedly designed for." Suddenly, a
mad beady glare electrified his eyes and up came that long jut-
ting chin, stiff as a poker.

"But the situation down there nowadays?" he queried
me. "Trumpery! The way they run it? Slubber. African timetables? Bumfuzzle. Efficiency? Slag, right to the core. Anticlockwise
thinking, rum officials. Rail service? Nonexistent. Reservations?
None. Stand up for hours, a full day with uncouth bosthoons
through the Great Karoo, 1262 kilometres, stony hills, absolute
desert, prickly pears, cacti, jump-jerking along until your spindles go weak, the entire operation an imperatorial goatfuck." He
leaned in to peer closer to me, his eyes out on stalks. "Grab a
ticket on the train and hold onto your wallet! Trust Tryps! You
are getting advice right from the castle! Such are the perilous
times we live in, boyo. Make a complaint? Sweet Fanny Adams is
what you get, the two-fingered salute."

"I remember back in—"

"Gone are the days, my friend. Your old Pullman porter? Brains smaller than shoe-peg corn. And talk about being
slower than ratshit? I could tell you stories. 'Over here, Rastus,
here, fetch me a Bulmer's Woodpecker Cider, pronto, no ice!'
Oh, you've got to love it. 'Yes, boss, right away, ma'am, anything
you say, sah. Comin' righty up, sah!' But nowadays? Not likely, no

way, no how. You hear only your own echo. Stupid as owls. '*Sasa hivi*,' he'll mutter in Swahili, bobbing in deference, wot? 'Rahhtht away, sah,' then the nine ball goes and disappears for the day."

He sipped his whiskey and wiped his mustache. The disturbing set of his mouth suggested inner ferment.

"Basically, your kaffir did his job, if supervised. Train boys kept mainly on task—with exceptions, mind you. I used to see lots of coons half-cocked back there in the lumber cars slugging down Kanonkop or Cape White or Wells Waggle Dance, rusty nails, nail-polish remover, weird pinotages, the worst South African wines you could buy, crappy bottled shirazes like ja-jar jerky, what you Yanks call 'Night Train' or 'Thunderbird' or Ripple or Cisco—bum wine, *burnt* wine, fortified piss, sweet, fizzy, cheap screw-top shit, tailored to the taste of vagrants and hobos and skid row dossers with cellar palates, 20% alcohol, peach and berry and grape, stomach-heaving and palate-crippling disappointment, cruddy flagship reds, undrinkable, with mocha and burnt rubber tastes. The aroma lingers like the bashed metal of an auto accident. I acquire a headache just talking about it!"

Tryps interrupted himself to take a dram. He queerly hummed when he sipped a drink, a murmuring satisfaction as if to remind himself of the pleasure, and he *chewed* liquor, mouthing it about like gum.

"Fact is, our boy is a thing of the past, extinct, dead, defunct, a distant memory. Nig-nogs? Shiftless as Canadian thistles. Their looks even skeeved me. Sambos out of Pimville and Kliptown all with a devious look, horny-looking, like a Dartmoor pixie—you know, the antique doorknocker—and with ears open. Bantus, kaffirs, dangerous ANC troublemakers, love to sing, Soweto blokes who got on the railway police, angry tattooed blokes just out of leg chains from Pollsmoor prison, the number gangs '26s' and '27s,' hard as woodpecker lips. And how about the way the wogs currently handle your luggage and trunks? *Wogs?* Can't even say the word out loud nowadays! Put it in brackets, right? All disability allowance and buck-passing. Breaks your heart. Your coloreds"—he whispered a soft aside—"Gormless mingers, if you want the truth. Malingerers, *mompies.* The Tories had the right idea all along. Backbenchers of dog-whistle racism? Friends of apartheid?" He answered his own question.

"Bollocks, I say. It is about reality, my man! Chapeau up to Enoch Powell! Oh, but it's a sight now the way the municipalities look. Take the line run, Transkaroo. Piggate housing all along the city tracks, worse than the bloody Gorbels. Hovels. Shanties, dog-trot cabins. If it's not that, it's public housing and the projects. Subsidies. It is a free ride for all of them nowadays. Mooching."

"But if you're willing to reason—"

"Are they underpaid? Oh well, they give you that all day, don't they? Stiff cheddar, I say. Dopeheads, duffers, plonkers, wallies, wankers." He burped. "Why humbug about it? You are courting disaster simply disembarking the *train,* my friend, never mind exiting the thieving dark terminals of Johannesburg, where no end of baleful buggery and brutality awaits you. We can't have any of that here. Can't have it. Unsafe. Blacker than chocolate! Like your Chicago, real whore of a place, I'm told, overcrowded, raggamuffins, rummies, living cheek to jowl, desolate in a way, like your Utah, an unholy piss-poor—"

"But no, Utah is out west, by the mountains in—"

"Safe? *Safe?* In downtown Jo'burg? The train station is literally crawling with jungle bunnies, Kaffers, brigands, back-country hawbucks, pickpockets, barn-door primitives, cracksmen, second-storey creeps whose genes might have been scraped off a septic tank, and murderous dacoits as black as a Newgate knocker, any one of whom will relieve you of your belongings faster than a wife can find a way to spend it. Too black to whitewash, my friend! Trust them? I would trust a Bedouin camel trader or a pawnshop kike with an eye loupe screwed into his head sooner than I'd trust a one of them, let me tell you, and I'm not exaggerating. Your Hottentot? Pull the other one, it's got bells on. Dirty bucks out for a shag, every man jack of them. It is no different here in London. Look at Lambeth! Brixton! Never mind the West Midlands. Merely looking at a nog, you can *hear* him evilly machinating to cut your throat! Oh, no, your corner-boy will give you chin, every Jim Fish and jungle bunny and boot-lip. Can be as cheeky and insolent as he wants. It's been proven time and again."

"But surely every time—"

"Jo'burg is Birmingham in spades. Why, I've seen many a good white woman openly insulted down on Wolmarans, Rissik, and Noord streets, Oh, and directly there in front of me, how is that for starters? Doesn't even *begin* to explain the meaning of offensive, right? Me, I would sit every one of them down on a long grid of hot-fired Fenny Poppers and blow their arses off!"

To Major Tryps, foreigners—any, many, almost all of them—were not worth anything for lacking sufficient resolve. "Russians? Boers? Krauts? South American browns and blacks and duskies? They have for centuries not only given birth to violent and hardened criminals but, face it, are down to a man nothing but a bunch of lazy shiftless cucumbers. No energy. Cream-crackered. Would sleep all day. Make a dog's dinner of the smallest task. Faffing about. All pants, let me tell you." Something of a hair-on-fire tone entered his voice after taking a hefty slug of another bright whiskey, on me, incidentally. His chesty proclamations were accompanied by tweaking his mustache.

"Italians are macaroni eaters. Your Spaniard is blood-thinned and weak as water, given the long lame tradition over there of intermarriage with inferior Latin races. Take your Indian: it is a race, is it not? A race of millions of kedgeree-munchers and towel-headed rail-thin macacas who, squatting like yobbos, allowed themselves to be placed under the dominion of a little remote island in the north of Europe? Superstitious cow worshippers! Curry house odor. Is it the fenugreek? Open the windows! Let me tell you, my friend, they could drive a saint to hell in a dogsled!"

"But—"

"Fickle as weathercocks."

"And yet—"

"Dogsbodies, menials, drudges."

"If they only had—"

"Crossing-sweepers and budges." He shook his head. "No room for the bleeders. No," he affirmed, "wogs begin at Calais."

"The thing is—"

"I mean, Churchill thought the Boers were hideous —'grim, hairy, and terrible,' he called them—with their long drooping beards and ratty coats, and filthy shagbags with feet like longboats in wooden shoes? He should take a butcher at these blokes with their Ruby Murray breath, right?"

"Still—"

"There are classes much worse, it's true, but not much more contemptible, if you get my drift. We Brits have shown them too damned much ruth all along. Why so? We have the disadvantage of civilization. Hear me? *Dis*advantage, I say. Too liberty-loving when we should have been cracking heads. That's the capstone of progress, my friend. Did we put paid to the Hun back in 1919? I'll rub-a-dub we didn't. The result? *'Fuhrer gefehl, wir folgen.'* Fuhrer command us, we'll follow. Get my drift? The mother of idiots is always pregnant. No, I'll take the white man," said Tryps.

"'Let the buffalo gore buffalo, and the pasture to the strongest'—your own man there, Mr. R. W. Emerson, if I'm not wrong. No, reason goes walkabout with your average coon, my good man. And I say woe to us if, content with only our legendary pride, we flag in the matter of cultivating the rugged, the forceful, oh yes, the *virile* virtues."

Anxiously I checked my watch. "But before you—"

"I've bulled out of South Aff on the Capetown-Buluwayo line; know the Canton-Kowloon run—poorly lighted bleeder, she—like I know my own mother's footsize; rode the old 'Orient Express' when the poor lass was just a poor, neglected, wood-burning thingamabob, rocking along on her just-as-poor-as-outworn antique buns and rockers; and then the 'Copper Nob,' the 'Baden Powell,' the 'City of Truro,' the 'Sudanese Jumbo,' and even the Austrian 'Röllbocke' with a kick like a mad snorting stud out-of-pocket and a blast pipe that'd blow your sweet nickers off." He polished off his drink, wiped his chin, exhaled gas with a wheeze, and stood his glass down.

"Aye, I shunted about, my friend, rode the hefty Pacific of the London and North Western Railway, the elegant brass-capped Castles out to the West Midlands and most of Wales, oh, on pert little steam trains, lovingly restored, did your heart good, you know, brisk breakfast tea and marmalade, the best, beaten and smooth, oh no, none of your 'chipped' or shredded-peel versions, I will not touch shredded-peel marmalade, a right little Teasmade set down in front of you, right in your lap, maybe a bag of boiled sweets, no smelly food, be clean, you know, pick up your debris, no littering, all that, racing from London to Cardiff, Shrewsbury to Swansea, streaking along the Bristol Channel Shore, you want to see blue water, my man? Oh yes, by the by, no more respectful or attentive a lot on earth can be found than those gangers, wheel-tappers, linesmen, and locomotive engineers. Ask me!"

He leaned in under my face, bending close to me, as if he were less ready to share a secret than inspect my chin.

"And now you're going to learn something, dear fellow. I'm going to tell you about a fierce explosion we had taking out, oh years ago, from Chipping Sodbury, for, my goodness, of course there are dangers, *res ipsa loquitur* and all that. Touch a toasted sandwich with hot cheese? Get the picture: it was an old 'fire-horse,' this one, six wheels coupled radial tank engine; cylinders 18 inches by 26; total wheel base, 21 feet 3 inches, with a real overhang at the trailing end; standard boiler, a beauty in her time; total heating surface, 1174 square feet; area of fire grate, 17 square feet. The side and bunker tanks had a capacity of 1416 gallons, all juice; bunker capacity here, oh, 2 percent tons of coal. A powerful steam brake acted on—"

Next thing I knew I was in the men's room, just leaning with one arm against the wall and staring down disconsolately into a dribbling urinal. I couldn't take any more. I remember walking around in a nervous circle in there, nipping at the cuticle of my thumb. I was in knots. I swear to God, I was in knots.

When I returned to the bar, my wife, calm-as-you-please, was sitting alone at one of the stools sipping her drink. She shrugged and, with a self-satisfied smile, coy tongue to upper lip, told me—nodding, gesturing vaguely toward the front door with a swizzle-stick—that what's-his-face, just before he left, had asked her if she would like to visit St. Paul's.

    "You? And without me," I asked with some shock, "alone?"

    "He said you were, let me see—"

    "What?"

    "Well . . ."

    "Tell me."

    Closing her eyes, she pronounced, "'A crashing bore.'"

    She was drinking, I noticed, a Dusenberry Snap.

The American Tourist Home

"Hey, sport, got a light?"

I had.

"Them nicks you see," he said, puffing hard, his face a scowl cemented shut against the billowing smoke, "ain't from the mower, uh-uh. Nope. They come from pickin' my strings. That thumb there is harder'n a Mississippi pine-knot, look. I play the gee-tar and am fixin'"—he winked—"to do that very thang up in New York City first chance I get, and you take that to the bank."

Duane's mother ran the tourist home in Beulahsville, Virginia. Amicably, as I had pulled up in my old Chevy, he appeared leaning into my car window showing a face as ugly as a hedgerow fence. He was a long-faced, thin-headed, delicate-necked specimen of real country stock. He had a moose's banjo muzzle, an oversize upper lip that drooped. His eyes looked like convex shank buttons, while his hair confettied in the rude snippets of grass he had just cut was cropped, bristly, prairie-grass rooted, and straight, like the hard mane of a stubborn mule. He was wearing bib overalls, but while I unloaded some things from my car, he changed into a faded-blue frayed 4-H club sweater, a string tie, and gigantic jodhpurs. Why? Who knew? Came dusk as we sat there on his front porch there, smelling the heady sweetness of tedded grass.

My room with its walls out of alignment was small, covered with faded pink sheep-hopping-fences wallpaper with one window, its shiny frame heavily varnished, open to a meadow, some railroad furniture, a nailed-up wall calendar fat with illustrations, and a Bible lying on a deal dresser. A sign in a natural wood-twig frame—bold Clarendon type—stated "God Bless Our Home."

We sat outside and rocked in our chairs, sucked Nehis, and stared out at a dull savannah of bushes and shrubs growing dim in the dusk through which occasionally a few bunnies darted. I could see on a hill faraway fields with flax blossoms like waving water. Duane was just sitting there blathering and rhythmically twitching the right foot raised above his left knee to the sounds of the radio reaching us through the window of the kitchen, where his mother was making cobbler and singing, "If You Take Two Steps Toward Jesus, He'll Take Ten Steps Toward You," and the music, the radio's, reminded him, he said, of his Nashville dream, his sweetheart Lorinda, and the old Ford pickup he totalled going jukin' one night over in Chattanooga, a name I have to say I can never think of, frankly, without smirking.

The porch we sat on, faded white wood, smelled like stale bread.

I nodded. "Where does that pathway lead to?" I asked.

"Nowheres."

"Not a pond?"

"Nothin', nope."

Duane yawned.

"Want another Nehi?"

"No, thank you."

"A Grapette? A TruAde? A Dr. Pepper?"

"This'll do."

"You ever been to Nashville?" queried Duane.

"Never."

"Neither've I. You plannin' to?"

"Probably. One day," I replied. "You?"

A cat skittered away.

There was a long, long silence.

"Oh God," I heard. It was a sigh borne from the footsole, pregnant with respect and expectation and a slight unworthiness.

I myself, fatigued utterly, had pulled off the road for lodgings on my way back from Florida. Beulahsville was the compromise between the fretfully depressing Danville, it of the mills, and Thomas Jefferson's more effete Charlottesville, where I had promised myself an open day, though for the life of me I couldn't reach it, for the sharp crick in my neck and a pinched zygomatic arch. Initially, Beulahsville meant a night's sleep (at whatever cost), but to those on the *qui vive* for such things, demonstrably me, I found something far more interesting. There is a phenomenon easily overlooked by the inattentive, empanelled deep in the heart of America, especially in the South. It is the odd fly in our mythic amber called—

"A tourist home, oh yeh, huh-huh," said Duane, nodding with closed eyes and showing positive conviction when I had asked him what, unlike himself, his parents wanted more than anything else in the world. "In other words," he clarified, "a home just for tourists." Duane mentioned that he was thirty years old.

He seemed aimless but intense and had a severe stare that collapsed into a cheerful grin when he was amused.

"And you just cut the grass?"

"Generally—and sit around, 'ceptin Saturday night when I have a right good time, but—"

I looked up.

"—but I'm own go to New York City come the opportunity, and ooo-wee, lemme tell you, ain't no tellin' what's going to happen, friend, 'cept lock up them girls ever one of them and throw away the dang key, OK, 'cause when I'll be blowin' through there like grist through a damn dwarf, I'll be totin' my everlovin' gee-tar, which"—he winked—"really attracts 'em." He surgically licked the creases on his thumb and seemed to study each of them. He grinned. "Broads."

"Yes?" I said.

"You set with your drink?"

"I'm fine."

"Mom likes a Grapette."

"No, thank you."

"New York and zoom." He jerked his thumb backwards and shook his head. "I ast no permission from no one, un-uh. None"

I yawned.

"I'm not married," he clarified.

"Not yet," a voice blurted through a window.

"That's ma. My mother," he helpfully clarified and whispered to me, "A few peas short of a casserole."

"What about, um, Lorinda?" I thought to ask.

"Oh, we go walkin' now and again. She's a good ol' gal.

Was goin' with Evelina, but she crop-dusted me."

Long silence.

"Ma makes the same dang inquiries. I always tell her, 'Reason not the need.' Get me? No reason, no need."

"He tells me nothin'!" A squawk from inside.

Duane winked at me. "Broads," he mused. "Can't live with 'em, can't live without 'em. Can't use their bones for soup."

Whether he knew that remark, one of badass Sonny Barger's memorable apothegms, was a well-documented lament of the Hell's Angels I couldn't say. Rednecks love lore, think they invented it.

"I had a crush on Anita Bryant once." He looked at me. "The singer? I noodle for catfish and carp. By hand. Hand-fishing. I got lots of books about pythons, mm-*mm*. Lots to do here. Can fix a weedwacker. The most expensive gas is found in Norway. I like fried pies and collard greens." He seemed to be scanning the treetops. I found him a bit like the old His Master's Voice sitting dog, peering in stupefaction down the horn of the gramophone, except up. Duane seemed nice enough, room-temperature intellect, lots of good will, not a reader certainly. "I'm a Republican. Democrats? Don't know shit from apple butter. No, Republicans gone get this country back on its feet, huh-huh, don't you worry," he promised. God as his witness.

"Ike Eisenhower on the D-Day there? Won the war is all, how's that? I'll yank a knot in the man who says no."

He was *political?* Worried about the national debt? I had rather thought the economy down here was roughly similar to that of the Congo. Keep the plantains coming. Free baobab and kola. Singing loud at church.

"It's peaceful around here, anyway. Some may say bowring." He shrugged. "You want the water, you get the wet."

Cicadas buzzed and clicked in the post oaks and syca-
mores and a stand of pines. Noises like scratching itches.

"Expect it's going to be warm tomorrow."

"Excuse me?" I said.

He nodded toward the sky.

"Crows flyin' in pairs."

He wiped his hair and set down his empty soda bottle.

The American tourist home, fanned, usually, by the inevitably local meadow smells of mundungus and warm grass, is that
small, sub-memorable clapboarded little accommodation that
you pass and almost immediately forget, an unpigmented little
dwelling-with-porch with a frontage of wilting geraniums and
grimacing plaster elves, all of it, generally, under the protection
and blessings of two soap-faced marrieds, ca. fifty—arms folded,
white socks, square thumbs—exercising to and fro, at dusk, in an
unoiled porchswing, pausing at moments in shocked obmutency
over The Recently Fallen Away World (perpetually urban), and
exchanging in mournful numbers slowly pronounced comments
on the merits of teat-dip; this year's quality snaps; the bugs in
the swiss chard; the weird rash of blewits found that morning by
the ha-ha; the new treasurer of the Jaycees; and apposite matters
touching generally on farmhouse pharmacopeia. The tourist
home is crucial Americana—as common as corn fritters, as time-
proof as Main Street, and as much in evidence as the fruited
plain.

"Shay-it," pronounced Duane out of the blue. "Sure'd
like to be in Memphis right 'bout now. Ain't got enough strength
to blow the fuzz off a peanut around here in Beulahsville. All
sapped out." He whistled dryly and leaned forward, jaw in hand.

"Now Memphis, well, that's more like it. Saturday night sippin' on a hailstorm julep made with real peach brandy? Fancied up with sliced fruit?" He clapped his hands, once, one dry clap. "Oooooo-*wee.*"

He let out a deep sigh. "Need money." He spat. "Lots." He spat again. "Who don't though? Right? I ain't shiftless. Right now, things are tight. What do they say, too poor to paint, too proud to whitewash?"

He told me about an early farming ambition to grow and sell okra, "Out back," he said. "I grew it, boxed it, and sold it out front a buck the quart. Done right good, too. As they say, it ain't what you do, it's the way how you do it." I told him I thought those weird pods grew down Biloxi way and warm places like Louisiana. "Not if you plant the seeds indoors, Doc. In peat pots under full light. *They grab to grow!* Shoot up like a herd of turtles. I fancy I can grow most anything, I put my mind to it. Shoot, Ezekiel saw spaceships, right, wheels upon wheels? I also grew muskmelons. Cantaloupes. 'Superstar' and 'Eclipse.'" He jerked his thumb. "She ast me to. Crows played havoc with 'em. I'd like to see ever crow alive dead, ever dang one. Course, they hear any old thang you present to 'em. Smart as paint. Of all creatures alive, they have the hide to know what's goin' on. Crows don't never roost nowhere's there's noise. You can start your okra directly in a garden a month 'fore the last spring frost date, long as you cover the dang plants with a cold frame, which I made solid out of old wooden belvederes I liberated from the Wegman's here—he shaped a large square in the air with his hands—"liberated, by which I mean borrowed, if you catch my drift."

"Oh, pallets" I said.

He shrugged. "Belvederes, I call 'em."

His mother yelled out, "*Pallets!*"

"Make sure that the covering is two feet or so, so that the plants have room to grow," said Duane. "Okra thrives in full hot sun. Good for okra but keeps the melons back. He stretched. "I love 'em, soups. You harvest the okra when it's about three inches long. Cut the stem 'bove the cap with a knife. Toss 'em if the stems are too hard to cut. Wear gloves, right? 'Cause them suckers are covered with tiny spines that will irritate your damn skin, unless you have the spineless variety."

His mother shouted hard, "*You're* the spineless variety!" I imputed this obloquy to the fact that Duane quickly lost interest in his farming scheme, frustrating his—very agitated if loving—mother.

"Plus, I hurt my shins, right there, all that bending over there and what-not. I take a pill for it, Perna Canaliculus Green-Lipped Mussel Extract." Wow, that came out fast. I could see that Duane liked to say it and had said it many times. "A capsule!" yelled his mother. Duane stretched, settled back, folded his hands. "Fishy taste, for poky joints, said to help, cain't say. Just a pill."

His mother shouted, "A capsule!"

The tourist home is in the world, not of it. Folks travel. These folks put them up. Folks, they say, are generally the same all over. Folks got to sleep. Folks, as they say, don't want sashayin' around and fussin' and bein' up 'til all hours. Folks passing by then are more or less grateful for the folks that run the home, everyone, all things considered, being just plain folks in the first place, except maybe up there in New York, which is a cryin' shame and a thing that makes you wonder and a horse of a different color.

I looked around and smelled the tang of soil and sod, a warm cat's-paw breeze blowing from a field pasture. Had I discovered a place, as Kipling put it, where "the dead who did not die but may not live"?

A *donneé* in this business of the tourist home down South is that they are almost always found in quiet, dull, motionless flat-iron towns with open-ended wide-A suffixes suggesting, so seemed the intention, a kind of neo-Masonic esotericism, Greco-Roman ersatz, a kind of star-gazing, forward-looking gestalt of Columbia, the Gem of the Ocean: Alma, Eulalia, Moravia, Utopia, Batavia, Swannanoa, Bonhomia, Fantasia, Amazia, etc. In such places many Gothic Revivaland American Foursquare and Prairie Victorian houses from the Bliss Carman and Thomas Bangs Thorpe era abounded, with welcome mats, serviceable carpets, and savanarolean rooms. And to these rooms, studiously obliterative of every trace of pretense and generally fitted out with a Gideon Bible, cotton priscillas framing each window, and heartening signs everywhere you look (e.g., "There's a Heaven to Find, a Hell to Miss"), come the intrepid Polos and pan-animated wanderers of America who, in point of fact, have usually taken the wrong road, missed the right bus, incorrectly booked a train, blinked the key incidentals of a highway sign, got waylaid or parlayed at the eleventh hour, or whatever—people, in any case, who, even if for a night, have simply retired from life into the gloaming of rustic privacy for a supper of nutritious soup, the sound of crickets, and a good night's sleep.

Duane's mother, thumping the window sill, set out two servings of cobbler in rumpled-glass dishes.

I took a spoonful. "Raspberry."

"Yup,"

"Nothing better."

"Nope."

By nature, types convene. They gather by brand, link by lope. I have long been familiar with George Orwell's complaint about "the horrible—the really disquieting—prevalence of cranks wherever Socialists are gathered together," with his "impression" that "the mere words 'Socialism' and 'Communism' draw towards them with magnetic force every fruit-juice drinker, nudist, sandal-wearer, sex-maniac, Quaker, 'Nature Cure' quack, pacifist, and feminist in England." It was no different, I've come to see, with the type of travel-weary folks on the road who take solace— find sanctuary—in the country tourist home. There is a pronounced comfort in the replenishing quiet, predictable mores, and subdued sameness that guarantees nothing unexpected, merely the same creaking rockers, slanted old porch, possibly a swing, and rumpled quilts.

"Pretty dishes. Sandwich glass maybe. Pebbled edges."

"Them are old."

"Antiques."

"Did you know that the solar system's most distant known object is a body called 1996 TL66, which lies some odd eighty times as far from the Sun as Earth is, and twice the distance of Pluto?"

"What in the world—where did you, I mean, get that?"

"Oh, I sit here and think."

This kid was a marvel!

"You could become a philosopher."

"Might could."

He set down his dish.

"Shoot, maybe—" Duane folded his arms, leaned back,

poked his feet out, and squinted suppositionally at the horizon, "why maybe I'll take me to Jackson like my daddy told me he done in that big-ass Buick of his. Steamin' over and clunkin' to pieces? Hell, like to near killed that boy. He was born in Jackson. I been to Richmond, twicet," he said, taking out his wallet, "for the Glory Baptist church outing," and he showed me a photo of an older woman and Duane himself, smiling there in front of a barn wearing what I believe is called a Canadian tuxedo, a denim jacket and denim trousers, and holding a small trophy. "Look," he said, pointing to his face with a thumb. "The lady there was head of Positive Youth Development. Mrs. Uhle. Homelier than a stump fence built in the dark. Look, there's me. Hell, happy as a puppy with two peckers. Why not? I had won a 4-H Silo Wreath Award and even a three-legged race but then went ahead and hurt my foot on a harrow last summer, so I cain't race fast any more, but I used to could. It was my ankle, actually, the fibula bone, pinched it somehow, sent me squealing like a pig under a gate. Nowadays, shoot, can't jump over a nickel to save a dime."

He turned to me earnestly.

"Tell you the truth? 4-H see is where I got my first beginnings in okra. Well, I also grew peas. Sugarsnaps. Oregon sugar pod. Meteor. Feltham First. Douce Provence. But mainly okra. I ordered from them illustarted"—he obviously meant illustrated—"gum catalogs. 'Park's Candelabra Branching,' 'Cajun Delight,' that there one has spineless, dark-green pods and grows, oh, 'bout four feet or so. 'Annie Oakley,' compact plant. 'Louisiana Green Velvet'? Well, dang good for big areas, yes, but only—they are mean, vig'rous plants, grow 'bout six feet tall. No lie, friend. Head damn high and growin'. That's what mine shot up to. My method? Had only to do with God's soil. And wanna know somethin'? The hand doesn't hold blood to improve on it. Smooth and spineless, oh yeh. Shoot, even ten feet."

"That big?" came a squawk.

"Ignore her."

"He's tellin' porkies."

I had begun to think he had a head harder than dental enamel, but his entrepreneurial drive impressed me.

"Some folk prefer fiddlehead fern to okra. The fractals in a fern form a first-rate function, don't you think?"

More idiot savant stuff!

He spat, squinted at a cloud. "Didn't earn enough money to burn a wet mule, my farming. That was the reason Evelina walked off the campin' pitch. Claimed I wasn't a deft hand at nothin'. You know what they say, if you cain't run with the big dogs, run under the porch. But, hell's bells, Jackson's just the best damn ol' place to be in ever, son!" He cackled. He looked over at me—and his face grew nostalgic, wistful. "Jackson? Shoot. The best." A minute of silence passed. "The best," he said again. He reached down and grasped his ankles, looked down, and sighed. "But heck who knows?" he said, "The only truth a wave knows is that it is going to break, right?"

I looked at him and almost fell over. How the deuce did he *come up* with these gems? Duane was a philosopher. There is in the country boy's head a small nut of genius, I've always thought. Twain. Faulkner. Elvis.

"So, when are you going to go?" I yawned. I was ready for bed.

"When to where?"

I had to remind him, "Jackson."

"Don't encourage him." The voice from inside.

"Me? Hell, Doc, damn yes, I'd go tonight if I could." He leaned to peer up skyward again. "Except it looks like rain."

"Rain? But wait a minute—you said it would be warm tomorrow, right? What with crows all flying in pairs, right?"

"Warm don't mean no rain, though, do it? Crows sitting on a fence means just that, rain gone come. See." He nodded forward and pointed. Three crows were sitting on a far wooden fence. "I've also heard that rhymin' poem, have you, that 'when chairs squeak, it's about rain they speak'?" He quickly jerk-rocked his chair and looked over at me with a wide grin. "Damn straight."

"OK, that's twice." From inside.

But I assumed Duane, as I, would soon be in his room and asleep in lieu of, at that moment, motoring forthwith to Jackson. Duane, I, others—we would all be in our rooms asleep. The clientele of the American tourist home? The hardy perennials: Shriners; racist Elks (B!P!O.E.) and their shovel-mouthed wives, usually named Stella Loo or Linda Ann Bee or Erin Cornelia or Moxone; 32-degree Masons and their ball jars; vegetarian author-essettes with blue hair, a jilted heart, and a lecture to organize; henpects; herbivore professors, chasing down the bizarrest of fauna; old men, reminiscent, sucking at the knobs of their canes and waiting impatiently for the release of the Judicium Extremum; cuckolds, looking for reasons; the inevitable burgomeisterial middle-aged man in ballooning dotted underwear and gartered socks hobbling down an unlighted corridor with a pair of shoes in his hand; salesmen in snuff-colored waistcoats and adulterous dreams; and, always to be seen, those dull, cretinous, leathern-breeched, peasant-like Colin Clouts who roll by down some lonesome highway on their way to exactly nowhere, take a room for the night, smoke in the dark, pay, and are gone.

"Shit, damn right tonight, if I could. Maybe meet up with a good ol' girl. Someone real country. Down to earth."

I offered tentatively, with a wink, "Someone maybe named Annie Oakley Okra, with dimples, milk complexion. Who knows?"

"Now you're talkin'," he put in. But it sounded hollow. A silence fell. He seemed subdued. "You know, okra can be consumed in a number of ways—see, that's what most folks don' know."

"Well, I'm going to turn in," I said.

I heard a sigh, in the dark.

"Course, then there's downtown Baltimore where my good buddy spent New Year's Eve last year. Threw him out of the bar, they did, some city boys, and beat up on him right bad somewheres in downtown Baltimore. He lost his vertical hold. Went loopy as a crosseyed cowboy. Shucks, let 'em try it with me, though. But, cripes, Baltimore's just where I wanna be, my man." He clapped his hands, once. "Downtown!"

At the noise, an irked bird disengaged from a tree top.

I said, "*Squawk!*"

"Wrong, boss," interposed Duane. "Crows caw, ravens croak."

"Really?"

"Their tail feathers are basically the same length. When a crow spreads its tail, it opens like a fan. But ravens have longer middle feathers in their tails and appear wedge-shaped when open."

Who was this guy, Roger Tory Peterson?

"Anyway, don't matter, that there was a grackle—"

Again, from inside. "You're a grackle!"

"—black buggers but smaller than crows. Look like they done been stretched. What you heard was a guttural *readle-eak readle-eak*, like a rusty gate. Little bitches, me tell you. Pull up sprouting corn!"

"And there you go again!"

His mother was a real sheriff.

"Put out a feeder, why, they'll eat the seeds, then they'll eat the *feeder!* Thing is, you cain't kill a grackle. Uh-uh—it's illegal."

He sighed and looked, sighed and looked, sighed and looked, and sighed again. I listened to all of those homespun sounds and their accompaniment, a squeaking porch swing, crows, ravens, grackles, presiding and moderating mothers. They all seemed to be saying goodnight. Silence elsewhere. The ruses of trade, the abuses of traffic and horns, the muses of the city hotel and motel were all very far away from rustic Beulahsville, indeed. The tourist home in the autarchy of its isolation somehow stood like a sentinel at the fag-end outposts of Protestant America and represented everything white, basic, noncomplex, unscientific, non-European, non-Catholic, and populist and plain as anyone could conjure up. It gave one the memory of some kind of prelapsarian disengagement and the possibility of an infinity of non-events, pleasing especially to those who took their coffee black, their flapjacks dry, their days ordinary, their chat unfussy, their sleep alone, their visits short, and their dreams limited. It simplified, simplified.

Night fell, and I was on my tired feet, stretching. I told Duane that I was going to try to make it all the way to Boston next day and, if he wanted, I'd drop him off in any of fifty cities on the line.

"Damnation to hell, I'd love to, stranger," said Duane socking his fist in the air, "but have a look-see at that big ol' patch to mow down by the dark-fired tobacco barn, and if that don't beat all hell. And me, too. I'm work slap out. Next time you come by here, dammit, I'll be with you, you remember that. OK?"

I did remember, I remembered it as forgettable.

Summer Bellerophon; or,
The Agonies of James Querpox

> Longing is the agony of the nearness of the distant.
> —*Martin Heidegger*

Summer Bellerophon, a junior from Ames, Iowa, who was also considered the most beautiful girl at Graybar Hall, the elite prep school set in the low, verdant, rolling hills of northwestern Massachusetts, played the flute.

The girl was strikingly good-looking and regarded by many as Scandinavian because of her carriage, poise, fine bone structure, and shiny blond hair. She had presence. There was an air of springtime in her quiet smile. Her fine golden tresses surrounded a face—O paradise! O sweet Renaissance garden!—that was an oval of almost faultless beauty, backlit with soft alabaster light, its lines, from her perfect temples to the delicate perfectly straight lines of her philtrum to the slim, delicate, ivory volutes of her nostrils, sculpted as if by Phidias himself. She had the milk-white shoulders of Elpis and walked in a lilt, at certain times with a long stride and at other times with careful colt-like steps. She was as tall as Dido, and her skin, candle-pale, was exceptionally striking when tanned, as dark and bore-smooth as stained mahogany that has been rubbed to a fine luster. Her gentle eyes, which had a pure clarity to them, were a mild unclouded green like daylight through seawater, brightly clear, and soft as a gazelle's.

Almost everybody who had ever seen the girl fell in love with her. But for James Querpox, the quiet mathematics teacher who lived alone and who had few friends, things were far worse. It was his ill luck to be smitten with her—indeed, stricken was the true word for it—a passion capturing him with such pulling force, such intensity, it constituted virtually a fairy house of dreams, and yet, as well, a decided sense of penalty and no small amount of disquiet and unease.

He read a lot, he never married, and he had a clubfoot. With small, round glasses that seemed to magnify his eyes, Querpox could have passed for a street preacher, an anarchist, or an aggrieved socialist pamphleteer walking the streets handing out leaflets. "Live unknown"—Epicurus—was one of his mottos. He harbored an odd sensitivity. In a cinema one night after hearing, "I am told the lights often go out in Vienna when it rains," lovingly spoken by Greta Garbo to Conrad Nagel in *The Mysterious Lady*, he felt in the tight grip of its unaccountable transformative magic for months afterwards, uncannily so.

It turned out that one evening he happened to see Summer in a school play, where she was playing the role of Beatrice in Middleton's *The Changeling.* A perplexing mysterious fire had split some rock in him that night, and in an instant he knew that after so many years had passed, years of bleak solipsism, he had found the one passion that was stronger than his mistrust of himself, a revolutionary transfiguration, however, that compounded that mistrust even more. Walking home, Querpox heard high in the branches of a linden tree a meadowlark with charming and heart-bursting accuracy effortlessly singing the first two bars from Alfredo's song in *La Traviata*. He loved birds and felt in their feathered proximity a best attachment to life.

There was something elevated in his stride now. The way he walked was often mocked, for it was a forward-determining trudge done with explosions of eagerness, club-footed and all, that usually put him a step ahead of everybody else, and his mind worked the same way.

Oh, the delight! thought Querpox, feeling horses riding through his heart. *The mad enchantment of it, as I go aimlessly walking through the air! Oh, beloved, oh inamorata! Come to me in a spangled gown with scintillating galaxies on it! Come to me in a blaze of electric light or in the brume of fog, I shall be here for you! Bewitch me with spells and sorcery and abracadabra! There is a secret garden for us and only for us alone! I sing, I rave, I turn in stricken quest of you!*

No more momentous a feeling had ever come over him, ever, certainly never in this extraordinary way. It was at the very instant that Summer Bellerophon left the theater that night, gracefully passing by him with her head pensively low but with a long purposeful stride, that he scantily whispered under his breath with a truly terrible kind of prescience, "Not all the wasteful years, heaped in all the scales of one consummate hour, shall this moment ever outweigh."

Instantly he felt wind like cold zeros flowing through him, a gust of abstract numerical passengers emptying an essential being warily within him by way of a waning, a depletion in some kind of kenosis. He thought of a line from Emerson's

"Self-Reliance": "In every work of genius we recognize our own rejected thoughts. They come back to us with a certain alienated majesty." Still, majesty he felt. Her name alone, with its sonorous and lilting supra-enchantment, pierced his heart ever awakening to it the comeliness of it, a pulchritude of sound, because in his deepest soul an eroticism endured as much through names and words as through images.

Dionysius had conquered Apollo, overcoming him forever with a power impossible to gauge. A romantic soul hiding under science was freed, an expression of personality released. It avoided structure and order in favor of wild hurtling emotions, broke rules to create new ones hitherto undreamt of. He looked for complication now, mystery and magic, not solutions, and, no, no, there was to be no ruled paper anymore, but open canvases. The time had come to put away absonant Hindemith, Schoenberg, Weber, Alban Berg, and Edgar Varèse.

Bring on Beethoven, Schubert, Frédéric Chopin!

§

Nothing else would ever fully matter to him again, except the singular art by which, exclusive and deliberate and extremely rare, fashioned out what much deeper appetite he knew not and could never say, while nevertheless born of love, he was driven to see this incandescent girl over and over again, while yet contriving—insistently, for his own peace—never to try to *meet* her. An uncertainty principle Heisenbergian in its scope, cantankerously nagged at him. He figured that if he located Summer in his life, as it were, insinuated her somehow as the peaceful, loving being he so needed to survive, the more precisely—clearly, distinctly, strictly, desperately—her specific position would be held in place in any of the thousands of ways he wanted to be with her, the less precisely her momentum (or stimulant) could be measured.

And vice versa. It was quantum physics. To him, Summer was very like both a particle and a wave at the same time. The better you knew her position, the less precisely her momentum—her dynamic force, her drive into his heart, her strength as a hold on him, her aesthetic propulsion—could be measured. Whenever you knew the momentum, you could not know where to locate her. Was a universal dream lost in the particularizing over it? Logic said yes.

Smitten utterly, Querpox nightly dreamed of the young girl—just to kiss the tender inward of her hand! But he feared coming close to her or loitering aimlessly too long within range of her chemical message or even making the slightest attempt to try to converse with her, lest he become consumed, burnt up, and split down the middle like some tall pine tree in a forest struck by a bolt of molten lightning. Still, he could not stay away from her. He tried to do so. He failed. He was frightened that he failed. He saw her every day, adjacent in corridors, proximate at tables in the refectory, walking outside. He looked at Summer with all of the shepherd Silvius's hopeless ardor for heedless Phoebe, who had no taste for metaphor or for him.

His only waking thought was: *Would that I were gifted with a language floribundant enough to turn my fantasies into fact, my haplessness into hopes, my aims into aspirations without continuing delusion.* He indulged in poetic flights he never had before. *Sigh for me, night wind, as if from an epidemic of ruin I trudge across the desert of my soul, waterless and unsafe . . .*

Consequently, he contrived to become one with her by a

deliberate act of mind. Was that why Kierkegaard once pointed out that genius is sin? A relentlessly close observer, Querpox now found that the plenitude of his heart—love? obsession?—invited alert vagabonding, and in walks through the woods, across meadows, by brooks and along river streams he began to search the inscape of things. Walks he took were rarely taken without a sense of mystery. The hush of forests intrigued him. Woods to him always looked as if they were waiting while he passed by, a felt suspense in the darkness that seemed like a sort of breath-holding.

But walking through nature this time, instead of feeling comfort in simplicity he found it a realm of imposing patterns, a labyrinth of confusing whorls, zigzags, and mandalas, enough that, upon reflection, his mind began to resemble the floor of the Cathedral of Amiens, crazy with multiple unbeguiling designs.

Querpox started to realize that consciousness is a pure appearance in the sense that it exists only to the extent that it appears. Was that crazy? Was he defective to think that was insane? He was swallowed up in his own indescribable happiness, it was true. He was also ironically spiked from within, prisoner of a pinched universe whose unreality he had queerly begun to glimpse in small inevitable lightning flashes. He tried to recreate with words the wonders and fears he felt, gloomily toiling over lifeless adjectives to explain.

He was now often bewilderedly of two minds. He was at times feeling buoyant, then not. A dark sense of unworthiness would then be followed by hand-squeezing joy. Plagued by a sense of incompetence, he took on the problems of other people as a way to escape from his own—one or two neighbors he looked in on—but then as if demonically, cursedly, access to any one, true, solid way of thinking ebbed.

A lame man whose name which, when pronounced, often brought forth peals of laughter from many students seemed disconnected from the complicated realities of the school, never mind life, but this was nothing new.

He took out his old tin chess set. To while away time, on rainy days especially, he sat alone in his room and shifted the glum, silent pieces around the board, creating new rules in an attempt to bi-master two sides. Was the single idea that one side had to lose while another had to win fully healthy?

In his dreams, in which fictitiousness played both a saving and damning role, Querpox wanted—ached—to arouse promises in her that her insight would insist seeing to fulfillment. He would somehow insinuate into and so possess her heart to the degree that she would see in an epiphany that ignoring the helpless remoteness in him was a cruelty she could rise above. In a kind of paranormal panopticon, for example, he wondered, when Summer in a senior recital performing part of the difficult examination piece "Flute Concertino in D Major" by Cécile Chaminade, of which she did only the central section, "*Più animato agitato*," did she somehow have a glimpse into his adoring heart as he sat in the dark, eyes shut, along with other faculty members of the school, listening to the interstellar gold rush? He truly believed so and held tight to the thought for as long as he could. Suddenly the idea vanished when she followed it with the aria of Parasha from Stravinsky's haunting "Chanson Russe," the maiden song from the one-act opera *Mavra*, which, by way of the overflowing ripple of the audience's delight with each increasing flight of notes, broke the spell.

He walked much of that night, strolling into the starry

firmament. The echo of the rainbow-scored music softened the air, and it magically brought to his mind bright images of Virgil's shepherd Tityrus and Frederick the Great and Giulio Briccialdi solacing their leisure with the flute and strains of melody so transportingly rare as to tempt the dryads out of their barken hiding places and the incandescent water nymphs from their high festivals sporting on the silver flood.

Were those the sounds a starling he heard, that lustrous songbird with its gift for mimicry, who makes just one appearance, in Shakespeare in "Henry IV, Part 1." *Wee cleeesclakeee*, liquid trills and clicks?

§

At one time, he almost did not remember, he *was* another person. What had mattered to him once, greatly, happened when he was but a mere child, for his father had given him a telescope, and he saw—began to study—Andromeda's light, a barred spiral galaxy, a golden whorl also known as Messier 31, approximately 2.5 light-years from the planet Earth and the nearest major galaxy to the Milky Way. It is a collection of a trillion stars lying 2.5m light years distant, an ultraviolet luminosity close to God!

A living question for James Querpox, one that long kept a tight but delightful grip on his soul, was the nature of primordial light. Light travels at a finite speed, as everyone knows. But he had held the educated theory that light from the very early universe—a primordial light known as CMB, the cosmic microwave background, which of course no one has ever seen or indeed could ever see—might possibly be observable and so statistically determined, in spite of the fact that vast intervening gravitational radiation, barriers not only stretching the mysterious primordial clouds of gas, haze, and dust by way of the curvature of the Earth and of course also greatly affecting the nature of the CMB, could be mathematically studied and indeed measured. He was keen on looking behind the bold front of which the vast young universe sat and to try to describe by mathematics the most distant objects we could see!

Although gravitational waves squeeze and stretch anything in their path as they pass by, he knew they were *not blocked* by those barriers, in spite of the fact that the rippling fabric of spacetime obviously affects those barriers, as Einstein had explained years before. After astronomers had discovered tell-tale signs of gravitational waves in the polarization of the CMB, it was Querpox's goal to glimpse and chart certain literally un-seeable wonders. All through college and graduate school, he had applied himself to this project, doing research at such high places as the Center for Astrophysics at the Smithsonian's Astrophysical Observatory in Cambridge, Mass., that hosted the well-known Chandra X-ray Center which operated the satellite, processed the data, and distributed it to scientists for analysis, and in quiet intervening years working at the LIGO observatory in Livingston, Louisiana.

No one at Graybar knew of, or even if he or she did know, would have been remotely interested in Querpox's palimpsestic preoccupations, and he not only preferred it that way, it had been the very reason he sought out a small secondary school in which to teach. Being ignored was a consolation, consequences reckless driving. It had been the perfect choice. Prep school teachers, who come to the aid of no one, are a shallow lot. Walking by you is the way they parade. They function on disdain and revel in their facility to ignore. Self-regard is the pond they swim in. They are the reason they call a mouth a trap.

At an earlier time, a young ambitious Querpox confided to his father with an insistent but overconfident assurance that constituted a prediction—and always with the kind of inappropriate laughter that became unpredictably characteristic of him— that every first Monday evening in October, as he often dreamed, he fully expected to receive a telephone call from Sweden—the Nobel Prize!

He was now in the grip of a new suffusion. It was not merely having seen Summer Bellerophon playing Beatrice in *The Changeling*. A volcanic eruption had taken place in his life, a molten upheaval spouting magma and fire, but with scoria and slag. An elemental gravity shift had taken place in him—a full fascination simply had ebbed, making room for another, a deradicalizing adaptation that, exploding in his hot heart, traveled through him in a visceral renunciation of all he knew before, borne of such a need for love that the accommodation created a seismic shift in his very being. Nothing was lost, he felt.

He rejoiced as he wept and, weeping, tasted in his tears not the salt-taste of anxiety or apprehension or regret but only gratitude.

That night he dreamt of distant tropical islands full of hot purple sunlight and long white beaches flown over like music by scything Pink-footed Shearwaters and Flying Resplendent Quetzals and Austral thrushes.

No, nothing else would ever fully matter to him again. And, paradoxically, that deeply mattered.

§

Querpox always saw Summer for the first time, with something like worship in his eyes. When the girls on afternoons played field hockey out at Rafferty Field, Querpox often stationed himself by a distant tree that reminded him of one painted by Fragonard and looked on, simply observing. In the late spring or fall, he often went out early in the fresh air to wait at some remove as the mist vaporized before his eyes, lifting its veil from the rows of poplars with their graceful fluttering leaves and the now gleaming sunlit apple trees, their ripe fruit shining a bright message from the sun. There was an aura of living color whenever Summer beautifully appeared on the field, ready for action, usually often wearing a shirt, he noticed, of bright Provence yellow and blue, her lustrous hair woven into a six- or seven- or eight-strand French plait, a quirt so sleek, shiny, and sharp that it resembled a cowboy whip. A beautiful girl, curiously, hardly ever leaves a clear-cut impression, however, and, later, try as he would, Querpox, finding only a blur, could never remember exactly how radiant Summer Bellerophon was, until the very next day when he saw her again.

The hockey got rough. Competitive. The shining shins of exercise, the flashing legs. And with a low-level frenzy of frustration, Querpox watched the heaving breasts. Was it not the observant, if spying, Tennyson who in quite specific admiration of the human body upon observance subtly wrote so insightfully about motions of the back and the supple-sliding of the knee?

He stayed by the tree. Self-conscious about his limp, he was never unaware that in appearing to walk on the side of his club foot, as did King Tut, the French diplomat Charles Maurice de Talleyrand, Lord Byron, cranky Josef Goebbels, and, among others, the stuttering Roman emperor Claudius, there was a nefarious connotation to the deformity which seemed to him to lie in the order of iron necessity, an order in which he did not feel at home. It gave the illusion of corruption, unholiness. No, our illusions are not real, yet it is real that illusion itself exists. Specters, phantasms, mirages of being another self had always haunted him. He perceived himself badly flawed. He realized it well enough. His idealization of Summer, which was both a magnification of as well as a suppression of reality, carried with it a kind of stalking.

Across the field, throughout the afternoon, chattering, shouts, soft prattle, laughter, unspoiled and harmonious nymphs in Arcadia, choral turn upon turn, while Querpox quoted Philip Sidney to himself,

> My sheep are thoughts, which I both guide and serve; Their pasture is fair hills of fruitless love, On barren sweets they feed, and feeding starve. I wail their lot, but will not other prove;

A good-looking girl with blonde hair that hung down her back like a slab of wood ran round her, hockey stick raised, and, while her pert face took his attention, not a note registered in his mind—this was revealing to him—that compared with the feeling in him of Summer that struggled in his soul. She and other girls were pretty but what were they in contrast to Summer and her buttercup-colored hair and entrancing beauty? There was Gina Genesis from his math class with her coconut coiffure and wonderfully lithe figure, a very good athlete, and competitive Jonquil and Jocelyn Wetwool, twins from Johnson, Vermont, whom he called the "Dolly Vardens" for their good humor and blooming beauty like the Dickens character.

Play stopped for a moment, He watched Summer sip water from a ladle. *Zhizennia voda.* The water of life. *Aqua vita.* Vodka, dear little water. My water, my life, my Vodka. Summer Bellerophon was as graceful as a silver poplar, fruit globed, *chatoyant,* shining in his dreams unfolding and unfolding, petal by petal, waxen and immaculate.

Vodka, he whispered.

Can observation effect and determine our realities? Was it possible—indeed, was it true—that what cannot be observed should therefore not be an ascribed reality? Chance, indeterminacy, and probability began to supplant certainty in the conjectures that poor querulous Querpox torturously began to devise that involved, by way of fantasy, various means by which the two of them might be together. A tomorrow now began fully to mean life itself for him.

Querpox listened to their squeals as they ran the field, hockey sticks clicking and clacking, loud imprecations, laughter, groans. Laughing and shouting. He marveled at the hermetic language that the girls used. In the refectory their conversations floated on a sea of slang and informal speech, by prep school patois. The interlocutory school chats they engaged in seemed a language all of its own. Most of the Graybar Hall girls spoke mainly in particles, or so it seemed: *well, like, anyway, totally, so, you know, OK, really, actually, honestly, literally, in fact, at least, I mean, quite, of course, after all, hey, sure enough, know what I mean? Just sayin',* a vernacular of endearing backchat filled with clicks, coos, and enclitics that in a sort of breathless, racing way, streaking and scuttling, fairly seemed briskly to hop over nouns and verbs in order to give voice to an already shared understanding.

The girls, many of them, were lovely. But while others, inculturated to flirt, often did so, Summer did not. It was a true beneficence to Querpox, as well as a continuing irony, that she never seemed to notice his presence—or even look up at the world. At times she appeared to be dreamily absent, a tranquil daze of preoccupied enchantment, princess in another world. It was nothing like lethargy or inertia, rather almost a wanton languor at the heart of a calming lull. She might yawn, softly, with the kind of grace a lotus might unfurl to reveal its complex blooms. It was an abstract beauty. And yet all the while, specifically because of her, his days, although poeticized by sweet expectation, were surrounded by subtle shades of fear.

By these specific fears he suddenly came to discern an inner truth. He determined to exclude her fully from entering the solid fact of his life, lest any defects of correspondence in the real world become apparent, and, by becoming so, ruin the rich possibility of their being together in his mind. It would be of no consequence if Summer had never regarded him or spoken to him, provided that he could bind himself to her by a fealty of adherence, a fastness born of simple, if self-effacing devotion, a bond of loyal obedience, a private allegiance of pledging his abstract troth.

It was absence as a kind of presence. Paradox ruled the very minutes of his life. And so, while the two-and-thirty winds of passion loudly beat about his breast, their apocalyptic effects affording background for his anxiety, he refused to recognize anything of fact in what he felt. It was perversely as if reality was the one fantasy he should dread.

It was tunnel vision. His insight demanded a kind of blindness, his ardor isolation. He wanted to know exactly nothing of her parents, her address, her home life, no potentially limiting facts, no thorny intrusive details to spoil their—*their,* thinking the word he tremulously closed his eyes—still frail and unconventional distinction, the fairy-tale exceptionalism of it all. He read in her green eyes the wistful confession of a young girl on the threshold of adulthood filled with the sort of dreamy self-absorption that accompanied the familiar condition she daily met of being ostracized by her rich and egregious beauty, helplessly longing for the deliverance of a special love, eagerly awaiting, under the light of a pale moon, say spell of fate, with patience, trust, simplicity, and organic growth, to be transported, helplessly, by an enchanted love, taking her unawares, to some superlative and peerless, enviable and unsurpassable kingdom, like a disguised or unknown princess, which Querpox alone would provide.

Or was he deluded entirely?

Was the light of his hope a *lucus a non lucendo?* Could it be the case that the solipsistic state of his being in which he waited, he wondered—always by himself—ultimately be a grove in which light did *not* penetrate?

§

A cripple, he also felt deeply unworthy of love itself and kept in his wallet a slip of paper, where he had copied lines from one of John Keats's letters to Fanny Brawne: "My dear love, I cannot believe there ever was or ever could be anything to admire in me especially as far as sight goes—I cannot be admired, I am not a thing to be admired." It was his way of never losing either her or his soul. He was something of a puritan. He dunned himself with demerits whenever the real possibility of his being with Summer entered his head, and he began to collect chits in a cough-drop tin that he kept on a shelf in the house in which he lived at the end of Winterbourne Lane, where a distant prairie view seemed to lead nowhere. It was his way of never losing either his or her soul. He would gaze out of its northern window down a long trail and daydream. "Dear God," he prayed, "may I please be taught to learn only to want what I have when I have what I need." Every night now he began having dreams of escape, like moving to far Scotland or driving a XR-750 Harley out to the far west through interminable roads into the mountains where no one would ever know where he was.

Live unknown, he heard, he repetitively heard.

There were rules fixed in him she shattered. He began to appear less and less on campus or be seen. It was not only his graceless gimplike walk but a method, a contrivance of his, to try to slip in and out of a day without contacts. There was about him something of a barrier not his own, and he was unable to get through the day without spending a good part of it by himself. The act of trying to keep darkness visible threw no light upon a shadow still looking to see.

Avoiding the girl, in short, was paradoxically his way of keeping her close to him. He brought into existence everything he could not face. Only by denial could he love. Rain began badly to congest him. Querpox suffered from various allergies like Christmas tree asthma, which caused coughing and weeping. The oleoresins in paprika, egg yolks, and solvents badly bothered him. He kept them mainly in control. But other things plagued him. Dog dander. Humid shirts. Cinder blocks. Orange juice. The mere sight of such things as artificial turf and latex gloves and plastic toys and rubber basketball shoes actually sickened him, bringing on bouts a kind of nausea. Was he living alone, he wondered, on a teardrop-shaped island?

At school James Querpox had a local reputation for aloneness. He would make offhand comments that were meant to be funny but were not entirely so. He had an odd humor and used it to express the aggressions his shyness created but it always came across, he thought, as biting wind.

Meanwhile, Miss Fingerspitzengefühl, the departmental secretary who disliked him and was old enough to fart sand, began crabbing that he could never be reached and, often calling him to her office, proceeded despite the effrontery to ask him personal questions in an irritating sing-song. He replied to her with solemn monosyllables and when speaking he looked as if his voice were putting his face to sleep. She cruelly enjoyed keeping him standing before her desk, making him abide, forcing him to heel. It gave her immeasurable power. She had his number. Her cold, unforgiving eyes were pistols aimed at a target. He found her triangular head reptilian as she sat there before him with an icy stare, jangling a set of keys.

His colleagues, meanwhile, cared nothing about it and only clucked with amusement in the faculty lounge at his misfortunes, teachers like Kelly Photz and David Crabbe and Tom Lee Drump and Leah Dova Silverglate—who sported a mustache and once wrote an awful pedestrian novel, *Scroylewind*—and dumb, faggy, beaver-faced, sharp-elbowed Kenlowe Manning, and the earnest and idiotic chinless Protestant chaplain, Phil Flummerfelt, who bored everyone rigid on the faculty with what he self-inflatedly called his "pastoral calls," when out of the blue, calling cold, he would appear on your doorstep on a visit (always unwel-

come) merely to snoop—a man who then deeded everyone at
the school a bright holiday gift when one Christmas vacation he
committed suicide in a motel in Herreid, South Dakota, later the
occasion for a gloomy memorial service which the headmaster
ordered everyone to attend but which James Querpox, characteristically ill-disposed to obey, refused and stayed home.

The peevish, knife-hearted headmaster of Graybar Hall,
J. Uranus Paltrey, III, or "Urineman," or "The Inhuman Grig," or
"Joey Three Sticks," as he was variously and derisively called—a
small, thin, inarticulate, glad-handing empty suit, a non-en-
tity not very bright, but with a big acquisition fund and lots of
political connections—was convinced on no evidence whatsoever, needless to say, that Querpox was a deviant on some level
or other, for charges of sexual misconduct, whether lies or not,
always tended to bolster by proof the idea that the headmaster
was vigilant. He had once asked Paltrey to intercede with the
Board of Visitors to fund on his behalf a short project to visit
and study at David Mountains, Texas, the location of the Hobby-
Eberly Telescope with its major 10-meter aperture glass, and the
headmaster laughed out loud, sneering at him, and not only
openly refused to do so but subverted the chance.

A low-bred, well-connected, calculating politico, the
headmaster kept his own private little *Kameradschaftsbund* working for him, a secret society of spying elves. He had even gone so
far as to order his bratty 16-year-old daughter, Pook, a short, nosy
little busybody with small eerie snow-white eyes, a set of space-
age ears, a protruding lower lip, a neon sprig of a haircut, and an
endless fund of gall to report back to him with any and all gossip
that she had heard about Querpox, simply declaring, "That man
is dirty." It was this man who presided at Graybar faculty meet-

ings, which always turned into a Portuguese parliament with everybody trying to speak at once and always to no consequence.

More than once Querpox was called in to Uranus Paltrey's office to have to explain—while rudely left standing to be interrogated by the near-midget headmaster with his glowering bugle eyeballs and little nose like an avocet's upturned bill—why he felt such a need to spend so much time out on the fields during the girls' afternoon sports times and venues. It was all part *Einsatz Querpox*, an investigation to get to the root of this man's subversion. His opposition to everything was noticed. He was placed on a list of radicals to be monitored. With utter contempt for this kind of inquisitorial officiousness, Querpox acknowledged nothing. The gesture of not doffing his hat—he often wore one, completely out of date, but a habit—allowed him to feel within the psychic comfort of ignoring such people and their ilk whenever he happened to pass any one of them on campus or in a shop or on the street.

But he was out of date himself. He divided the world into three parts: the beauty of nature, the significance of art, and real life—and while he sought refuge in the first two he badly tried to ignore the third. Coldly high-hatting the third part seemed virtually the only possible way literally to exist.

One afternoon at the library Querpox pretended to pass Summer on business, lingering hopelessly without the audacity to do so. She was talking to Rachel Forrestal, and, although he could not hear, he watched the thrilling effect of the way her mouth moved in speech, the small boss in the center of her upper lip, her lips, so smooth and shining, thrust forward into a sort of open pout. Her movements, even as she shifted, were more bewitching than a panther's. How can a beautiful girl fail to recognize just how powerful a drug she yields, every part of her, her eyebrows, her calves, the edge of the mouth meeting the cheek, the valentine-shaped buttocks that were so taut, firm, modeled virtually to a moon-sheen? Later in the day, approaching dinnertime—he had lingered there alone—quietly within the library stacks with just the briefest scintilla of courage he managed to brush by her, just catching the sillage of a lime-fresh perfume as delicate as the fragrance of rain.

The scent of her hair, framing that exquisite Fra Lippo Lippi face, was like honeysuckle. He had the sensation of the smell of newly threshed oats, of meadow surf and of butterscotch tallow, of rich wet fragrant peonies and freshly cut grass. He thought he touched her candy-striped shirt. He walked on almost in a stupor, peering back through a small aperture in the shelves at her holy Christmas-white beauty and, as she paused, was about to speak—what on earth was he thinking of?—say something, when, turning her head around, she paused for no reason, walked to a round table, and joined her hopelessly ordinary—mortal—friends.

Could she be a brat? He would spank her! Her kiss would taste like a wedding cake. He wanted to buy her a rare earth bracelet. There was a frog-pin in a store he saw that she would love. Life would be a mere yoctosecond with her, too brief, the smallest unit of time. *I know about enantiodromias* was a sudden thought that flew into his knocking head, *and it may save me!*

He walked outside and giddily found the stars were so bright and white that they reminded him of the frost of enchanted winter. He leaned against a tree and craned his neck, watching the Big Dipper pour space upon the grounds that seemed as mistily beguiled, bewitched, and transfixed as he. It seemed as if she inhabited a planet different than other common students.

That world was once his domain. It was in the region of the empyrean, the far upper reaches of heaven, that his mind once walked, the planetary motions of which that once stirred his spirit, the primordial light of the early universe that at another time and place alone brightened his soul.

It was through the force of gravity in another realm, however, by obeying its ineluctable laws, that he fell in love.

§

Most of Summer's classmates, several of whom Querpox had taught, were of the shin-bucked, crumple-faced, stone-bruised variety, physically unmemorable and not Graybar favorites. Camille Petacci, her hair crimped like mafalde; Taneka Yoops, who had experienced same-sex love with Lida Rose Rittenauer, sang beautifully but was unattractive. Vibrissa Hare, with large, snowy-white arms, met town boys behind the gym every week. "That's what she don't do nothin' else, except," said roommate Debbie Ann Vinyl, who wore a silver nostril button. Morose Phyllis Grizzlom with her beet-red *gershnoskel* always sat by herself in the dining-hall with such wishful self-orphaning pretense that it only infuriated the snobbish upper-class clique all the more. Jean Thouless, mouse-eared like hawkweed, a girl who had transferred from Phillips Andover—a school everyone at Graybar mocked as a distinctly inferior rival—was always trying to dissuade her roommate, Cipperly Groom, from taking another dessert, she being a compulsive eater who was constantly taunted by the elite hoydens who predicted that. growing even fatter, she would end up in a mental ward wear rubber underwear and living on reducing pills—cruel girls, of whom there were not a few at the school, called her "Bicycle Helmet" not only because she was ugly but wore her hair terraced like a Portuguese garden bed.

Ambrosine Wolfit and Eulalia Bundles, who often held moist hands underneath the table behind the Ralph W. Emerson bust at a far corner of the library, both had big undeclared crushes on Summer but wouldn't tell anyone. Many of the girls were very good-looking and frankly alluring. Gorgeous Lois Blessington, who was her partner in biology lab, had a brother who once invited Summer to attend a Groton School Evensong service with him, but she had refused. Hatshepsut Jordan who had olive skin and ravishing almond eyes looked like a beautiful sleek greyhound and wore rings of arm bracelets of real Egyptian gold. Haughty seniors Natica Metcalfe, Edwina del Monocol, and Trinity Sedgewick Bunce spoke to nobody, virtually lived in a higher atmosphere, and only dated older men whom they met in Boston.

Prep school girls, so many of them, bright in their youthful intoxication, endlessly cocky, gave off a heady fragrance like blooms in a tropical garden, scarlet roses, the scent of pink spring peonies or lilacs redolent of misty rain, woodsy, floral, hot-house moist. They were rich, spoiled, and their very names were jewels. Pleasing Street, Celeste Overdrive, Marietta Treadgold, Joline-Lee Serpentine, Malgorzata Kohl, Shenandoah Sprott, Iris Bonechill, Citron St. Jacques with her narrow bright silver medal of a face, Arabella Drinkrow, Sieglinde Dansk, Dido Biniaris, R. W. S. G. Sizar—named after the initials of Richard Wagner's four-opera *Ring* cycle—Jane Nophins-Wald, Nguyen Mirador from Ciputra, Hanoi, in Vietnam, Sigrid Bagarfjorder, Bunny

Gligoric, Christmas Spenser-Bourne, Tulip Grenadine. Freya Ghost-Cardinal—strongjaw, six feet tall, steady dark-blue eyes, robust packaging—Katrina Van Greete, who had already been tapped to be in an actual Hollywood movie, the twins Portia and Perdita Falconbridge, Jemima Gateacre, Gudrun Evigheten, and an international skier, Pippa Beddingfield, were select. Brash young beauty gave them an enchanted, sort of foreign look that, reflected in their faces, told how dangerous it was to have a personal stake in loving them.

They never wept softly like a watering can on flowers. They were above sin and beyond pity. They were bred like prize racehorses, all money and manners and magnificence. They lived high in the sky on puffy clouds of privilege, a passel of Jaguar-driving trustifarian braganzas getting fifty-dollar manicures, too rich to care, too indifferent to confess, too pretty for make-up, except for the sticks of opaline gloss kept in their jacket pockets to use on lips to fake-kiss the world.

There was also Daphne Phatne from Texas who wore snakeskin cowboy boots; prim Sarah Sharp Ouzel, who affectionately called Summer "Snowbunting" and who cherished an amber bracelet that Summer had given her in exchange for a book about Amelia Earhart; pretty Ptarmigan Hare, who had a reputation for once kissing a black guy; skyscraper-tall Mariastella Cristiani, who when she flunked math said, "Always crisises;" Swan and Madrid Wivenhoe who read Nietzsche and said we were all meaningless; Spokane Filsinger who was going to become an actress and who wrote sonnets about lemurs; Ariella de Chartreuse, Layla Merritt, and Aubrey Jellicoe, all on her field hockey team, always sought to include Summer in the cheers of their victory circles; Charlene Poats, whose voice sounded almost heliated; lovely Cupping Bradley, a cottage loaf of a girl; fetching Fenella Belle, with her blonde curls and cute, sweet, pie-shaped Ginevra de' Benci face; Dawn Silvermail, who wore her hair in squash blossom whorls, like a Walpi Indian maiden; and languid Belisha Bacon who was known for fetching tight leotards with black-and-white stripes and amber blouses.

Confidence characterized them—and worldliness, for many of them had traveled widely and had had international experience. Houston Popple-Bottom had personally met Queen Elizabeth II. Skyley Van Genteen's father practically owned Seattle. Textor Houghtaling, Bijoux Greenmarket, and Jennifer Whiteside Esterbrook had all been to China, several times, while Victoria LaFramboise-Courtemanche's father was the Ambassador to the Sudan. Querpox remembered overhearing one particular exchange at a table in the dining hall on the subject of eating asparagus. With cool demeanor Tyndall Makepeace, tweaking back her perfect hair that fell evenly round her shoulders from a blade-sharp parting, in her blithe and lordly way told fat little Posy Bowden, watching her shiny appleface fall, "When asparagus stalks are firm and are not sauced, it is fine to pick them up with your fingers, one stalk at a time. Asparagus is traditionally a finger food and is so regarded by the English as such."

And she was correct!

Some of the girls were forward, brazen, and overly forthright in seeking the approval of teachers and in the passions of their rivalries. Chastity as such was held up as a praiseworthy ideal, but flirtations of all sorts, conflagrations of many kinds, were in the main impossible to stem. Victoria Muchmore, who was religious and whom cruel girls uncharitably referred to as "Bibleface," made a special Christmas card for Querpox every year without fail. Bunny Gligoric once left a copy of Willa Cather's *The Troll Garden* on Querpox's front steps, a fairly rare thing for a very beautiful girl to do, but she had divined her teacher's love for Summer Bellerophon out of some sort of panoptical genius and was jealous in competition. Wistful Amber Pistyll, of the elfin hair, was always sitting on the library steps eating an apple and missing her father who, divorced, would only visit her when his ex-wife would not be there. Whenever Querpox walked by, as often he did, she would needfully bound down the steps to run up to him with questions, inviting derision from many of her classmates, and once declaring, "Do you like Tuberose lipstick by L'Oréal? I am wearing it, and also black panties."

Summer herself was almost always accompanied by a devotee or two, often a slightly chubby, dallying enthusiast, her hair bouncing in long curls like apple parings, a pleated skirt, and white Oxfords, effervescing toward the tall beauty with an admiring neck-reach as she tried, by quick-skipping, to stay in stride with her. "I always fought my hair until she taught me how to blow out side-swept bangs from wet to straight with a round brush and a blow-dryer," said Zephyr Nee. "I have a girl crush on her," venerating Taneka Yoops confided to her roommate, "she can sing, she's gorgeous, and she's intelligent. I want to *be* her."

§

Comparing Summer with her classmates in the school, Querpox always found the others wanting. Distinction is *involved* in numbers, could not people accept that? In her uniqueness, as he saw it, Summer was always different in the contrast and in the distinction incompatible, for the discrepancies always tilted in her favor. He would run through the complicated mathematical logic of the Peano Axioms to prove her distinctiveness and singularity, whereby, when the first axiom asserts the existence of at least one member of the set of natural numbers, she became to him—memorably—that one member, that first number, that ineluctable palmary number to whom no one else on earth could compare.

While an individual can add a distinct set of apples to a couple of oranges and obtain five pieces of fruit, as Gottlob Frege pointed out and James Querpox reasoned, you cannot add the class of all numbers to the class of all couples. Nor was this concept so novel a discovery, for had not Plato, who had already made the claim that numbers exist in some mind-independent abstract heaven, already asserted that they cannot be added? The two sides of an equation have common reference, but always differ in sense.

In his deep but agitated love for Summer Bellerophon, Querpox in his private ontology of mathematics saw her in terms of mathematical logic as the totality of her own set. The philosopher Bertrand Russell took the German logician and mathematician, Gottlob Frege, to task for such reasoning. The significance of Russell's Paradox, as he pointed out, was that it demonstrated in a simple and convincing way one cannot both hold that there is meaningful totality of all sets and also allow an unfettered comprehension principle to construct sets that must then belong to that totality. The Cambridge seer spoke of this situation as a "vicious circle."

Querpox admired perfection. He was a devoted reader of and an expert on Frege and shared that man's interest in trying to remove the blemish of arbitrariness in an attempt to show that pure mathematics was merely an extension and prolongation of logic. Thoreau was correct, who cynically wrote, "Men go to a fire for entertainment." But our Graybar mathematician in his own right hated to admit the allowance of such conflagrations, even if there could be found a flaming passion in his own heart. The two of them were very much alike in having discovered the indentations and staggering empty holes in the universe with its roaring illogic and lunacies on which they trod. The anti-social, eccentric, and hyper-analytical Frege was known to his students as a highly introverted creature who seldom entered into dialogues with others and while lecturing compulsively faced the blackboard. He was indrawn, ill-disposed to general chat, refused to join clubs, and never spoke in public of his politics. He was, however, known to occasionally show wit and even bitter sarcasm in a lecture.

In college, in the grip of hero worship, a restless Querpox, as only a Pilgrim of the Absolute would with a view to examining the way of the world, traveled to far Wismar, Germany, expressly to lay flowers on Frege's grave—in his younger days he often made such spur-of-the-moment trips, animated by zeal and mad conviction—just as, later, he would voyage to Amsterdam to look at the eerie jungle-brown painting, *The Fall of the Leaves* (*The Garden of St. Paul's Hospital*), *1889*, one of van Gogh's at-the-time mentally troubled later works, which portrays a sad, and isolated individual, all alone, surrounded by eerily otherworldly and serpentine natural growth seeming to envelop him. It was not difficult for him to see himself as that dwindled figure, with only one foot—a crippled one—on an established path.

§

There were occasional scandals at Graybar Hall. One of a rather significant sort involved an impropriety after a basketball game when three town boys at a spontaneous off-campus party stripped and covered with gobs of honey an intoxicated Gerda Revolvy, who was discovered, asleep, by campus police the next morning on a bench in front of the Holmes Library, looking not only rumpled and half-dressed but as toffee-sticky as a Portuguese *nogados*, one of those big towers of tiny honey balls of fried dough. Another girl, Daphne Extrapopoulos, a hectic-haired garden gnome, lovelorn and self-hating, who had an incipient case of De Clerambault's Syndrome, used to sit for long hours on Querpox's front steps and made claims to friends that he had invited her to do that. Another troubled soul, Maria Clingfilm, a young woman who often found herself down in the doldrums, just before the Christmas holidays had attempted suicide by locking herself in her cluster down room and eating a bowlful of rhododendron leaves. No one knew why, but she had intimidatingly left a note behind on her dresser claiming that, upon visiting his office, and so cruelly implicating him, she had sought out Mr. Querpox for help but he had made no response at all other than to say to her before walking away, "The universe is an octadecagon."

The reputations of most girls were clean, Summer's especially, for she seemed worlds apart from others. But teachers were questioned. Short, weird, wiry Headmaster Paltrey, who had it in for Querpox, twice summoned him into his office and, working his parrot mouth—an undershot jaw—but never asking questions, began lecturing him about sexual boundary violations.

Passing through his office just then Miss Fingerspitzengefühl, whose wide rayon dresses *shushed* and whose Red Cross shoes with sensible one-and-a-half inch heels clunked, gave

Querpox a nasty look

Several girls hated Summer Bellerophon on principle, however. Homely rubber-lipped Dale Weeks, who was known for stealing, boosted her hockey stick out of sheer jealousy. Fat, short, unprepossessing Cathy Atkins, schadenfreudedly delighted, once saw the girl trip and invidiously cried out, "Bust!" Priscilla-Ann Burton with her huge dent-corn teeth and bulky draft-horse legs insisted—to the general amusement of others—that she herself was prettier. (She herself harbored a competitive crush on Querpox and, when he ignored her, as constantly he did, she moped, she brooded, she pouted like a pewter pigeon stalled on a limb, and in the dramas of her self-absorbed moodiness you could almost hear the thwapping of her sulks.) Homely Prissy Picard from Biddeford, Maine, badly over-rouged and hopelessly stupid, feigned to take down telephone messages for her that intentionally, cruelly, she never passed on. Bitter Esther Zupnik, whose nose had the exact shape of a wet bar speedpourer, reported in an evil hour to her nosy friends she saw Summer, ossified after a drinking bout in Masterson, a dorm room, who, outside with a boy, besides kissyface, went "downstairs inside." "They saw her?" "That's what they said." "But maybe they're telling lies." "Who cares? She wears Yves Saint Laurent lipstick, the fuchsia one, number 19, doesn't she?"

The fact is, non-alcoholic parties were held by wealthy seniors, or uppers, late at night in the cluster dorms. They drank "Virgin Coladas," "Vanilla Colas," "Unfuzzy Navels." "Pour me a Shirley Temple!" said one. Another yelled, "I want a Hop-Skip-and-Go-Naked." "Ever hear of a Pousse Café? I want a Pousse Café! Give me a Pousse Café!" But Summer was never involved.

Raccoona Waybill, the walking broomstick, spitefully

scissored every single photograph of Summer out of the soph-
omore section of the one yearbook that was kept in the student
shelf of the Upper Library where librarian Edna Potentia Pluck-
rose, a Graybar careerist and proto-monstrous gossip, spent all
day every day spying on students from her desk where she knitted
cashmere goat sweaters as furry as her cheeks. The sole joy in her
bejezebeled life was spying, which in a very real way gave regula-
tion to her universe. It was Pluckrose who reported Rachel Forrestal and Summer once coming out of the woods "in disarray."
Waybill told Prissy Picard, whispering incantations behind her
back, imagined lighting Summer's long blond hair on fire. "Let's
do it while she is wearing her ice-cream pajamas that she thinks
she looks so cute in." Zephyr Nee, who overheard them, declared
that was cruel, and they shunned her all month.

Querpox, who could not help but make note of much of
this bad behavior, referred to these backbiters as "The Phylloclades," those trivial appendages clustered near the tip of a beautiful asparagus spear. He knew only too well how young girls in
their savagery could gang up on anyone they chose to dislike,
closing in on her like sailfish at sea making short work of a sardine ball.

Then of course there was the jug-eared headmaster, busy
little "Urineman" Paltrey, busily ferreting about the campus like
a white mouse, and of course irritating Pook, able to turn up anywhere looking for any cruel gossip that might be heard that she
could pass on to her father. There is a mercilessness at the heart
of all envy. Jewish girls with Hittite noses and curly hair buzzed
around Summer in the dining hall but never welcomed her to
their exclusive table, where all sat in a coven eating odd-smell-
ing sandwiches and snarping at each other competitively about

grade-point averages.

At one point, Geraldine Oikle, her hair up in vise-tight Medusa braids, a girl who thought if you ate your food in the dark you would not put on weight, commonly asked Summer if she would like a blueberry-filled doughnut. Like so many others, Geraldine had a crush on her. "Want a powdery one?"

"Yes," Summer exuberated. It was the very first word Querpox ever watched her say—watched, that is, because over a stairway he tightly held both of his ears with an almost crazed anticipation lest he hear her speak and break the spell. Summer usually ate with her friends upstairs in Ropes dining hall, with its drab WPA mural of chaotic green Babylonian grapevines curling up painted Corinthian columns. Situated at a distance, he habitually watched Summer eat, always delicately with precise finger and thumb, as on this day, with one hand resting in her lap on a striped apron of mattress-ticking she had worn from her art class and her work at the kiln. As he watched, he heard the metallic cut-glass jingle of a goldfinch's rapid chirps with sounds like the bird was quietly saying *po-ta-to chip* with a very even cadence.

Summer had got powdered sugar on her cheek from the doughnut, which made her suddenly bow, bend forward with laughter, as she removed it quickly with a flash of a yellow-and-blue handkerchief. Her laughter had the ripple wash sound among stones along a blue running brook. She was perfection. She imprinted his rare imagining. It was heaven. It was impossible. It was hell. It was a moment filled with dizzy confusion and an almost completely unbearable, unsurpassable joy.

§

Two bizarre alternatives in his desperate life now presented themselves to Querpox: he could try to hear her voice for real—recognize the living fact of her in relation to himself and die—or he could somehow privately continue to sustain a false fancied life with her in order to survive.

The fact is James Querpox was merely trying to cope. He mainly kept to his office all the time now, never socializing with other faculty. He felt suitably shunned. Small-minded, gossip-prone, and petty, his colleagues at Graybar Hall sharing a table with him could not bear hearing Querpox delve into his confusions. That he mattered at all to them was merely as a Merry Andrew, a crackpated pantaloon. A hardness in him spread itself into their own shallow lives.

At one point he tried comporting himself with disillusioned wittiness, the academic primal scream, and took self-dissembling walks down street upon street, not to forget her, but to be with her in the only way he could. He saw his face in scenarios fashioned solely out of his own disturbed projections. He was a hero in all of them. Or was a resemblance merely the persona of a difference? He watched some common ravens, black as cassocks, spring from a tree, hoarsely cawing *kraaaa–kraaaa*. They circled about. He circled. He walked the length of a long lawn, watching his feet. The fluttering leaves in the trees seemed to be an insane green. The sun was wrong. Light is glare. Its sharp rays sorely began to hurt his eyes.

Glaring light, murderous rays, fiendish solar horror, seaweed-green leaves turning as toxic as acetoarsenite. Sick and dying animals revolve in circles in a rabid vortex, round and round. Mars limped.

Querpox fought off such horrors.

Impulsively, he sat down to write a letter to Summer Bellerophon, but of all those he began he was able to finish none of them. "In my soul a forcible sympathy accumulates to awaken a logic . . ." "I believe as Ralph Waldo Emerson said that every face is an atrium, and when . . ." "They say that there is a tune actually forbidden to be played in European armies, one so lovely that, upon hearing it, soldiers are driven to desert, and I would compare . . ." It was impossible.

He sought diversions. Now he no longer went outside but began staying closed in his rooms, with the curtains pulled, flipping the discs on his View-Master, his eyes circled hour upon hour, *snap, snap, snap*, oval discs clacking, some showing the Yoshino cherry blossom trees around the Tidal Basin in Washington D.C. and others, ludicrous ones, revealing General Douglas MacArthur out of monstrous vanity striking poses for the history books. Repeatedly, Querpox took refuge in fugues all of his own devising. He would lie back in an overstuffed chair in his dark room and posit warm, elaborate, highly detailed dreams, all built exclusively out of airy intentions and feeble projections, of taking beautiful Summer in hand and, sitting together, a loving couple, quietly over a chessboard, just the two of them, teaching her the difference between the Giuco Pianissimo and the Colle System. She learned fast in his fancies. He tented into himself. He conjectured in the close shadows that everything he was experiencing was a dream, was inside his head. It was a circular kind of nightmare, for who was dreaming? He began to question whether reality was real, sustaining arguments in his mind that others either did not exist or that their existence could not be proven. Sometimes he played Respighi's *Ancient Airs and Dances* on his phonograph and dreamt through a window. Twice he made muffins, often stopping in the middle of cooking them to try to remember what he was doing. Several times he was looking at himself from the ceiling.

Stasis. He found himself immobile, stopping in place, now considering bunched-up thoughts. He felt stock-still, stationary, rigid. He stood in the middle of his wooden room. Zeros again, trivial zeros, began dissolving in him, the self-emptying he had felt within before as a kind of physical experience of a columnar meltdown. It led him to speculations of dissolution, odd, juddering Cubist-like perspectives on the idea that God is self-emptying, a self poured out to create the cosmos and the universe and everything within it. He sat down and began madly to scribble out all sorts of equations, fumbling up quirky new insights regarding analytic number theory, which led him to acute, razor-sharp speculations—suddenly—on the Riemann zeta conjecture, arguably the greatest unsolved problem in all math. In mathematics, the Riemann hypothesisis is a conjecture that all non- trivial zeros of the zeta function have a real part equal to 0.5. He was fumbling over number primes when he looked up. He heard a noise. Dawn Silvermail, a student who seemed to divine his unhappiness, before racing off left a note on his doorstep: "'*Melancholy is fine gold'—Vincent Van Gogh.*'"

After a school assembly at which Querpox was supposed to hand out flyers, he was found standing in a telephone booth and Miss Fingerspitzengefühl snapped, "You are preoccupied!" *And you are as ugly as death eating a dirty doughnut*, thought Querpox, regarding her cronelike head rising above that hairless fur coat of hers that exuded a strong ferrety odor as she jangled her keys at him before she triple-locked her office door, leaving him alone there on the landing. "'I resemble the pelican of the wilderness,'" he muttered, quoting Psalm 102:6, and, walking over to Room 101, sat quietly in Summer's third row seat, bowed his head, and wept.

"Vilate Fingerspitzengefühl will cast his ass in plaster," giggled Tom Lee Drump to Cesar Puig, the math teacher, when someone had seen him there, and later at the graduation ceremonies in late May when June Zinnabar told Puce Dobkins, both from the history department, that she had seen Querpox standing up on a hill near a pine tree far away pointing to a star! "I once saw him talking to a goalpost," said Puce. "And it answered him!" guffawed Zinnabar. "I see Iris Bonechill sitting outside his office all day," said stone-hearted Kelly Photz. Plagued with merciless, endless days of evasion and concealment, James Querpox decided to follow Goethe's suggestion that turning outward to the world was health, while turning inward was disease.

Would making himself unavailable prove his worth? Was an absent figure a prevalent one? Can resignation be an assertion? Does the missing become more loved or unheeded? Scorned or revalued? Might truancy win her? Who that have vanished do not solicit pity from the absentminded?

§

James Querpox traveled to Rome that summer. It was the opposite of a vacation: self-denial and exile. He limped quietly from museum to museum. He went into cathedrals and found them pointless. He regarded fountains. He stood in the sun on empty European streets and fed pigeons and listened to music and was alone. On one rainy day, he stayed in and read Hazlitt's strange *Liber Amoris*. He meandered down the Via Giulia under a hot sun and found he had developed a focal dystonia, a misfiring that may have been the result of the loud crash of a dropped tray behind him in a restaurant bar which had caused a severe muscle contraction. One morning when he woke up in a sweat he imagined that he was in Germany, but he was not. He was spectacularly alone. There is nothing left of me. I am a remnant, he felt, the residuum of lost love. I died a while ago. I do not know who it is that is traveling.

A sense of forlorn remoteness never seemed to leave him at peace. It was meaningless. He was meaningless. He had taken some photos of Summer with him. He would often take walks, carrying his photos, and sit down on the grass to look at them. He would hear swallows twitter *quit quit.*

One photo he had snipped from the annual Graybar facebook. Another he had seen of her in a school field-hockey photo thumbtacked on a bulletin board near the dining hall, and, when no one was looking, he took it down and placed it in a book to save. Smiling, perspiring, she held her hockey stick horizontal and was wearing a thin sleeveless jersey, a blue kilt with side-flap, handsome blue knee-socks with one rolled down, and bold white soccer cleats with black criss-crosses on them. There she bolted, in mid-run, her hair the color of Nebraskan corn, warm apple-blossom skin, and an alertness in the five-fathom green of her eyes that fairly shone.

Querpox for hours pored over the photos. Was Heisenberg correct? Did the very act of observing something or someone affect the observed? Do we onlookers in some way effect our subjects? An electron does not even have a definite position or path until we observe it, or so it was said. Was there even an objective reality—even an objective position—outside of our observations? These were recurrent questions that began nagging at the poor man as he turned Summer's pictures down and up. It was just about the time that he started wondering whether the universe obeyed strict causal laws that he began to believe he might be losing his mind.

A swallowtail settled on a flower, then a short-tailed blue, and a cabbage white. Querpox reflected on Darwin's theory of "pairing," a kind of splendid co-evolution in the world in which we discover like magic the wonderful natural partnership among living things, whereby an issue of purpose is amazingly joined, the pairing of trophic feeding-dependence of so many insects on certain flowers, along with the reciprocal dependence of flowers on insects to pollinate and so produce seeds.

Why not in some parallel world the possibility of such a natural bonding between him and beautiful Summer Bellerophon?

He got lost in pointless thought and began to wonder what it meant to their souls if his loving her led to nothing. He pondered the One and the Many problem as he walked along the Tiber. Didn't we live in a world of infinite objects that are constantly changing, and yet even in this imposing world of objects and change, was there not an underlying unity and stability? One of the things that putatively so tortured him was that a legitimately atavistic metaphysics admitted exactly nothing of ethics or moral values or questions about what it is to be human. By lovely fountains he sat, watching the water play beautifully out of spouts. My water, my life, my Vodka.

Vodka, he whispered.

In the Piazza on Capitoline Hill, he saw how the travertine design set into the paving was perfectly level: around its perimeter, low steps rose to die away into the paving as the slope required. Its center sprung slightly, so that Querpox sensed that he was standing on the exposed part of a gigantic egg that was all but buried at the center of the city at the center of the world. His own egg was cracked.

Was there no hope? What about Domitian's strange dream, shortly before his own death, when a golden hump grew out of his back, portending the moderate rule of the emperors who would soon succeed him, and a raven perched on the Capitol flapped and cawed *All will be well?*

Missing in him was a shape of love scooped out he needed to survive. He coped by delusion. Who was it said a thinker is someone who has deliberately decided to kill part of himself in order to make life bearable?

He sat day after day on a low hill near the Forum. It was a brooding heat. He spent much of his time pondering with melancholy the pagoda-shaped arborvitae and sorting through the photographs he had brought of Summer Bellerophon. The air seemed to vibrate with sunlight. He was a strange lonely man on a hill. He sat in reverie. One of the pictures was a special favorite. It showed the girl very alive on the green hockey field, in plaid knee-socks, strong full thighs, blonde hair swinging. Artemis among the Oreads. Lovely Camilla outrunning the wind, so lightly. She had just looked up but was yet in mid-run, a real long stride. Her teeth were white and feral and showed a wild, competitive drive. He had taken the picture. The rare photograph that resulted, with its apricot-colored tones and a blue bloom on the surface, was almost Sophoclean in its sadness, but he had saved it. Saved? O, hoarded!—cherished!—*treasured!* One afternoon he bought several postcards and with a pen carefully wrote on one of them, "'I kiss you 1,095,060,437,082 times,' as Mozart wrote to his love, Constanze, on April 14, 1789." But he knew that he could never mail it. He ripped it up and dropped it fluttering into the river instead. It didn't matter. And as long as he dreamed, it would not.

Imagination, like a guardian angel with its warm, bright, enveloping pennons enfolding him in an embrace of protection, shielded him from reality. He began leaving room for angels and, like Pascal, now refused to sit in a chair without an additional chair at either side of him so as not to fall into space, for one thing, a new worry, but in order to accommodate "visitors." He engaged in circuitous monopolylogues that grew out of his despondency like a bolting stalk of rhubarb. Seclusion led to isolation and remoteness to an even sharper sense of isolation, which, developing out of a friendless sadness, ever constant, became a howling loneliness.

Were his imaginative flights contrivance? From his furtive imagination grew paranoia and no end of nightmares involving, inexplicably, and born of nothing that he could explain, the frightening appearances of great bounding prehistoric megacerops, duck-billed iguanadons, savage massive pleni-toothed creodonts, fat rhino-like titanotheres, and threatening green bistahieversors from the Cretaceous. It occurred to him that they were no worse in any anti-world than the belittling set of vegetative Phylloclades, who so plagued the beautiful girl of his dreams. What space was he inhabiting in his feverish fugues and esoteric mind-flights? Could he be actually returning in time?

Space is a form of thought, as is time—and, not being empirical concepts, both allowed Querpox, as he pondered the dithers he was in, a kind of excavating freedom to wish away the unforgiving need to come to terms with his obsession, the endless consuming and compulsion preoccupation, this monomaniacal love, and push it further and further toward abstraction.

§

The following autumn Querpox returned to Graybar and the academic year. Summer Bellerophon, he saw, had registered to take his course in calculus, which he knew must not be. Didn't Meister Eckhart tell us once that an angel in hell flies in his own little cloud of paradise? As Summer was with him already in his mind, most pressingly so, he wondered how could he dare take the chance of losing her in real life. So, much to Miss Fingerspitzengefühl's anger, he dropped the course, giving the secretary weeks of extra work. He spoke of his ill health. She immediately reported this to the headmaster, who called him in and made a long grave speech to him about rules and regulations and told him that if he had health problems, he should see a doctor. The short, bantling headmaster asked him if he took drugs and inquired why he seemed so anti-social and queried him about several of the school's more attractive girls, Hatshepsut Jordan, Natica Metcalfe, Partita Palandjian, Graybar's tennis champion—she was slated for the Olympics—and Lois Blessington. Hadn't he once invited Bunny Gligoric, Christmas Spenser-Bourne, and Sieglinde Dansk over to his apartment?

He replied exactly nothing.

Hadn't Nguyen Mirador's wealthy father coming from abroad recently taken him to lunch, and now why would he have done that? Shenandoah Sprott had signed up for every class that he taught and for each had repeatedly received the highest grade of A. Was this typical? What about Iris Bonechill?

James Querpox maintained a cold silence, merely looked away, infuriating his inquisitor. He correctly judged Paltrey a ball of spite. Querpox remembered once seeing the headmaster terrorizing a heron. It all seemed to fit. The very act of being born ruined my health, he reflected, as he walked dolefully among the shadbush, the sweet gums, and the beeches, fingering the small spearpoints and scales and steep spirals of their fall buds, as he walked aimlessly in sorrow.

Absolutes nevertheless buoyed him up. Not once had he ever heard Summer speak, nor had he ever talked to her, but her voice, he knew, would be sweet and exact and have a certain tissue-paper vibrato. In his mind she slept with him and hugged and kissed and loved and danced with him and whispered hope into the well of his mouth and squeezed his hand without ceasing in the paradise of his dreams. He lived as a man who had been touched by heavenly light. She came to him as if poured like photons of light, quanta, an infusion of fairy dust, tiny particles of which light also consisted, not merely a wave, but an enchanting stream.

At the Christmas assembly, during one sequence, she stepped out to play "The Holly and the Ivy" on her flute, the clear haunting notes of the carol vibrating soft and smooth like an enchanted ring around a rain moon. She followed this with Carlos Gardel's "*Por una Cabeza*" and John Stevenson's "The Last Rose of Summer." He sat there in the darkness, way at the back, all alone. The whole idea of the mystical feast for the first time came alive for him. Mistletoe. Snow. Candles. Querpox was so moved that his thoughts went through the ceiling of the auditorium, through space, past the ether of love, up into the high reaches of the empyrean itself even, past the towering and cosmically immense blackness of the infinitude of space itself to a still point. He walked home alone that night, heady with thanks, following as best he could his halting, his sad halting, his long halting awkward shadow across the snow.

When he woke up the next day, snow on the ground bright as a knife blade, Summer Bellerophon being so near to him, taking in the four corners of the Earth, was in the joy it imparted allegiance enough.

Weeks followed. From his classroom, as he taught, he habitually looked down through the branches of stark empty maples where sat below in metal stalls a zareba of bicycles. He knew Summer's. Hers was the Atlas 1000—a blue-and-white speedster with a basket but which had no lock or horn. He knew her bike routes as well. She pedaled up Webster, down Forest, turned up the drive, and pulled in every morning at 7:50. She was seventeen, she had one brother, she played the flute, she drank Diet Pepsi (in bottles only), she collected thimbles, she hated sewing, disliked card-playing, country music, and meat, loved sandals, desserts, earrings, manicures, geometric haircuts, daytrips to Boston, the color lavender, acting and theater, and lying on her stomach when reading. She owned a cat, had no father, or even a boyfriend—at least no one he ever saw. Her telephone number was (508) 362-5162.

One time, daring himself to do so, Querpox coming across them across from Rafferty Field asked Summer and two of her girlfriends if they had ever heard about the woman who complained to her psychiatrist that she had two repeated dreams, first of a wigwam, then of a teepee, and what the psychiatrist had said? Querpox paused and said, dryly, "You're too tents." There was no waste in her laughter, which was quick—a single, merry, high, descending lilting triplet.

Actually, this never happened, thank heavens he had only dreamed it, for in fact Summer Bellerophon might indeed have hated jokes, and neither in his mind nor in fact could he bear to offend her. The truth was, he could not allow anything to take place in reality that had not been probed by, vetted by—and so paradoxically co-opted by—his mind. *I have become insane with long intervals of horrible sanity,* he thought, conjuring Edgar Allan Poe. Querpox had not told anybody, confided to no one, but for some time now he had been going to see a therapist in Hartford. The sessions began on January 19, which was, as a matter of fact, Poe's birthday, and the significant reason he knew that was simply because it happened to be the day that he himself was born. An echoing grief like the distant rumble of thunder he could not seem to shake. It came from faraway as if from over the pale of distant hills. It seemed as if he were hearing sounds through his knees, as crickets do. At first, the doctor thought it was chronic nonspecific anxiety disorder, then some odd phobia, until after some months—of talking, of listening—he came up with an even worse diagnosis.

His patient was dying of love.

One palmary afternoon, on his way back from the school squash courts (where he liked to read in peace), Querpox happened to see Summer Bellerophon in the incandescent light of a spring morning at the pool, where she let her hair down like a golden veil over her shoulders. Her bathing-suit the color of celadon, when wet, clung to her like varnish, in its shining having something of asteroidal light. She tweaked the tight nylon over her perfectly rounded buttocks, dove, and surfaced in a jetlike moment to an explosion of foamy white bubbles. Her legs were strong, shaped to divinity, and though muscular, obviously as soft as cheveril. Golden hot sunshine poured through the high wall windows of the pool that afternoon, as he noticed her silhou-etted against the bright light, as if she were being photographed *profil presque perdu*. Goblet belly of Canticles. Strong young arms and singularly shapely legs. The gentle blades of her back sym-metrical. Light hair a sopping shape as naturally as the whorls of a seashell, but with far more beautiful freedom of curve, twirl, spiral, helix, and arabesque.

But in seeing her, he had unfortunately been seen. Nosy Pook Paltrey reported that. So did librarian Edna Potentia Pluck-rose, she of the goat-hair sweaters. Chinless Philip Flummerfelt, feigning concern (but actually nosy) stopped at his house late one afternoon—bicycle clips on both legs—and knocked to make a pastoral visit. Querpox had seen him through the windows and, knowing him for the Maryland Parson he was, a person skillfully adept at fitting in any company, refused to answer. Like a shrew, whichever way Flummerfelt moved, his fur never mussed.

So, days passed. Summer played preternaturally inside his loneliness in ways he could not begin to describe and that he could only cope with in the framework of madness and mono-logue. He walked in circles under the albescent moon. He wanted to hurl his heart against the clock of time to stop its ticking, to beg of the gods that she never leave the school, to implore the gods that she always stay, to beseech and entreat the gods to let her remain forever as young and lovely as she was that moment. Going round and round. It was his fate. Living on the edge. The mystery of the circle. An infinite number of sides. A circle has one curved side. A limiting curve, the curve defined as the limit of the polygon with an infinite number of sides and with numberless edges.

No, but a circle is a shape, not a polygon, so it does not have sides. So, I cannot have infinitely many sides, concluded the man bounded in a nutshell, although I do have too many sides. No one can have an infinity of something. Yet in my emptiness I have an infinity in my heart, as a king of infinite space.

With his back to her, Querpox would typically whisper, "Look at me, child, who will never leave you, although you will never know it. Wheel me into the sun. Let me die on the thorn of a rose. My eyes catch fire. I live in wind!"

§

Then something terrible happened.

One week a faculty member had asked Querpox to proctor one of the dorms. It involved maintaining general order and watching curfews. Summer Bellerophon, unbeknownst to him, was staying over with her friend, Geraldine, as the following night was a big school dance—the boys, their dates, had names like Atwater Kent, Sheraton Commander, and Larch Tamarack—and one evening, late, Querpox heard a timid knock on the door. He answered it. Summer Bellerophon was standing right in front of him. There was the scent of a eucalyptus breeze. She was wearing a wispy black diaphanous nightgown sprigged with tiny roses and delicate damson lilacs. He stepped back, unable to believe exactly what he was seeing. She was crying. The wetness of her eyes, a lightning-flash cadmium green, glistening and tinsel, were wild with a viridian that burned like fire sprinkled with copper salts, glister-snaps, like the blue electric sparks set off in all sorts of directions by the catenaries of a tram. Her hair was down, a golden waterfall. There was in the way she looked up something arresting. Her eyes, formidable, were an exact pair—most people's eyes are not. The intoxication of her suddenly being in his presence demanded all of his attention, indeed mastery.

Seeing her close up, he instantly thought of Pallas Athena, climbing from her bath in Tennyson's poem "Tiresias,"

> ". . . yet one glittering foot disturb'd
> The lucid well; one snowy knee was prest
> Against the margin flowers; a dreadful light
> Came from her golden hair, her golden helm
> And all her golden armor on the grass,
> And from her virgin breast, and virgin eyes
> Remaining fixt on mine, till mine grew dark
> For ever, and I heard a voice that said
> 'Henceforth be blind, for thou hast seen too much,
> And speak the truth that no man may believe.'"

It had a synergistic effect on the control of his nervous system, all of it, that is, what he was able to muster to see through the misty fog and insistent beat of suddenly thumping emotions, he who had so often palpated her hair and warmed her arms and kissed her eyes in the inner secrecy of dreams. "*O amantassimia mia diva,*" he thought, as his heart, drenched in pain, swollen with love, almost gave way, "your tears will be running down my heart long after they have died in your eyes."

Summer spoke. *She was speaking.* She told him that her date for the dance had been hurt in a car accident. Apparently at a red stop-light, playing "Chinese Fire Drill," all of the passengers playfully jumped out to swap seats, and he fell. Her voice was musical, soft chimes, but a halting patina of tears clouded them. She continued speaking. But it was not her intense concern for someone else. Nor that she had looked into his eyes. Or that she was even grieving. Simply, she had spoken—become substantial—attained reality—actually came alive. Could she not see that they who for so long were one without her were now divided, crucially separated? Segregated?

Partitioned?

Querpox, who went onto the roof, was perspiring badly, stricken with pain as would a stag, sheet-white with love. What is vertigo but the foretaste of a deep, an infinite, a fatal fall?

How even when she would but raise her eyelids slowly with a smile could he adore her at a distance, how utterly safe he was at that remove, and how desperately had he prayed to God not to give her eyes to feel the worshipful heart within him, beseeched God that nothing come true of the many things that could. There was no "pose" in her smile, merely the openness of a guileless heart. By it, however, had she stepped through that veil, and by so doing, entered history, to become frail with the possibility of vicissitude, change, alteration, shift?

It was a black Thursday in March, worst weather, worst day, worst month, raining like a fire-hose on a fat rat, with clouds rolling black down from Maine. Poor Querpox in his room began walking in circles, the film of his mind racing far too fast, and, like jumping sprockets, it began to unravel. His health began to suffer. His skin, turning rubious, was beginning to roughen badly and took on the nap of mica or isinglass, flaking and dehydrated and seemed to corrode in the same way as his lost but hectoring, centrifugent dreams. He was driven to go outside. Panicking, he reflected: *Whatever has Jesus Christ done to me?*

As he walked he heard a catbird high in a hemlock tree—or was it in his mind?—and the lawless freedom of its song. It became very disturbing. The bird with its sense of almost ventriloquist-like imitation seemed not only to entertain no regard for any set rhythm but proceeded to sing, to squawk, in a confused series of muddled, interrupted twitters which bore no relationship at all with each other and in their meaningless died in a dopplerian echo far away. Did the bird in his mimicry, in his impersonation, possibly have no idea what he was singing about at all, merely squealing cartwheels, miming the song of a thrush, the yowl of a cat, gobbles of a hen or rooster, all, anything, as the grist for its musical mill? Tears filled Querpox's tired soul. Prince Lágrimas. He became fearfully conscious of a kind of *terribilita*. Remorse of baseless sort, guilty thoughts, began drifting in on a black mist, shower, floor, rain, torrent, sheets of rain wafting in like the seaborne hieratic winds to his mind.

Was his the Fallacy of Misplaced Concreteness—the fatal error of mistaking ideology for reality?

Without the defense of dreams, the fact of fancy, he began to bite his fingers. He began to appear in public with his coat turned inside out, becoming petulant and vexatious in ways no one had ever seen before. Then one morning he stopped and stood up facing a window in which, by mournful reflection, his face became nothing but the apparition of a stranger, as though he, it, had arrived from nowhere, from nowhere at all, and he proceeded to say to no one in particular, "Now that I've memorized your name shall I throw my head away?"

There were conversations he had with Summer's ghost, with his thoughts, with his fears, with his lost dreams. *Are you cold? Have more wine, dear heart. Do not be sad. You'll never know the pain of losing someone like you when you are someone like me. Faithfully yours, Hephaestus.* A muttered curse he flung at the assassin sky overhead that, brooding, seemed to ask darkly for an explanation. It was now as if the soul of a dead person had entered his living body with its own crown of thorns. Grief fit round his forehead like a headband.

Querpox felt the magnetohydrodynamics of his hot tears burning into his cheeks, as he revolved about the desolate room, squeezing his hands, uttering, "God save me! God save me!" As he cried out, he heard only the feebleness of a hollow echo in this age of the death of religious conviction.

A book lay on the table. It was the copy of Willa Cather's *The Troll Garden* that the student Bunny Gligoric had left for him. He turned to a page and by mere hap saw Summer again in a last pleading surveillance as he read, "Thou art the Spring for which I sighed in Winter's cold embraces."

He felt the very language was crying that night saying goodbye to her in his room. Something had happened inside of him that he could not reverse, reclaim, or reset, something portentously unalterable, deeply ineluctable, inescapable, unavoidable. Wasn't the idea that one must conduct oneself in such a way that the principle of one's action can become general law—Kant's Categorical Imperative—based upon the necessity for rational thought to agree with itself? Then agreed with himself, he was! He had climbed as it were to the top of his head, as it were, to take a last long deep neuroimaging glimpse into the projected experience of what it was he was supposed to know. His sad fault was having tried to reach beyond his grasp, and his sin was *hubris,* followed by *ara:* fall from pride. I am merely an element, other people's needs, deets not data, a ghost in a machine, a tick-tock-ing, digital, geo-engineered robot in dark winter.

He was suffering a schism between fact and value.

Nothing is fixed. The twins, Anicca and Anatta, seesaw.

If nothing is permanent, there is no soul. It is only because delusion remains, we imagine our imagined selves to be real.

Can one have false axioms within a logical system? he wondered. He roamed the room in an existentially inauthenticating mood, seemed not to be able to locate his own reflections. Must not false axions produce systems that could prove anything including their own invalidity? And if they are finally false, would they not be tautologies, improbabilizing statements that we assume to be true?

He remembered goofy red-headed Phil Flummerfelt, the chinless—and sententious— gossip-mongering Protestant chaplain at Graybar telling him on one of his hopelessly dull and intrusive pastoral visits, invariably the objective of just plain nosiness—passing on to him, as rubbernecking, he snooped around Querpox's rooms—the Gospel message of Jesus in Matthew 10:38, the gist of which seemed to be aimed at him alone, or so the minister implied: "And anyone who does not take up his cross and tread in my footsteps does not deserve me. The man protective of his life will lose it, but the one casting it away on my account will preserve it."

What hard road had that fool ever trod? It is precisely the sanctimonious who never feel the importance of God.

The cross was all Querpox *knew*—and why not cast away one's life when the final truth is that life is suffering?

Querpox thought one can always go back if back is where

you can best strike from, but what was going back but, aping reclamation, merely mean retrieval, which is salvage? All that is reclaimed from the distant past are ghosts that in the fetching only possess you. Nothing is repaired or rectified but through tears. Who was it that said that a person who does not enjoy his own company is usually right?

"I will undertake myself," quoth he.

He opened the window to avoid his reflection. He watched a murmuration of starlings cross the abstract sky and disappear. *Goodbye*, he thought. If only a like flight could take the irremedial chagrins of my darkness, doubt, and unrest with it. Querpox walked back across the room. His club foot ached.

"I feel chained to a dead man," he gasped out loud over a sink, speaking aloud simply to make sure that he was still there, even alive. It was pure *zerrissenheit*, a torn-to-pieces hood in his numbed skull. What did any one thing matter? he wondered. A preponderance of matter in the universe does *not* emit light, he knew. The horror of it all is that most of the universe is actually *missing!* Dark matter prevails eons wide, a vast ultra-expanse of endless space. Gravity is stronger, fiercer than we can possibly know. Galaxy cluster collisions will one day detonate in a spectacular nightmare of solar masses, and we will all of us suck in death. If math was the language that nature uses to describe its wonders, why was he not consoled?

With a face as pale as bloater paste, James Querpox wrote several notes, pointless, unsatisfactory ones. He put down his pen slowly and deliberately. How he wanted to drink the ink! But, instead, he squeezed his poor hot forehead with his hands, muttering some mystic words. He then picked up his pen again, deliberated, and proceeded to write out this equation on a card:

$$A + B$$
$$A = B$$
$$A + AB$$
$$A - B = AB - B$$
$$(A + B) (A - B) = B (A - B)$$
$$A = B = B$$
$$1 + 1 = 1$$
$$2 = 1$$

That was all he needed, and it was enough. Whereupon, he walked out, found the Fragonard tree by Rafferty Field, threw a rope up over a gnarled but sufficient branch, and hanged himself.

A Wordstress in Williamsburg

"The writer," sighed Miss Rosemary, the tournure of her phrases as precise as cut glass, "has *noooo* time whatsoever for such things. No, I'm afraid, she has not. The devotion which asks her to feel the deliberation of art asks also that she choose the blessed single life." She looked through the window of the bus studiedly. "I am a novelist, my dear, which is spelled s-a-c-r-i-f-i-c-e."

"I see."

"Oh," she replied, patting her bun of hair, "but you are so young."

"I suppose so. But novelists," I added, "know people so well."

She silkily thanked me.

We had met coincidentally, the upshot of my having been seated at the table directly next to her that morning, and where, over hot lemon tea and plump raisin scones, I had found myself—along with others—a fretful auditor to one of her many (I came to see) inexplicit, polysemantic chats, for she was one of those starboard-leaning High Anglicans, famous and innumerable in the Commonwealth of Virginia, whose factitious sense of vanity in a private conversation makes it frankly public: the raised and punishingly assertive voice of the Insane Queen which includes, willingly or no, everybody within earshot. Hers was a loud, lessoning voice. Wherever she went, presumably, went her parthenon.

She was a limitless fund of psychobabble about self-reliance, lots of the socks-up, Albert Ellis/Dale Carnegie/ "Personal Growth"/"Human Potential," Bliss Carman-like, pseudo-neo-Stoic, self-esteem, ringing self-assurance, learning-to-like-your-self, being-your-own-best-friend sort of cant, filled with palliative language of therapy that favored expressions like "share" for "tell," "relationship" for "romance," "reach out" for "call or visit someone in pain or trouble," "challenges" or "issues" —for "problems" or "troubles"—and (emotional) "closure."

Miss Sweetshrub, *aetat.* fifty, was classically affected and wore a patterned dress that looked like Morris wallpaper, a striking manner of dress that made her seem not so much clothed as upholstered. She had a perched Jacobean nose, like a dogvane, a long neck suggesting that she could feed on the topmost leaves of a tree, a waltzing oversized bottom, and wore her rusted hair in an outlandish bun at the back and anchored by several severe combs. I became fascinated with that hair-bun. I kept thinking of the many references in English poetry—Lord Tennyson is an apt example—which call to one's attention the crucial contrast, iconographically shown, between one's hair worn tightly up and hair unpinned and flowing, the latter of course, unlike the former, almost always a symbol of sexuality.

But Rosemary Sweetshrub, as she herself had often pointed out, had never married, never having been struck, like Queen Dido by Cupid's arrow, with a "living love in the long-since-unstirred spirit and disaccustomed heart." She was—how to put it?—an "unclaimed blessing."

Miss Sweetshrub had what a person might call antique manners and it seemed at every turn sought to make them manifest. It was her joy to cultivate knowledge of proper etiquette. She still employed formal calling cards, for instance, knew that a fish fork must be silver and a caviar spoon horn. She gave small, lavish dinners, preferring service *à la française* and never *à la russe*, which she thought more graceful—"An answer will oblige," she fastidiously wrote at the bottom of her invitations, but never the more common RSVP—and with pride not only owned, but actually used, an epergne. She lived alone somewhere in Richmond in a large, half-finished structure that used to be called "Late General Grant" and had grown up in an era of horse cars and hackneys. Once every two or three months, she took a teaspoonful of powdered charcoal mixed with sweetened water or milk, in the firm belief that it would prove efficacious in making her complexion clear and transparent. When stepping off a curb, she out of tidy habit gently raised her dress a tad with her right hand—doing so with both hands was vulgar—and of course never in any circumstance whatsoever, pointed. I have often wondered if, when she sat down to write, she employed a quill pen.

"You perhaps know my work?" She was looking at me with her eyes closed, her lavender gloves buttoned shut and crossed immaculately in her lap.

"Er, could you name some of them. I may have—"

"My novels? Let me see. My first was *Answer Came There None*, then, respectively, *Rouge from a Pyx; I, a Stranger;* and *The Big Regret*. And my volume of early verse, *Naps upon Parnassus.* I followed that with a critical work on Robert Browning, called *The*

Snail on the Thorn."

"Mmmmm."

"My most widely reviewed book? Difficult to say, in all truth, but I'd say it was my *Tlot! Tlot!: A Biography of Alfred Noyes.*"

"Gosh," I tactfully observed, "you've sure written a lot," I said, cross-charging her, smiling thinly, knowing what her response would be, but her beaky satisfaction was fun to see. "Permit me? 'A lot' is a parcel of land. I have written"—she arched an eyebrow—"much." Then she smiled sweetly at me. Her long, pronounced, sloping snout reminded me of the peculiar face of the queen triggerfish, a visage seemingly calm but yet, in the slant of another odd light, suggestive of stress and, changing color to match its surroundings, giving more than a hint of aggression and peevishness. Stroppy, she could get. More often than not, she walked about, with seemingly meandering quizzicality, her mouth turned down like a croquet hoop.

I could not avoid listening to what she said during much of that afternoon. Her speaking prop was her eyeglasses. She used half-glasses (horn-rimmed) worn on a fashionable eye-glass cord, carried a Moleskine in which, at intervals, she made entries with a tiny pencil, and by dint of age or fussiness or whatever, she lorded it over the rest of the company. Random remarks that she made seemed to cry out—in her mind, at least—for a Boswell. I listened to her much of the day. She referred to raw vegetables as *crudités*. She made it quite clear in her extravagant praise for Herbert Hoover the nature of her political cast. Sweetshrub whenever possible opted for the obfusc, the oblique, and the scholarly. In an excursus about flowers, one of her most serious fascinations, she distinctly preferred "calendula" to marigold, "antirrhinum" to snapdragon, and the high-brow "myositis" to the plebeian forget-me-not or scorpion grass.

"Are we all not later in the afternoon being fêted with a lecture on Old Williamsburg at the lyceum?" asked Ms. Sweet-shrub.

Not a hall. A lyceum.

That was her all over.

Her work was her *oeuvre*, her hair her *coiffure*, a tomato was to*mah*to, and, to her, problems were merely "challenges." The biblical Ten Commandments she always referred to as the Deca-logue. She preferred "plethora" to *plenty* and whenever she had the chance employed, I noticed, "whilst," "methinks," "whence," "behoove," and never failed to opt for "cognizant" over "aware."

Williamsburg, the historical capital of Virginia up to 1780, lay before us. The bus shuttle swung out into the sun-shine from under the arch near the information center, where we had all boarded, and slowly moved toward the historic colo-nial area. A recorded voice gave a running account of the high spots along the village route: the Old Windmill, the Capitol, Christiana Campbell's Tavern, the Old Jail, etc. Tourists—in sun-glasses, peachblow-colored Bermuda shorts, fat straw shoes, with Leicas slung over their shoulders—cooed, gabbed out loud, and pointed everywhichway. The wheezing bus stopped frequently. At one stop—I believe that it was somewhere near the Bruton Parish Church—a young couple of college age noisily boarded, and, excited, laughing, and encumbered with several large bags of groceries, both tumbled into some seats. The boy tousled the girl's hair and kissed her.

I then suddenly heard from the seat next to me a cluck of discord, both—the cluck, the discord—Miss Sweetshrub's. She was blinking furiously, and I was able to follow La Modesta's icy admonishing stare (the effect) to its cause: the beautiful girl, her head thrown back, was shaking out her soft golden hair and brushing a comb through it. The boy beamed.

The authoressette's eyes glinted menacingly.

"It's apparently the fashion nowadays to—"

I swallowed nervously. "To—"

"Why," she unhappily snapped, ring-fencing her phrase with withering emphasis, "to go *marketing together!*"

She looked away.

Before I could reply—a difficulty in itself—Miss Sweetshrub was up and off the bus, self-efficiently having refused the assistance of a courtly middle-aged gentleman who, at the foot of the bus's steep steps, had thoughtfully doffed his hat and cavalierly offered an extended hand to her. Head high, she raised her chin and waggled him aside with an admonishing index finger, and, as we pulled away, wended her way with a turkey-gobble strut across the street to some greenery. I watched her from my window stuffing her cartwheel garden party hat into a sling bag and without so much as looking right or left go nutting across one of the open meadows off the Duke of Gloucester Street in foolish, golflike strides. And she was alone.

The old Capitol building, its architectonics perfect in eighteenth-century brick, was our point of disembarkation. We collectively bounced like happy jellies all over the old town: to watch paper made, silver wrought, wool spun, flour ground, handbills printed, barrels staved, books sewn, and to see locals garbed in the period fashions of tricorn hats, doublets, and buckled shoes or sally hats and flounced dresses, each of those, at his or her cue, to rise and provide round and eximious summaries of various aspects of American history.

But was this historical? Or even American? A curious fact is the town of Williamsburg as presented was a simulated construct, an imitation—a copy—of what the village once looked like, restored and rebuilt, as it was, by Rockefeller money in 1926. I was whimsically reminded of what the satirical writer Evelyn Waugh saw on a visit to this country in a few horrid glimpses of Hollywood's Forest Lawn cemetery, not only that that hideous "Garden of Remembrance" defined the goofiness of Tinseltown but also that the United States in general, which he mockingly referred to as "Substitute Land," was a place of secondhand experience, phony culture, ersatz buildings, imitation architecture, fake costumes, debased language, counterfeit art, fraudulent politics, bogus sects, spurious music, and, worst of all—at least in his cynical, scoffing and misanthropic point of view—barbarous behavior.

Miss Sweetshrub told everyone that she felt in this reconstructed town, however, the lilt of the period and the same elegance that gave inspiration to the place in old colonial days. Touring various houses, she loved the ladder-back chairs, fold-top card tables, old wine cellarets. It was the same with the various patterned colonial gardens, both the crape-myrtle-in-the-dooryard type and the box-bush-by-the-front-gate. The woman had a tendency to take over, being large and in charge, and in her self-approving way assumed the right by her very nature to begin talking ten to the minute about converting many of the Williamsburg back lots to flower gardens. She was lavish with her opinions while she walked down the garden paths of the Pitt-Dixon House, the gardens of the Governor's Palace, and the Coke-Garrett House.

"I really do not 'get' hostas, if I may say so, although I

suppose they do fill in a blank spot here and there. But when people plop down perfect rows of hostas and, well, nothing else—it just screams, '*I give up.*' Most hosta landscapes look antiseptically corporate to me, like something you would find in a chiropractor's office. I tend to think of them as a different kind of weed."

She stopped to comment favorably on a far wall of espaliered pear trees, trained and grown along one plane.

"Too fussy," I said. She whished.

"Nothing should be noticed," I offered. "Bunny Mellon's mantra."

"Red cedars clipped to simulate the English yew somewhat affright, I will give you that," she proclaimed. She pointed to a clump. "To my eyes bearded irises seem way too fussy. Yarrow always look scraggly to me, and I cannot stand the stench—scent, if you insist—of petunias. Barberry, inevitably planted for its 'evergreen' color on something that is not green, is always plonked too close to a path so that at their maturity one cannot walk by without it snagging one's skirt or leg. I loathe the smell of privet flowers, oriental lilies, and paper narcissus and cannot say that I like most hybrid tea roses—scraggly plants with mutant flowers demanding far too much of one's time. Striations on leaves in the extreme tend to bother me." No one of course was listening to her, no one I saw, anyway, and, if anything, she was given a wide berth.

I myself have never credited the ingenuity of topiary. Anything too clever or overconsidered in gardening always lacked charm for me. I used to sit studying in the gardens by the Serpentine Wall at UVa. and often had the feeling of Martians hovering over me. Boxwoods. Worse, *poodle pruned* boxwoods! Privets. Even worse, poodle pruned privets, they were just too insipid to hate.

"I hate forsythia for its brainless yellow and have never liked that color in flowers, which seems too garish," Miss Sweet-shrub expostulated, waving an arm and pontificating as if she were Gertrude Jekyll herself. "Sometime ago, I planted some prim santolina after several ascetic years of not having it, and I must say I still think that its blooms were a little too bright, flashing, and took away from the beauty of my orange dotted salvia nearby. I would add gladioli to my list, which look fine when cut for a floral arrangement but grow top-heavy in a garden and tend to invite thrips. Also—unsettlingly—one always finds them next to a casket!"

Barging, talking, pontificating, hair-fluffing. It was a hot day, somewhat muggy, and trooping the paths began to pall.

"My least favorite color combination, I have to say, is the Lime Mound *spiraea*, chartreuse and pale pink—and with all that relentless bright lemon-yellow foliage trying in its pathetic way to woo you? Good heavens. These are *green* gardens, notice," she clarified for us, pointing by way of quick staccato bobbing nods of her head. "A true-to-type Virginian always prefers pastels, subdued colors, nothing garish, you see. I abhor the 'riot of color'—wake up, people—which so many over-fond gardeners today insistently apply to their informal plantings and herbaceous borders."

I decided to pipe up again. "Did you know that the only green pigment in nature is chlorophyll—the color in plants. As plants are abundant in nature, we find green all over, but it is in fact a rare color to find indeed." Sweetshrub glared at me. "To illustrate the difficulty nature has in making green, rather than making a green *pigment*, frogs for example have yellow crystals under blue skin cells, creating the color green. Amazing, isn't it? I mean, *what is truly green?*"

Sweetshrub steamrolled my observation as irrelevant and continued talking, correcting with a fluffing hand that *à la concierge* hair-bun of hers.

At historic Christiana Campbell's Tavern Restaurant, around lunchtime, people—tourists—fell in to have their repast at several neatly arranged outdoor tables. It was a lavish set-up, banquet style, mainly colonial fare—boiled ham with brown sugar and cloves, fried lye hominy, scalloped potatoes, fried apples. A hearty fellow in a loud plaid shirt and big chrome watch, one who had asked Miss Sweetshrub—while pointing with his thumb—to pass the potatoes, also grabbed for two ears of corn. I happened to be sitting between them. Gnashing at the ears with gusto, typewriter-fashion, his mandibles working, he began quidding kernels like a starving draft horse, urgent, dropping them sloppily onto his messy shirt front as he ate. With closed eyes, in reaction, Miss Sweetshrub—shocked—anxiously pressed her bosom.

She was now whispering a few words to the young women on her right, pointing out that, when eating corn on the cob, not her favorite activity, she hastened to add, one should do so with holders, and went on to explain that one should properly butter and salt an ear of corn only three rows at a time—two was childish, four was gluttonous—and people with good manners correctly chewed from left to right. Going in the opposite direction, for some particular—and inexplicable—reason, was barbarous. She noticed no beverage spoons were provided. *Beverage spoons?* She also began grousing that Mr. Plaid had failed to cut his meat into bite-size pieces, drank white wine inappropriately from a big-bowled glass meant for red wine, and inconsiderately left his napkin on the table when he temporarily left, although it belonged on the chair, since he was returning. She explained to the young woman sitting by her that cream pitchers—as with other dishes with handles—should always be passed with the handle toward the person receiving them. After all, was this not the Olde Williamsburg?

Upon leaving, I heard her declare, invoking something in the mood of antebellum Virginia, "He ate like a cornfield darky." Touching the young woman's arm, she stressed that the ignorance of the man in the plaid shirt with his napkin was all too characteristic of bad behavior, adding, "Napery means the world to me."

She was exacting, finicky, fussy—what the French call *difficile*—and in a very real sense distinctly outmoded, a person from the bygone era of Squibb toothpaste, Lux toilet soap, Ronald Colman movies, the twelve-cylinder Franklin, Atwater Kent radios, and squat cap-sealed beer cans—not that she ever deigned to imbibe, and certainly not cans of common workaday beer. I believe she came from the era of automobiles with running boards, mud scrapers, celluloid windshields, and a folding entrance-step. She spoke of dame schools, referred to erasers as Indian rubbers, would only eat Wolf River apples, referred to yeast as "saleratus," lauded the designs of Lilly Daché, and to her fish meant only cod. (Haddock in her day was given away as trash.) She wore gloves, kept fire screens at home, waited until men opened doors, left calling cards, and kept an old-fashioned Tiffany lamp in her front hall, right by a silver dish for mail. She hummed melodies from *The Merry Widow*, loved the poems of Bliss Carman, went on at lengths about Frozen Pudding ice cream—an outdated flavor—and lamented the disappearance of lyceums.

She was a formalist critic and a traveler.

"I was raised to eat at a table with an epergne," I heard Miss Sweetshrub tell one of the girls there when the subject of antiquity came up, as often it did that day, "a silver one, mind you, not a glass one, which some households chose. Mother thought having a glass one slightly—and I agreed—slightly *mesquin*." She sighed and raised a shaky hand that showed the venation architecture of a willow leaf and touched her brow in a piteous lament for all of us moderns. "You will not have heard of them today, I daresay. It served for side dishes, fruit, or sweetmeats. It saved on passing dishes around as is commonly done nowadays." She also had what could be called a tiptoeing voice. "But what is common, we avoid, *mmmm?*"

I thought: *but wasn't the act of saving anything slightly* mesquin?

Walking about from one venue to another, I got to talking with one of the young women in our group, a disaffected student of hers I assumed. She had been sitting at our table earlier and seemed to be the only one uninterested, say bored, in the chat. I was confirmed in my conviction that Rosemary Sweetshrub was sorely, almost comically, out-of-date when my new acquaintance confided to me by way of gentle correction that she insisted on *Dr.* Rosemary Sweetshrub in her college classes where she dressed in cabbage-rose chintzes with patterns of feathers and ferns. I asked, "Did she happen to know John Greenleaf Whittier?" I was given the full picture. "She calls biscuits 'ratafia,' grits groats, and still refers to *poires* Melba, braised clod, and baked shod—I mean, who eats food with such Victorian names anymore?"

Was this Sunday in Cicero Falls? But my new friend

was on a roll, and it was more than I could do to keep up. "She adores Lady Apples. She says she likes to taste rose water in her pound cake, and fastidiously will have it no other way. She told us that her lamb chops had to be served in *papillote* and insists that the word *Brie* always be capitalized." I was laughing. "She once explained in detail how Owen Wister perfectly described a Lady Baltimore cake in that 1906 novel of the same name—"with a boiled, or 'Seven Minute Frosting,' a must for her."

I asked her about Sweetshrub's books. A scrawl of amusement flashed in my friend's eyes, and, with a laugh, looking behind her to make sure no one was listening, she said, "Outright self-basting turkeys, and"—she paused—"I shouldn't really be unkind, but, well, a bit long past their keep-till date, as the English say."

Curiously, I had the dubious opportunity sometime later to flip through a paperback book of her—call it verse. It was of the James T. Sapp variety, mostly sage moral advice in bouncy fourteeners ("Avoid any conceit by every means, temptations to pride deny / Maintain though you strive a humble pose, but reckon forever with a sage surmise that you were born to die . . .").

She had a passion for—and her literary tastes were apparently confined to—all of those three-name-using serotinal authors, educators, and poetasters of yore, all of them late, rather overripe visionists harking back to a previous century, like Ella Wheeler Wilcox, Sarah Orne Jewett, Constance Fenimore Woolson, William Henry Venable, Charlotte Perkins Gilman, William Bliss Carman, Eleanor Henrietta Hull, Rebecca Harding Davis, and Mary Elizabeth Braddon.

Rosemary Sweetshrub also painted, *plein air*, I was told, sitting on a folding stool, wearing a big straw hat and a smock, nibbling filberts as she slapped away on the canvas. No human figure didn't look like a mitten. Any house could have been a bread box. Every cloud had the shape of France.

At an opportune moment I randomly inquired of my acquaintance, "How old do you think she is?"

Came a pause.

"Um, look up the word 'cupressinoxylon.'"

"Pedantry comes easy enough to her," I offered.

"Do you know Byron's *Don Juan?* '. . . she looked a lecture / Each eye a sermon, and her brow a homily.'"

I took a glass of sassafras tea at an *al fresco* table outside the Raleigh Tavern, and then ambled about the lazy morning for characteristic snapshots, doomed beforehand, I saw, to forgo any pictures excluding visitors, who insinuated themselves just about everywhere. They lemminged about in pushy and determined squads and stuck either their own heads or those of their balloon-headed kids into my every angle. I stepped idly into a small house with bow windows, its glass old and marvelously rippled, which turned out to be the *perruquerie:* the barber and peruke shop. What was my surprise when I noticed a bun, the bun becoming a head, and the head turning into a person, whereupon—lo!—there in the crowd, her half-glasses at the edge of that nose, stood Goody Sweetshrub.

"Wigs, see?" loudly whispered a cat-faced mother in purple slacks to her little goofy son, smudged and filthily becrumbed from the wedge of chocolate whoopee-cake he was cretinously misshoving into his ever-widening mouth. "It comes from the word 'big-wigs' and—oh my god!—Sonny, will you look at your mouth! I swear, I will give you such a belt."

"Permit me?" The voice was unmistakable. "You have it

wrong. Our word 'wig' is from the French *perruque*, spelled p-e-r-u-k-e in England and the colonies at the time, and cannibalized therefrom to *perwyke* to *perewyk* to periwig and that, by abbreviation"—and here Rosemary Sweetshrub, novelist, carefully lifted off her glasses and patronizingly, by turning her head from person to person, lessoned us all—"to 'wig.'" She folded her arms, triumphantly.

Our guide, a pretty young girl in colonial costume, had gathered us around and was disquisiting on one of the many historical subjects there (they never really talk, rather speechify by rote in formal rehearsed paragraphs): "May I draw your attention to . . ." and "You may not have noticed, but . . ." and "Now if we look to our left up near the ceiling . . ." and "Contrary to popular belief . . ." and "I'm now holding in my hand the original . . ." and "Mr. Jefferson himself once actually . . ." It was a charming, if machine-learnt, lecture which plucked the roses of the past and left the thorns behind—but none the worse, really, for its wild surmises, adroit half-truths, and impossible-to-be-documented garnishings that bleached away irksome facts and somehow got American history all pointlessly arsy-versy.

We were treated, then, as we all stood there to a pipped-up survey of powdering masks, bone combs, yarn caps, wig blocks, hackles, curling irons, nipping scissors, yellowing wefts, and—held up, spun around, turned out—a gaggle of eighteenth-century periwigs. We were shown brigadier wigs, queue wigs, bag wigs, square wigs, natural wigs, knotted wigs, double pigtail wigs, cadogan wigs, and even clerical (i.e., tonsured) wigs, with a little half-dollar size hole at the crown. Wigs, it was pointed out, were primarily for men.

"If," a voice cleared itself, then softened declaratively,

"if you'll permit me, my dear? Milady's hairdress, roughly dated to the period of Louis XIV's court, found expression in a many-tiered and very attractively bejeweled *fontange*, piled high to a gracious beauty and often feathered. Now am I correct," Miss Sweetshrub asked, her eyes fluttering with her advantage, "or am I incorrect?"

"Oh yes," recovered the embarrassed guide, blushing profusely, "I had forgotten. And weren't they called, um—"

"Yard-high heads."

The girl snapped her fingers in recognition. "Yes, they were called 'yard-high heads.'"

"They were. They were indeed called 'yard-high heads'—and, may I add, that they set a chaste and attractive fashion, a vogue, a trend," clarified Bossyboots, "which we today in our period of moral permissiveness indiscriminately, I think for a number of reasons"—this punctuated with a delicate snort—"fail to follow. Yes, fail to follow. Oh dear, fail to follow. Indeed."

"And actually in those days," smiled the guide, "only country women wore their hair completely down, and—"

"Exactly," exploded Miss Sweetshrub. "And why?"

Good grief, *that* was a firm question. But no answer came.

"And why? Ask yourself: and why?"

Rosemary Sweetshrub, incarnadine, stood there in place, twisting her fingers angrily like some medieval hysteriarch.

A bewildered silence held.

The guide recovered: would we like to learn how wigs were made? We—if a sudden combustion of *yays*, tongue clicks, hoots, *oohs* and *aahs* were an indication—certainly would. So. If we would pay attention, the eighteenth-century wig was built up of rows of hair—in the preferred shades of chestnut, black, white, grizzle, piss-burnt (here her pardon was begged) but not red, which generally was considered disagreeable—and woven at the root ends to cross threads, each row then being sewn to a net-and-ribbon skullcap or "caul." We may not have noticed (she continued) the hackle which she held in her hand, through which, contrary to popular belief, the chosen hair—mostly goat's and horse's—was combed or carded and then, in the wigmaker's vise, separated into parcels of different length, rolled in a curl-paper onto curling pins made of pipe clay, and boiled for three hours. Now if we would look to our left up near the ceiling we would see a tripod-base wig block. Did we notice it? Yes, we affirmed, we did. Good, good. On that, then, the wigmaker would sew to the caul the strips of weft that he had previously woven, using a simple straight stitch and probably kept uniform and neat with the help of that original looking-glass by the hearth over there— could we see it? Fine, excellent. Finally, the craftsman would add a rosette, a bag, or ribbons and pomade, powder, and perfume, all according to the whim of the customer. In fact, we were told, that Mr. Jefferson himself once actually. . . .

Now much the wiser, our little group, having turned to each other with glad nods of approval and wide smiles, shuffled out of the house in file. Wasn't it interesting? Indeed, indeed, floated responses.

But then a relatively inexplicable incident followed, though perhaps best explained, I suppose, by rather realistically pointing to—and therefore indicting—little incorrigible Sonny, the aforementioned he of the chocolate whoopee-cake; for, while bored and lurching antagonistically against his dear mother's hand, he had managed quite successfully to rip himself free of her and bolt viciously for the door, in front of which—alas!—languished Miss Rosemary Sweetshrub, poor thing, pedantic old trout, in a reverie that would be all too brief. For—thump!—she was bashed unceremoniously against the wall by the filthy little fugitive, and, at the crash, most of the combs and pins fastening her hair clattered to the floor. She went breathless utterly—and then let out with one bone-chilling shriek. She clutched for all her life at her hair, now slipping in silly loops down to her very shoulders. But the tourists there shrugged vaguely and passed by her and out into the sunshine. I believe only I alone caught her, pale, terrified, in the reflection of that warped and antique mirror, snatching savagely at each loose strand and blocking and re-pinning the whole with a speed I can't describe into a closed nest as tight as an angry fist.

And it was only I, I believe, sitting in my seat in the waiting bus at the Capitol later that afternoon, who saw Miss Rosemary Sweetshrub like a small moving dot walking slowly and aimlessly toward us up the long wide Duke of Gloucester Street.

Permit me? She was alone.

Scugnizzo's Pasta Co.

I am a woman. I stand for no nonsense, never have, haven't the time for it. I edit the international gourmet magazine *Hotcupboard*. You recognize? Doubtless—the not overly demandingly specific requirement here being probably (a) that you are not a man and (b) that you know the galley-ship the kitchen once was (though our whole tack needn't be), having felt like we and others do the depressing simplex, but for our women's "liberation" otherwise tragic, of scrubbing pots, dishpans, bread tins, egg-cups, Marmite spoons, and filthy cylindrical molds. Ain't no way, let me for a minute be cute and colloquial, that we will go back to that. Oh, and (c) you are a discerning reader with an educated taste for food.

Agreed, sisters?

I hear you.

We think of our magazine, frankly, as not only tunefully current but frightfully aware of the needs of the American woman, any selection of whom, of those on any day flashing through magazines, could be seen with a copy of *HCB* at the ready and scissoring out one of our scrumptious recipes, boxing a household hint, recording the new versatility of an herb, or, simply, time permitting—because ours in America, but for the periodic lift magazines such as ours give, is hardly a life of leisureful or spoon-licking la-de-da—pausing rapturously over the vivid, mouth-watering Ektachromes (by which we monthly enrich our issues), of, well, crisp buttered broccolis, smoking barmbrack, skewered pieces of charcoal steak, lush desserts, and hot bowls of conch gumbo. It is a woman's magazine, not theoretically to exclude men, of course, but there is to be found an undelineated, felt, though paradoxically unobservable, line drawn around us—I like to think of it as a circle, an exclusive one—our work, and our thought over which, for my money, they need never step.

We have one male with us in our offices here in Manhattan, although he is rarely seen. He is a janitor.

I don't touch on this point idly. I will momentarily introduce and, gainsaying a resolve I made some years ago, with a view to some advice about the workplace, even discuss an Italian person named Scugnizzo, archetypally male, and the mere memory of whom gives me the fantods and has more than once forced me angrily to taking abrupt cold showers and salving ice-packs. But I see I am getting ahead of myself. Let's to an airport and a crossed ocean.

§

Pisticci, Italy. Who knows of it? Few, I'll wager.

Thither, however, had I gone—you cannot believe the risk, by the way, of the bus-ride alone at night out of slatternly Naples and its blanket of stale sudoriferous air—to research an article for an Italian number we were doing. My focus was to have been in the area of pasta. Its A, its Z. How often, it one day occurred to us sitting around the offices in New York, had our patient readers, female predominantly (exclusively no, we cannot be certain), been shunted hither and yon during the process— ignorant of what it quintessentially was—of ritually preparing pasta: cooking it, straining it, crumbing it, saucing it, or, say, shoving cheeses or meats through it? Or, bless such who do, even making it from scratch? Well, *Hotcupboard* jumped on the subject right away. American women would soon know, if I had my way.

May I add that I usually do? Have my way?

The reader—may we a minute pause?—will perhaps recall the biennial "special numbers" of our magazine, over which for just about every last copy, rumored nearly priceless the very day of printing, people fought each other right in the open? For example, there was our first special, on Bombes (as of a month ago a collector's item); there was our number on Winged Game, seminally crucial, that one (with photos) to the basic knowledge of an abstruse subject. There was the one on the Gourd Family, and the photographs alone from that issue have since become legend. Our special on Frostings I am told was seen in the hands of our First Lady, and it brought letters to us from as far away as Lapland, as did the devilish little one we ran on Meals to Be Eaten Only by Hand, a big hit, that one, in the South. Let me see now, we ran them—I hope this list is complete—on Chowders, Asian Hors d'oeuvres, Biscuits (everything from pull-aparts to bran), Peppers (the vivid color spectrum alone sold it out within weeks), and, our most remarkable I guess, the special that we did entirely on the Camel, whose hump, feet, and stomach by the way are very much appreciated by connoisseurs. A strictly Fruitarian issue people are begging us for. Someday soon.

But pasta? Well, hell, this was something we knew everything about but what it was! Go for the story!

§

Pasta factories, though history credits the invention of macaroni, spaghetti, perciatelli, bucatini, casarecce, fiori, ditali, and similar "pastes" to the Chinese, are best found in southern Italy and in Sicily, especially in the areas of wheat cultivation. As I said, I stand for no nonsense, never have. I wear hard brown shoes. Well, let me get on with my story. I had managed to secure for *Hotcupboard* and her subscribers the perfect "paste" factory imaginable. It was one set up high in the small and unpredictable sienna-colored hills outside rude and rural Pisticci. I had demanded a tour and a few days inspection, and then after gathering notes—my wet nails drying in the warm breezes that blew far inland across the fabled bay—I efficiently telegrammed New York from my pensione the following message:

HOLD FOR DUCKY PIECE ON FARINACEOUS. SEND
PHOTOGRAPHER.
PISTICCI WOPPISH AND SWELTERING. MUST RUN.

§

It was morning at Scugnizzo's pasta factory.
"*Semolina*," yelled the proprietor.
I wrinkled my nose against the dust and noise, and nodded.
"You like?" he howled again and his grinning mouth widened and opened like a nutcracker under a gigantic beak of

a nose, like Punch. He was cross-eyed and all hands. He wore a pigskin hat, which with his antic eyes—swiveling and electric and almost comically irrational—made him look all in all rather like the bedlam figure in an English medieval mystery play.

"Show me the machines."

"*Precipitevolissimevolmente*," said my guide mockingly and bowed.

I found his foolish smile hard to take, following his dopey stare already looking me over. I had already put up with a few of these scribinis, gindaloons, and cucuzzi outside my pensione. Dipshits, blue gums.

"*Barili*," Scugnizzo redundantly pointed to the barrels and kicked one of them with his heel. "*Vasche. Botti.*"

"Rather," said I. You don't want to give yourself away. "Rather." I scooped up and weighed several handfuls of semolina from only one of the fat wooden barrels filled with this hard, glutinous wheat, known, generally, as durum in the States. The barrels surrounded us in a phalanx in the middle of which, it had just then come to me, we alone were standing, an occasion Scugnizzo found propitious enough as he waggled a knob on the machine for a sudden inquiry: had I a *fidanzato?* I was flabbergasted. He stood there, smiling, stroking the huge length of his nose with three fingers. I ignored him, needless to say, and exaggeratedly stooped to smell a fistful of semolina. I felt the nap of it—and made a note. More questions obtruded: had I *fidanzato*, my hotel a bed, my heart a void, and the sky a moon? I suddenly just plainly stood against him, put my hands on my hips, and hissed. He mooed and sidled off, crestfallen. I could tell his mood by the back of his head when he took off his hat. It tightened.

At the far end of the company's one long room stood six

weirdly angular and unrecognizable machines, chuffing away. I
surveyed them, handles, dials, and levers for about five minutes,
trying as best I could to divert my attention from my companion,
romantic Cagliostro who, not ten feet away from me, I suddenly
noticed, had turned away, but not far enough, and was micturat-
ing through the doorway onto some tomato plants and whistling
snatchers of "*Mamma, quel vino è generoso*" from—I thought it suitable—*Cavalleria Rusticana*. He finished dramatically, how shall I
say—with, well, gestures. I had a real one on my hands.

"Gum." He flicked his head.

I frankly couldn't tell whether he was looking at me or
not.

Asked to come (he was looking at me, oh joy), I followed—the alternative, in point of fact, not really mine in that,
my fretfully unwilling hand in Scugnizzo's effortful grip, I had
been haled along at an unenjoyable skip over the floured plans
to an imposing guillotine-type machine with a large round
drum instead of a blade, roaring, whistling steam, and spitting
out droplets of hot water from around its moonscape of pressure
gauges and meters. He was chewing fennel, an Italian habit.

He reeked of garlic and sausages.

"*Il nostro bambino!*" exclaimed Scugnizzo at the top of his
voice, poised and beaming before the machine, butting it with
his belly, the plate of his face a mere inch from mine and showing
that maniacal sense of pep and proximity we associate with the
excited but simultaneously troubled in eye. He tapped the metal
sides of the machine lovingly, then he reached down and—I swear
to God—goosed it! He winked and cacked at me with inner-drawn
snorts, indicative, one perhaps rashly assumed, of his having
done something witty. And, indeed, this probably was wit for the

Italian—and the male. The combination is disastrous. Scugnizzo now began fondling some long pipes, brainlessly assuming the American woman incapable of seeing—and immediately—linked analogies, the damned fool.

I sought a displacement activity.

"What is—" I reached up high and tapped the drum, "that?"

"Ah yes, Mrs.," he pronounced. "This is called the *trafila*." He gave an orchestral lilt with a finger. Scugnizzo turned me to him (and to those juggernaut eyes) by the wrist and, with jaw extended, pointing to his lips, tried to be helpful by tripping out for my educational benefit—slowly, cretinously—the demonstrably overstressed dental/labial/dental "*Tra. Fi. La.*"

I repeated it aloud, accurately I might add.

We are not talking high Dantean vocabulary here.

He shook his head, the prig. "*Traaaa. Feee. Laaaaaaa*," repeated Scugnizzo slowly and presumptuously moved closer to me. I repeated it quickly to avoid, I said to myself, the nearness of you.

Scugnizzo reached over and touched a metal plate. "Aach—*scottaditto! What-a you calls* 'hoat,' 'vum,' 'varm'—*caldo!*"

Crazy with delight, he leapt to the side of the machine and pointing here and there, as it were, presented it. In an inclusive wave from top to bottom, he said, "*Ecco! Il mobile di cui ti parlava. La macchina madre.*" He bowed like an idiot. "*Uno pezzo*" (one piece). "*Pianura*" (plain). "*Spilla*" (pin). He spoke like a boar pisses, in jerks. I began writing down the terms, as he hopped from foot to foot. "*Una campana*" (a bell) "*Laggiù, la bocca.*" (down there, the mouth) "*Allora, collara*" (then, the neck piece) "*Ciascuno*" (each one) "*Eh, finalmente, signore, scarpa metallica.*" (metal foot). He stepped back, proudly. "*Vecchio. Antico*" (old, antique), "*Ecco qua, dalla testa ai piedi*" (head to foot), "*Cappello da soprabito*" (hat to overcoat).

In any case, it was then explained to me—as my article fleshed out—that boiling water used in very small amounts moistened the semolina, which was then worked up into a powerful machine kneader. The process wasn't complicated. The finished dough goes into the drum of the press, flop-flop, where the pasta—compressed tremendously by revolving screws—is squeezed slowly out of the base of the drum through the small effective holes of the perforated plate called, as, God help me, I only too well knew, the *trafila*. It exudes like beautiful golden hair. The pot was already gravid with fattening dough, and Scugnizzo, while ostentatiously singing snatches from "*La Donne è nubile*" (a joke, preempting his, he was not aware my three years of high school Italian also afforded me), shoved into the bottom of the drum one of the *trafila*-forms or slugs—there are a plentiful many—which, by the way, fix the shape of whatever variety of macaroni or any pasta one wishes.

Semolinas are multiform. For instance, there are "pipes," "solids," and "ribbons." There can be found in each hole a steel pin which give the macaronis their hollow, tubular, form; the "solids," using smaller holes and no pin, yield spaghettis; and for flat, noodle-like ribbon varieties a flat opening takes the place of a round hole. The roar of the working machines in the room was close to ear-splitting, with chunking, whirring noises, all of it made more deafening as Scugnizzo babbled on about this and that, all with gestures of, what—apology, accomplishment?

There were pasta shapes both familiar and exotic. "Wuddy you wanna me *rendere*, um, you wishes?" asked Scugnizzo, bouncing about me, who with the manual accompaniment of flashing fingers began pompously ticking off all the different shapes that he could make for me. It became in a sing-songy way a virtual operetta. *"Mafaldini, malloreddus, occhi, pappardelle"*—he flatted his hands and made a zooming gesture—*"rombi, broccoli, pizzaccherri, strangozzi."* (He brazenly reached over and touched my hair!) "Anading espesh—you name miss, OK?" He proclaimed a full mastery of them all. I couldn't help but notice the list became progressively salacious. "You wisha *occhi di lupo?*" He made googoo eyes at me, fluttering lovesick eyelashes! "I fa you the *testaroli fatto*"—he winked and grabbed his genitals like a common muttjack—*"fatto apposta per te*, gusta fa you, unnustan'? *Cavatappiu* corkyscrew-shapah, like, like *amo fare l'amore con te.*" I thought, *this is a goddam monkey!*

I stepped outside and wiped my brow. This was becoming an ordeal. As he explained the pasta shapes, I realized that Scugnizzo, if he could metaphorically be one of the shapes—*represent* one of them—it was *maltagliati*, an irregular shape of flat pasta framed from scraps of pasta, and badly cut! I reentered the room. Scugnizzo killed the machine, deftly nipped a piece from the oozing *zitoni* there, tasted it, closed his eyes, and smacked his lips, saying, *"Troppo dolce."*

Then he burped.

He gave me none of the snip to taste, such is the Italian cavalier, and, I suspect, most men. Why should he hand me a sample? I was female. So, I presumed to yank out of one of the holes a little wettish wad and drop it into my mouth. But Italian manners? There's a topic, believe me.

"This is you like, Missus lady?"

He was looking at the machine. No, he was looking at me.

"It seems very efficient," said I, lying. I had come too far to see so little to make overmuch of it. What the thing was, you see, was only some queer backwater noodle-house in someone's backyard looping out comic little pastas as slow as a wet week, basic if lumpish product to be sold dry from drawers only to be overseasoned and twisted around in the local and surely indiscriminate platters of the neighborhood. But what the deuce, it had color and was magazine-worthy. If the dough here was humming with mites and animalcules, well, that was more Pisticci's worry than mine, thank you very much.

Now he was popping hazelnuts.

"Is peautiful, yes?"

God, the Italian was such a—! "Yes, Mr. Scugnizzo," said I, my eyeballs rolling skyward and sighing, "it is beautiful, all right."

"*Romantico.*"

Romantic was hardly my word for the machine, as you can well imagine.

"Eh?"

"*Romantico,*" repeated Scugnizzo, winking "*Provocante. Sensuale, mama mia!* He decided to pour it on. "*Stammi più vicino! Che begli occhi che hai! Hai un sorriso stupendo!*"

On my left side, he dodged around to my right.

"I you take to *Celebrazione de Pasta de Fin de Semana?*"

"No. Yes. I don't know."

What was he talking about?

But it didn't matter.

He saw he was getting nowhere.

He had his goatskin cap or whatever slipped off and with his hand was nervously combing back thick, pomaded shocks of hair. He raised his eyebrows and looked at me (I surmised) puppylike. His throatball bounced. He did a wee little jog in a circle and grabbed my arm.

"You, um, a-give me boogie-woogie?"

"You say?"

"Wee, yoo, me-yoo, two we?" He began rubbing his two index fingers together, side to side. "You knows, *rapporti?* Fog? *Come* da mink? You unnerstan'? We make-a the *giambatta*– hodga-podga?"

My god, I realized, he hadn't been pointing to or talking about the machine or discussing the factory. He had been refer- ring all along to himself! Well, I stand for no nonsense, believe thee me. I gave him unshirted hell, I can tell you—how's that! I stamped my foot and abruptly marched away, notebook in hand— along with, should I have pointed this out to him, a sharpened pencil?—to the outer drying rooms. I heard him further humili- ate himself by clutching his hands at a semi-squat and crooning like a butcherbird and blubbering out things, like "*Far l'amore?*" and "justa *bacio*" and "I am kood, peautiful, yes, no?" Funny, down on 42nd Street, I would have instantly vised somebody like that right in the gonads without blinking.

I quick-flipped my pocket dictionary. All I could find in the back were "common phrases," so pulled one out, and snapped,

"*E chi se ne frega?*" Who gives a damn?

I couldn't take that moony look and checked my book.

"*Sto per ammalarmi*," I tried. I am going to get sick. Noth- ing. "*Mi fa cagare!* It makes me puke. *Mi fai vomitare!*"

The photographer telephoned from Rome, assuring me that he was on his way. "What's the name of your pensione?"

"Villa Grissini," I replied.
"Your connection there?"
"A guido."
Silence.
"That bad?"
"If you took his brain and put it in a bird . . . it's going to fly backwards."

§

I needed a break for a day or two and took to a bus to Taranto, saw a few Greek temple ruins, looked at the Ponte Girevole—a swing bridge—and had the chance to watch through a shop window dough being rolled and filled—potato-stuffed *tortelli* and thick, worm-like *pici*, which, although famously a Tuscan specialty, was popular all over Italy. I was particularly interested in *maltagliati*, so-called "badly cut" pasta—also variously called "*fregnacce*" or "*pettole*" in various parts of Italy—squares, rhombi, or irregularly-shaped flat pasta pieces that had started out in life shaped but ended up, not unhappily, as remains of rolled out tagliatelle pasta dough or re-kneaded ravioli cuttings. In a very small restaurant owned and run by a gregarious family named Dittami, only four tiny tables in a wide room that was virtually an extension of their own house, I had a delicious bowl of *maltagliati con fiori of di zucca*, "badly cut" fresh pasta in green and white with zucchini flowers, and was in heaven.

I managed to sample all kinds of pasta shapes, *linguina*, "little tongues," *orecchiette*, "little ears," *zito* from *ziti* meaning "bridegroom," and capped it off—after nibbling from a gorgeous platter of San Vito Mozzarella Caprese—in the United States, you cannot find San Vito buffalo mozzarella, made from the milk of water buffaloes, just try!—with a heavenly dinner of Spaghetti Aglio Olio Peperoncino with garlic and zucchini and carrot coins. Every separate thing that an Italian cooks with, she can eat plain—cheese, tomato, basil, even an onion which you can munch like a pear! I finished with a *bombolina con crema* and some taralles, dunking them, with my cappuccino. I walked about, sat by the Lungomare Vittorio Emanuele III fountain, smoked a cigarette, and tried to organize my notes a little bit before retiring.

I had on my last night a superb *cozze alla Taranta* at Momo's, a dish of mussels, dry white wine and cherry tomatoes, and have to say that the relief of being alone was a bracing tonic but then the matchless views of the sparkling Ionian Sea, blue and wide and far-reaching, was enough to make me want to stay there forever.

But of course, I was due back in Scugnizzoville the next day.

Lucky me!

§

It turned out the pasta festival back in Pisticci was, indeed, to be held that weekend, an annual free carnival that was more than anything a street fair. A crowded piazza. Pennants flying in the marketplace. Local hobbits. Two days filled with tastings, about twenty recipes, a cooking show held on a wobbly wooden platform up front by a couple of regional chefs and a special guest, Mayor Dago Lumbago or whomever—a fat little man with a fat little mustache and a fat little belly under a fat little hat, a few loud food demonstrations that I stuck around for, I didn't really care, some street food ladled out in dollops, maybe a work-shop, I wasn't paying much attention.

I was wearing bright colors and heard the usual twaddle from the street boys, shirts open down to their navels, gold neck chains. "*Che begli occhi!* "(Nice eyes!) "*Come sei dolce!*" (How sweet you are!) "Sei una bella donna!" (You are a beautiful woman!) "*Che bel sorriso!*" (Beautiful smile!) "*Sei molto simpatica!*" (You are very nice!) "*Adoro i tuoi carciofi!*" (I love your artichokes!) "*Guarda le grandi angurie!*" (Look at the big watermelons!) They were all variations of Scugnizzo whom I had demanded—*ordered* in no ambiguous terms—to stay away from me that day, but then look what I got?

One little goon, blinking and winking, and doing little dance steps in front of me like a blue-footed booby or a rifle-bird, bowed deeply and rose to salute me with a waving Renais-sance hand, gloriously stating in the loudest voice, "*Fata!*" (fairy), "*Andiamo sulla spiaggia, voglio perdermi nei tuoi bellissimi occhi fino all'alba!*"(Let's go down to the beach, I want to get lost in your beautiful eyes until sunrise!) What is particularly reptilian about these *strada roma* in cheap silk shirts and *imbroglioni del sesso* in tight pants is the overriding cow-eyed presumption they all have, the smug and puffed-up weisenheimer expectation, that they are actually *making progress* in winning your heart with all of those fatuous compliments!

I smoked some sage, that helped—although I had to be careful, I was really down in the boot, lower Italy—and munched a bunch of Mulino Bianco cookies. I wandered around, ate some salami on a locally-made bread without salt, quite good, listened to accordion music loudly played on records, and in the hot sun enjoyed myself touring tables filled with various foods and booths selling scarves, sandals, gelato, pamphlets on Communism, managing to side-step all sorts of hawkers of *shmatta* and hats and questionable jewelry.

I filled up on *schiacciata* from a vendor—the word means, crushed, broken, squashed—which was a nice salty, golden flatbread, which I enjoyed with oil and basil. It turned out I was still hungry, so for lunch I found a small trattoria in a side street and sat in the shade to enjoy a bowl of "black cabbage" with mushrooms and garlic, pepper flakes, and Parmesan cheese—*cavolo nero*, the signature vegetable of Tuscany, is a kind of kale—but here it was good. All went well, except I was served by the tricky *coglione* some crappy wine, a homemade chianti diluted by too large a percentage of white grapes.

Everybody went to church. So, I joined them. It was part of the town's *spettacolo* and involved, if you can believe it, because I can't, my being trapped and having had to stay for the entire sermon. Loud, endless booms echoing up and down the nave—the subject of the day being on the "Farewell Discourse," John 14:7–9—"*Discorso Di Addio*," that's right, daddy-o, you know, the one that was given by Jesus to eleven of his disciples immediately after the conclusion of the Last Supper in Jerusalem, the night before the crucifixion. I managed to follow along, just.

I made notes on the passage. *Philip said to him, "Lord, show us the Father, and we will be satisfied." Jesus said to him, "Have I been with you all this time, Philip, and you still do not know me? Whoever has seen me has seen the Father. How can you say, 'Show us the Father'? Do you not believe that I am in the Father and the Father is in me? The words that I say to you I do not speak on my own; but the Father who dwells in me does his works. Believe me that I am in the Father and the Father is in me."*

The priest made up in volume what he lacked in finesse. His chosen text accommodated the weekend food theme, of course, but it was the same old hooey. Raving and gestures à la Pisticci. The gender-insensitive use of "Father" as a synonym for God went down really big with me, as you can well imagine, for, never mind speaking of God in general terms, it had to be sexist, as well? How better than to flatten the vitality and depth of discourse of religion than to have to hear on a sweltering day in rural Italy—right here in the heart of medieval wopville—the old gender-befucked assumption, the patriarchal assumption, at work in the context out of which the Fourth Gospel emerged that the word *Father* is not simply the Gospel's preferred name for God the Almighty, Maker of Heaven and Earth, but—hello! —the Gospel's primary metaphor for having all theological discourse on the subject, a designation, let me add, because we had run several articles on this same topic in *Hotcupboard*, that appears solely in the words of others, most notably Jesus's, but never in any direct speech of God's!

Don't you find everything paternalistic and patriarchal patronising, paternal, pathetic, and perverse?

§

During the following weekend, Scugnizzo became my shadow, tripping along by my side like a loyal spaniel, making the same overtures.

It was pathetic, really, wasn't it? Here I was in the last outpost of Pisticci on a sweltering day in July and there finding myself being bargained for like some market sow by a swivel-eyed peasant noodle-maker and the uncomplicatedly common face of a rustic poltroon. Naples proper would have been no different, of course. I know the score. I've been around the block. I knew what in Naples one could expect in the way of male Italian promenaders; of being trailed as a tourist into dark caves on the Herculaneum/Pompeii circuit; of being sized-up and pinched blue in the (it is my firm belief) intentionally less-than-well-lit Galleria Umberto Primo; of being sent into abrupt shock by jaunty middle-aged would-be tenors, white mustaches a-curl and with horns on necklaces, who come suddenly bulging out of creepy Neapolitan doorways in silk shirts singing through their wet lips, "*Maria, Mari.*" As I say, I'd seen them before. But, I mean, in rural Pisticci where goats and stoats meander in the piazza?

I stayed on briefly, in my pensione, the time that it took the recently arrived photographer to take a suitable number of pictures for the project. He summarily departed, with me to follow in a day.

§

My final day became a *rite de passage*, a hellish one, to be sure. With his usual vile energy, Scugnizzo tried to sugar his sourness that morning (following a night in which he had tried to blunder into my bedroom with a cracked mandolin and an incredibly presumptuous estimate of what was to happen there) by gallantly opening the factory door and accompanying this with a low, nonironic bow from the waist, this last a *bella figura* I beautifully snubbed, walking past him, as I did, breezily—and with a single arched eyebrow. We found ourselves in the company yards that morning. I had finally gotten all the information that I wanted on the drying process, which, in sunny Italy, it turns out, is done by simple exposure on long racks in a room. The pastas, I saw, looking out at what seemed an orchard of looms, were draped over canes or frames and there dried, sorted, inspected, weighed, and packed.

"*E bellissima, no?*" asked full-of-himself Scugnizzo, surveying in a martial walk as if through his own private camp of devoted *soldati* the row upon row of limp pastas—crackable if too cool, souring if too hot, mildewed if too moist—drying under the warm window-light of the hot Italian sun: short flat lasagnes; thinly threaded fidelini; healthily ribbed rigatonis; curled vermicellis; exotically cut bombollotis; and all the foratinis, linguines, mezzanellis, and on and on past a hundred and more. The names! It sounded like the roll-call of steerage on a rusty ragbag ocean liner, *SS Capra Cornea in Colore* from the 1930s. I scratched away at my notebook. I looked around for Scugnizzo, who had suddenly disappeared.

Once again inside, I blinked at the cool darkness of the shed, relaxed until Scugnizzo (with his infantile humor) pivoted from behind the back of the door and—urgent, perspiring—likerishly whispered, "Blink at me with *approvazione, prego?* I wants you to habby make you, Mrs., *capisce?*"

"Uh-uh."

"*Con permiso, il mio cuore, la mia anima, signora gentilissima, voglio dartelo,*" he whined. Was he pitching woo?

"Blease, I am young and good. Much hair like Valentino widd da shine like you stare at! I have dirty years old."

Catching me just on the brink this time of my indignant run to higher authority, Scugnizzo, crushed, generously but nervously began quickly bagging me some samples of tinted pastas right there under my nose, a colored medley of greens, yellows, and reds (respectively from spinach juice, eggs, and beets—anything tomato-related was out!) and then with racing speed but blundering he parceled out some of the more artistically cut and styled variety: alphabets, stars, dots, crescents. "*Molto pazienza.*" More pasta. "*Una signora bellezza.*" He kept muttering, apologetically. "*Lo mi diverto.*" I couldn't help but watch, due to his eyes, him spilling scoopfuls. He was nervous. "*Mi dispiace.*" He blinked. "*Mi pare che tu sia stanco.*"

I saw further that I more or less had what I needed to do my piece, *meno male*, as they say, and quite needfully wanted to be off. (Actually, I had been packed for three days.) No one will be surprised that Scugnizzo's lengthily pondered farewell *auguri* he thievishly tried to transmogrify into a sloppy kiss, the impudent monkey, but lurching at me—close enough at least to reaffirm, I grimaced, the one absolute in this world: the Italian abuse of basil—he found himself quickly fumbled, if that loud shriek was not faked, by your ever vigilant editor and the molten handbag I swung more or less directly at his extremities. I cannot stand nonsense, as I say.

He was crushed, broken, squashed—right.

I hurt his feelings, you say? Tough!

You know what I say?

"*Schiacciataaaaaaaaa!*"

§

A few months later, *Hotcupboard* ran its already by now coveted Italian number, a classic issue, snapped up by women all across the country and certainly an undertaking fulfilling all of our own expectations, not only in the tantalizing wine and food area but also with its *complement formidable* of the truly lush color shots of lovely Naples and environs, the only exception, alas, a photograph printed in the "pasta" section, sad only because so beautifully written, of a machine, me, and a man with dislocated eyes in a pigskin cap at my right. The man appears to be looking at and earnestly gesturing to the machine. No, I mean, the man—anybody would vouch for it—is definitely looking and earnestly gesturing to the machine. A damfool janitor here, until I—particularly *when* I—fired him, disagreed.

The Copernicus Affair

"The center, the center."

"Zontle?"

"Listen, the *middle* of town. Put it that way."

"Ah, meetzle!" he recognized, somewhat chuffed, and then sighted his nose down the street in the direction of the Rynek, or Square, of Warsaw's famous Old Town, the oldest part of the capital city, which I had noticed, especially for its tall, flat-faced mansions of fading pastels—there was a bohemian look to it all, and I loved the old bricks—while being taxied from the train station to the hotel the night previous in an old black 1939 De Soto. Remember those little rubber propellered fans above the driver's seat? Rumpled steering-wheel covers? And running boards?

We stood in the doorway of the old Orbis Europejski Hotel, me and Wietzel, my waiter—and, let it be said, my first real Polish acquaintance—who, in a comradely way, held my elbow amicably and glanced up at me with the fondness of his little snowman eyes, two wee raisins set in a doughy face round as a ducatoon and the color of that apron of greasy duck girdling his paunch. I can honestly say I did not know what to make of him.

His hair was wild-whipped and looked like pot-warp, straggly and limp. A few double chins which he would wobble with a finger while thinking looked like a set of lino stairs with rubber nosing. His complexion was a pale, sickly green. It fit. Death, the so-called "pale horse" of the Apocalypse, is a weak translation from the book of Revelation for *chloros*, which actually means a frail or feeble green. He farted, loudly. It didn't really matter. I love a contactee situation.

"I see, I get the bus at Old Town then?"

"Yes, your honesty. There is not any ruler without an exception." Then Wietzel peered closer. "No automobibble you?"

"No," I sighed. "I'm afraid not."

"This too is as you vish," he smiled, dipping a shoulder. "Put your confidence at my."

"Good."

"Kood," came the choric response. Wietzel scurried about me, nodding. "Must," he managed, cutely walking two fingers across his cuff, "must to go this way on your foot, krab the bus, and, um, best for luck, also too. Don't interompt me. Because is so varm, please to take *woda sodowa* for sips who make you cold." He then slid from somewhere a bottle of garishly bright orange soda, and, allowing for no refusal—this was affected by closed eyes and clucks—pressed it onto me, and frankly I wasn't ungrateful. It was August, month of the sickle. The sun bore down, shimmering all. My shoes were melting. I was anxious to be off. "Someshine," Wietzel grinned, picking up a handful of mud, "is making pisses on airth."

Yes, well.

I buckled my gear and was about to say goodbye. But his face, suddenly, creased wistfully like a slowly deaerating balloon.

He humbly bent deeply over his two cupped hand, the dots of his eyes snapping sheepishly. I leaned closer, only to hear the whisper I believe I had already heard twice before.

"Carmel tigarette?"

Poland, smaller than the New Mexico from which I myself hailed—and where at a recognized university I proudly, and for some time, have held a chair in radio astronomy—found me a passionate pilgrim. I had logged into Warsaw, with a frightful case of railway kidney, only the night before, my very first visit, in a dung-brown train screeching to deaf heaven, my sole reading diversions all the way from dim Berlin nothing more than a microscopically-printed copy of Mickiewicz's epical *Pan Tadeusz* and the loose, garbled conversation of a ballet dancer from Poznań who, attaching himself to me, kept trying to put his hand on my shin, calling me "Lelitchka," and attempting to ply me with the national drink, the mere noxious smell from which pinched shut my nose and caused shooting pains in the area of Wirsung's duct.

Contactee, yes, but with limits, OK? I mean, I had a job to do. I was on a mission might be another way to put it. You see, I had secured my papers, letters of introduction, visas—even got several injections of iron from a neighboring neurologist—and set off, with a cud of anticipation in my throat, outward bound for legendary Poland. I was hot for facts, discoveries. I adore science. I am a birder, amateur, of course, a member of the Audubon Society. *Premium* member. Six issues a year, read religiously cover to cover. Reading is my dram and drug. The cost of membership is high. Point is, I was in the process of writing—and simultaneously, of course, updating the earlier spatchcock works of Starowolski, Broscius, and Gassendi—a biography of Copernicus. The astronomer Nicholas Copernicus? Exactly.

I am a frequent contributor to *Sky and Telescope*.

Fortune, then, immediately smiled. Some background: this waiter Wietzel, he that morning seeing me off on my lateral trip to the birthplace of Copernicus, had dropped a bombshell. A. Bomb. Shell, let me tell you. In the course of serving me my dinner of hot *krupnik* and fat, devoted Wietzel casually mentioned, out of the blue, that he himself actually owned Copernicus's very own alpenstock. The original *ciupaga!* It seemed a highly unlikely prospect, but he was convincing. He told me, but garbled, its history. Never you mind, I thought, I would have that alpenstock, no matter what the cost, or the sun would never be as bright for me again. Well, the poor gormless fellow just blurted it out—and should I sit by? I'm not an Albuquerquian for nothing. But then—get ready!—he apprised me, also offhand and in his laughably malapropistic English, that he alone knew some secrets which he had never told anybody about the relationship between the great genius and his mysterious mistress.

How shall I put it? *Pourparlers* were arranged. For a biographer to know such a thing? To be thrown such a bone? I was aquiver.

I can't honestly say what I was expecting to see, although I envisioned an old-world and probably well-made shepherd's axe—*valaška*, in Czech or Slovak, *бартка* in Ukrainian, *fokos* in Hungarian—you know, a mountain stick with the handle in the form of a small axe. A true *ciupaga*—pronounced "chew-PAWH-gah"—was once considered a dang *weapon*, although the colorful Gorals of southern Poland actually wore them as an element of folk costume, and versions of them you can find in many souvenir shops today. I was breathless, I must say, wondering what I was going to see. The classic *ciupaga* had a steel handle, but faux versions, souvenir jobs, have handles made of brass or wood, with colored inlays. The bars are decorated with carvings. I owned one which I made myself, after finding a couple of tomahawk heads years back. So have a homemade *ciupaga*, right? *Wrong!* I gave it away as a birthday present to a bubble-headed nephew of mine, and he broke it the same day! When a person sees you wielding one, he can become terrified. Someone trying to push you around can meet a very unhealthy end that way, for after all they're designed to kill wolves and bears and things. One good belt with one is all one needs to flatten an adversary. You can split his skull like a melon, he'll be dead before he hits the ground.

Thanking jolly old Wietzel, and resolved utterly to return that same night to jimmy him of some of his secrets (to say nothing of niggling that 500-year-old antique), I trotted away with glee toward the Old Town in order to catch my bus. I had not gone a hundred steps when, lo, I heard—"Hey, meester man!" I turned around. There stood Wietzel in the middle of the sidewalk—his arms raised and circling wildly, his head melodramatically thrown back, his bullet-shaped nose fast in the air like a cartoon elf. It was a picture of an opera singer, poised for high C. Then the little devil let go his clamorous and effulgent note: *"Mikolaj Kopernik!"*

The old hissing red and white bus wound up, backfired, and we swung around a corner past the stained statue of King Sigismund and jerked out of town with one last flatulent poop of exhaust.

I was heading to Toruń—about 115 miles from Warsaw—an old Hanseatic city of about 70,000 inhabitants, the place famous, of course, as the birthplace of Copernicus who had lived, died,

and was buried in Poland. Having arrived, I rented an old pret-
zel, which they called a bicycle to look around, but one of its vul-
canized inner tubes blew and on an unremarkable country road
left me for the hour it took to wheel it to a garage and remap
out my bearings and resume my small tour not overly absorbed,
if the truth be told, in the drab peasant cottages and four-sided
windmills made of wood with flukes that just about cleared the
ground.

Roads I followed were meandering and circuitous. I spoke
almost no Polish; my friends claimed I knew about seven words,
kołaczki, my favorite dessert being one of them. I kept stopping to
try to sound out the directional signs but was confounded by the
language—words based on the Latin alphabet, yes, but including
too many of them nipped with diacritics, like the *kreska* or acute
accent (ń, ó, ś, ź) and the overdot or *kropka* (ż), and the tails or
ogonek (ą, ę), and the strokes (ł).

I saw a horse staggering to and fro in a furrow and lapsing
under a wooden droshky yoke as I meandered past wheat-colored
landscapes and sunken barns and queer houses and, becoming
more optimistic, I not only picked some small sprays of cosmos
and rudbeckia and threw them sillily at indecipherable signs but
took out my camera and shot some rosy babushkas mangling flax
who, for me, for my Leica, looked up with embarrassed frowns. I
cajoled several of them to pose for me and today still run through
the photos in my snap album (at least I have these for remembrance): bulb-headed, arms akimbo, and even some women I
later snapped on a street corner dressed in their beaded doublets
or "frogs" with braided seams, their legs wrapped in the usual
Polesian way, and their white bandannas shining like samite in
the hot glare of my hero's central sun. One loon, an older moon-

faced lady with eyes too close together, stuck her tongue out at me for no reason whatsoever. Some people nowadays are like this. You wonder where the nice ones are, you know? Lord. In any case, my babushka photos I later printed for friends.

Allow me an anecdote? I was backing up at one point for depth-of-field and unwittingly, not seeing the cow-fold I should have, won the captious hearts of those kind ladies by sliding—then slop!—right into guess what? Right. I can't quite forgive their whoops of laughter nor their toothless exclamations, so often were they repeated, as they pointed at me and bawled, "*Krowa gowno! Krowa gowno!*" *Krowa*, I figured it out, cow. And *gowno?* Right. Exactly.

Then I bicycled back, disgusted, to Toruń.

The house in which Copernicus had lived and the dark-red brick observatory where he worked—and over which flew the flag of the white eagle on a red shield—looked like a massive Edwardian toilet. I managed to see his astrolabe, his daybook, some wooden yardsticks which composed part of his crude telescope, a chart of the planets he had fashioned in metal. (His father, named Nicolaus Koppernigk, so spelled, was a copper merchant from Krakow.) The observatory! The thought of what the great man might have seen! Our galaxy contains 100 billion stars, and there are more galaxies in the universe than there are stars in our galaxies *alone!* Three or four old chairs stood around. There were rows of ancient Galilean "telescopes" with out-of-date concave eyeglasses. On the wall hung a series of prints of the great fellow: a keen, bright-eyed gentleman, usually portrayed with a pageboy haircut sitting before an astrolabe in his scholar's fur-lined robes. Why, I even saw a vial that contained the dye he fastidiously used on his hair. (May I mention here that, hard as I looked, I noticed no *ciupaga?*) I was given permission—putting on white gloves—to poke around the library.

I took copious notes on everything, thinking all the while, as I threaded from glass case to glass case, that I had at last got to the center of things. There I was, in the house of the great astronomer of heavenly bodies. It was astrospectroscopal! The Bachelor Canon himself, Pan Nicholas Copernicus, the very man who refuted Plato, Aristotle, Ptolemy. I was hoping to scour though and possibly fumble up some old texts to show that the great astronomer had actually discovered accounts of Aristarchus of Samos, born about 300 B.C., a Pythagorean who had actually been among the first, maybe the very first, to suggest the unique notion that our Earth orbits the Sun, a rebirth of ancient Greek ideas in 16th-century Europe! Am I suggesting plagiarism? Well, it surely would have won me some approval among my peers—or scorn. Academiciana are competitive and among the most envious people alive. Still, I shall never quite forget the reverence I felt as I skipped hither and yon through his observatory, softly whistling snatches of *Fidelio* and corroborating a thousand odd details for my book.

I had a vision: I looked into the land of the Jagiello kings at the University of Krakow, about May 1494, and saw a handsome youth—one fascinated with revolution (get it?)—standing before the stone-faced rectors there and not only daring to gainsay the earth's importance but also courageously articulating his views on the fixed sun, which later became the life-imperiling Book I, Chapter 10 of *De Revolutionibus orbium coelestium* (1543). You know, it all reminded me somehow of that most memorable of Christmases when—a mere tyke—my father gave me my very first telescope, the formal cause of my assuming the profession, as I believe I mentioned for a little autobiographical fun in my monograph, "Do Planets Sneeze?" in the periodical *Wortcunning and Starcraft*, XXI, pp. 801–9, and how I had it screwed together and pitched on its three pods that very night on my roof. To see the Hair of Berenice?

At seven years old? Money can't buy things like that.

Well, no, actually it cost my father quite a bit.

My return stub for Warsaw showed I had almost an hour to kill. I wandered around some, found myself in a little forest at the end of a long street, and watched birds in the sky. What if I saw a white eagle? I wondered. A white eagle, the noble emblem on the Polish flag! How thrilling that would be! Not merely white-bellied sea-eagles, I mean the real thing. Partially albino, or leukistic, birds are rare, of course, occurring in about one in every 1,800 individuals, according to the Audubon Society. I scoured the sky, in vain.

I meandered down unpaved country roads. I saw many shacks, falling-down barns, water troughs, poverty. Was it any worse than in my own country? I knew better, believe me, who had traveled around quite a bit. Telfair County in Georgia. Conditions in rural Mississippi. What about Centreville, Illinois—the poorest town in the United States. Talk about low median household incomes! Why, New Square, New York has the highest poverty and SNAP recipiency rates of any town in the entire republic—70 percent of the population there lives in poverty. My feet were getting sore, swollen. So, I took the time to sit down on a narrow bench by a park and collate some of my jot-takings, especially matter touching on the part where I was refuting step-by-step, Gnapheus's *Morosophus*, which hundreds of years ago nastily ridiculed Copernicus. When I got hungry I wandered off down a dirt side-street and found myself in front of what I assumed was a store, for the pictures, in deference to the illiterate, drawn in the margins of these kinds of signs (the which, ever the scholar, I took down):

APTEKA

Lemoniada Musujaca	*Kosmetyczny*
Fabryki	*Chirurgiczne*
Blochowka	

Fabryki, that would have been fabrics. Cosmetics you can get out of *Kosmetyczny*, right? And then *Lemoniada*. Easy. You just drop the letter *i* and substitute the letter *e* for the second *a*. I was always good at languages. But it was science stole my heart. Anyway, as I said, I was hungry. Ravenous. Two eyes, as I entered the store, peeped over the counter. It was a tiny lady with a few rags on her head and gumless. I ate a few *kielbasa* and at her request—a twitching head, a cheeping sound, a grin—tried the local *pierniki*. Washing it all down with a beer, I set out in what remaining time I had for souvenirs; I bought a red rooster carved in the Zakopane, a pair of birch-bark sandals I could use on my patio, barbecuing, and, well, an amber tie-clasp I wasn't going to mention because I got gypped. It was Lithuanian.

You should understand me, no one could ever mean *all* contactee situations, if you get my drift. I think you're liable to misunderstand the whole point, now that it's come up again.

On my way to the bus, I paused and watched the pinched face of an archbishop in sunglasses, a tiny magenta cap, and all his ridiculous red robes nobbling several old men at a street corner for a donation—*złotys* showered into his briefcase—to Our

Lady of Częstochowa. It made me want to—

Good god, I suddenly noticed I had forgotten my manuscript! I raced back to the food shop, having made several crucial wrong turns, only to find the gumless little twit grinning at me and serving up her steaming *kielbasi* on sheets ripped off my pile of notes to the thirty or so Poles, it being noon, sloughing around there and eyeing me resentfully. I sagged back with an empty heart to the bus and boarded dejectedly, and we eventually pulled away. I thumbed over my purchases until it grew dark. Then my hands held each other.

A big moon, its wake a silver shimmer across the Vistula, saw our bus rattle into downtown Warsaw. There was a peaceable glow suffusing the front of the Europejski Hotel that promised, inside, a respite from the merciless jouncing. I flopped into a chair in the bygone old lobby and circulated, with relief, my stockinged feet. I heard soft piped-in background music on what I am sure was an old Hammond B-3 with a Leslie model 122 speaker, circa 1959. Out-of-date melodies, from the 1930s, with the mind-bending reverb of a skating rink. It made me want to pee.

The bulky over-stuffed chairs with long backs were monstrously huge, like leather tombstones. Travelers from all nations stood around, gasbagging in groups about the dreadful money exchange, the charming embroidery they saw, the proliferation of nuns in the dark aged streets ("You'd think they'd die out, wouldn't you?" asked someone), the memorabilia in the Frederick Chopin Museum and Marie Curie's house, and so on. I saw some folks, so contagious it must be, playing pinochle. These were my fellow Europejskis. Speaking of which, by the way, old peasant names in that country never ended in *-ski* or in *-icki.* Only the very rich bore them. Initially, they formed the endings of the names of the nobility, etymologically adjectives formed from the names of estates. We have to put up with such pretensions from Indians back in New Mexico. OK, natives. Native Americans. Look, I hate pretentious people, always having to be at the center of things. Republics like America have no room for such things.

I yawned and continued sitting. I rotated my sore stock-inged feet, which gave me blessed relief. I considered the idea of a few possible side-trips. Copernicus was thought to be buried in the cathedral at Frombork—it was called Frauenberg at the time—a small town on the Vistula Lagoon in Warmian-Masurian Volvodeship, where the great man worked as a canon ca. 1512–1518, although I was told no marker existed. It was in Frombork that the astronomer wrote the epochal *De revolutionibus*. I was told that you could smell the Baltic Sea from the bell tower.

I began to feel peckish, I must say. Down with a ringing clatter came the elevator, which I summarily rode up that I might change clothes, bathe, and send a few postcards. Stepping off at my landing, I was almost on top of the several bags of laundry for some reason stacked in large white bundles on my thresh-old, when suddenly—my heart club-fisted!—it all began to stir, it moved!

"Halyo, meester man."

"Wietzel," I gasped.

He looked like a battered old squirrel.

In one way, it was touching. The retainer asleep at the door of his master. Loyal as a tapeworm. He slept until his face got fat and, waking, yawned like a camel. A loud fart seemed to propel him to his feet.

"Carmel tigarette? Gif it for me."

I waggled a finger. "That's for later."

"Lugcky Streeks, to go puff." He bounced expectantly. "Make these"—he held up four fingers—"tigarette of America in my hand, pleased?"

It was when he entered my room that, intending to show him my small purchases from Toruń, I realized with a thousand stinks and curses that I had gone and left everything on the bus, including my camera, which would now be, I remembered, on its way to Łódź—pronounced *wodge*, if you can believe it! I felt murderous. I pressed my temples and began walking swiftly in circles. I sulked. Wietzel, the poor simp, did not know what to make of it, I imagine. I managed to repress it all over the three or four schnapps-and-Piwos that we drank, celebrating after a fashion in the darkish old room where we alternately watched the natation of several blueflies in our bottle caps and shared national toasts: "Polska!" "Amedicare!"—and afterwards I dined. By the way, forget negotiating the menu. I tell you, it was alphabetical kookooland! *Szczęście* is their word for happiness. A beetle is a *chrząszcz*. *Bezwzględny* means ruthless, which is what I felt! For pencil, try *ołówek!* Polish sounds so nutty to Russians they even have a verb for Poles trying to speak their language: *pshekat*. So, I call them "pushcarts." To top it off, many Czechs think that Poles when talking sound like Czech children with speech defects! Oh no, there was no ordering anything from a menu, not on my part!

About the *ciupaga?* No, no, I had not forgotten it, not a chance. I am no dummy, although I suspected Wietzel was. We all hate stereotypes, like all that ethnic prejudice against Poles, right? But, oh well, God forgive me, did you hear about the Polish rapist? He was standing in the lineup, they brought in the girl, and he says, 'That's her!'"

The dining room of the venerable Orbis Europejski was huge and shadowy, the ceilings barn high. At one end an orchestra of sorts was playing something heavy, the entire atmosphere 1950s American Drab—one saw double-breasted suits; thick, solid hideous telephones; padded shoulders; dated hairstyles and low hemlines; stirrings of fox furs biting fox furs; and, outside, the limousines were only those lumpish pachyderms-with-fins. And the music? In the lobby my first night, the orchestra leader—a plug-ugly in a mothy tux and dumb as a felt boot—walked over to me and earnestly asked, "You am liking the Shubby Schecker? Alwus Pooshly? Vukk and Voll! Fyets Toorminoo!" You cannot make up stuff like this. I did a double take. I took a look at this poor fool. Forgive me, but I couldn't help thinking of one of Copernicus's expressions: "the obliquity of the ecliptic" (*De rev orb coel.* III, 6).

I asked Wietzel for a wine menu. Scratching his buttocks, he just stood there and seemed not to understand. Could he possibly be the moron I suspected him to be? Or was that unkind of me? I felt guilty for thinking so. Were Poles any different from Americans? Frankly, just as no amount of epicyclic complication could adequately describe the observed orbits, so also the ratio of the square of the period of revolution to the cube of the mean distance from the sun turned out to be the same for all planets. Humans were surely no different, I had to be patient with Wietzel. So I called for the sommelier, a tall Bela Lugosi look-alike, *très lugubre*, and asked for the wine menu. I felt suddenly European. This is my day, I thought. So, I ordered an expensive Chambertin-Clos de Bèze, the favorite wine of Napoleon. *Grand Cru!*

I shouldn't have? Be a devil, I thought. Why not push the boat out. When would I ever be here again? I would write it off.

Then came dinner. I had thought of formally dressing for the occasion. It amused me to think that dressing so in such a quaint antediluvian setting might have fit perfectly. The dinner jacket seems to have remained obstinately uninvented until 1898, but sitting there I felt that could have been yesterday. I drank deeply of the wine and smiled, it was heaven, and refilled my glass. "Pouring forth its seas everywhere," I quote Copernicus, "then the ocean envelops the earth and fills its deeper chasms." Wietzel waddled out with the entire affair balanced on his arms, his fat thumb, I noticed, comfortably macerating in my soup-bowl of *chlodnik* all the way across the room.

"Peerfect sloops," he breathed.

I sipped my Burgundy. Pure velvet.

He set down the soup bowl, with a tilted spill.

"Yes," I said and salted it. Wietzel sucked his thumb and uttered a long satisfying *mmmm*. I took up a tablespoon large as a ladle and tasted the soup. A tad conglutinate, I thought. A bit mushy.

"Bigos with mushiereems," exclaimed Wietzel, bowing over the main platter before me, a central slab of meat mantled in sauces, be-crumbed, and surrounded by a coven of what looked like blackish okra.

"Oh look," I managed halfheartedly.

"Meats is language!" What was he saying? He stuck out his long horrible tongue and began pointing to it and then to the small gray slab on the plate. "*Jezyk!* Speaks! I give you wooots, word-es. Made important for better than nothing is was! You eat with lovely fingers." My God, he was serving me a *cow's tongue!*

Wietzel squatted down by my ear. "There is not better

sauce who the appetite. I won't," he added, "to blease meester man, upon my live." I thanked him. "This is yurple to yump, make for taste tongues."

He asked, "Wodka?"

"Vodka," I repeated.

"Wodka he is." And Wietzel poured.

A chubby violinist with a great imperial mustache and wearing a long black velvet vest, embroidered with flat beads, then stepped forward and, swaying romantically, began to play "Cherry Pink and Apple Blossom White" and a few other old 1950s hits. Wietzel, three quarters of the way across the room, paused, stopped, farted, disappeared, unmortified, through the doors, and returned with my dessert, a potato *babka*. The Poles all love it. It means grandmother. I love words—well, let's face it, I love knowledge. I had hoped to have a dish of strawberries and cream cheese, John James Audubon's favorite dessert, in his honor. No such luck. So, I took the babka. I spooned it in while Wietzel told me that food in Poland was inexpensive (he had told me the very opposite the night before with equal conviction). I nipped the vodka and sipped more wine. I tasted notes of raspberry, blackberry, cherry, some unidentifiable spices, and even gamey flavors. It was zesty with a fruitiness found in the big reds.

The menial paused and, almost drooling, began regarding me, expectantly. I simply thought: *ungulate.*

To tip or not to tip? How many times had I been paralyzed by the problem. But what after all is an emolument in aid of? It is a consideration, but of what? Protection? Hush money? Appeasement? And exactly what had he done for me so far but put a clamorous and noisy dent into my visit here and squeak with half-witted pleas for my attention? Who was it said, "Cunning is the dark sanctuary of incapacity"? I patted Wietzel's hand, that was good enough. He beamed at me.

I finished my bottle. I pocketed the cork. I adjusted my jacket.

I decided to trump the small chat.

"Is that, ah, alpenstock of yours expensive?"

Wietzel leaned over to ear level. "*Tso?*"

"Your alpenstock. Much," I spelled out, "*złoty?*"

Beyond humiliation, I acted out a little charade. You know, the happy wanderer kind of thing, with groping motions uphill.

"Ah, *ciupaga!*"

This was it. Yes, I agreed, the *ciupaga*, and what about it?

"Must for we to upstairs be going," said Wietzel. "*Ciupaga* for"—he closed his eyes and licked his nose—"twee hundres of Amedicare dollars in the shiny kold." He rubbed his thumb and forefinger. "Mummy. Gif it for me."

"Twee hundreds? You mean two. Two hundred."

"Don't you are ashamed to gif me as like?" Wietzel poked his nose at me. He held up seven fingers, then pried down one. "Make me dat."

"Too much," I rejoined.

"*Cholerni Żydzi,*" he muttered.

"What?"

He shrugged, cagily, and said "*Nie dla wszystkich skrezypce graja.*"

I took out my Polish phrase book and, flipping for proverbs, tried looking what he said. *Wszys! Wszys! Wszys!* Did every word in Poland begin with those same five letters? Wietzel snatched the book from my hand and finding the phrase pointed to "The violin doesn't play for everybody."

I stood up. "I'll give you five dollars." Tapping each finger—separately, to help—I spread my hand and waved it in front of his beady eyes.

"*Nie rosumiem*," he said, leaning forward shaking his head. "Was not twee hundres?"

"Knee what?" I grabbed my wordbook again. He didn't understand me. He was whining and kept shifting his feet like he had to pee. Were police involved? He kept looking behind him. "Don't for *narobic bigosu*"—he was pleading for no problems, not making a mess, something like that—"gif Wietzel more much and you smile big like most Amicamerica man fun thing!"

That was Wietzel all over. Always wrong. Never in doubt.

He shook his head up and down. "Twee hundres? Six fifty forty eight shiny kold? To make dat you do?"

There was a cold scrape in the air.

I pulled a strategy: *employ passive lethargy.* I sighed and stepped aside and leaned against a wall. Trick him. Trade space for time, time for position, while he prepared a counter offer. Anxiety in all of its jittery, jiggery ramifications had scooped all the matter out of his headbone.

"Look, I snapped. "I." Pause. "You." Pause. "Give. This—fiiiiive dolllars."

"*Taaallers!*" His face wrinkled into a ball. "Dis much, *dot-knąć.*" He spread his fingers in front of him. He blinked. His nose, which was bulbous and comic to a degree, I could see, intruded on his vision. He was perspiring as if he were a tree with mucilaginous inner bark. His stomach bulge seemed to bring him forward. He was now bent over, forward, like a weasel looking at a crippled hen. "I luff you mak, makes, too much twee hundres?"

"Good?"

"Wpfive? Fpwive?" He held up his hand. "These?"

"Fiiiiive, yes."

He shrugged, grinned, shrugged again.

"Good?"

The Slippery Elm cogitated.

"Carmel tigarette? Gif it for me."

I handed him a pack of cigarettes.

"*Kood!*"

I immediately snatched his oily hand and shook it. The umlaut of his eyes moistened and gleamed, happily. He was a pushover. A little figure of joy began dancing in my heart, as I counted my blessings.

Wietzel lived, it turned out, on the seventh floor of the hotel in a cubicle that smelled of foal wormer. It was a room with one large cloth chair and a shelf with square dishes and innocent tools of the carpentry sort, drills, I suspect, with round I think teak handles. There was a smothering quality to the fat blue dull curtains. On an old black stove sat a battered aluminum pot of stewed and spicy tripe—*flaczki*, I looked up the word—from which, when passing, he plucked a morsel to eat, crunching the cartilage and sucking his fingers with a slurpable noise. His wee raisiny eyes gleamed as he patted his paunch. I could see that, though repulsive to record, he was a dedicated innards and offals eater, a sucker of marrow, a gnawer of tendons, a muncher of entrails, intestines, viscera, numbles, and great skin-on bone-in gouts of meat.

He proudly showed me a statue of St. Stanislaus, under which burned a vigil light, recounted for me an endless tale of Szczerbiec, the legendary sword of Poland; and then—finally—

rolling back his sleeves, looking back at me with the pride of a collector, stooped to retrieve from under his gritty cot an oblong box about five feet in length. He unlocked it and stepped back proudly.

"Lordy," said I.

The antique alpenstock lay before me, its handle cut by hand and buffed to its high walnut was designed with delicate carvings, chased, and inset with ivory pieces in beautiful buhl-and-counter. Its grapple, of old iron and peaked, was perfectly balanced. It was unbelievable.

"He has a kood beak?"

"A wonderful beak," I replied. "Just a wonderful beak, Wietzel."

"Djarmans in seconds vult var, um—" Fidgeting for a word, he pulled his mouth. He never looked more charming, so I spoke.

"Germans? Tried to steal it? Damned right, Wietzel, damned right."

"*Kraść.*" One hand angrily snatched the air.

The word obviously meant *steal, grab, seize.*

Whatever. "Yes," I nodded, encouragingly.

He continued. "This nineteen-zirteen me find"—he knocked on the treasure with his knuckles—"in bull-steeples of a chairch."

"A church?"

"Chairch," he repeated. "Gethlicks? Breests?" He bit the air in frustration and tapped his forehead. "Bluss me fudduh?"

He seemed truthful, although, I must say, I wondered. The liar can often be detected by his smarmy insistence on a strange detail.

"And you're sure, this belonged to Copernicus himself?"

"Kopernik," he nodded vehemently, lifting the piece up and pointing with that cracked, serviceable thumb to a dramatic Polish eagle stamped at the flat of the handle, under which was hammered the mark of a single fading letter: *K*. I put my arm around his shoulder and together we left the cubicle and walked down the corridor. The gesture was the best icon of friendship I could muster, short of kissing his feet. At the elevator, I paused. I looked at him, so he could see me see him. I eyed him and snapped five crisp ones into his hands, beseech-side-up. His nose was aflame with the great bargain. He suggested a drink; I complied. He suggested a party; I complied. And then he looked up at me, saying: "Carmel tigarette?"

And I complied again. "Of course."

"Which pleasure! Which fom!" giggled Wietzel, puffing.

The fat was in the fire. I leaned closer. "You also, Wietzel, you also suggested that you were aware of some secrets between—"

"Din't interompt me," squawked Wietzel, guffawing, the butt pasted in his mouth wagging up and down, and he lurched forward. But then Fright Itself plucked at my sleeve. Screams will always characterize for me what followed, screams and utter chaos. The elevator had been rattling toward our floor from above, and, having several times shoved the bell, Wietzel, in a moment of curious infantilism—whether motivated by the antic or the urgent I still can't say—moronically interposed the alpenstock into a slim crevice there, which, while only momentarily jamming the falling car, splintered the historic stick like slate in a loud dithering crack, a hopeless splintering fracture, and then ripped the astounded waiter clear off his feet and sent him instantaneously crashing through the fences of the door, nose first, when simultaneously came a sickening whirr and snap, and out were torn like thread, a mad ripping of the unraveling ropes and pulleys from inside the orlo, sending the coffin of the old passenger car free-plummeting down the pit of the shaft—along with my *chakera*, my secrets, and, alas, my waiter—like a dead weight into the explosive crunch of dust and dunnage 120 feet below, punctuated all by a screech so loud it hurt me in the eyes: the horrifyingly eerie decrescendo and dopplerian echo of Wietzel's desperate "*Gooooooowwwwwnnnoooo!*"

Trembling, I looked down the long shaft. Smoke rose. And with it, having passed through the dining hall and then through the thinnish shaft, I heard the paradoxical strains of that weird little orchestra's finale, bowing the evening out. The piece was the Polish national anthem, "*Jeszcze Polska nie Zginęła*," which means "Poland Has Not Yet Perished."

It had for me. But why aggress so fulsomely against that country? Or the earnest and confiscating constabulary who in a day-long inquiry asked me no end of questions? Simply and briefly, I found myself next morning racing—and with a throbbing kidney—toward Poznań and the Polish-German border. The sky of this earth, I saw through the speckled train window, was now giving over with dark watery stains.

I sat terrible-eyed, regretful, staring at my valise: dispossessed of my souvenirs, beggared of my priceless papers, rifled of my lost "secrets," and unhoused utterly of the sorely coveted alpenstock. The actual alpenstock of Pan Nicholas Copernicus *himself!* Left only were a jumbled mess of my photographs, foremost among them that disgraceful Ruthenian she, obviously humble of brain, with her fat tongue sticking out at me.

It seemed to symbolize the haplessness of my trip. I had to bite my knuckles to keep from weeping.

My one reflection? The earth *couldn't* have been the center of the solar system.

Am I unkind in saying that it should have occurred to a Pole first?

Watergraphs

The auction had begun. A rapping gavel brought the crowd to order, and immediately an inconspicuous little man in the third row started perspiring into his shirt collar. His name was Irving Biegel, and he was still in a near faint, for not two hours before while rummaging through a box-lot of otherwise inconsequential books and papers he had suddenly discovered with no one the wiser—right there in a Moose Hall in Chelsea, Massachusetts—what he instantly knew to be priceless: the rarest autograph in American history.

Goods were already moving, they were already into Lot #5—a pair of art deco bookends—but intense Mr. Biegel felt in his heart only the kind of despair that is hope deferred. His coat was knotted into a lap bundle. He closed his eyes anxiously and began the long, long wait.

It had in fact been a long day. Irving Biegel had the previous evening taken the "Night Owl" up from New York on a job for the Atheneum—he did appraisals for a fee—and finishing by noon subsequently found himself, for no particular reason, walking around the Public Garden which he disliked and always found a shabby imitation of Central Park. The area, although green and patterned, was still a jaywalker's heaven—a despicable Bostonian vice—despite the fact that it was an obvious grid of walkways and paths. He remembered pausing idly on a footbridge and peering down into the shallow water to see his reflection, a reflection, the face too few in the world, having seen, frankly ever liked. He looked like a waiter.

He had a big stubborn nose, slicked-down black hair, vexed in shape, and a thin, perpetually quivering mustache, which gave him, along with an egotistical little walk, something of a Chaplinesque stamp.

He hated the city of Boston. He came up occasionally and only on business and usually left the very same day. It was a city of filthy pigeons, frightful traffic, no place to park, ridiculous back alleys, and crooked Irish politicians who had enough wind to blow a soft hat through a concrete ceiling. The skyline looked like a set of broken teeth, and the people were all incautious and loud-mouthed provincials who quacked when they talked, which they did all the time and always with that hideous regional dialect of theirs—mispronouncing everything—that sounded like 1930 radio percolating through ripped mesh. Regular cwoffee! No *pah*king! Half a dollah! You flyin' Delter Rarelines? That's mi-en, not yaws! How about them Red Sawx, Tony? You wanna hit Fenway Pahk tomorrah? Nah, the weather's rawr. You a Hindu, from Indier? Our Lawd and Saviah. Are yez retahded? Wicked pissah! Wanna go to Tamper Florider or fly alla way to Cuber, where it is really hawt? So wanna go?

"Watergraphs? *Watergraphs?*" they would invariably ask, chewing the word shapeless, "you collect watergraphs?" That one of course he heard all the time. Bostonians—not one—could pronounce the word at all. Collecting autographs, unfortunate phrase, was an activity—why?—always associated by the popular mind with movie stars and the paramenstrual urges of any teenage girl with a pencil, but it did scant justice by way of description for the work that he did. His was a profession, thank you very much.

A former assistant curator at the Metropolitan (manuscript division)—fired in 1973 for what they called "irreconcilable disagreements" with his colleagues, who used to call him "Buglebeak" behind his back—he still specialized, but privately in this same area of interest, a small but not inconsiderable province of which involved autographs, yes, but also prints, rare books, that sort of thing. It was his livelihood. It had brought him to Boston on this particular day. He had had an early lunch at an inexpensive diner—the heartburn special: a short-cut stew, coffee, and pie—and having survived that found instead that he had the afternoon to kill and so bought a paper which in the market basket section happened to list an auction that night for 6:30 p.m. in some place called Chelsea, wherever the hell that was. He knew auctions, did Biegel, and frequented them whenever he had the opportunity—they had become something of an obsession after his wife died, and often he could be found driving of a Sunday through Scarsdale or Yonkers or up along the Taconic Parkway on these little mousehunts he so loved looking for junk and jumble. He knew auctions better than he knew his way around Boston, but finally, given directions, he thought what the hell, picked up his attaché case, where many a great scheme was always in duress, and caught a northbound bus across the Mystic River Bridge ending up after a few wrong turns on foot in front of a silly goddam Moose Hall where inside six or seven nosy herberts were already one step ahead of him pricing out the goods.

And that, that, was where in one of those unlooked-for reversals of fate, so long denied him, he had stumbled upon something so rare, so extraordinary, and yet so maddeningly now within his grasp that for the first time in his life, he saw himself at last on the brink of becoming rich.

Irving Biegel's reverie was brief. The bidding became suddenly fitful, but it was the usual stuff: an assorted box of ruby glass (Lot #13), three bisque-headed dolls (Lot #14), an 1861 Civil war musket (Lot #15), and now a small cider pitcher with a Fu dog finial on the lid. "Don't drop it, you damfools," warned the auctioneer to his help, "we don't want two of them. Now," he continued with little mutt-like snaps, "start the bidding at 50, do I have 50? 50 anyone? OK, 50-55, 50-55? 55 over there! Now 60, 55-60, 55-60. Talk to me, talk to me!" *Twalk to me*, mimicked Biegel under his breath, *twalk* to me! The regional working-class Boston accent had to be among the ugliest displays of vocal abuse of the English language in the waking world.

It was awful, a smoke-filled room of accumulating all-sorts who didn't know a bargain from a blivet: working men in paddyhats, women with cigarettes wagging up and down in their mouths, couples whispering too loud, and everywhere pie-faced little kids tearing through the hall chasing cats. The place sounded like bedlam. An old Muntz TV with the gubbins hanging went for $50, a crumb-cake iron missing a plug for $17, and a bronze something with a broken finger actually commanded an outlandish $75. "Now we have a speah heah," cried the auctioneer, brandishing a slender, iron-tipped, hardwood spear, what Biegel knew to be an actual assegai, probably from southern Africa. "From Afriker. Start the biddin'! OK, Ova heah!" he barked, adding, "Watch it, that tip's shahp!" Biegel snorted derisively. *Afriker! Shahp! Copley Squayah! Saddadee! That guy's wearin' shots! Chowdah! Kegga beah! No suh!* Idiots, thought Biegel, morons.

He sneered at the vulgar bundle of Boston nut words—cellar, package store, sprinkles, rotary, frappe, bubbler, tonic—for soda!—cleanser, "bang a uey," beach wagon, and "subs," for sandwiches. In Boston he always felt as if he had landed in an outback of primitives, hottentots, and aborigines!

He patted his chest for his checkbook. Let them go broke, let them lose their shirts. He really couldn't have cared less. His mind was concentrated with a single defining concern specifically on Lot #72.

Was that where he had found the valuable autograph? Not at all. It was where secretly when no one had been looking he had *placed* the autograph, concealed it in fact within the pages of a red Victorian oversize on ornithology and underneath the opaque pounce paper covering the last chromocolor in the text where it had been tucked so tightly into the signature that the particular bird exampled next to it couldn't have pulled it out on the hungriest winter morning in Vultureville! But that was not the end of it, not by a long shot. Again, waiting until no one was nearby or standing around, he had then secretly clamboxed that special book under a pile of other books at the bottom of a disabled carton and then set on top of that a handful of old, dusty magazines from the last century, the entire lot of which, even taken altogether, couldn't have been worth less than the last pair of monkey knickers on earth! He smirked and cagily thought: these are called strategies, OK, dumbos?

In the pile of auctionable items, he had overlooked—but did not care a whit to look at or buy—a rare 10-volume set of Ralph Waldo Emerson's *Journals;* an original $500 Orvis antique fly reel; three full boxes of ruby glass; three New England 1774 "samplers;" a silver-banded Colt "Texas" Paterson No. 5 Holster Model percussion revolver; a stack of old Uncle Wiggily books; a framed photo of Alla Nazimova, signed; a valuable Megan Boyd Atlantic Salmon fly "killer" tie, formally mounted in a mahogany case; a beautiful reproduction, framed, of French artist Pierre Auguste Cot's "Springtime;" a large original wooden Howdy Doody puppet, stringed and ready to play, freckled and friendly, with his arms spread out to hug you.

Why all this trouble? For what? On whose behalf? Fair questions, fair questions. The answer to them all was of course a name, one name, a special name, and it took almost more than two hours before Mr. Irving Biegel of New York City, ex-assistant curator of the Met (manuscript division), could precariously utter that name, even to himself, merely to frame the words. It was as painful to concede as it was to conceal, but then, as if to verify a fact that he himself desperately needed to hear in order to ascertain, quietly, in a near silent confession, he closed his eyes and ever so faintly heard himself whisper the words, "Button Gwinnett."

He repeated it: *Button Gwinnett.*

It was a name almost more familiar to Irving Biegel than his own, and like all specialists in the field he knew the facts: Button Gwinnett (1735–1777). American Revolutionary leader. Born, Gloucestershire, England. Resident, Savannah, Georgia. Member of the Continental Congress, 1776, 1777. Killed in a duel by his political opponent, Lachlan McIntosh. And the signature—a tight little calligraphy beginning with an unclosed B, the eighteenth-century G of the surname rising to the double t's in a kind of funny stairway—appeared on a document upon which because of its singular location, on the very top, upper left, he may in fact have been the very first to sign! The document was the Declaration of Independence.

Here, but were there not fifty-six other signatories? There were. There were, indeed. But Button Gwinnett—to the best of anyone's knowledge—had signed exactly nothing else! Not an IOU. Not a tavern chit, not a diary entry, not a poop-sheet! Not even a letter to dear ol' Mom! There is no record of the man having appended his name anywhere else. Nowhere! The signature was worth millions! It can scarcely be imagined, then, Irving Biegel's astonishment, reaching into despair as so often he did, only to fumble up in a Moose Hall or a Goose Hall or whatever the hell lived there a 200-plus-year-old letter that bore the single most sought-after signature in the country! It was literally unbelievable! He had backed bum-first into the Kingdom of Oz and had become the Wizard! He saw yachts! Trips to Rio! Gold fields!

And yet while he came, and saw, conquering was another thing entirely. The night was passing. The lots were tolled and the goods were sold. Bed sets went. Step-back cupboards. Ivory pie-crimpers. A foam "We're #1" finger from the '74 Super Bowl. And jars of hatpins. And beveled mirrors. Some Pupi Campo records. A broken zither, an old box of marbles, and a long Indian pipe of the Manitous. Lot #70—some Smith Bros. Opal Ware—took so long to flog that Biegel almost bought it himself to speed up matters. Some peckerhead bought an ice cream scoop. A flea-bitten Amish quilt came up for which a ransom was paid by a lady in the front row with a feather in her hat. Eat it, thought Irving Biegel. He almost couldn't bear to hide his contempt for the tasteless and the uninitiated, for, while his ongoing battle with the world was fought only on the field of his mind, he radiated a great and somewhat forbidding authority in matters touching on his profession. Someone tried to engage him in conversation—the man with a thirty-cent haircut on a twelve-cent head sitting next to him—but he wouldn't answer, for suddenly, moving up in his seat, he heard the crying of Lot #71, a gimbaled crystal head-lamp, for which as the noise level rose the bidding became intensely ferocious, jumping by tens past a hundred.

"Now 125, now 125!" shouted the auctioneer. "Over here, 125! Do I hear 130? 130? 130. Now 135. 130-135! 130-135! 130-135! No one? No one out there? Come on, folks, this is crystal! French! Louis something! One of the Louis, I forget which! Do I hear 135? 135? 135! That's more like it! Now 140! Now 140! 135-140, 135-140. 140!" Two factions on the right were in combat, flashing cards like semaphore. Fight it out yourselves, thought Biegel, with not a jot of feeling, choke on it. Justice is only the balance of competing interests, right? Wasn't that right? Good, he thought, screw each other, you goy bastards! He as has, gets. It was the golden rule: he who has the gold, rules. The auctioneer, meanwhile, continued. "140-145, 140-145. No one for 145? You're stealing it! Stealing it!" He paused. "Last chance, last chance. Anyone anywhere?" He banged the gavel. "Sold."

The auctioneer quickly motioned up the next item. It was a box of—

"Books," he shouted. "Lot #72!" Some working dunces brought it up front, immediately confirming Beigel's view of the world, for the box was so bent and overfilled that in the process of being shifted forward its contents spilled onto the floor spreading brighter than a royal flush! Some little brats dove for the magazines. But this was impossible! The lady with the feather in the front row leaned over slowly and picked up the large red book that was the last to fall.

Irving Biegel clapped his mouth in horror!

"Old books. Valuable books. You name it," cried the auctioneer, impatiently reaching over to snatch the large book from the slightly surprised lady. "Check out them bindings. That's Spanish cordovan. OK, let's call it a lot and let's start the bidding at 20 bucks."

Biegel shot up his card.

"20 to the mustache," crowed the auctioneer. "Now do I hear 25? 25? 25? Come *onnnn*, 25?"

There was only silence. Biegel paused like a puma. But then his bid was suddenly met up front—he could not see who it was. He did not even want to look, so perspiringly anxious was he. It didn't matter. These were illiterates. Moose didn't read, and if nonsense were solid this place would have been the goddam Chrysler Building, he thought—and again held up his card.

"Bingo!" cried the auctioneer. "And now 30? Where's 30? 30? 25-30? 25-30?" He found his 30, Biegel went to 35, and the increments quickly went to ten. Why? wondered Biegel, why? But there was no time to reflect! "45-55! 45-55! 45-55! Spanish cordovan! Ancient bindings! Illuminations by the Old Masters! 55 and lookin' good! Now 65-65-60-65!"

But 65 jumped to 75 and 75 to a hundred. Who was bidding against him? wondered Biegel. It was almost diabolical. He heard no voice. He ducked his head left and right to see. His mouth went dry. He strained forward in his seat at 110, and it was then that he saw the lady with the feather. The Amish quilt! She was a twinkly-eyed woman in her seventies and had a thin, slightly high-shouldered prettiness who, smiling vacantly, held her card in a tilting birdlike way.

"Attention! Attention! We have 110, do I hear 120?" But suddenly the auctioneer had 120. And then he had 130! Biegel wiped his dripping nose. Could she have known? Could she possibly have known?

"140?" A card.

"150?" Another.

"I told you these little beavers were valuable!" shouted the auctioneer, hitching his pants up with his wrists. He had smelled something and now jacked the bid up to 200 dollars. The crowd oohed. Biegel bent over double and squeezed his thumb red like a squirt bottle of ketchup and then sat rapidly up with a high hand—just in time. But again, smiling, the Amish quilt wiggled her card.

Irving Biegel almost bit his tongue. He fell back in disbelief. He exhaled crazily. The man with the twelve-cent haircut next to him shook his head and chortled. "Mrs. Sneape," he said, nodding in her direction. "Game old thing, don't you know. Don't miss her Thursday nights, she don't." He twiddled his thumb and forefinger. "Money." He winked. "Lots."

"Two hundred dollars!" yelled the auctioneer, measuring out each word and nailing Biegel with his eye. "Hike it 25," he cried, "and don't play with fire unless you're ready to cook!"

Biegel was swallowing bile. He wedged into his underwear. Button Gwinnett, Button Gwinnett, he whispered to himself, crouching and looking about. He thought of all his failures. He thought of his reflection in the water that afternoon. He thought of Shlomit and her disapproving scowls who, tied in with her nagging sister, Gila, had often scolded him for stupidly wasting his money on airy schemes and dead-end ventures. He thought of those lonely afternoons by himself without a friend in the world driving along the gray, endlessly empty Taconic Parkway—and, hoisting his card, took 225. But the auctioneer immediately drove into the breech. "Now 250! 225-250! 225-250!" And now people were bobbing up and down and craning their necks. And again, madly, urgently, Biegel waved his card.

"You're bidding against yourself, Jack," shouted the auctioneer, and Biegel gasped at his stupidity and almost tumbled over. The ball then bounced into Mrs. Sneape's court, bang, it came back a quiet drop-shot—punctual as pain—$250.

Biegel down the baseline. $300.

A backhand for $350. Advantage, Mrs. Sneape. Irving Biegel to serve. "400? 350-400! 350-400!" The seats had now all turned to him. There came a pause. His hands were damp. Closing his eyes, Biegel only shook his head—up and down! A wild murmur passed through the crowd; no one could believe it! But just as 400 went to Biegel, 450 went to Mrs. Sneape.

Irving Biegel's knuckles whitened.

Christ on a pony, he thought, hissing.

It was too much. Biegel was suddenly on his feet in the grip of passion and yanking out his checkbook and wildly waving it in the air bellowing, "$500! $500!"—just at the very same moment, and as inexplicably, the sweet befeathered lady in row one shook her head, sideways. It was concession! Capitulation! And now the crowd was beside itself, jumping out of its shoes in delirium and cheering, but the auctioneer as all hell broke loose began swinging his arms crosswise fashion like a referee and banging the gavel's head again and again and again until order was finally restored. And then he leaned forward to speak.

"That a check?"

Everybody turned to look at Biegel. Dead silence.

"A check? Of course, it's a check," snapped Biegel. "What did you think it was, a lunchbag?"

"Local?"

"What?"

"Is it a local check?"

Biegel peevishly shook his head.

"New York. New York City."

Everybody burst into laughter as if he had just told the funniest joke on earth. Perhaps it was the funniest joke on earth. The auctioneer simply shook his head and looked disgustedly away. "I have references," screamed Biegel, with a yelp like a dog run over. "Take my pen! It's gold! Call—" But it was of course too late, and Lot #72—box, books, and baggage—was handed over to sweet Mrs. Sneape with a price tag of $450, no tax required, whereupon Irving Biegel took his card, tore it across and across, and to hoots of derision, mispronounced hoots of derision, stamped angrily out of the hall with a stumbling lack of grace.

Bostonians.

Morons, muttered Biegel, *actual morons.*

I am actually dumber than I was an hour ago.

I am officially dumber!

§

That night he took rooms in a small nearby hotel where he sat up in a chair in the darkness staring out across the gray harbor to Boston. The shadow of the room behind him was only another grim variation of night pulsing inside, the window answering his stare not only with this cursed city in the depth of field but with what was worse in the foreground: Buglebeak.

It was too late to go home, he knew, as he fumbled-felt the torn half of his return train ticket in his pants pocket. It was too late, too late for everything. He stretched out desolately on the bed, horizontal in the heart of the room, an illusion of levitation, quiet, rigid, unregarding, his mind a blank. Or almost a blank, for there was yet a shifting, changing picture before his eyes, bits of glass in a kaleidoscope that, shifting, shifting, turned and turned. It kept turning. It was first a fire. Then it was a folding flower. And then it was—a feather.

Irving Biegel sat bolt upright. His sparrow eyes tweaked and landmark beak twitched. He snapped on the light, stumbled over to a table, grabbed a Chelsea telephone book, wet his thumb, and with a rising sense of inner demand, began flipping desperately through the pages for a name. One name. A special name. He paused, peering closely. Suddenly his mind felt like a slate completely cleaned. Then he slammed shut the book and went to sleep and dreamt all night, for some odd reason of what, never patriotic, he had never dreamt before—the Declaration of Independence and, above all, its apocalyptic promise of freedom.

In the morning he awoke with a new sense of resolve and was on the street and in a taxi, handing the driver an address, before the slum-dark buildings and deserted warehouses of the area could oppress him any longer, and in what seemed only a matter of minutes he was dropped off in a smarter neighborhood by far. He checked the number and looked up. It was a house on a hill eloquently bespeaking the mood and significance of a past generation, generous in height, imposing in view. He rang the bell, twice. An old woman peered through a window and then came around to open the door. He was not certain that she recognized him.

Biegel cast about where to begin. But that was unnecessary. "Of course, you're the nice man from last night," said Mrs. Sneape tactfully. She invited him inside and blessed his blood with her tiny winglike hands. "Wasn't that fun?" It was a delicate silver smile. Thin, frail, silver. A light seemed to shine through her. Would he perhaps like a cup of tea? Some biscuits? But he wasn't listening. He was urgently taking in the rooms beyond her, an alcove white and gold and spacious next to a full library hung with very fine paintings. There were blue vases of delphiniums everywhere and a profusion of large white wicker birdcages, Edwardian and grand, from which emanated the twittering chatter of parakeets and canaries and cockatiels, all of whom had clearly long flown into the owner's heart and lived there exquisitely. Her veins were full of bird blood. She was indeed the bird goddess.

The room into which he was shown was octagonal. It was papered in plum and silver stripes. Three sides of the octagon were mullioned windows, half open on pivots, and the hollyhocks from the garden on that side of the house peered into the room. There were floral appointments here, as well, and more birds, finches, parrots, budgies. She told him it had been ages since last she had visited the city of New York and wondered if it were still as splendid as she remembered it. But Irving Biegel never heard her, he was not listening. He was suddenly staring. She made no scruple of noticing but in her innocence only gently smiled, slow but eventually to understand. "Ah, these you recognize," she said, motioning to the familiar pile of books on the floor which Biegel had already counted, weighed, and assayed, taking special notice of one in particular, were he lucky enough to buy it from her, he professed to have thought of as a gift for his wife who'd recently been hospitalized.

"Have them."

He stepped back.

"Excuse me?"

"Take them."

He swallowed.

"All—all of them?"

She sweetly put her head at a prayerful angle. "It would please me."

Biegel spoke a croak. He cleared his throat. "This one, too?"

"Well, you see," said helpful Mrs. Sneape, "that was the one I wanted"—she pressed it onto him—"but then, dear me, I own so many of them, don't I?" She looked towards the library. "I've collected books on the subject, you know, for donkey's years. Birds are my life. There, there, I have already looked through it."

"I shouldn't," he said, dissembling, opening the book very slowly, cautiously. "I really shouldn't."

"Favor me?"

Then his heart misgave. Something was missing, and he mentioned it as he felt suddenly clammy.

"A piece of paper?"

"An old piece of paper." He tried to control himself.

"An old crinkly piece of paper?" put in Mrs. Sneape. She suddenly remembered and tapped his knee. "Oh yes, that piece of paper. I put it to good use." And she led him over to a large cage of cockatiels, encouraging him to look closely. "They're all on special medicine, you see."

Taking a step, Irving Biegel peered closer, closer, closer.

"You don't mean—"

"Oh my, yes, globidiosis. The poor things can't help it. Some call it scour, flux, enteritis, and some," she added blushing, "diarrhea. I much prefer my dear old grandmother's phrase." She smiled. "Oh, old Boston proper, you know. She called it, and not without disapproval. I'm afraid"—Mrs. Sneape took his arm gently and softly whispered—"being urgent."

Blackrobe

Camp Truro was the first and last camp I ever attended. It was run by a severe, officious couple named Beebe, had Roman Catholic affiliations, and all the counselors were seminarians, candidates for the priesthood who for the duration of the summer tyrannically ruled the hundred or so boys sent there, mostly from the inner city, to get them off the streets. It was an inexpensive place, predominantly for boys from poor families, and there were even charity cases. My frustrated parents had sent me there as a last resort for another very specific reason: to be cured, finally, of wetting the bed. I had turned eleven-years-old that summer and had never been away from home before, and, looking back, I remember that when my parents dropped me off and drove away, I had the sudden feeling of being deserted.

The word *priesthood*, when the counselors used it, for some reason always, chillingly, gave me an image of cobras.

Was it because of the counselors? They wore black trousers and white T-shirts, and seemed never in sight, until slyly sliding out of some corner they appeared pimply-faced and tall with big black shoes and shiny, round "miraculous medals" around their necks. They were most of them of Irish descent and sex-starved and jut-jawed and repressed and angry, and they always spoke down to us, usually barking and overpronouncing words as if talking to complete idiots. Our lives seemed of no consequence to them. Seminarians lived alone, unattached, with no wives, no children, with an authority that had a fierce hardness to it. A counselor by the name of Drebber had wild whitish hair and big teeth and with disgust and a cold dismissive hiss called every boy at the camp "Johnson." Bulger snatched at his long hair, hanging loose and cut in a Brutus fringe, whenever he screamed at us. Curran went into blue rages and disparaged us without qualification.

The very worst one of them all was Monsky, in charge of C cabin—mine. We all noticed sadly that he always attacked the one or two persons least able to defend themselves, made insulting remarks to even the smallest camper, and troubled everybody often by nothing more than maintaining a certain cold, vicious look in your direction. He had a short quiff of hair with an odd white spot in it, a fat, humorless head, rather like a professional bowler's, and a feral-looking case of underbite, with fanged yellow teeth. He was also humpbacked and mannerless and had a missing kneecap and held his fork like a screwdriver.

He shouted at everyone and with disgust, called us "quats," and could cagily pick out features in each of us to ridicule. He picked on Ad Fitler, "Run, don't walk, Pissler! Get a shine on, crudman! What, you got webbed feet?" and told Piggy Gerasim, "You're going nowhere in life, this is one-strike-and-you're-out territory, you hear me, fartdog?" and hated Brian Godalming, who was my friend, screaming, "You're too dumb to pour piss out of a boot!" He barked orders. "Hey, wallio!" "OK, you, over here! C'mere, mister, right now, and I don't mean maybe!" I met

Monsky right away because the very first day I got there and was waiting anxiously for my cabin assignment, he began shouting at me, asking, "Why are you sitting on your footlocker like a fairy and not waiting outside with the others?"

The camp was a circle of old barrack-type cabins in a clearance of scrubby forest in Marshfield, Massachusetts. Dusty fields lay all around. At the end of the main field, in front of which stood a very tall flagpole—we fell in at 6:30 a.m. for reveille—stood the administrative hall, where Bill and Phoebe Beebe, the administrators, ran the programs. Races, activities, things like that. Canoes were launched along the small river, a narrows beset with woody islets where the summer air was redolent of hot pine, spruce, and cedar. Blueberry bushes sprouted up everywhere. Spongy pine needles were lovely to walk on in those faraway dark dingles and dales under the kind of tall, massive, sky-pointing evergreens that I once read could once be seen all over North America when this was a young and beautiful country, which I began to think it wasn't anymore. I cannot tell you how much I loved the woods, just the smell of them.

Over the office door hung a sign with the words written in black letters, then dots, "*Quibus rebus cognitis. . . .*" We were told at camp assemblies, several times, it meant *which things being known* and was from Julius Caesar's book on the Gallic War. I guess it meant they spied on us.

Nearby the camp lay a malodorous marsh that stank at low tide and which we called Fart Harbor. I stared at the moon by night and communed with it. Cool mists gathered in valleys in the early morning when no one was up, except me, many mornings. Most of the ballfield grass got yellow by the middle of July.

It was, all in all, a green, deeply forested, and isolated

place which became even more so in the rain-dripping darkness. I remember warm lazy afternoons, a droning plane somewhere in the distance, writing postcards home. Many miles away rose the kind of hills, I knew, that Indians once lived on, always facing south, near water. Direction meant everything to an Indian. Before skinning an animal, the Apaches always placed it with its head to the east, and they approached the animal sideways or from behind, always making sure never to straddle the carcass. I knew about stuff like that. I don't know, maybe many people did. I owned a book with many amazing photos, in his tent in the frozen wastes, of Richard Evelyn Byrd, whose name wasn't a woman's.

My favorite book, thick and green, was *Trader Horn*, about a daring adventurer who once made a comment on one page, I remember, regarding the lack of softness in nature. I wrote down some remarkable words from it in a blue leather book, the pages in which I confided various personal thoughts and copied out out-of-the-way sayings like "A cranberry bog is the color of alizarin crimson" and "The Chinese refer to us as 'white devils'—*lo fan* or *fan guey*." I recorded proverbs like "Bring me men to match my mountains" by Sam Foss, a poet. My favorite song was "The Heather on the Hill." My favorite painting of all time was da Vinci's *Lady with an Ermine*. I owned six rolls of wheat-sheaf pennies, a short-wave radio that I always kept by my bed, a toy bird-pecking toothpick dispenser, and an amazing Sheffield Farrier SNAG, made of horn and with a tremendous snap, one of the greatest jackknives in the world. I wanted to know and I needed to feel and I hoped to learn and I had nightly dreams of strange, mysterious landscapes on which, unlike anyone else who ever lived even from the beginning of time, I alone walked. *A beautiful legato blown by the wind through the trees* was a sentence I copied out of a book because it was amazing.

Many times I used to look up at the black sky at night—*past* the sky—and when I realized that 50 billion planets in the galaxy of the Milky Way sat out there alone unseen, unheard of, and unnoticed I got goosebumps.

I can honestly say that most of the time I lived a dream-life. So many times I saw people, strangers, passersby, and out of nowhere thought: I will never ever see that person again. Everyone always walked in different directions in the world, lost to logic or loyalty or luck. What was fleeting was temporary, and anything temporary broke my heart. Nothing one experienced ever remained permanent or recoverable, I realized with melancholy—not the moment, not the place, nothing. Whatever it was we encountered or happened to pass by was immediately and forever in the past. It was so strange that the things that I longed for had nothing to do with the future. I always looked into the past. I pondered in consequence—and with mad concentration—the way things used to be. I was always wasting my time as a young boy trying to squint back through space and time or some dimension, making an effort to look into and then past crowded neighborhoods and urban blight and city blocks in an attempt to see, as if by way of photographs, the ghosts of the past. I would sometimes look at a point in a painting or an aerial on a house or a certain word in a book and think, I am the only one in the entire world looking at this right now, no one else.

And I knew about druids. Who knew, I thought, maybe I had been one of them once. I could read signs in nature. I wanted to sleep in the open air without a blanket, live in the woods, eat berries, and find mushrooms—I believed that trees had rights—

and trek over trailless mountains and meet Pontiac's holy ghost, attaining the tippity-top of their highest mysterious peaks, silent in their primeval sleep. Become an explorer! That word. I loved it. That, and the words *author* and *scout* and *Shenandoah* and *frontiersman.* As soon as I closed my eyes, my mind went to one place, the same place. It was a refuge for me and was always in the Black Hills of South Dakota, where the wind caves blow, the most sacred ground for the Sioux who called it *Paha Sapa,* "The Heart of Everything That Is." I made friends in school, grew quiet in the presence of girls, whose beauty and mystery I loved and feared, but still, because I was going to be an author, I walked alone by the lake, tossing in stones, listening to the silence in clearings, and taking long looks into the world. I got goosebumps.

Phoebe Beebe, who gave out mail in the high hall, where the chapel stood—daily attendance was required—looked like a bag of russet potatoes with earrings. Augie Doggie had a joke about her and told it every day. "Why is it good Phoebe Beebe has the face of a vulture and the voice of a crow?" And we'd all sing in unison, "Because if you threw a rock at her, you could kill two birds with one stone!"

There were campfires at night, when we all sat like Mohawks *sur leur derrières,* crouched, our knees as high as our ears, and fed pine-knots to the snapping fire as we listened to scary stories about creepy madmen like Grippo and Three-Fingered Willy and Mr. Mendocino, a sentient vegetable, and Fat Ping, the Chinese warlord who bit people to death, and Dripple the Cripple who strangled women and when they were screaming whispered in a horrible voice, "Thuffer!" Sometimes we threw on pieces of old driftwood, which are never straight but gnarled and with gribbles and shipworms and have part of the ocean in them;

whoever has seen driftwood burn with all its magical lights, hissing and spitting sparks, odd bursts of powder, will never forget it. I cannot explain the feeling it gave me of eternity coming. It was thoughts like this that the frontiersman Kit Carson probably had every night when he walked through the mountains with only his rifle. The moon would be out. Foxes barked some nights, and I think I heard coyotes. I felt the wind. It was wild and wonderful to be alive.

We heard crickets. "I know how to get the current temperature in degrees Fahrenheit by listening to them," I said. "You simply count the number of chirps that occur in fourteen seconds and then add forty. That's the snowy tree cricket, the most common variety in the United States." They all laughed. Nobody believed me, and no one would listen long enough.

At times Mulligan and Obie, two of the nicer counselors, asked us questions. I often knew the answers and put up my hand. It was because of my reading—and knowledge of James Fenimore Cooper and spirits that came from the loveliness of the deep green woods and being able to survive if I got lost on Mount Katahdin and all the time I put in dreaming about American Indians and their way of life and especially about Glooskap, an enchanted spirit who never grew old and lived at the south end of the world with the lion and the wolf.

My parents promised me a pony if I stopped wetting the bed for a year. They also said they would buy me a Daisy copper-bonded Red Ryder 111-40 carbine air rifle. I wanted a warrior pony and, many a night as I slept, used to dream of having one. The Indians in the Plains had a great dependence on their warrior ponies, which could easily outrun the U.S. Army horses and didn't need saddles or shoes to do their jobs. They required very little to eat—no grain at all, just clumps of grass and very little water. They could also stand for hours without moving or neighing, which allowed their riders to sneak up on deer, buffalo. Anyway, I never went a week without soiling myself. I always woke up wet. Something was wrong with me. I once banged my head against a wall when I was crying at my failures.

Curfew was for ten. And the counselors were strict. "Don't you trust us?" asked Shellnut, as in the dark we filed into the cabins by flashlight. "Yuh," said Atkins, "like a nigger doing pushups over dollar bills."

But I didn't mind the curfews. Or the work detail. Or even Monsky. My nightly affliction was something else. I found it impossible even to ask permission to go to "The Sheds," camp lingo for the bathrooms, which were outdoor spruce lean-tos. It seemed that merely bringing up the subject was something I could not bear to do, I can't explain it. "Flush your ugly buffers and be clean about it," screamed the bully counselor Curran, after giving others permission to go. He had a ram's head and a limp and a harelip gave him an incoherent manner of speech, which suggested a minor palatal defect. I feared him as much as I feared the oncoming of night much of the day. On many nights in the close, forbidding dark I dreamt of my mother often trying to comfort me, sitting by my bed—I could hear her in my memory—soft, humming the bewitching "Sailing By." She sometimes also sang "Little Sir Echo."

After a time at camp, I had not only friends, but admirers for the first time. At first I had a hard time just talking to my fellow campers. I only wanted to be down by the water by myself poking around with a dowel looking for crayfish, clippers, and hellgies—hellgrammites—to use for fishing bait when I went on solitary walks to the pond. Some looked up to me. I knew things others didn't and it won me some esteem. A button is a good fish lure. Snow is a leavener for cooking. A walnut sapling makes a good bow. A leaf is a photograph of a tree. All seaweed is good to eat. Never plant a seed deeper than its width. A blueberry is red when it is green. Spring moves north about thirteen miles a day. The bark of a dead tree holds moisture on its northern side, and the center of the damp or rotten area is usually slightly east of north. The bracing fragrance of evergreens in the woods is like a diet drink. Did you know that dry oak leaves rustling sound exactly like rain? I could build a *spunhungan* and knew the shrill *ah-tetle-tetle-te* of the white-throated sparrow and admired Fr. Isaac Jogues, the Jesuit—a "Blackrobe"—who was a martyr. I even knew that people wiped their bums with stones in Samoa, but I didn't feel that was right to mention.

It was due partly because of the lore I passed on and maybe because I seemed so strange that I acquired the nickname "Blackrobe." It didn't bother me. The counselors mocked me with it, my friends used it with ironic respect.

I felt that there was a kind of honor to the name Blackrobe. At night I tried to tell some of the boys in my cabin about the brave pioneering fathers—Louis Hennepin, Pierre-Jean De Smet, Père Marquette, Antoine Daniel, Charles Garnier, Gabriel Lalemant, Jean de la Lande, Noël Chabanel, and René Goupil—who voyaged from France to the terrifyingly dark, deep mysterious forests of a strange country to convert the Indians, to bring them the message of the Gospels, not to torture or to mock them or to exploit them. How pathetic our camp counselors were compared to those fearless, heroic Frenchmen! They started no wars, sent no witches to the gallows, and left nothing behind them but

the gentle names they devised that sounded like poems: Belle-
fontaine, Saint Croix Island, Fond du Lac, La Salle, Prairie du
Rocher, Cape Girardeau, Espérance.

Ad Fitler told me the English explorers were better. That
was not true. So I got up, opened my foot locker, took out my
book on Audubon, jumped back into my bed, and by flashlight
quietly read to him:

> The French alone accepted America as she was.
> They passed through the wilderness reverently and
> with lightness of hand, leaving no scars, no memori-
> als to themselves. They were the only Europeans who
> were ever successful at keeping peace, and their own
> honor, in their dealing with the Indians. The voya-
> geurs as they passed though left not a trace of their
> footprint. The sword of France had passed through
> this country and cut no more than the wind.

"Too many big words," grumped Fitler. But Brian
Godalming said I was right and that Lafayette who was French
was one of our national heroes and that he did a library report
on him.

We sneaked out at certain times and smoked pipes, not
corn silk as I once did at home, but real Edgeworth in the blue
pouch and Model tobacco from a red can with the cartoon of a
smiling bald old man with bright comical eyes and a mustache
that the Jackdaws bought, two brothers named Shoffner who
looked like birds of prey but were great at the art of soap-carving
where you glued together two or three bars of white soap one
on top of the other for whittling totem poles or human heads or
buildings. I thought I'd never get as old as that old geezer with

the white mustache on the Model can. The wistful postcards I mailed home were speckled with nonsense, puns, and Latinisms and the self-protective lies I advanced to hide my complaints. Sometimes out on the field Monsky stared at me in games. He was cruel and, I felt, dangerous.

But even down there I got in trouble. "What are you going to do with all that shit, Johnson?" asked counselor Drebber who stopped me once and found me all muddy. "I was looking for clippers," I tried to explain. "Don't birdturd me, boy. Get back to your cabin." I abruptly left. "And straighten out sometime, will ya!" he shouted after me. I believe that he was referring to my bed-wetting.

Fishing was an escape for me, a place to get lost in nature, to leave the world behind. The Nez Perce were skilled fishermen, too, who lived off the salmon on the "River of No Return" in the middle of Idaho. They were the last native tribe to be defeated by the U.S. Army, but not their great chief, White Bird, never, who neither surrendered nor was ever captured. He fled to safety in Canada, unlike brave Crazy Horse, the Lakota war leader, who was stabbed with a bayonet by a soldier that had been guarding him. Crazy Horse refused to be photographed by the white man. He would not let them.

Sometimes people, even good people, refuse to obey. Just do not want to and will not. They are not bad, only different, is all.

Bed-wetting—I don't know if I read this or thought it up myself but I knew it was right—is the result diving deep, deep into sleep, hugging pillow, and refusing to face the world, descending, plummeting, submerging, a way—*a reason!*—not to wake up, as I repeatedly told Dr. Skinner, a psychiatrist in Boston whom my mother sent me to every Friday afternoon on the elevated train. I told him I once took a vocational test that indicated that I secretly wanted become a forest ranger. I tried to explain to him, I don't know, that in school whenever all the boys were walking in one direction, I always walked the other way. He listened and told me, "You're always trying to get out of the world."

But I liked fishing flies. My father told me that he would buy me a Woodcock Green, a Yellow Sally, or a Royal Coachman, if with a firm purpose of amendment, as he said, I would not wet the bed for a full year, but I never came through. I failed, always, every time. Still, everywhere, wherever I went, Monsky never took his eyes off of me. It seemed to me his stare was like a cold searchlight, sweeping across distant spaces to try to find me, *discover* me, doing something wrong. One day, Drebber snarled at me, "Johnson, you hate this camp, don't you?" I believe that he had opened my letters to read my mail. I denied what he said, feeling ashamed and turning scarlet red. Seminarians always screamed if we used a double-negative, I remember, calling us ignoramuses, but Drebber the bully went ahead and once used a double-positive that was a negative, when he snapped, "Yeah, right!" I loved that.

I got to know my bunkmates. Billy Gilday could mouth and spitshoot 300 BBs into the small hole of a Daisy rifle. Richie Zambino was a good egg. So was Andy Bitesnich, who had epilepsy. Derek ("Bok") Choy was Chinese and had a missing thumb. There was Harshbarger, the Nazi, who went in for "mailbox baseball," smashing boxes with a bat whenever we took a walk to Rexhame Beach. Paul Rappleye, a genuine mutant, had webbed toes, a twist of nature he often pointed to with pride. There was Snover, Warren Ruck, Sonny Lemitina, and Brian Godalming, my friend.

Ad Fitler, who was always flipping a Zippo in his pocket, had a bad temper. Richard Center went home with rheumatic fever after only a few days and then later died, a small, slightly wall-eyed, frazzled-hair kid with a childish mind who always hopped after me eager to show me the different pine cones he found.

There was Slupski. Julie Zuk from Danvers who collected leaves (oak, maple, catalpa, etc.)—"telling leaves," he called it— and Gammon ("Piggy") Gerasim, who, although he was thin as a reed, weak, and pale as the underbelly of a fish, would stand up during dinner prodded by the older kids and squeeze sandwiches through his fingers. There was Edd ("Bona") Harding, a clown. And even Blackerby, who was from Athol, Massachusetts, and always turned blue in the ocean and whom we called the "Unidentified Flying Oddball." I liked them all, most of them anyway, but whenever at night I thought of Richard Center, I wept into my pillow. I dreamt about him in his grave, alone out there, in the rain. I remember lines my mother read me,

"All that we see or seem
is but a dream within a dream."

Was it possibly true that everything is but a dream? It was in a poem. And "No event is truly deathless unless its monument be built in rhyme." That was in *The Knave of Hearts* by Louise Saunders, another book I loved.

In my cabin was Billy ("Useless") Uelses, Gurney Saturday, and Al ("Mini Guinea") Zirpolo from Ironton, Ohio, who once boldly licked a car battery just for our amusement and who one time, when there was nothing to do, publicly ate three grasshoppers just to show off. Billy Polk who had muscles walked around feeding a pet squirrel that he had baptized "Algebra," and he claimed that on a bet he once skindove to the bottom of Wright's Pond back in Medford, Mass., and always added to anyone who doubted him whenever he told that story, "Nobody say nothin'—or I'll kick their asses for them!" Davy ("Fools") Rushin owned a pack of dirty playing cards with pictures of naked women on them. John Flurkey, who sported a sharp whiffle, challenged everybody on a bet that he could magically jump through a hole in a single cigarette paper—the trick was, you cut along drawn inner lines and opened it into a wide circle, careful not to tear it—and who had a terrible case of acne.

They gave names to everybody. Big-eared Horatio Nowl had ears so big that when the sun shone through them everyone yelled out, "Red sails in the sunset!" Jack ("The Hallmark Card") Goodwish. Donnie ("Two Dinners") Bufferin. Joey ("Sleepy") Scarfo. Mo ("The Grasscutter") Wing, a short, thin, Chinese kid who spent all of his time in the Ping-Pong room. Wayne Wagonrod got the name "Penny-in-the-Slot" because of the brief answers he always gave. Pryzbl Kriwaczek they called "Eye Chart." Chick ("Cha Cha") Ciarcia, for laughs, made up comic names for everybody like "Al Fresco" and "Donatello Nobody" and "Whobitchacockoff, the Russian composer." He had what we called "Hawaiian feet," which were scratched and horny.

On rainy afternoons, we did crafts but in C cabin Gurney Saturday, who was wicked smart, took out a pack of cards and showed us card tricks—"Snap It," "Cutting the Aces," "Card Case Escape," and the "Sandwiched Genie." I swear, he knew card-handling techniques no one else in the world knew, like the Ribbon-Speed Turnover and how to flip the laid-out deck or do the "Ripple Revelation." Horatio Nowl became an expert right away on the "One Hand Cut." He taught me the "Hindu Shuffle," the most important card trick of all, he said, because as a basic move it allowed you to do lots of other hidden maneuvers.

Once, Monsky burst through the door and shoved everyone aside, loud and butting in, when Saturday was showing Billy Polk a thing he called the "Overhand In-Jog Control," and to prove that he could not be fooled selected a card, replaced it in the deck—then grabbing the full deck, suspiciously turned his back to re-shuffle it again—but guess what? In less than a second, Gurney made his 10 of spades protrude from the top! This embarrassed Monsky, as we were all watching. With his fanged yellow teeth, angry, Monsky—this time pushing him nastily against a back wall—barked for Gurney to do the trick again. Same result. Losing killed him. Want to know something else? Monsky hauled off and punched him in the face and spat out, "Nobody cheats me, peckerhead!"

Not a word was spoken. The aftermath was so strange. We all went to our bunks and stayed there, dead quiet. I heard Gurney sobbing.

Monsky thereafter became truly infamous. No day passed without ritual hate. No limit was put on the pain he deserved. We gnawed his name like a bone.

Paul Rappleye wanted to know more about Indians when I told him that on a raiding party by canoe they—the Blackfeet tribe especially—were not allowed to scratch their bodies with their hands or even look up at the sky, because that would bring rain. It was considered weak by the Mohawks to shift or move in a canoe. Weak and effeminate and dangerous. Fr. Isaac Jogues, the Jesuit who was ordered on paddling trips, went for whole days without once flinching. He was later blamed by the Indians for crop failures and diseases, so they chewed off his fingers. He was then tomahawked in the neck and killed.

I also told him that it is the flexible white side that is on the *inside* of the Indian's portable birchbark canoe, not the opposite. The yellow corky surface is kept for the outside. Most people don't know that. The Indians also favored the root strings of the larch to sew their birchbark canoes tight.

I knew everything about Indians. Mostly.

"Apaches never ate fish," I said. I knew most of the rules of that people by heart from all I read. We talked about them at campfires. Chick Ciarcia said that he loved my stories. "They believed that fish or snakes would cause evil," I told him, excitedly. Others gathered around. "They ate only one large meal a day, in the evening. No Apache ever thought of calling another person by name, only at war dances." "Why?" asked Chick. "I don't know," I said. "They had their own habits, because those were the rules by which they lived. They never joked with their sisters and would never even be found alone with them. Looking directly in the faces of their mothers-in-law was never done. They were all taught from childhood never to walk in front of a person or to step over a sleeping person. They never spoke of their dead. They believed that black crows aided them in hunting and they always generously left for crows the intestines of any animals they killed." I explained, "The old Athabaskan Indians would never eat a wolf or a wolverine or any member of the weasel family."

"Geronimo!" shouted Fitler, leaping onto Richie Zambino and taking him down. "I'm an Indian chief."

"Geronimo was not a chief," I corrected him. "He was what they called a shaman—and a prophet. He was a Bedonkohe Apache. The Sioux never used the term *chief.* They preferred

'Head Men' or 'Big Bellies.'"

Warren Ruck always wanted to talk after taps. I remember him as a quiet, fragile, stuttering boy with exquisite but somehow feminine manners who had a wicked cowlick and always used to ask me why I got up so fast from breakfast—our table was always sticky from spilt maple syrup—to get back to the cabin before anyone else did. Inspection followed breakfast, not just a quick scan, but a probing going-over by pitiless and unforgiving eyes, and I had to race to open the window and talcum the sheets whenever I had an accident, which was all time.

Hazing, and often bitter, humiliating, relentless teasing were absolutely savage procedure there. Taunting was encouraged among the campers by the counselors merely by example. Thuggery came natural to them. Drebber, Bulger, and Monsky all mocked Ruck—and of course us, too, but they mocked Ruck more—about girls. They called him "S-s-s-speedo" and snatched his hat, played *salucci* with it, and squeezed the bum of his pants and never picked him for patrol leader. Fiendish, even bloodthirsty punishments awaited any campers who were disobedient or willful or anyone who lied. They made us kneel on a broomstick, our hands gripping it, with knuckles underneath, for example, or kneel down with both arms fully extended, with each hand holding a boulder. It was painful even to watch.

Fistfights occasionally broke out. Any real fights during the week were settled every Friday night, a peculiar and paradoxical justice, in a makeshift boxing ring surrounded by a frayed rope outside of which sat the smirking counselors who sat with their legs up picking the rubber on their sneakers and barking at the contestants to stand in and not crouch like fairies. The Oglala Sioux never beat their children—young males who were especially pampered were allowed to play at night, to practice games of stealth—and those so-called "savages" were actually shocked to see the white pioneers savagely discipline their own kids. Sometimes the counselors would pull us aside expectantly to ask us if we wanted to become priests. But from the sound of the sheets shuffling at night, and from what I heard about it from others, there may have been sins being committed, which is why one Sunday after Mass Phoebe Beebe had small pamphlets called *The Difficult Commandment* passed around to all.

I pitied Warren Ruck so much that my heart hurt. I was overcome by sadness and felt a crying in my wet heart and solemn dead feelings within. I used to have dreams at night that a vengeful Maushop the giant would come alive and meet up with cowardly Drebber, Bulger, and Monsky and fix them good. After lights out, because they had asked me to, I told my new friends in the cabin about this figure.

"Maushop was a mythical hero and giant who protected the Wampanoag Indians. He was strong as a Massachusetts maple, but much bigger, a mysterious creature who roamed the forests with several companions of his, including a giant frog and his wife named Granny Squannit, who could both cause storms and heal people. He was not like Wendigo, an evil spirit, but had the force of Manitou along with a huge head in the Wampanoag tongue called a '*bosquoquo.*' No Indian ever saw him, but all of them knew that he was forever on guard against their enemies and would protect them in every way. Indian mothers, who never struck their boy children for fear they might become cowards, would tell them whenever a storm raged through woods bringing thunder and lightning, 'Maushop is gathering his firewood.'"

Everybody in the bunks loved this story. Counselors rustled by the doors. I waited until the spill of a flashlight disappeared,

"According to legend, he came from Cape Cod, specifically a place called Aquinnah, which was a sacred clearing not far from right here at Camp Truro, and he provided food for them and taught them how to hunt and fish. But the Wampanoags became too reliant on him, according to old legends, and he decided to go away and leave them, so that they would learn how to survive on their own. Maushop was so huge that his diet consisted mainly of whales. To catch them, he would throw boulders into the sea to make stepping stones, and then he would walk out and pick them up whole as if they were nothing but clams or little squirters! At one point, a crab bit him on the toe, causing Maushop to jump around, leaving large footprints in the ground. Moshup's Rock is named after him in his honor, before the missionaries—the '*Noeshow*,' as the Wampanoag called them— renamed it to 'Devil's Footprint' as a part of their battle against tribal traditions. During one celebration a long time ago, he emptied his pipe ashes into the ocean, and they became Nantucket. During a bad storm, with thunder and lightning, when the trees are blowing, old people on Cape Cod to this very day still say, 'Maushop is gathering his firewood.' The only thing that could injure him was the blue cone of the fir tree."

"You know something, Blackrobe?" said Brian Godalming, who had shiny chocolate hair and kept all of his treasures in a slim red Prince Albert tobacco tin. "You might grow up to be President someday."

We had races at camp on Saturdays. I could run and was fast—faster than even I myself knew—and won the 100-yard dash. Drebber's jaw shut like a rat trap. Do you remember when the

Count of Monte Cristo is thrown into the sea, how when he manages to cut himself loose and swim to freedom, he climbs up on the land and shouts, "The world is mine"? That was how I felt—just how I felt. Before that, I had no real pals to go about with. All that changed.

We often went to the old tractor shed, with its old pitted tin signs advertising Moxie and Lucky Strike and Jell-O that rattled loudly whenever we bounced small green apples off them, me and Warren, Brian Godalming, Eye Chart, and Sleepy Scarfo. There was stuff to do. I fashioned a popgun of pith elder. We practiced making gimp lanyards and twill-woven potholders and rawhide wallets and leatherhead drums and birch birdhouses, but while we worked I explained to whoever wanted to know that none of the Sioux up there in the Dakotas who were hunter-gatherers ever bothered to weave baskets or fabrics, bake pottery, or make stone jewelry, and I explained that they even looked down on farming and constructed no permanent lodges. They were warriors, as tall and as bold and as daring as Sequoia trees.

We talked about other things like when is the best time to plant and where to build lean-tos or how the Pilgrims survived the first bad winter in Plymouth. "Eating groundnuts, birch syrup, pigweed, even antlers when in velvet," I said, which was the truth. "Large Leaves," I said. "That's what the Apaches called summer. Cold winter they referred to as Ghost Face." I got to know a lot of this stuff from libraries. I knew a "fetch" was wind over water. Andy Bitesnich loved pancakes so much—he gobbled them down. I said to him, "Indians called maple syrup *sinzibukwud*," and Augie Doggie said I made it up, which was not true. I remember never saying much about myself, having developed formidable defenses against reality at a very tender age. Bedwetters must. It is required. But I remember being very happy. Not happy really. Busy, I guess.

Other days I felt sad for no reason. Hurons and Iroquois who hated each other were part of the same nation. The Sioux hated the Chippewa, the Lakota the Cheyenne. I began to see that opposing things often went side-by-side. It was confusing but it was life, I guess. Harshbarger punched Derek "Bok" Choy but then was friends with Jack Goodwish. Who can figure?

"What did Apaches call spring, Blackrobe?" asked Joey Scarfo, elbowing The Hallmark Card, "De-pants Season?"

Everybody began hooting with laughter

"Little Eagles," I said, soberly. "Early fall was Large Fruit. And winter was The Time Our Babies Cry for Food."

With a stick Billy Gilday pointed to Blackerby. "Not Little Fruit?"

Cha Cha golfed Wayne Wagonrod in the groin who said, "Quit it."

That made everybody start mocking Richie Collins, who was called Wingnuts because he lost one of his balls climbing over a fence to get into a football game free. Throwing away the stick, Billy Gilday got a splinter.

I lanced it and took it out with a knife point.

I was always prepared. It's a concept young boys alone can understand: being prepared, not for anything in particular. But for everything. Like the Minutemen. Was it what they call an escape mechanism? I rat-holed all sorts of things in my khaki foot-locker: string; pamphlets on ventriloquism and throwing your voice; a jackknife; a Roman Catholic missal; a bottle of Vitalis; an army compass; a flashlight; a book about Audubon; several packages of Clark's Teaberry gum; a McGinty, a fishing fly that looked like a yellow jacket—the best, the great writer Ernest Hemingway used one, which should always be tied on a number eight or ten hook; a copy of *Saint Among the Hurons;* a pair of sneakers; chestnuts; a hatchet; baby powder; a rubber sheet; copies of my favorite comic books, *Strange Tales, Sad Sack, The Purple Claw, Wild Bill Elliott.* I had some copies of Jimmy Hatlo's *They'll Do It Every Time.*

I also kept my copies there of Horatio Alger's *Ragged Dick* and *Timothy Crump's Ward; or, the New Years Loan and What Came of It* that had been thrown out at a church sale. I read them both many times. My father promised me a new suit of clothes like Ragged Dick had, if I stopped wetting the bed.

I wanted to be an author, mostly because, at least to me, writing books with quills by flickering candlelight seemed to be about the best thing a person could do, no matter what, and also, I think, at least partially, because I also had the same first name as the French author, Alexandre Dumas. I once made a list. It included all the things I could think of and was entitled:

Things in Nature That Hurt

sunglare
jellyfish
horseradish
hot peppers
locust bark
poison ivy
yucca plants
dry ice
stinging nettles
snakes
an echidna

onions
rhubarb leaves
mosquito bites
African thorn trees
thorns
hail
hornpouts, which is a fish with spines
wolverines
bluefish teeth
sea urchins
spiny-backed orb weavers

Camp food dorked. We marched to the dining hall every morning to a march by John Philip Sousa called "Fairest of the Fair," an old scratched 78 rpm record playing on a Victrola up in the wooden fire-tower and blasted over a loudspeaker. I remember at breakfast watery scrambled eggs and rubbery pancakes and clogged syrup-pourers and the cool scent of pine blowing through morning windows thrown wide open. Gilday once winkled some silverware from which we fashioned long spears, to fight sabre-toothed tigers. We left messages in the woods by shaping tree limbs. Tapioca pudding we called "fisheyes," donuts "shotputs," apples "Mrs. Beebe's Bubbies," and certain white, round, desert-dry old New England cross crackers that they gave us—which were impossible to eat with peanut butter without strangling—we called "hockey pucks." Fitler used to walk around holding crackers up to his ears, goofily mocking Horatio Nowl, repeating "Red Sails in the Sunset." They were so dry that even "Two Dinners" Bufferin wouldn't eat them.

It was cruel of Fitler. I remember once wanting to cry when I saw Nowl's reaction, which was blushing and sorrow. The soup we were served was so thin we used to say it was made from boiling the shadow of a pigeon that had starved to death. Sometimes we stole Oreo cookies, which we ingested all at once with big gulps of milk, trying to see who would pass out first, which we also did with Table Talk Pies, lemon being my favorite. Some of the campers made completely unspitoutable paste from the Oreo and milk mess—"Look!" they howled, gagging and waving their arms—which was thick enough to brick up Fortunato, the man in the Poe story that the counselors read to us at night by the small bonfires in an attempt to spook us.

Afterwards came inspection, as I say, which always terrified me. Sometimes, Monsky checked out only a few beds. He walked softly, to catch us, and spied into our lockers. I came to align all my hopes to the fact, wondering, still, whether if I were found out, I would be forgiven. My bed was in the farthest, darkest corner of the cabin. The section of a Sioux teepee opposite the entrance is called a *catku* and was a place of honor; in my case it was a place of shame.

I remember the growing panic I felt before we lined up by our trunks and stood there. I desperately shook baby powder over the stained sheets or doubled up the blanket or did both, praying to God under my breath that no one would notice what my mother called my *incontinence*. It worked for a few days. But then my luck abruptly came to an end. I can still remember the morning. Monsky strode in and, his jaw out, hump up, paused, flinging back the covers of my cot, singling me out in front of all the others, and screamed, "What's that stink? C'mere, fart harbor, and explain this! You went and done that? Want to pee on your wife? Are you a homo? Handwash them blankets, mister! Spray the slats, springs, and frames of this bed now! Get them thoroughly wet, then borax them, hear me?" He called me zip-perhead and a quat and a fairy and, in his mocking way, even got my friends to laugh at me.

My face heated balloon-red from humiliation, and, for a minute, in a hot flush of vertigo I honestly thought I had actu-ally disappeared. Or was upside-down. I remember hearing only echoes in my head of his infernal shouts. "And spray that pig-dog of a mattress, shithead! Do not soak it! Pay particular attention to seams and tufts! And brush the box-springs, for godsakes, because they reek!"

As a punishment, I was forced for an afternoon, in front of the entire cabin, to sit on a stool like a dumb penitent and wear a rubber sheet tied around my neck. I will never forget how much the seminarians enjoyed it. Forgiveness is important for a Christian, But forgetting? "Forgive us our trespasses, as we for-give those who trespass against us," as it says in the Our Father. It says nothing about forgetting. I would never forget, never, ever, not in a thousand million years. I could not even take comfort then in thinking of Wovoka, the Indian messiah, whom I once did some drawings of in school who was born of a Paiute Indian but raised by white people as Jack Wilson, who gave to the world the Ghost Dance which was fed by despair but at the end prom-ised hope, when the buffalo, deer, and elk would return and food and warmth, joy and peace would replace hopelessness, disgrace, and poverty.

"They should shove an umbrella down his throat and then open it," Chick Ciarcia whispered to me later and gave me a lemon Pez.

Many things have happened to me in the intervening years, good and bad, but from that day on I was never the same person again. I was only worried and anxious. I never wrote home again, or, if and when I did, I rarely told the truth. To tell you the truth, I lied. It was like I never was. And when I was given jobs at camp, like putting paracrystals in the old storage rooms and cleaning the garbage pails with chlorine bleach and buffing the chapel floor and lining up the trashcans and brushing the radiators and boraxing the toilet molding, I always wondered whose hands were doing the job and who was acting under my name.

So many times, when that happened, I wanted to go home, I remember lying down on my bunk, arms by my sides, palms downward, fingers bent, like they were hand-cuffed, listening to the white noise inside my head. I kept repeating in my mind the words I never forget that my father read to us of what the Count of Monte Cristo wrote in a letter: "All human wisdom is contained in these two words—Wait and Hope."

I was going to say I never went out after that—I wasn't even alive anymore—yet I did go out once, to the top of the old wooden fire-tower where I sat alone for hours trying not so much not to be seen, but to be able somehow to turn back time, to reverse everything and somehow start again. There, see? The past, again. I kept thinking of that sentence: *a beautiful legato blown by the wind through the trees.* The whole last week of camp it rained, and we stayed in those musty cabins with their cedar walls and silverfish in the wood and naked light bulbs, and it never seemed so lonely. I was so homesick that if anybody even blew on me, I knew I would start to cry.

The day my father came for me, I was so happy to see him I went mute. I could not talk. My throat was filled with tears. It was the strangest thing. But I was cynical, too. Since I figured nothing ever came true, especially what you wanted, when I wanted something, I prayed for it *not* to happen, just so it would, like my father coming to get me. But then was that really a prayer, praying for nothing to happen and for nothing to be answered? I never attended camp again. Nor did I dream again of woods or compasses or Glooskap or wolves or the best way off Mount Katahdin. I was never again in life called Blackrobe. I was a bedwetter, you see, and so knew I was worthy of being neither an Indian nor an author.

One thing I never wondered anymore was what hurt most in nature, only because I knew. It wasn't jellyfish or locust bark or dry ice or thorns or eating rhubarb leaves. It was people. Camp, they said, always taught you something. And now I knew for certain that they were right.

Genius

Genius, in its singularity, always seems to imply a detachment from the sublunary world, its proud possessor ever ready to guard and protect a wisdom which he owns but never—somehow, for its uniqueness, for its strange and uncanny characteristics—manages to reveal. He is seen, peered at, even *ogled*, almost exclusively from a distance. Little of the real person interferes with the myth. There goes about him, fable, legend, fantasy, something of the unicorn. It is all mystery, except that I knew one, knew him, directly, from the age of five to the age of seventeen. Sporadically, we stayed in touch until he entered prep school. It all went pretty much downhill from there. But I see I am already getting ahead of myself.

My name is Stonesthrow.

Although I am now in my late forties, I have to go back in time to explain how this all came about. I had never forgotten the boy, you see, not at all, but many years had passed since he came again fully to my attention. Last month I came across an item in "Notes and Obituaries" in the UVa. *Alumni* magazine:

Professor Beauregard Relative Found Dead in NYC
Under Mysterious Circumstances

that struck a very deep chord in me, one that brought me instantly back through a hazy blue vision to my days of student life at the University of Virginia when, having had little money, I was dependent on a small scholarship and any servile work I could scare up to pay my bills. Thanks to a thoughtful French professor and his wife there I was, at twenty, well into my junior year, able to earn a small wage almost every week, at first by helping out as a sort of butler/waiter for the small social or academic get-togethers that he and his wife occasionally gave in Pavilion IX on the west side of the Lawn where they lived.

The couple needed that kind of help at parties, being older, although they were often visited by their older daughter, Claire, a young divorcee, who lived over in Staunton and sometimes left her only child with them for days, even a week. I myself spent time with him.

It turned out that my charge, the professor's grandchild and pretty Claire's only child, was five years old and unique in more ways than one.

He liked games and puzzles. Secret codes entranced him, beginning when he was a boy after I got into the habit of telling him stories from Edgar Allan Poe, the dark and ghoulish poet who, as a matter of fact, had briefly attended the University of Virginia himself. My own versions of the tales were less scary, much funnier. Outside, my little friend would often look up toward the sky, as if pondering its blue nature. What surprised me was that at five he was able to name fifteen or so kinds of birds. He liked finger-painting, large disturbing whorls. I remember his absolute fascination with mazes. He drew little puzzles of them on sheets of paper, zig-zagging ladders with many dead ends and the essential template always the same: pairing a chicken at the start, corn at the end; a cow, grass; an Indian, a buffalo, and so on.

The little boy's name was, unimprovably, Leon Noel. When I first met him, I was an undergraduate studying English literature and brought into his company by mere hap and chance. I was living on the West Lawn at the time, a privilege given to few UVa. students. While special housing gave me a sense of pride and due distinction—the individual rooms, after all, were designed by Thomas Jefferson—the facilities also required that residents go outside to use the chilly lavatories and to fetch their own firewood, as well, which was kept stacked out by the doors in cold winter months. All rooms had fireplaces, small inefficient brick-framed hearths without grates that lent much dust and dirt to the old wooden floors. Back in my day, the only personal items that were allowed outside your door were your rocking chair and firewood. It was my third year of college. Things were tight financially. I was a scholarship lad.

§

My family was not well off. I hale from up Vermont way, the Northeast Kingdom with its terrain of wild forests and mountains. During extended holidays I found it far too costly to go home, busing up to D.C. and taking a train up north, only to have to turn around after a week and return the same way. So, I stayed on the grounds over the course of the long Christmas and New Year holidays to finish my two term papers, having been given whopping homework assignments. I worked on those papers, but went to the movies several times, alone. To save money on food I would cook hamburgers in my fireplace, rashly, using a wire coat hanger to balance the raw patties, holding them over a small fire, precariously, with the hazard sometimes of almost burning my hands. It became a kind of Walden-like experience.

My compensation was, virtually the sole occupant, having the feeling that I virtually owned the entire college, walking the grounds there as if it were vast Blenheim and I were a young Churchill. No one was about, not a soul. The premises had been vacated. Everyone else had gone home for two weeks. It was on that one vacation that Professor Beauregard took notice of me. He was head of the French department. Coming and going on the icy walkways, we would formally nod to each other and smile. He had a mustache, wore a brown rumpled hat, galoshes. We eventually talked, thanks to his good graces. I had been climbing over a large snowdrift right near the Rotunda when I fell flat on my face. He tottered over, smiling broadly, holding the strap of a green book bag over his shoulder, and, laughing, helped me up as best he could, winking and saying with his accent, "*La vie est une chute horizontale.*"

"Thank you," I managed to sputter, dusting off the snow. I had been carrying back to my room a bag of groceries and was sloppily wet for, in my fall, I had not only broken a clay bottle of Lancer's Rosé wine but had quite severely hurt my right elbow, which needed some sort of attention.

"That is not my own wit. I was quoting Cocteau," he said, adding with laughter, "Is it true? I suppose so, yes, if you have the blood of a poet." Concerned, the professor inquired about my circumstances, being alone and all, and I explained how staying over the holidays was saving me money. We walked slowly across the Lawn together. He invited me in for tea. I felt awkward, too embarrassed to inconvenience him and his wife, and told them that I preferred to get back to my room, take off my soggy coat, and see to the painful elbow myself. But his thoughtful wife duly dressed my wound, I had a glass of wine, and since it was just before Christmas, they invited me to join them for family festivities, surely out of pity. I was doggedly committed to get done as much work as possible on my term paper and so I didn't linger. A few days later, I found on my doorstep a small gift. It was a silver bell, and attached to the clapper an invitation to join the professor and his wife for drinks that same evening. It was such a gracious turn that I put on my best shirt, appeared at the Pavilion, and had a wonderful time.

Another heavy snowstorm had blown in. The professor's daughter, Claire, Leon's mother, had a job working in Richmond. She was in her early thirties, lovely, and after suffering what I was told was a painful divorce became sorely dependent on her parents to help her out with all the attention required by her little son. This was the way I managed to meet little Leon, a self-reliant, unparalleled, and extraordinary child, irresistibly bright as a penny from the first moment I saw him. A handsome face—pretty—was right off his singular feature, that, and his beautifully formed, delicate-looking, aristocratic coloring, with a pert nose, eyes ardent, dark, wide-open, and his shiny chestnut hair, which was kept long, shoulder-length, framed it in a pageboy fashion.

I remember seeing at the Royal Academy of Arts in London Henry Raeburn's splendid *Boy and Rabbit*, that famously tender painting of an innocent, sweet-faced child wearing an open ruffled shirt while caressing a bunny with his right hand and looking directly at the viewer in such a trusting way without a hint of guile, that one melted looking at it. I was struck by the fact that as a child little Leon had that same almost sculpted face, soft, intelligent, relaxed with wide but knowing chocolate brown eyes. When he was told that I had fallen down in the snow he stepped over to me, put his head down on my arm, and then began gently to pat my elbow.

How could someone so young show such concern, I wondered? His nuzzling interest in me found equal expression in his probing fingers, although in the love that he so freely gave, I noticed at the same time that he seemed so paradoxically needy. His caring stubbornness refused to let him relinquish an interest in me. I distinctly remember the first words that he spoke to me as we sat together in a window seat, looking out while he traced a falling snowdrop on the pane: "Why don't the tears of water drip off the bottom of the world?"

§

As I say, I first met the boy when he was only five years old.

He asked my name, and, repeating it, savored the word. It was something, I noticed, that he did with just about every new word that he learned. I would soon come to see that he was compulsively curious. Professor Beauregard, who seemed impressed that his grandson took such a sudden liking to me, confided that the little boy had no immediate friends about and encouraged me, if I should have the time—if I might take the time—to look in on him whenever I chose to do so, which I did, at first casually, but then, finding his funny company an utter delight, did so quite often, for I quickly came to see he was a special, even extraordinary child on whom nothing whatsoever was lost.

I bought a gift for Leon and stopped off at the Pavilion to give it to him on Christmas day, making certain in doing so that I first went to the back door, for a few days previously, just before I left, he grasped a finger of mine and, wistfully peering anxiously past me, as if searching for a ghost, soberly asked, "How does the world go around and around, but my back door is always in the same place?"

I spent much of the next winter week creating snowmen with Leon. Was that snowsuit warm enough? "I can wear any clothes I want," he said. "That's how nature works." "Isn't the good of pictures that you can call them whatever you want?" "I have a lot of room for dessert." "On a piece of paper, why aren't buildings lumpy?" "Are you driving a car to Yew Nork?" "What would happen to you if you got your head chopped off by a car door?" "Am I going to congratulate [graduate] from The Hundred Acre School?" "Pencils are like fingers but dry." That's correct. He was a perfect fund of these ingenious little trifles. The color white alone fascinated him. "If we had white hair, white heads, white necks and legs, we could hide in the snow and hibernate." "See that white car over there"—he pointed across the road toward Alderman library—"it has a face, but that yellow truck doesn't." "Are snowflakes good for cakes?" "Devils have coach lamps for eyes." "I sleep at night with a frog named Popjaw who eats insucks and chickmunks." "Does a hard-boiled egg wear a shell for pants—Humpty Dumpty does?" "Are colors buttered?" "Did you know that Rapunzel *ate* rapunzel?"

I detected quite early in the boy an instinct to rock rather than row the boat. No genius can stand the run-of-the-mill, however, I could see that, for such a creature is an original copy, odd, peculiar, unexpected, atypical, whatever—the word egregious might best apply, for the word actually means to stand out from the herd. I read to Leon "Henry the Bootblack," "Alice's Supper," and "Ralph Wick" ("When he could not have what he wanted, he would cry for it . . .") from an old McGuffey's *Reader*—I would eventually come to live in a hill dormitory that was named after that particular author/educator when I first began my graduate studies and once I took Leon over to the university cemetery to show him William H. McGuffey's grave and obelisk—and the tale about the eagle swooping down to steal a child which intrigued instead of frightened him. He observed, "Girl eagles are bigger than boy eagles and they have hollow bones and can even swim."

We scared some squirrels. "Animals run away but flowers do not, do you know why, the mud holds them down." We threw snowballs at each other. Leon laughed and exclaimed, "I couldn't see because my eyes are in the way"—followed by, "What do eyebrows do?" "Will poison ivy kill you?" "How did Jack make the beans talk?" We set out a bird-feeder, but he got frustrated and worried that, because birds only swallow their seeds, they couldn't taste anything and so were nutritionally deprived. I told him that because they select certain types of seeds, something was going on. It was the first time he ever scolded me. "I want to tell you something"—here he would wait for acknowledging attention—"their bones are hollow," he pleaded, "so nothing fills them *to enjoy!*" "Know something? All people's human skin is waterproof!" I mentioned having seen a dead skunk behind the Serpentine Walls. "Was there a body and a foot on him not together?" Told at the age of six that Santa Claus was no more than a myth, he immediately asked why God was not a myth, as well.

He was a gifted listener, but talkative. I could see he was quickly exhausted by any facts he heard that he needed to digest, pausing—sometimes as if actually straining to see if everything jibed—to test their verisimilitude. It was clear that he had spent much time alone and actually craved the chance to be with someone, anyone, most probably a person who was older. Where was it that I read that intimacy is the neurosis of solitude? Surely the capacity to be alone without drowning in loneliness, I thought, mirrors the capacity to be with others safely.

I had an aunt who had treated me like a grown-up when I was roughly his age, so I found it easy to do the same with my little charge. It helped that he went to kindergarten three times a week, where he learned to read at four, and I mean polysyllabic words, as well. I also had the ill-luck to have a sarcastic and unfeeling uncle who was a brute to me, a priest, by the way, whose mockery over my bedwetting at age six or so bordered on child abuse. I saw myself in Leon, in the way that, like a reverberation or reverse-cast, I found not only his singular curiosity but the pain he suffered an almost explicit match to a good many of the ups and downs of my own childhood, exploring with him, I remember—with him, through him, whatever—the countless mysteries of identity one struggles with in trying to grow up and how one's persona is often a mask or guise, a simple face a front.

Snow fell often that long winter in Charlottesville. There was a Trappist-like peace to the fully deserted college grounds during those intervening weeks, my working vacation, and, as I worked on my term papers, I felt it an accomplishment to be getting things done, alone, typing away in my room on the Lawn, using my wood supply well and self-reliantly cooking my hamburgers on the wobbly wire-ends of a coat-hanger, even if, at times, irretrievably dropping one or two burgers into the flames. I loved being able to compose sentences the long days allowed me. I wanted to become a writer all through my student years, even before that. On afternoons, I would go over and take Leon sledding over on the hill by the old gymnasium—they had a Molson runner sled, among the best—when he never showed fear thundering down through the drifts, never failing to ask his many innocent questions, when we took time to sit in repose on a bench at the cusp of a gray afternoon. "What are noises made of?" "What happens to a noise after you can't hear it?" "How heavy is a telephone pole? Were they once trees, and how did they change to become a telephone pole?"

I remember not only starting to write down his remarks but recall even buying a notebook to do so. *What makes rubber snap back? What happens inside a cat when it purrs? Do fish have voices? Can you say a piano has teeth? How do they catch air to put in your tires? What color is the wind? Why do we need two eyes to only see one thing? What makes soap hurt? When you're electrocuted, are you cold or hot? Spoons go up, and forks go up, so why do knives stay flat? What's faster, fire or dust? Why don't the heavy dark clouds fall down?*

Where did all this stuff come from?

§

A wonder child, Leon's upbringing was privileged but contingent. His mother was fragile and moved jobs. When I was told that he wet the bed, I saw he shared with me what Matthew Arnold called "the fever of the differing soul." As a habit, it is an escape from reality, not due to laziness, a deep dive down by way of sleep into a realm of safety, to a subjective world that becomes an alternative to the cold reality of the living, the fractured world one otherwise has to face upon awakening. Not getting out of bed is a subconscious attempt to seek refuge. "You two get along well together, like Sauvignon blanc and trout!" said the professor, on the occasion of his sixth birthday. It was true. I was truly fascinated with the workings of this young brain, the gifted possibilities found in someone so young. "I know what a fiasco is—a glass bottle, not a mirror," Leon told me. I had no idea where that came from, but such was often the case with him. It was always out of the blue, and fast, and frank. He loved my name. "Did you ever throw a stone at something, like a elephant?"

"Emptiness can be pretty because you can fill it with your dreams," he told me once in an earnest, confiding way. Six years old and ready with a seminal theory of art! Defending loss—shoring up identity—seemed to be a theme in much he ever said to me. It was as if he needed surety, everywhere. Assurance. A pledge of allegiance of sorts. I recall many times that he would be sitting outside on the Pavilion stoop waiting with his eyes full of extra-eager expectation for my appearance that broke my heart.

Any child who compulsively wets the bed—set upon by nature in a stigma that is also an enigma—is both mystified by, but peevishly disgusted with, the mysteries of the body. Leon told me simply he could not wake up. He had no end of other questions about bodily functions: "Why do you need spit in your body?" "How deep is under your fingernails?" "Why when you hit your body, is there a bump instead of a dent?" "Why do mirrors let you look upside down?" "Can all bunnies sleep without their ears hearing?" "Where does your lap go, when you stand up?" "Why don't people have earlids?" "When did I first step on my feet?" "Did you know you can make a magic mountain by pushing a bed sheet together?" "If we were all born with three legs, what would we do with the other one?" "Can you bite upside down?" "Why doesn't it hurt when they cut your hair?" "What do black and blue marks look like underneath?" "Why do your teeth need all that pink stuff [gums] to hold them up?"

I linked his jejune sexuality to the precious questions he asked so gently, so lovingly, asked—lisped—when, even as a mere poppet, he showed quite clearly that he harbored an inner drive, almost compulsively, to see the many sides of things, to ascertain a unique view from various slants, angles, and approaches in the cognitive need to see, to grasp all sides, especially about boys and girls who of course at his age was only about one gender having long hair and the other not, one wearing dresses and the other pants.

I would occasionally read to him when he went to bed, books like *The Wind and the Willows* and Hilaire Belloc's *Cautionary Tales for Children*, and Munro Leaf's *Story of Ferdinand*, and Robert McCloskey's *Make Way for Ducklings*. He loved the nonsense poems of Edward Lear and pleaded to hear them again and again, especially "The Courtship of the Yonghy-Bonghy-Bò." I regaled him with weird stories that he craved, both from my own imagination, dredged up on the spot, and others contrived from summer travels that I had made, of Kundlifresser, the Child Eater of Bern; and Necropants, the Icelandic Loon; and the Emaciated Ferryman of Wicklow; and Space Face, the Supergranny of Medicine Hat. He particularly loved "Ali Baba and the Forty Thieves"—genies gobsmacked him with the infinite possibilities they offered—and he once precociously asked me, "If a genie comes out of a bottle to offer a person three wishes, shouldn't he begin by wishing for—*more wishes*?" It was at such times I wondered, is this little guy going to end up on Wall Street?

I narrated the Wagnerian tales of the Nibelung treasure and Alberich the dwarf and his cloak of invisibility. Leon loved to hear the Grimm fairy tales and stories of wily foxes, devious elves, repulsive frogs, and beautiful daring princesses who secretly slipped out at night to dance holes in their shoes. He was wide-awake and vigilant as perhaps only an only child can be, watchful and quick on the uptake. At five, when we happened to see a movie on television together beginning with rolling credits, he would alertly ask me, "When do those words go away?"

He played alone. At age seven he read *The Red Badge of Courage* and with playing cards he ordered Union and Confederate armies into battle across the field of the polished library floor, complete with a running narration.

He also loved riddles. "What's black and white and red?" he would blurt out with challenging glee. "A raccoon with a diaper rash!" "What is brown and sticky? A stick." I always tried to get it wrong, naturally, for nothing more delights a young child more than a slow, dopey, blundering adult. Language and riddles intrigued him. "What do you call a fish with no eye? FSH!" (He dutifully wrote out the big letters for my edification on banana-colored paper, of which he had reams, for he loved to draw.) "What do you call a deer with no eye? No ideer." "What do you call a grandfather flower? Poppy." "What do you call bears with no ears? B." "Why don't you have to starve in a desert?" he asked me. "Because you might eat all the sand which is there. Why *are* the sandwiches there? Because there the family of Ham was bread and mustard!" I would later learn that he had asked his grandfather earlier about Noah's son as well as the cognitive connection of that verb/noun combination. But it was his understanding of *mustered* that got me, a word that he used without missing a step.

We exchanged talents. I taught him how to fill a bird-feeder, and to play "Chopsticks" on the piano, and the words to the Jelly Bean Prayer,

> "Red is for the blood He gave.
> Green is for the grass He made.
> Yellow is for the sun so bright.
> Orange is for the edge of night.
> Black is for the sins we made.
> White is for the grace He gave.
> Purple is for the hour of sorrow.
> Pink is for our new tomorrow."

He sought to entertain me with that old hands-and-fingers maneuver: "Here's the church, there's the steeple, open the door and where's the people?" I delighted in his energy and found it so easy to praise him, for it seemed that just about every turn of his warranted admiration. He glowed like a little girl when complimented, with a fetching blush on that beautiful poetic face, tender lips, and eyes that you could swim in.

One particular riddle never got by him, about the geography of the Earth. "It is called the globe," he told me, "but it is not perfectly round. Did you know that? I know that! The diameter at the equator is 27 miles larger than the pole-to-pole diameter, just like a—like a—fat man!"

I had my own riddle to solve touching on Leon's precocious cognitive powers, let me add, or, I should say, his driving need for cognition, seeking all the whys and wherefores of things. Doing some wayward reading in the library, I looked into Kant's famous distinction between *Verstand*, or intellect, which seeks to grasp what the senses perceive, and *Vernunft*, or reason, which is concerned with the higher-order desire for trying to understand the deeper meaning behind such sensory input; while intellect is driven by cognition, reason is concerned with the unknowable. I could deduce little or nothing, of course. What amateur could?

Then there was Leon's spate of mirror riddles, what seemed to be no end of them. Mirrors. His fascination. "What turns everything around without moving?" "When you see me, you also see you!" "When you cry, he cries. When you laugh, he laughs. When you ask him who he is, he says, '*You know*.'" "There is something behind a mirror it cannot see." "Mirrors have a shine like ice but it will never melt." "What can make my left hand my right?" He would gleefully bounce up and down on the sofa and as a challenge sing out,

> "They're sometimes on a wall
> And sometimes on a shelf
> And when you look at one
> You always see yourself."

"My name is a mirror," he used to tell me, more than once. Soberly. Could he have possibly meant that there was nothing behind it?

§

Claire, his mother, was grateful that I became a sort of big brother to Leon, more a studious and loving uncle than anything. Dacre, his father—"faker" would have done well enough—

whom I never met, was a French Canadian saxophonist. I spent many an hour wondering what that man was like, speculating that, in spite of the divorce and his semi-show-business inattentiveness, he had to be a man of some virtue to have sired such a spectacular child as little Leon. Being with Leon was such an intriguing daily enterprise that, to amuse her, to give her a better idea of her loving and gifted son, I began to pass on to Claire compilations of her "wise child's" questions: "Santa's and Grandpa's bellies are the same height." "Am I too handsome to get a tan?" "My blood is always happy." "Why are there holes in bread?" "Where exactly is north?" "Is barking talking for dogs?" "Why doesn't rain come down all at once?" "Can you blow up a house with water?" "Is lava sticky?" "Where exactly is the bottom of quicksand, in China?" "Why is rain thin?" "Can you make walls of air?" "When a window's open, where's the glass?" "Why can't we skate on the floor?" "Is all soup round?" "Is electricity fire?" "Are they called watches because that's what you do with them?" "Do combs bend hair?" "Do beaks have teeth?" "When crayons get short, are they still good?" "Copper and zinc got married and gave birth to a baby, Bronze!" I laughed. "But they didn't get married," Leon added as a surprise for me. "They got *alloyed!*"

He read avidly, including many of the works of Robert Louis Stevenson from an inexpensive set that I bought him. It was if he had memorized every scene from every story, somehow always leading him to jump out at me whenever I appeared, crying out intrepidly with gestures, "I'll duel you!"

The act of discovery brings constant joy to a child. I was always met with excitement and laughter, for the curiosity that feeds the jouncing energy of a seven- or eight-year-old is endless and no day long enough. "Oystercatchers are birds, not fish." "My pillow has puffin feathers inside and squeaks under my head." "A boy duck is a drake and swims on what he drinks." "Never laugh at a crow—it will count your teeth as you do it, and they will all fall out one by one." And that was just birds.

I told him the wonderful story of how the secret of attaining the perfect world without pain and where all human beings loved one another was written on a green stick buried in the woods, a happy fantasy that his elder brother Nikolai once told the young Leo Tolstoy.

Leon loved the role of playing helpful doctor and, with me supine, could often be found busily taking my temperature. "7 8 9 6 11 is your temperature," he would say, winding a thread around my arm. Oftentimes he would put on a solemn face and gravely tell me, "Forty pounds" or "30th 98"—whatever outlandish figures came to mind in gauging my fever. He would in all seriousness confuse temporal enumerations with dollars, but there seemed to be a nutty reality in his crazy figures and reckonings, mimicking a real doctor. "The clock says sixty dollars— *and you are late, sir.*" And there were of course those continuing comments about mirrors. "When they shine, that is when they work the best," he said. And "You can never see your whole self in a mirror, did you know that?" And, "Do you always love what you see when you look in a mirror and see what you see?"

It was, this mirror business, strangely prescient of the questing motif in Leon's little life. The mirror knows what you are, but you know nothing of the mirror. You catch yourself at moments surprised where, maybe in parts, or places, you cannot even recognize your own reflection.

Skepticism is the province of adults. Leon eased into his

capacities—thoughts, words, and deeds—without the slightest efforts of concentration. It was left for older folk to probe and question. Vitality trumped self-consciousness in him. He was a fund of openness. Samuel Beckett was right: "The only fertile research is excavatory, immersive, a contraction of the spirit, a descent."

Touchy and defensive Leon could also be. One rainy day after he did some drawings of raccoons and pigs with missing noses, he paused and scowled a bit at me. "I don't like drawing noses these days." The arbitrariness alone intrigued me. Another time when his mother could not manage to get to Charlottesville and she left him at the Pavilion for a long winter week, he spent much of it moping, although I never saw him weep. He told me huffily, "I am angry at God."

Well, I did see him weep once. "Leon, you better be good—or I am going to put a stamp on your forehead and mail you away," his grandmother told him when he refused to pick up a pack of pencils he had scattered. He came to me with a strong hug for solace. I remember that it made me blush.

He was virtually visceral with intellection, lively and unappeasable. We engaged in no end of Q's and A's, of course:

"*What are little girls made of?*"

"*Flesh and bones.*"

He wanted to know what flesh was made of.

"*Cells.*"

"*So what are cells made of?*"

"*Molecules. Complicated ones like DNA and simple ones like water.*"

(I was often tired and said whatever came to mind.)

"*What is water made of?*"

That was easy to answer, but as I got down to electrons, neutrons, and protons, I knew trouble was coming.

"*What are protons made of?*"

"*Quarks,*" I said.

What did I know?

"*Ducks?*"

"*No, quarks.*"

"*Quarks?*"

"*Yup.*"

"*What are quarks made of?*"

I simply shrugged and gave up.

"*I don't know.*"

Lest we forget, children are very rarely deceived. Fabrications are swiftly detected. Having themselves experienced the great delight of telling lies, children detect them in others with remarkable ease.

I decided to keep to the honest route.

§

I took my degree from the university, stayed on in Charlottesville, taught Upward Bound for the summer, and in the fall began graduate school in order to avoid getting drafted—a notable side-blessing—for the Vietnam War, then five years along, was raging badly in the year 1968. I moved to a cozy room on the West Range and continued earning money working as a butler for the Beauregards. At age eight, as I was in his, Leon Noel was still very much in my life, an anchor to windward, so to speak, in the sense that his innocent and buoyant company was a delightful alternative to the swots I shared classes with in the four courses I had taken on. I saw the boy more or less every week. He had developed an interest in collecting Civil War bullets, buttons, pipes, relics. I had an old black 1957 Chevy and took him down to Saylor's Creek one open-ended day, down past the James River and south of the tiny little dorp of Farmville, where he went grubbing away in delight with a small spade looking for old souvenirs and found all sorts of .58 calibers, ringtail bullets, and mini-balls he kept in a pail.

We stopped on the way home for a hot dog at a roadside café. He sat quietly on a bench, shaking a foot, and out of the blue said, "I know that Europeans eat outside."

"You know what I didn't find?" he added solemnly, shaking his pail of balls, shot, and slugs. "The green stick that tells about the perfect world." I looked to see if he was smiling, but his face was dead serious.

I was sitting in the Beauregard's parlor one afternoon later to be serving guests that evening. I always tried to come early for special instructions—whence came a telephone call. A teacher in the third grade was calling his grandparents and somewhat flustered declared, "Master Leon insists that the word '*the*' is an adjective—and he demanded that I call you." His grandmother repeated the remark and asked me to respond. "He is correct," I said in confirmation, sharing my thoughts with the professor, who agreed. The boy's gifts were irksomely foreign to that teacher, his demands for attention nettling. She was a different pre-school teacher than the woman they had gone to see another time. Every eight-year-old draws curved and straight lines. Nevertheless, a child rarely makes a circle with lines crossing the perimeter before the age of three. Leon had been drawing visual impact gestalts and mandalas at the age of three—he got his ideas from the ingenious scribblings he commonly made on his own and took off from there—and the competent teacher, the former, had sent drawings home with a favorable note. That teacher clearly saw thar the boy was exceptional.

The reading textbook they used in the early grades was an affront to Leon's dignity, I could tell. He didn't complain, but was merely bored. Do you remember *The Little Red Readers*, a book many grew up with and in places still in use? "A cow went in the cave," "A boat can float"—and even harder ones!—"Tall trees grow close together." I took time to look up Stanford-Binet tests, checked out the noted Wechsler Intelligence Scale for Children (WISC), probed various subjects like verbal knowledge of words, of pictures, of designs, and I read through a lot of what seemed out-of-date topics like "Prehension Provoked by Tactile Stimulus," "Comparison of Known Objects from Memory," and, I don't know, "Suggestibility."

They gave him a WISC, which is supposed to measure the mental acuity of as child at a given age. It turned out that Leon, who took it at age seven, had the capacity of a sixteen-year-old. His IQ was listed, if I remember correctly, up there in the 170's—in the 99.8 percentile of scores.

Who was surprised?

As he was growing up, a little tyke, a mere peppercorn, his grandparents, or so I concluded—and a distant but wealthy aunt who lived out in Keswick, a grand old lady in the great tradition of female directors (I met her once)—settled on his head the weighty crown of genius and inculcated in him from the earliest age an intense and demanding training in the rigorous efforts needed to make fine distinctions, the premise of which also involved a kind of skepticism. She was proud, and who could blame her. Forming his character in an oblique way, however, inculcated a certain vanity in him, the upshot of which carried with it a good deal of pedantry, dogmatism, quibbling, and perfectionism. I was not being nosy but was simply intrigued by his brilliance that in curious ways echoed—quoted—the precocious qualities I was reading about in the lives of certain English geniuses, such as John Stuart Mill, William Wordsworth, Isaac Newton, Robert Boyle, David Hume, and Gerard Manley Hopkins.

I seriously believe in a way that, prior to meeting Leon, I measured my own life, my own prospects, in ways that I had not done before, simply because—seeing what he would be up against in the world, for all of his brilliance—I saw that the need for courage and endurance did not encourage reflection.

It had long been confirmed by now how bright Leon was. I saw with escalating awe the prodigious curiosity exampled by the many astute questions he would ask, each one as if chosen to demand as considerable if not as substantial an answer. Around the age of eight or nine, he went through what I guess I would call a religious phase. It was not of course spiritual but something romantic, juvenile mysticism, a kind of supernatural enchantment. He would carry a crucifix about him at times, wordlessly hold it up toward you. One Sunday I decided to take him over to a service at the Westminster Presbyterian Church on Rugby Road. He was a perfect gentleman as he sat through the sermon and said upon leaving, "Jesus took clothes off the soul, so we could see it." His schools by now knew that he was special, a truly unique child.

But how many eight-year-olds desperately wanted to know the facts about St. Paul? I told him the story of Saul—St.

Paul—on the road to Damascus and what strangely befell him. Leon exploded with fascination, probing me about the horse, the road, the fall, the blindness, and, above all, that celestial voice.

I decided for once—as a lark, yes, but also as a sort of epistemological test—to give Leon a graduate-school answer, a sophisticated, adult's response to his questions, one as round as possible even from a graduate student's point of view, and replied, "Any history or study of the Greek world that omitted St. Paul would be wildly incomplete—he was one of the greatest figures in all of *Greek* literature. He thought in Greek. He wrote in Greek—all of those letters of his that we read in the New Testament were written in Greek and actually preceded the Four Gospels, by the way, *by half a century!* It was the official language of the Eastern Roman empire. We know that Jesus spoke Aramaic. When Jesus came into the world, the Greek language was spoken throughout all parts of the Roman Empire. You should know that Jesus would have spoken in a sort of 'marketplace' or a common dialect of Greek to Pontius Pilate, since Pilate did not speak Aramaic and Jesus probably knew only a few words of Latin."

Leon loved to *know.* I continued and explained to him, "St. Paul had a great teacher, Gamaliel, and a deep knowledge of Greek rhetoric was instilled in him. He could quote Scripture from memory, all of it taken from Greek translations of the Septuagint, that is, the Greek Old Testament, which is also called the Hebrew Bible. Paul came from Tarsus in Cilicia," I told him—I would take out a map later that same day and trace for Leon the route of Paul's travels—"which is now southern Turkey, on the Mediterranean, a very Hellenized city. St. Paul was as a man on fire, because he loved Jesus so much." "Were they friends?" Leon breathlessly asked. (Later he did a bearded drawing of St. Paul.)

"They never actually met," I said, "—but yes."

I skipped certain refinements, of course, in talking with Leon. St. Paul actually *did* meet Jesus, who actually appeared to him, "as by a delayed birth," after the resurrection, as we read in 1 Corinthians 15.3–9. Of all those who saw the risen Lord, in fact, Paul is the only one whose own words we possess.

Nor could I find it in my heart right then to disclose to impressionable Leon that Thomas Jefferson, founder of the University, being offended by the supernatural aspects of Jesus as reported in the accepted Evangelical gospels, went on in a passionate burst of revisionism to create his very own, to him, more acceptable and platitudinizing religious leader instead, not the holy Messiah we know of such devastating greatness and splendor but a mild, sententious dullard and moralizing goodfellow who says nothing—is not *allowed* to say anything—shocking, unexpected, challenging, original, profound or even obscure, a completely sanitized secular wise man in an expurgated and farcical mock-up—no original copies of the thing exists today—that by way of creative editing and snipping rejects not only the divinity of Jesus, the notion of the Trinity, all of Christ's miracles, the atonement, and original sin, but indeed the Resurrection itself. To Jefferson, the Greek philosophers, Epictetus, the Stoic and Apollonius of Tyana, the Neopythagorean—both, roughly, contemporaries of Jesus—were equally as great. My thought was why infect a young and suggestible lad with a sterilized and blasphemous account, when his own little genius was a miracle in itself?

Leon and I went down to The Corner for an ice-cream soda after church. I remember the event for two of his questions, both of them, I found, remarkably unanswerable. "Why has God got a hell?" he solemnly inquired. "If faults are failures, why aren't all failures forgiven?" I was trying to frame an answer, when Leon, who seemed to be configuring something else in his brain, swiveling in his seat, turned to me to state, "When you said that St. Paul was a Pharisee, the son of a Pharisee, and that his relatives Andronicus and Junia, who became Christians before he did and were famous apostles, doesn't a Christian who says that the Pharisees are wicked, um, commit the same crime for which he is, um—"

"Denouncing them?"

"Yes."

"Correct."

Leon loved the hymns, "Soldiers of Christ, Arise," "Come, Thou Fount of Every Blessing," "Praise to the Lord," "Crown Him with Many Crowns," and "Be Thou My Vision." There were spates of questions he asked about God, heaven, and death, of course, where we go when we die. I remembered with delight when at the age of five he told me with great reverence and earnest piety. "Jesus died wearing a tissue and they stuck pins in him." Life sequence—mutability—intrigued the boy: "When I die will God want to make me again?" "How do you remember what you did yesterday—by doing it again today?" "Guardian angels eat clouds, but did you know the bigger angels near God eat light?" God occupied his world!

Little Leon embraced end-times prophecy by interpreting various cloud shapes as indications of God's warning, mirrors of a supreme personality: nimbus clouds were threats, cirrostratus clouds scraped the sky like forks, cumulus clouds were happy angel food. "Where does your name go after you die?" He was a sky-gazer, like most lonely children. Flaming sunsets delighted him. He once declared to me, over a sunset, "Westward in the sky the crimson children sport." Good God, where did that one come from? ("The sun goes below the horizon due to Earth's rotation," he explained expressly for my benefit.) He had a Bible his mother gave him; I was astonished to hear him say, "In the book of Judges, trees speak."

Trees intrigued him. He could have been a young Henry Thoreau. "Is it cold to be a tree?" "Why are trees stuck?" "What's inside of wood?" "When exactly do trees become metal?" "Are forests dog's toilets?" Observations grew in sophistication from age five to six to seven. "Buds don't come out in spring—they are fully formed in the fall." "Bark grows from the *inside* of the bark, but the tree trunk does the opposite, putting on new layers of wood on the outside of the trunk, underneath the bark." "Trees set the angles of their branches by gravity." "Yews bring bad luck and bleed sticky sap." "Did you know that trees are the world's greatest water pumps? There is an unbroken column of water in every tree from the deepest root to the topmost twig." "I know about battleship oaks." "See that tree behind the wall? That's a locust, who has a bark sharper than anything. They used them on ships to make tall sails, because, when they are straight like those are, they make lovely sail poles." "Rhododendrons"—he pronounced the word perfectly—"show popple flowers." He grabbed a page of my book and with popping eyes rattled it. "Even that—*this*—is wood!"

I feigned total surprise, bluffing, and went properly amazed. My sham ignorance, a masquerading stupidity that I always delivered with exaggeration, always immediately elicited new lessons from him, free little seminars I loved! Teacher as student, an inside-out idea. He was irresistible. During his pompous little object lessons—on *any* subject—so earnest was he, and yet so

comical, while cute, that it was all I could do to keep from dou-
bling-up in laughter.

He was an excellent mimic. He had hand puppets. And
how about his acting gene? He loved greatly to perform and,
assuming the role of different characters, would dress up accord-
ingly—the usual things, a pirate, a Civil War soldier, the witch in
the story of Snow White—one day even lovely Snow White herself,
draping himself in one of his mother's sequined dresses. For one
spring school pageant, Leon dressed up as Little Lord Fauntleroy in his black velvet court suit with lace ruffles and paste shoe
buckles. Quoted the earnest ten-year-old with delicate lovelocks
waving around that handsome manly little face, "'Are you the
Earl? I'm your grandson, you know, that Mr. Havisham brought.
I am Lord Fauntleroy!'"

I read him from the N.C. Wyeth edition of Jane Porter's
book, *The Scottish Chiefs*, which he loved to distraction. He was so
impressionable and loved the warfare and the paintings, both,
and William Wallace became a new hero of his. Oh yes, and I
became one, as well. Thanking me for reading, once before I left,
he pinned on my shirt a note on which he wrote,

> "The cube root of a million is six big zeroes.
> You are one in a million my best of heroes."

But, of course, he had to add, as if talking to a benighted and less
intelligent dummy, "Some problems cannot be figured out without zero, though. Did you know that the value of zero divided by
zero is unknown?"

§

I have an interest to declare. I began to date Claire Noel, if dating is what you would want to call it. It was all sporadic and ill-defined. I am certain that I was attracted to her through him, for I loved what she had made. I brought her a bottle of Taylor port wine and a bouquet of yellow freesias one Easter Sunday and asked if she would go out to dinner with me. The two of us drove out toward 250 West for beer and pizza. She was clearly out of touch with herself after her sulfurous divorce. As we had pretty much only Leon's welfare in common, I wondered if that presaged—in her mind—a match of any sort between us. How awkward it was for me to be acting in any morph the boy's father. We would return and sit in the dark in her car in one of the university driveways just talking, with nothing of clarification ever made between us. Sometimes she wept. I thought I knew why at the time, by which I mean her loneliness. She kept thanking me for helping Leon. "Your last name in a way means you're close by," she said, laughing. I would look deeply into her eyes and see the kind of complexities there I thought of as occultations— events that occur when one object is hidden by another object that passes between—and felt that by closer attention I could only do her wrong, more from neglect than betrayal. Different ages, divergent interests, separate tables.

It led to nothing. I knew it would. Claire referred to him as Dacre, but the full name of her husband was Abraham Lincoln Noel. That's all that I remember, it was so long ago. She fashionably wore white gloves, loved jazz, and wore expensive Roja perfume that probably had the greatest smell on earth, except—for me—peonies. As to details of their divorce she kept completely mum, discussing nothing of the matter in extenuation of her own personal behavior. There were suggestions of guilt. The eximious boy, her son, was our sole, and happy subject. We laughed at his uniqueness, the likeliness of the splendid future awaiting him, for to us there seemed to be no end to his blossoming aspirations. She wrote sporadic letters to me for about a year or so, filling me in on goings-on there, when suddenly they ended abruptly.

I was to discover inadvertently a decade or so later from the second-hand gossip of a disagreeable bookshop owner from Charlottesville, a random and intrusively loquacious acquaintance of Professor Beauregard and his wife, who took me aside after their funeral at a cemetery in outlying Staunton, Virginia, to tell me not only that the couple had died the previous Spring in a hotel fire while they were vacationing in Menton, but that, after having had several affairs, one in fact with the husband of that very same bookshop lady, or so the indignant and calumniating woman claimed—and yet even another, apparently, with one of her son Leon's older friends—poor Claire was eventually consigned by the courts to a behavioral health facility, euphemism, in Richmond, Virginia, where, in 1978, she died, all alone. A Roman Catholic priest had conducted services over two closed caskets. I flew back home.

§

By the age of nine, Leon was fascinated with books and stories. I chose to read aloud to him *Hard Times*, Charles Dickens' shortest novel, and did so in installments in the early evenings, but Leon was always inconsolable whenever I had to beg off to write a paper before I had finished declaiming the book. Out of frustration, he actually began to write out an end to the story himself! (I kept the amazing screed of that for years, ten rough pages or so, but mislaid them over the course of time.)

Sea-faring books predominated for a while. "Windproof furls I want! Hard up the helm!" he would cry out as the captain of a British fighting galleon. "See to the poles, you lubbers! If the wind catches the front of the sheets, we'll be taken aback! Lee fore brace and the masts will come down!"

Leon hated jigsaw puzzles, board games, and was also bored by Yo-Yos. He hated to swim. He showed a knack for drawing, always in pencil. He drew strips of "Phunny Phellows" cartoons. More serious projects involved doing watercolors. Many of his pencil sketches were self-portraits. What did that have to say about him? I wondered. Vanity is hardly an anomaly when it comes to genius. Were not Thomas Jefferson's own self-edited "Gospels," in which he eccentrically created a Jesus all of his own devising—in the end, providing us a portrait of a man *very much like TJ himself*—a perfect example of such a brilliant affectation?

I took photographs of Leon with a new Nikon F his mother had lent me, and every photo I took of Leon was blurred—a diabolical speed blaze—except for one taken in front of the statue, *Blind Homer with His Student Guide*, on the Lawn there on the grass to the north of Old Cabell Hall, which might have been a reverse-metaphor of us. He began to keep a diary.

Sagacity was always big with him. He poked into books of all sorts and even read in the bathtub. The word "radioactivity" frightened but intrigued him. "If you catch it," he told me, "you sparkle blue from atoms, making you a ghost. And you can turn into an earth metal like radium or a gas like radon which makes you glow." He was able to draw in almost uncanny detail the workings of the inner capsule of the twelve-foot command module of

Apollo 10, that little nugget or diamond about ten feet tall on top of the dynamic Saturn V moon rocket that, traveling 24,791 m.p.h., still holds the record for the highest speed attained by a manned vehicle. We were watching hawks in the sky, soaring. "If I was a flyer pilot," he told me, "I would always look below and use clothes on a washline to see which way the wind was blowing."

I replied, "But what if it wasn't on a Monday—wash day?"

Without pausing he confidently asserted, "But I would never fly over such a dirty place." Oh yes indeed, blind Homer was me.

What Henry James called "the visitable past" were my last recollections of the original Leon, the master print, the vital boy who with open-hearted innocence, never self-conscious, would always jump up to greet me with a cricket-like chirp announcing such outlandish things as, "I know how to say 'I love you' in Chinese: *Wǒ xǐhuān nǐ*" and "A beaver's favorite food is poplar wood" and "The giant Pacific octopus has three hearts, nine brains, and blue blood" and "A bowling pin needs to tilt only 7.5 degree in order to fall down" and "Did you know that the Tenth Legion of the great Julius Caesar's was the most courageous of them all and when they were engaged in battle they were always ready to die, no matter what?" I checked later, it was true, he was right. That particular legion was often selected for special mention in Caesar's *Commentaries*. Leon told me, laughing, that in school they called him "The Boy with the Lightbulb Head," adding, "But I told them I also have a mirror for eyes, so watch out!"

With some money I had saved, I bought Leon a kids' bicycle, a Schwinn Sting Ray with a banana seat and gooseneck handle bars. He loved it and could be seen on it many a weekend whizzing around the Grounds—the University, very fussy about it, never used the word "campus"—squeeze-clanging his bell. As a fair exchange, he composed a poem for me—oh yes, he had a gift for lyrics and rhyme. Written in ink on floral stationery—I saved the paper and have it today—it went as follows:

The Road

A lonely road goes into the sky
to the far region of Never End
where boys and girls will never die
and the winding road will never end.

I asked him if he still kept a diary. He did. "Do you put all your thoughts in it?" I asked, lightheartedly. He replied seriously, "I write in it every morning. Diary entries made in the morning are crueler." He paused, eerily, I thought, and remarked, "A diary that serves as a friend is an enemy."

My God, I thought, *what a brilliant remark*. Most people spend a lifetime without having a *single* reflection like that.

But where was my brave commanding British naval captain and what had happened to all of the "Clew the royals! Look sharp there in the buntlines! Slack away those halyards! Spill the wind!"?

I returned to Charlottesville only a few times in those intervening years and always the first thing I did on my arrival was to visit the Beauregards to ask what Leon Noel was doing. He was never there. But if *genius* was the guiding spirit or tutelary deity of a person, as it was in ancient Rome, I invariably honed in on such a being. I slept in his room and was generally apprised of what Leon was doing—"up to" was more like it.

The last time that I checked I was told he had grown his hair long, played the guitar, and wrote poetry, and Professor Beauregard, who was now retired, told me that he wanted to go to MIT. I was not surprised. Mensuration—of any sort, of all sorts—always intrigued him.

I remember that in the eighth grade when, predictably for a boy, he took on something of a challenging persona and loved trying to guy not only me with questions, all reminiscent of earlier ones, questions of his when he was about five or six, such as "Can you unwind time?" "Why do hot dogs come ten to a package while hot dog buns come in a package of eight?" "Won't we run out of songs?" "How can so many books come from so few letters?" "Isn't a clock a scale that weighs twelve hours?" "How many eyes does God have?" and so forth, all of that, oh, about the age fourteen or so, he was now apparently posing to an older boy, a neighborhood friend, one who worshipped him, I had heard, but who had vanished just as quickly as he appeared.

There was a cheeky defiance in Leon at this age—when in something less than ten minutes, just for his own self-delighting amusement, but of course to impress us all, he boasted that he had figured out the 144 palindromic sequences on a twenty-four-hour digital watch: 00:00:00, 00:11:00, 00:22:00, 00:33:00, 00:44:00, 00:55:00, and so on, ending with 23:55:32.

A pedantic Leon was nothing new to me. Playing basketball, he would abruptly ask without breaking stride, "What is the base ten logarithm of 100?"—and answering "Two," keep on dribbling the ball, and roar away with a hoot. I remember a challenge. He said to me (I later wrote it down to remember), "A tramp rolls cigarettes from the butts he picks up on the street. He discovers that four butts make one new cigarette. How many cigarettes can he smoke from a haul of sixteen butts?" I guessed four. "Wrong," exclaimed Leon, disappointed in me. "He makes four cigarettes and smokes them, see?. He then makes an additional cigarette from the butts of those four! Do you get it?"

He presented me with a math limerick: "Take $(12 + 144 + 20 + 3 \sqrt{4}) / 7) + 5 \times 11 = 9^2 + 0$." He waited cheekily for an answer. "What do you have?" I was supposed to know? "Answer?" he would brightly ask, then boldly reply,

> "A dozen, a gross, and a score,
> plus three times the square root of four,
> divided by seven,
> plus five times eleven,
> is nine squared and not a bit more."

Upon questioning, he confessed that he had not created the limerick but, rather, had picked it up from a math book—by one Jon Saxton, for verification he showed it to me—which was only one of a number of books that the precocious boy kept by his bed.

And in his head!

To show his grandparents—and out of sheer admiration and a sense of personal history—I made sure to write down much of what he said: "'The lawn is full of south and the odors tangle, and I hear today for the first the river in the tree.'" It took my breath away. "That's Emily Dickinson. I'm reading her poems." "Did you know that you can make a compass by piercing a cork with a needle of iron and float it?" There were postcards he wrote to me whenever I went home to Vermont, often signed with a flourish, "Master Christmas." His wobbly handwriting went through three distinct phases, I could see, and, toward the end, the letters never touched. As I say, he was a capital mimic. I also noticed there was something abnormal about him—or was it me? I had never met anyone before whose company drained my nerve power so much. I watched the motions of his mind, its ebbs and flows, and the gleams that shot through it.

I once witnessed him at the age of eleven or thereabouts talking on a street corner to a man in a white suit, accompanied by a white Alsatian. It took place on Jefferson Park Avenue. Was it a dream? Some sort of hallucinating projection of horror? Looking back, I kept seeing a handsome man who keeps coming up to him to shake his hand. But I've come to believe they were in my dreams, that they never took place. What conclusions I should have drawn about this, if any, were beyond me. But there was an unsavory foppish graduate-school classmate of mine from a Jane Austen seminar I knew who walked a hairless Mexican dog, a Xoloitzcuintli, who used to cruise young Leon Noel, but in the unrestrained world back in the Sixties in Albemarle County that was par for the course.

On that subject, there was an aura of dissipation in the extramural world of the University and in that pretentious horsey country club world in general—lots of money, too much of it, excessive drinking, self-indulgence, marital infidelity, and hedonism. I had not spent eight years in Albermarle County for nothing. A weird Mr. Rapino, a local *flâneur* in his sixties, white mustache, European manners, used to walk the college grounds sporting a cane and often looking in the direction of young Leon when he passed by. He was idle, a purposeless and brainless ambler, but his glances of ardor were brazenly undisguised. The man's surname—how could one forget it?—bore in it the repugnant and unseemly traces, all at once, of rape, of the Sabines, raptor, penis, rapscallion, rabid, and rapacity. The way the man strolled, his swagger as he sauntered, had too much of the gawker and gaper about it—a "botanist of the sidewalk," as Baudelaire would say—and without doubt no small degree of unwholesomeness in intent.

More than once it occurred to me that he and possibly a good many others ascribed an unsavory intention to my own affectionate guardianship of Leon. In those days, Charlottesville society within its louche, sybaritic manners had a debauched, pleasure-seeking decadence about it, and I can only imagine the gossip that I left behind in the wake of my own blameless stewardship of the boy.

What had I missed? Poor Leon, what had he seen? How had he coped? When did he fully come to recognize the cruel world? Whom could he trust? Did I lose him? If his heart was unaware of his head when both seemed to fail his imagination, I can say—would say, did say—the same of myself.

I did lose him.

But, please.

What should I have picked up?

§

By the time Leon was heading into the tenth grade, I had left with my PhD from the University. I took a position teaching at Raveloe Academy, an elite prep school up in Massachusetts, where I helped get him enrolled, no great task given his test scores and significant high-school grades. I had earlier mailed him an official R soccer ball and some school t-shirts with the prep school logo. In any event, he stayed at the school only one short semester, a period when I was so busy that I rarely got to see him personally there. Apparently, he had in the way of a fracas become intractable in some way in the cluster he was in—I never did learn exactly what had happened—but he decided to leave and go home. His mother wrote to me an apologetic, abject letter. At school he had become a snob and rarely spoke to me—I believe that I embarrassed him, I don't know, as a ghost from the past, someone to whom he felt he was indebted—a person who knew too much about him. I was a direct source of his vulnerability and self-exposure After such knowledge, what forgiveness, right?

I felt heartbroken that he had decamped. I found out later that he was booted for supposedly having had an assignation with another boy and so sent down. The stiff-necked, unbudging headmaster refused to listen to my good arguments that he should be called back, that he was a worthwhile boy, and that there had to have been a mistake somewhere. I remember Leon in adolescence as a sheepish, self-conscious, very handsome lad. I tried to see him once or twice. At Raveloe I walked over to his room a few times that semester. (I was overworked.) He walked in on me on one such visit, yawning, with a can of Dutch cocoa under his arm and a handful of raisin buns. He shrugged and nervously avoided my questions. I had the impression he was unhappy with his choice of coming north. I also think he took up smoking.

I suspected even then that he wanted to leave Raveloe, and I pleaded with him, using many arguments—banking on his understanding of me that I loved him—to try to take a second look at everything. He was not cold but very remote as he stood there and said to me, "Your speech is full of ergative constructions, like Basque and proto-Amerindian." It was rude, and now plain that Leon was no longer with me anymore. I ruefully called to mind Antonio's quip in *The Tempest:* "The latter end of his commonwealth forgets the beginning."

I remain convinced that he was deeply puzzled by himself. He was never truly satisfied that he knew what the nature of his particular genius was. He didn't quite know what to do with it, although he tried out many different ways, none of which were finally successful. What in the final analysis is a teenager, after all? Self-conscious. In consequence therefore? Shy. And, so, as a result? Standoffish. Cold. Leon had an off-putting repertoire of all different kinds of disappearance. I received a ragged postcard, years later, one prompted by nothing I could ever figure out—one of the last communications I had from him over a decade, a succinct attack on Raveloe and the many overadvantaged students he met there. He wrote, "They reflected what I most hated about myself."

Who or what had let him down—and when? Had he nothing to love, no one to confide in? (Not me? Never me?) "A feeling feels as a gun shoots. If there be nothing to be felt or hit, they discharge themselves *ins blaue hinein*," wrote William James in *The Meaning of Truth.* "If, however, something starts up opposite them, they simply shoot or feel, they hit and know."

Whatever he did or did not do, Leon was fighting himself. It was, all of it, a zero-sum choice between success and failure, a gain on one side prompting a corresponding loss on the other, characteristically mirrorwise, where the counterpart of a likeness is but the echo of an image in opposition.

I would not see Leon again for two years, and even then it

would only be for ten minutes, no more, no less.

§

In a letter sometime around 1976 or 1977 his mother told me that Leon had decided to go to New York and enroll at Columbia University. I would check later only to find that he had in fact done so but that, according to records there, he had punted all of his courses and dropped out of school in the middle of his first year, just as he had done at Raveloe. Apparently, he needed money, so he had taken odd jobs, one in a sandwich shop, and another overnight position in construction, from midnight to six in the morning working as a sand hog in an underground tunnel in lower Manhattan. To me it was standard stuff. When is an actual visionary not mistaken for a hand for hire, was my thought, when was great intelligence not handed a broom? Within mere months he was charged with disturbing the peace and assault with a deadly weapon, the latter after hitting with a pistol some hecklers who made insulting remarks to him while he was waiting on tables at night at some beanery, where he became addicted to narcotics, and was sentenced briefly to prison for illicit drugs. Claire wrote and begged me—pleaded with me—to visit him which I proceeded to do, posthaste.

The weight of the brain must be like a hump, I thought, a distortion, like the bag that trundling Silas Marner carries as a weight upon his back, resting it, sadly, not on the nearby stile where logic would have placed it. Maybe that was why the poor miser's myopic eyes were set like a dead man's?

§

I flew to New York City and there on Rikers Island found Leon behind bars. I waited in a chair for him to come to a window. It seemed to take forever for him to appear. Noises, shrieks, iron clanging. I peered out the window and could smell the orts and sorts of the East River. It was a ghastly sight to see my friend. He was thin, spoilt, even a bit thuggish. He looked exhausted. *I sleep at night with my stuffy frog named Popjaw who eats insucks and chickmunks and he loves me.* His shirt was a rumpled slate-gray, drab his loose cotton trousers. He sported a ponytail and a silver three-bell bracelet. He promised he was going to reform and said he knew the way back. *A lonely road goes into the sky to the far region of Never End where boys and girls will never die and the winding road will never end.* I had brought, along with some cigarettes, several wrinkled photographs of us two sledding in Charlottesville fifteen years before. He hesitated, smiled wanly, hugged his arms, and looked away. Our exchanges were uneasy, desultory, mechanical, superficial, cursory, and lukewarm. *Why don't clouds fall down?*

Silences held. I would have greatly preferred not to be there. I could see quite clearly he felt the same way. Pity surged in my heart for him. I told Leon earnestly, "When God asks Ezekiel 'Can these bones live?' the answer was 'Yes.'" I stressed it "*Yes!*" Leon replied, "Except, Ezekiel was living in a valley filled with dry bones." I made no reply. He pushed it. "Right?" I could not find an adequate response. When saying goodbye, I can honestly say that Leon did not seem personally to be anywhere—it all might have been a jumble of past, present, and future, suspended in a cloud of unknowing. We spoke briefly and haltingly for no more than ten minutes. He did choose to remark, "I have been looking into your friend, St. Paul, struck off his horse—without a warning, I believe. Remember?"

I nodded yes.

He added, "Heard a voice?" then cynically asked, "From on high?"

He gave me an amused, sheepish glare, more than anything a grimace of embarrassment, I believe—or was it the prominent ridge over his brow that the process of getting a few years older had given him by way of strain, worry, self-defeat, and being careworn? For he showed a superciliary arch, a sort of valorous, vital balustrade that constituted an almost commanding frown, a signature of pondering, mentioned by Tennyson in *In Memoriam* as a "weighty bar, ridge-like, above the eyebrows." It was an aspect of Michelangelo's David, to me—itself thought to be a depiction, at least in part, of the great Italian sculptor himself—and considered by some to be a physical mark of genius.

"And I have been looking for the green stick."

The green stick?

"Oh yes," I acknowledged. "Buried in the ground."

"The one that tells about the perfect world." He noted with a despondent and melancholy coda, "I never found it."

§

An instant upon reading the obituary in the alumni magazine, I arranged to fly down to Manhattan on the earliest flight I could book. The following days were a blur of false trails, dead ends, distorted stories, inaccurate facts, flawed accounts, imprecise dates, and invalid deductions. What I did manage to learn, I put together as best I could to try to satisfy myself as to what had happened to Leon during his misadventures.

After his release in 1979, Leon located in New York City, and, hoping to get organized, apparently focused his attention on the so-called avant-garde art scene there. I am guessing at all of this from the spoors that I have traced and facts that I was given, none of which ever seemed conclusive to me. He was known by Lower East Side residents who had listened to his constant stream of abuse, police officers who had broomed and arrested him, and social workers who had helped him survive. I tried investigating his junkie life later and the quizzical patterns of his dark last days.

A year after his parole expired, he moved and became a transvestite in Boston for a year, then moved back to Manhattan, where a classmate from Raveloe told me that some time ago he had actually seen Leon partying at a club called La Bombola—straight people there, apparently, were as rare as cowslips in a hothouse—wearing of all things a green suede dress, black patent leather shoes, and a pearl necklace.

In the early 1980s, the utterly penniless Leon apparently disappeared into the maw of the city's vast underground. From what I gathered, he was one of the more widely known street people in the city and, if they were not wrong, among the most reviled. He wore a woman's red-checkered winter coat that some nuns had given him, or some good caring soul at the Catholic Worker, where he often ate and even carried a handbag when one day he got shot, in the buttocks. Very seldom is such a wound fatal. But like everything else in his life, the bullet went the wrong way. The slug almost severed an artery and Leon, barefoot and wearing a blue winter parka, torn, with faux fur, was found on a sidewalk at First Avenue and 11th. He was hospitalized for a period, I never found out where and never discovered when.

Were rupture and conflict somehow ethical necessities for him in order to repudiate by degradation and loss all he found missing in himself—as, what, I don't know, a confirmation of the stupidity of fate? An apology for wasting the gifts God gave him? A sacrifice for the sins as he saw them he committed?

§

On March 30, 1982, about three or so weeks after Leon's twenty-second birthday, three little boys playing in a deserted Lower West Side tenement found his body lying half naked on a khaki cot in a sad abandoned building with its windows boarded up. They found lots of hypodermic needles, empty nasal spray bottles with "methamphetamine hydrochloride" prominently marked on them as the main active ingredient, and no end of drained vodka bottles and empty gin nips, along with lots of religious pamphlets scattered on the floor. A broken red plastic radio. Piles of empty Rheingold tallboys, crushed, and a flock of empty white-wine minis. There was no diary. Piles of clothes from thrift shops sat in a bin. Nothing else was found but a hot plate, crusty pots and pans, piles of discarded soup cans. Old chairs. A few ripped magazines, lurid paperbacks, green whiskey westerns and sagas about existential gangsters. Filthy crack pipes. He was a "low bottom addict." Lots of nose-inhalers.

Upon investigation by police, neighbors who had seen him mentioned stories about blackouts. He had filled his arms until they were blue. He had first-stage cirrhosis. In ill health due to major substance abuse, depleted of whatever funds he had at his disposal, he had died, all alone.

Nothing had mattered anymore for him. Apparently,

with the many drug exemptions allowed by Federal Schedule 2 opening up the pharmaceutical floodgates at the time, he developed a dependency on Demerol that kept him hooked for years, the lethal mixes of amphetamines—speed—and other drugs with alcohol, the doses of meperidine, injected, eventually proving fatal.

"Why don't you have to starve in a desert? Because you might eat all the sand which is there. Why are the sandwiches there? Because there the family of Ham was bread and mustard!" The curse of Ham, a curse made by Noah, and not by God, but a malediction nevertheless.

A medical investigation had determined that Leon Noel had died from heart failure caused by an advanced hardening of the arteries due to his longtime drug abuse. There was no identification on the body, and photos taken of it and shown around the neighborhood yielded no positive identification. When his body went unclaimed, he was buried in an unmarked pauper's grave in a potter's field on desolate mile-long Hart's Island—it can be reached only by ferryboat—where all homeless, indigent, and lost individuals who have not been claimed by their families are interred. I went to New York City and on that bleak island which housed at different times a tuberculosis sanatorium, a boys' reformatory, a homeless shelter, a jail, and a drug rehabilitation center, I identified the cold, dreary, desolate grave solely by number, and distinguished the body by way of a fingerprint match at the New York City Police Department. "Abyss has no biographer," wrote Emily Dickinson, and she was right.

Although Leon Noel's name appears on the aspen-white Beauregard family gravestone in Staunton, Virginia—I visited one time to tuck a single small note at the base of the plinth,

"Lie here, beloved dust, until the joyful dawn," a line from the poet Nikolai Karamzin—it is a cenotaph in point of fact, simply because his remains are still interred in that godforsaken place on the bleak island in New York. Many burial records had been destroyed by arson in the late 1980s, among which, I later learned, were those of my awkward three-cornered boy.

I was a lamplighter of sorts and sad as sin to see those lamps grow dim and eventually extinguish. Did I choose to share everyone's pain? It isn't always wise. Still, wouldn't he be a lesser man who would ignore the spectacle of the vultures sampling the corpses and merely keep walking? Leon went from innocence to decadence. We have all seen people do that. Somehow as their serious desire to live implodes, failing to have been reinforced by many vows, they can cling no longer to anything good or meaningful. No one can reach them and they cannot manage to come back to anything like universal harmony even if they wanted. Something breaks inside them, the light goes out, they don't even know right from wrong any more. Maybe there is such a thing as Spiritual Darwinism.

I felt only pessimism.

My one question? It involved the old paradox. If a crocodile steals a child and promises its return to the father if he can correctly guess exactly what the crocodile will do, how should the crocodile respond in the case that the father guesses that the child will not—will never—be returned?

I remember that last day standing by myself out at the end of a dilapidated wooden jetty and in the blueberry-blue sky overhead hearing the screeches of the gulls and watching their aerial gyrations, their wheeling aspirations. I loved Leon. Looking into the past is like staring into a mirror, where only the obvious, the obvious alone, is seen. Who knew better than Leon? It would have been pleasant to be like Elizabeth Bennet, who at the end of *Pride and Prejudice* recommended her philosophy to Mr. Darcy, "Think only of the past as its remembrance gives you pleasure."

To me that made perfect sense, for the past filled my heart. But, I must say, my thought was ultimately Leon's.

I was angry at God.

He giveth, yes—but also taketh away.

Chosen Locksley Swims the Tiber

Heartily know, when half gods go, the gods arrive.
—*Ralph Waldo Emerson*, "Give All to Love"

Chosen Locksley, who was a highly precocious and extremely sensitive girl, always entertained strange and wonderful dreams far beyond the telling. She had the visionary soul of a solitary. Her parents, who both perished in a plane crash off the Azores when she was twelve, left her to be raised by two great-aunts, very strict, formal, and proper but benevolent women, old school types, who lived on Joy Street off the Common on Boston's old, respectable Beacon Hill. She lived in her fancies and was transported by the books she read that were kept by her bed. She was fascinated by subjects on nature, on the beauty of birds, on skies, mountains, flowing streams, and especially on the kind of high majesty, holiness, and artistry that she witnessed every Sunday morning in the memorable stained-glass scenes and figures of the Lady Chapel of the Church of the Advent down on Charles Street, which she had attended from childhood, the stone front steps of which, during the penitential season of Lent, many years ago, Isabella Stewart Gardner, the eccentric American art collector, philanthropist, and patron of the arts, humbly knelt to scrub clean as a penance for her sins.

The Locksleys were not Episcopalians, but High Anglicans, and Chosen lived with eager anticipation for the books read her by her aunts filled with sacred tales as much as she looked forward to the stories told to her in the Creole patois by the loving nanny in that family, lovable Louise—"Loulouze"—who had come to them from Sainte-Anne on the island of Martinique.

Old Boston for ages had established the family mode. The aunts, traditional and conservative, confirmed in their habits, rarely if ever varied from their customs, routines, and patterns. They bought books at Lauriat's, ordered their groceries and delicacies from S.S. Pierce & Co. on Tremont Street, dined out (whenever they did so) at the Parker House, belonged to the Women's City Club of Boston, celebrated Evacuation Day, visited the Atheneum, took walks along Beacon Street, often strolled through the Public Garden, had a lunch every day consisting only of a slice of iceberg lettuce, always with their favorite S.S. Pierce mayonnaise, served on individual silver dishes, and kept open the venerable turnpikes by which traditions long traveled made that noble city what it was in the matter of refining civilization.

As to their Puritan cast of thought, typically, the aunts voted for the passing of Blue Laws, enforcing restrictions on business openings on Sundays and holidays and even badgered the Boston Licensing Authority to require by law that the entire interior of all taverns be visible from the street, in the hope that citizens would be shamed from standing up to bars in full view of the populace.

Their old house, built in 1861, although re-wired, refitted for comfort, and generally updated, still showed in a kind of creakiness many Victorian carryovers such as dumb waiters, a wall-grid of buttons for servants, along with brass speaking tubes, an over-laden gas chandelier (elegantly preserved, if no longer in use), several Tiffany table lamps with crystal lace shades, and an over-stuffed horse-hair-covered mahogany sofa set on a Wilton carpet. All baths were in the basement, no water ran above the kitchen, and heat was furnished in only two of seven bedrooms.

From her small bedroom Chosen and her white cat, Heiglot, named after the angel of snowstorms, could hear the church bells ringing, which always sounded in her ears in dactylic bongs, *"Come with me. We'll follow the bells, Come with me. We'll follow the bells."*

She shone for her intelligence even as early as pre-K at the Karen Mitchell Academy. As she grew into her teenage years, she often dreamt of becoming a lady. She was tall, well-rounded, sensitive, innocent—and very impressionable. Excitable not only in school but in all she did, Chosen often gave her aunts pause but Loulouze always consoled them with an island proverb, *"Chaque bett-a-fé claire pou lame yo."* (Every firefly gives light for her own self). She had eyes as candid as water, they were gray, and perfect skin like pear wood, smooth and brown. Her hair was a dark chocolate, which she kept pulled into Dutch braids with a special weave, and her lovely high cheekbones were the glory of a face that radiated uncomplicated beauty. One of her great-aunts, when younger, had taught in the literature department at Wellesley College on the subject of seventeenth-century poetry, and the nightly readings that she gave, measured, filled with passion and astonishing images, inflamed the young girl's heart for poets like Herbert, Beaumont, Quarles, and Crashaw. She especially loved Richard Crashaw's daring metaphors. She memorized and loved to recite "The Flaming Heart."

Every morning upon waking, after she stretched, she would close her eyes and, sitting in her bedroom with its warmly enveloping smoky, anchor-gray walls, recite to herself by heart the stunning words of John Donne's "The Good Morrow." At school, she alone was selected out of the whole class to recite John Milton's lovely "On the Morning of Christ's Nativity," ending,

> But see! the Virgin blest
> Hath laid her Babe to rest.
>> Time is our tedious song should here have ending:
> Heav'n's youngest-teemèd star,
> Hath fix'd her polish'd car,
>> Her sleeping Lord with handmaid lamp attending;
> And all about the courtly stable,
> Bright-harness'd angels sit in order serviceable.

Chosen loved that expression "*youngest-teemèd star.*" It said so much. It spoke to her youth, her girlishness. It lifted her hopes like liberating moonshine. She always went to sleep with her cat at her feet, upside down and snoring, while she floated in dreams of the beauty of bright-harnessed angels.

§

It was in the spirit of Isabella Stewart Gardner that Chosen harbored her dreams in her young bosom. Mrs. Jack! In her day, the high-spirited socialite walked down the middle of elegant Tremont Street with a lion on a leash, hired locomotives to travel on when she felt that coaches were not fast enough, and even appeared at lavish balls with a devoted page in tow to bear her train. She smoked cigarettes. She drove horses and cars at breakneck speed. She cherished a particular pair of expensive diamonds and wore them like aerials in her hair. She was not above standing at concert hall doors to hand out programs for the recitals of favorite musicians of hers. James Whistler painted her portrait. Gardner also befriended novelist Henry James, who immortalized her in his 1902 novel, *The Wings of the Dove.* A dahlia was named for her, as was the peak in a mountain range in the state of Washington. She would not be cowed by disapproving Brahmins. To many blue-nosed contemporaries, her fashionable dresses were considered too revealing. In one famous quip, a man tried to insult her by greeting her with the query, "Pray, who undressed you?" to which she proudly replied "Worth," referring to her daring Paris dressmaker. Renewing herself in many difficult circumstances, she ever remained for the aspiring young girl on Joy Street, the embodiment of a strong and indomitable identity.

Mr. Warmouth, her ninth-grade teacher back at The Hiawatha School who saw her potential, always took Chosen aside—singling her out as a special star—and never failed to remind her that she had extraordinary promise. Overweight, prematurely bald, with wide ears that stood out like hackberry leaves, and eyes set very deep, almost to the rear of an unprepossessing flatness of head, he spoke to her in sighing, allusive language draped with erudition and high flattery, stressing the need for reaching her goals, while praising her looks, a matter often reinforced on his part by massaging her clavicle with the accompaniment of indiscreet crooning sounds and fanciful endearments. There was a reprehensible sense of insinuation in his personal concern for her. Most of his advice was characterized by a kind of verbal tumescence, with notes of longing and immoderate and undue adulation breathed through with unhealthy extravagance. It is the bane of many if not most prep-school teachers.

Chosen captained the swimming team and looked fetching in her tight purple swimming suit. The leggy exercises of her poolside warm-ups and stretches brought her his increased attention. Several of his colleagues noted that the blandishments of this balding instructor dancing attendance on her seemed to exceed the normal parameters of a healthy mentor or disinterested guide.

"I love your eyes, gray as smoke bush." He beamed over her and cooed with indulgence as he paraphrased W.B. Yeats,

> ". . . her hair is beautiful,
> Cold as March wind her eyes."

Warmouth tapped her temple. "O, but there is a wrinkle in your brow as deep as philosophy!" voiced he, dramatically quoting Middleton's *The Changeling.* He was a failed playwright but not without high self-regard, fiddling with his ascot, one fussy finger pulling, the other pushing, daily gave her advice of almost unparalleled opacity culled from his experiences, all about life in general, and most of it touching on her special sport, such as,

"Dive too deeply and you strive too steeply," "To drown is a way of desiring to awake," and "False ambition in the end only gulps water." There is in every control freak a streak of the sententious.

She could frown. When serene, her eyes seemed a perfect shade of winter gray, settled and soft like wisps of clouds at sunset in the Scottish Highlands, the soft gray of a cygnet on the River Spey, with a silver shimmer of polished moonstones. But when angry, they could change into the unforgiving gray of quarry rock, a passion of smoke gray like the hot ash remnants of a fire full of heat.

In her innocence, Chosen took this attention of his for elderly charm, not unlike the wonderful stories that her aunts told her about gentle Lord Melbourne and the utter absorption and incessant devotion he showed to the popinjay, young Queen Victoria, in her teens, always fatherly and affectionate.

He strove to appear intelligent to her and with caring regard pressed onto her a library card stapled with a list of important books to read, some of them middlingly profane, most of which were way above her. He needed her obedience to look important. But he desired that, if she could become more mature, she could come around sooner to the ways of adults, and it mattered to him in the eyrie of his private thoughts where he mostly lived, sobbing like a queer vicar trying to form a new religion over his one mad intimidating love, that she come to admire him as having had the profoundest influence on her while growing up. He proclaimed to her, "I want you to reach the outskirts of every adventure!"

Dreams piled on dreams. Chosen was never sure what she truly wanted to do with her life, as so many options occurred to her. She spent hours of longing and palpitating self-doubt over this. Stepping in, gently concerned, Loulouze was always ready to advise her, the piquancy of her phrases analogous to the tune of the music in the words she spoke, "*Chien tini quatt patte, yo pas fouti prend quatt chimin*" (A dog has four legs but she can't take four roads).

It was sage advice.

§

At seventeen, Chosen decided that she wanted to become a fashion model. She yearned to be a real "lady," to walk, to sit, and to stand gracefully. She imagined in her bright fancies that she would change her name to something dramatic like Lark or Yarrow or Sequoia, a glorious appellation that in a poetic lilting grace would evoke bright-harnessed angels. She craved to be thin and willowy. She would rouge her cheeks by rubbing them. She walked about her rooms with a book balanced on her head with apprehensive toe-taps and an ever-discerning footfall. She had read of believers who maintained that one could achieve invisibility for a time by eating fern seed. She drank verjus and vinegar. She sucked in her cheeks and gazed fondly into mirrors. She peered wistfully through her window, staring outside at a stick-and-twine trellis—poor clematis!—which became for her a symbol of the futility she feared in not being able to reach her projected dreams.

And what of her model moniker? She thought an exciting name might be Tarrience—a bold three-syllable appellation—having come across the word in one of the poems of the English Romantic poet, Anna Seward, the Swan of Litchfield:

"O! if in that wide range by Muse's powers
May lure thy tarrience in her cypress bowers,
Shoulds't thou perceive that genuine sweets belong
To the pale flowrets of her pensive song . . ."

But she felt that she did not seem worthy of such an elegant, mellifluous word, so instead she chose simply Yarrow.

She remembered Wordsworth's lovely poems—two of them—about the Yarrow stream like a waking dream, "unseen, unknown:"

"O green," said I, "are Yarrow's holms
And sweet is Yarrow flowing!
Fair hangs the apple frae the rock,
But we will leave it growing."

"Bostonians do not go in for modishness," proclaimed the older great-aunt, Aphra. Such self-absorption and conceit were fully abhorrent to an established Bostonian. "We do not believe in fashion," interposed Amity, concerned. "Fashions are trends and so in that sense are myths." Aphra pronounced, "Fashion dictates, does not prescribe. The nature of fashion is to become obsolete. Nothing lasts that is fashionable. Fashion, my dear child, is precisely what goes *out* of fashion." Aunt Amity agreed. "Fashion always comes to an end with ridicule, as well. Fashion shifts are always baseless. To follow fashion is a kind of conformity of the worst order. It is disorder." "Models are menials, Chosen. Mannequins," firmly concluded Aphra. "They hail from and—"

"—and circulate with theater people, yes, exactly," put in Amity, "from which cads, bounders, and ruin-bibbers recruit

311

their mistresses."

Both aunts not only disapproved of modeling, but the very idea of receiving money for *any* undertaking was cringe-making to them. Accepting recompense for one's work was abhorrent, something Brahmins never did.

So, both aunts, who adored the girl, equally discouraged fashion. "We *have* our clothes," Aunt Amity used to say, a convention in Boston, walking to her wardrobe and pulling out an old *fourreau* as testament, a black satin sheath or scabbard that well-brought-up ladies habitually wore beneath any and all garments that were filmy or transparent. Amity held it up high in proud display. Their fears were that Chosen might head down the wrong path by default. They believed self-indulgence to have too many corrupting side-effects and, in all instances—following what unsympathetic onlookers considered to be a "skimmed-milk caution"—found intemperance in any form a vice, refraining in the febrile atmosphere in which they lived from frivolity and excessive enjoyment, especially of the contemporary sort. It was an aesthetics of refusal.

Lying down on her bed, Chosen pondered their remarks as she daydreamt, wistfully considering the array of mating purple martins in flight on her bedroom wallpaper, alternately staring out at the Boston Common, and, sniffing the scent of a *phlox petticulatta* from a vase in a corner on a wooden pedestal—it gave off a scent like candy—she realized that, if it is affection in a kiss that sanctifies it, it is the passion of a dream to do something effectively about it.

Chosen took time one morning to walk down to see 152 Beacon Street, the elegant house in which, so long ago, the controversial Isabella Gardner had once lived. She stared up at the dimpled purple-glass windows and pictured in her mind the daring and eccentric "Mrs. Jack"—a small woman, although never thought beautiful, yet nevertheless attractive, with ginger hair, eyes of startling blue, and a china-doll complexion, who, to staid old Boston's disturbance, wore pearls around her waist and rubies on her slippers—sitting serene with her magnificent paintings and shell collection. The young girl stood there, figure like a willow wand, the eyes in her porcelain face reflecting the lambent light of adulation.

The legendary lady as perceived seemed to give the young girl's vague dream a goal and, in a bold awakening, Chosen experienced by way of a sudden resolve the horticultural satisfaction of growing up.

The great-aunts were serving tea. Both knew of Chosen's wealth, the legacy of inheritance from the family ownership of several of the old fulling and waulking mills up in the old productively manufacturing cities of Lowell and Lawrence, factory models for burgeoning America, going back two hundred or more years, and they were word-perfect on endowments of her patrimony. The Locksley fortune was not small. But thrift, management, and prudence mattered. Declared Aphra from the loftiness of her experience often after dinner as they sipped cups of tea, "The Worth dresses we bought in Paris we would actually hide before letting them be seen at the symphony." Added Amity, "Only a lowbrow arriviste or churl would sport them right away in order to be praised by the common public."

But Chosen, who was never refractory or stubborn, rude or unruly, was nevertheless strong-willed. Upon her graduation from the Institut de Jean d'Arc she decided to follow a plan of her own, which she knew in her heart was exactly what Isabella

Gardner would have done. She had been endowed with a trust fund earmarked for her to do something notable and noble, she knew, and so, exerting herself in the gentlest way, she arranged her finances through the agency of Squinch and Pendentive, Attys, and took a train with all her luggage to the heart of New York City.

§

Chosen registered at the reputable Barbizon Hotel for Women on the corner of Lexington and East Sixty-Third Street in downtown Manhattan. She felt very alone, so sat up in her bed those first nights reading from her book of poems, Crashaw's *Divine Epigrams: To Our Lord, Upon the Water Made Wine*, to try as always to imbibe strong steadfastness of soul. On nights when she could not sleep, she looked out at the moon in the night sky. She felt lonely and said prayers and wished Heiglot were there with his white fur to hug. What could possibly have been in the air on one such night when she heard the ghostly echo of her great aunt, Aphra, whisper from Crashaw, "I believe without any levity of conceit, that hearts wrought into a tendernesse by the lighter flame of nature, are like metals already running, easilier cast into devotion than others of a hard and lesse impressive temper, for Saint Austin said, 'The holy Magdalen changed her object only, not her passion'"?

And what did it signify?

Who could say?

But soon things suddenly seemed to go awry.

Her first interview went off poorly.

"You are an alder," quacked Faleen York, the peppery-tempered director who ran the powerful York Model Agency in New York City. A Levantine, born Irma Snitz, she had legally changed her name to the distinctive York in order to give herself the appearance of being an upper-crust Englishwoman, which of course did give her profile of a sort, as, for example, when Chosen spoke of her heritage and her wealthy great-aunts. They were the very first words that York had spoken to the girl as she flipped through some composite shots for which Chosen herself had to pay. Out of vile one-upmanship, as a cheap ploy for superiority and height, York had sadistically made her stand and wait in front of her desk while with lowered head she affected to be elsewhere employed, bustling about for certain papers, intentionally, coldly, dismissively keeping Chosen standing in one place and unobserved for four minutes. At last, she raised her head and stood up, not shaking the girl's hand, and told Chosen right up front. "Alder trees are the black sheep of the birch family—the easiest trees to overlook. They mean zilch. A person can live for an entire lifetime without being aware of an alder."

York huffed.

"Are you listening?"

"Yes," said Chosen.

"No tree is blander," said Faleen. "It has no flash in the autumn. Alder trees contribute nothing to fall foliage. The tree actually reaches out to beat *back* people who walk by, notoriously greeting them with whiplike slashes. After the god Zeus struck down Phaeton with a thunderbolt, he punished his sisters for mourning their brother's death by transmogrifying them into alders."

She was shrinking the girl in front of her.

"It is a soft wood with a simple, straight grain, supple. It dents and scratches on cabinets. I call it the 'poor man's cherry.' You should know that its fruit and bark are toxic. It is not especially dense." Faleen smiled. "I am obviously not a woodsman, my dear. We occasionally use it as kindling in our summer house in Amagansett in the Hamptons, you see. It is a lightweight, closed-pore wood, but is easy to work with, does the job, even if of rather poor quality, so therefore among common people some might prefer it." She shrugged. "*Franchement*, I don't agree, and, although it is quite true that it does not burn well and gives off too much ash, it helps when a house runs low on kindling. It is a—a serviceable wood. An appurtenance, so to speak. They apparently use it out there in the Pacific Northwest when barbecuing," she smirked. "when they are grilling fish or some other boondock food out there."

Tears filled Chosen Locksley's eyes.

"You're five feet, seven, good, standard waist noticeably narrower than your hips, the whole mishmash flows, feet a bit long, I notice, good in a golfer, I suppose, from the knees up everything is long, extra, extra. Overlooking that in some shoots will be a big ask. Does your very white skin bother you at all?"

Faleen did not wait for answers.

"It will show up rashes, is all." She shrugged. "We can hide them with a concealer. 'No daylight on magic,' as they say."

She stepped back.

"The point of the chin is called the 'pogonion.' Yours is not quite—oh, I don't know. Your forehead is lower than average. I can put up with your Steiner S-line, it falls just short of being totally bad, I can say that much, but not very little more, and I could do with fuller lips. Your ears flout a bit. There is a slight slant to your gray eyes, have you any Chilean blood? Your shoulders sag. Teeth, let's see? Mm-mm. You're tall. Were you briefly a bunhead—a ballerina? Yes? No? Doesn't matter. I can't say I understand your hair. Your head of hair has a certain road-crazed something or other about it, blasted, wafted, whorled, I don't know—what the hell, fanned." She waved an arm. "Well, how you get about the city is the question here, I suppose, huh—do you or don't you take cabs? I ask, because walking in Manhattan pathologizes lunacy." She spoke poniards—every word stabbed. It was all so confusing and depressing to Chosen. Did this woman want faces that deviated from the norm or that conformed to it?

"Gray eyes, mmm," said York, appraisingly standing back with her hands on her hips, "like gloomy skies and drab and depressing color schemes. Very little melanin in the front layer of the iris. A common color for animals, birds, and fish, ranging in size from whales to mice. It is the hue in Major League Baseball of road uniforms." She wagged her head with closed eyes. "It is a taste, I suppose."

"Athena had gray eyes," said Chosen softly. "So did Sherlock Holmes and Abraham Lincoln. And George Washington."

She knew that if anyone took the time to look deeply into a pair of gray eyes, what they thought about the color might be quickly proven wrong. Anyone looking closely into gray eyes can find depth and warmth.

Chosen dared in pique to quote. "'The gray-eyed morn smiles on the frowning night, chequering the eastern clouds with streaks of light.' *Romeo and Juliet*."

"Oh, we're literary, are we?"

"I only wanted—"

Almost strangling with anger, reddening, York repeated with a sharp ferric voice, "*So, we're literary, arrre weee?*"

She abruptly walked out of the room.

In spite of her lofty pretensions, Faleen who was crude—
she resented Chosen's pedigree—used language riddled with a
street rhetoric that thrived on irony and the acerbic and that was
full of discourse fillers such as "kinda," "sorta," and "you know."
Reproaches came to her instantly and without reserve and always
with unapologetic delight. Her thin shoulders, the sharp blades,
shining through her blouse showed the hunch of a raptor. The
rotatory chumble of her jaws always meant war.

"I see I have very little time left," announced Faleen when
she breezily re-entered the room after five minutes. She icily
ordered Chosen to step on a scale. "You weigh in at 119 pounds.
You need to weigh 113 and are advised keep it there. So, we have
work to do, mmm?" Chosen was silent. York was in her element—
brutal advice. "34-24-34 is a strive-for shape, so keep that in mind
when scarfing down your next Reuben sandwich or a pile of
frosted cupcakes. Baked potatoes and caviar do wonders. Protein
shakes are even better. Do you understand? A model must give
dimension to couture, but not by poundage." She stepped back two
steps to assay her prospect with cold scrutiny. "Where I stand, we
like tall blondes." She blinked, "Oh, and are you wearing a handmade cardigan? Lose it. Sweaters are a street accident."

A silence held.

"Did you hear me?"

"Yes," whispered Chosen.

"NFFP," said York, wagging a finger. "Not for fashion
people."

§

A rubbernecking quidnunc who resembled a mole rat, York was wealthy, but, like all snobs, felt insecure and, knowing herself, suspected deep down that she did not belong, anywhere, which never managed to diminish, however, but indeed informed, the opera buffa that she constantly put on of celebrity as she breezed by her models, criticizing this and that, going up and down corridors, always on her way to important meetings, throwing out assignments to the two or three subservient if not quaking secretaries clocking along in her wake.

She had scads of warning stories for new models, always speaking with the know-it-all tone so many New Yorkers seem to have, and it was clear that she had road-tested each anecdote. She was a harridan who when frustrated or opposed or both irritatedly snapped pencils. She dripped with ambition, which, draining her and putting age in her face—muscle anger—gave her the look of a crotchety old crone. Being perpetually cross, she bore on her forehead a deep frown shaped like a surgeon's knot.

All exoskeleton, Faleen lived only for her job and the power it gave her. She was bluff, blunt, unrestrained. Nothing of vision lived inside her, not the slightest stir of interiority. Her soul was shuttered. She often proudly quoted the late fashion designer Karl Lagerfeld who in all he did seemed to have come from a planet like Pluto or Uranus: "I have no human feelings." Whenever she made the remark, her eyes flared and her saurian skin seemed to pull extra taut around the hard insistence of her skull in a mask of merciless contempt. Irony was her only humor. Bullying was her joy. Faleen couldn't laugh. She cackled—like a villainous goose. What drove her was a lust for money and a love of control, whose reinforcing urgency was her ambition, and the periodic need to duck out of the room for a hearty nip of Navy

Strength gin.

York had had so many face-lifts that her face looked like a catcher's mitt. It was ironic that someone so unprepossessingly repellent, so unattractive in every way, a woman whose hair was worn bunched up like skittering end-tips of celery leaves and whose skin was flaking with psoriasis, could be so cruelly critical of others. She was notably flat-chested and box-angular with narrow but sharp shoulders and a very, very large, outsized head which resembled in mordancy the sour, po-faced queen of clubs on medieval playing cards, the one with dark, troubled eyes and a truly glum expression, promising to bite, acid, caustic, and scathing. "As I say, alder trees—I believe that their wood was used for 1950 television sets and card tables for the *hoi polloi*. They are ignoble trees. Lowly—and bear hideous catkins that come fluttering down into one's face without regard. Shedding! Jesus! I have had that filthy experience in Central Park. God, how I hate the idea of *anything* flaking! To exude! To molt! To slough! *To decorticate!* No, my dear, alders are as common as paprika in Hungary," she declared, putting an edge into her stainless-steel voice. "Their rightful place is ugly, mucky bottomlands in the wild. Nobody wants an alder's timber, OK? Hello, goodbye."

That hurt. Irony is a legitimate form of criticism.

But York temporized—she was only trying to diffuse arrogance and to lower the cost of the girl's indenture. York had quickly seen that the girl was lovely. There was no small competition in model management, and she would brook no opposition, especially from those rising new ambitious glamorpuss Italian fashionistos, parvenu rivals—slick, tanned, wavy-haired Roman Catholics from Milan or Florence in silk suits and $850

sleek shoes of roasted autumn light—who had lately been drifting into Manhattan capriciously to set up agencies to try with
their glycerin charm to steal away her beauty icons, every penny
of it lost revenue. "Besides, technically speaking, the sister of
a grandparent is your *grand*-aunt," said York, with corrective
cruelty. "'Grand' shows that it is one generation away; 'great' is
supposed to be added to generations beyond 'grand'—plus, you
have no portfolio." York was either loudly braying or, with her
pronounced overbite, muttering, with the result that all of her
words by some baffling transformation seemed to be swallowed
up—in-huffed—rather than spoken. When misunderstood, she
bridled, of course, and accused everyone of being deaf. "Having
no experience—"

"But—"

"Recency is everything," snapped the vain directress,
yanking open a file cabinet and sliding a complicated contract
across her desk with a battery of machine-gunning stipulations—
there was no question the girl was bankable—which in a routine
and coldly business-like way she proceeded to interpret, the
exactions of which amounted to a few noteworthy commitments,
namely that she pony up a hefty finder's fee, fund an agency pub-
licist, and immediately reimburse the agency for twelve sessions
of prints, test shots, and photographs all out of her own pocket.
It cost a fortune to gather the portfolio that she went lugging
from place to place. *Monetizing*, thought cagey York. *Money-tizing.*
Tithing money. Tying up the money. Eroticizing money.

"I've decided. You for purple—the color of hesitant mea-
sures. It is restrained and evasive, by which I mean reticent, and,
if you must insist, diplomatic. Exactly my idea of old Boston,
an outmoded old conurbation where one goes to be civil and

uncommunicative and—oh, who cares. We'll cycle you through different looks at first in billowing shirts made of taffeta, carrying a damson Hermès Constance Bag Box Calf with matching bracelets, buckles, twillies."

York's inspectional walk-around was like a periphrastic series of questions to which she alone knew the answers. It was as if a parade drill. Her sole benchmark in arbitration was, of course, what's in it for me?

A closet alcoholic who enjoyed demeaning subordinates and undermining challengers, Faleen loved the mode of interrogation and was adept at question prologues, baselining her victims with sly elicitations and behavior assessment strategies. She had an eye for weaknesses of any kind, checking for denial behavior and searching for reluctance. Overly specific answers also raised her suspicions. She looked for—saw, *spied*—nonverbal deceptive indicators, unintended messages. Did a prospective girl hedge? Look away? Scan the ceiling? Was that an exclusion signifier?

"I envision you in mood fabrics," York blatantly lied, hedging her bet against the possibility of obstinacy in a rising star. Examining Chosen with an intensity which seemed unmannerly, she continued circling her—her face seemed to flare with insinuation—and a ghastly and contemptible crack came into her voice when she reached the higher notes of admonition, "Serviceable linens, plain cottons, nylon. Do not be offended. You have a grittiness that will highlight nylon and polyester, textiles that are not damaged easily." Should the young girl have cut a caper of delight in her apprenticeship or bowed to the somber exigencies of the business?

"You are now in the fashion game, my dear. It's no bed

of roses. Anticipate call-backs, go-sees, composites. Oh, and be prepared for fittings. This business is all about *pins.* Pins and patience! Snipping, measuring, taking out sleeves, backs, sides, collars, hems, whatever. Armholes. Coco"—sardonically looking up at Chosen over the top of her eyeglasses, York condescendingly added, "Chanel?"—"was a nut on armholes, at least according to DV"—again, the look, the patronizing question, "Vreeland?" —and yet never got an armhole quite perfect, at least the way she wanted it."

Brisk, impatient, York began impatiently flipping through an odd assortment of recent bride photos that had been handed to her, rapidly flashing one over another. She said to Chosen, "You may take a gander at these, if you'd like. See those ornate bodices. Nothing to get aroused about. I would save you for the simple numbers." It was if she had taken an instant, almost chemical, dislike to Chosen Locksley, but it was only about money and power and domination. The young girl who stood before her was a shining beauty, and the guileful Faleen York knew it.

"What do you tweeze with—Kelly clamps? Get *aboard!* Invest in a nickel-plated corrosion resistant steel Aiconics removal tweezer. Expensive but worth it." She fluffed at her hair. "Also buy a bottle of Oribe shampoo—or Pureology Naro Works Gold, just as good. Start a habit of using Philip B. Russian Amber conditioner. I also want you to employ a Mason Pearson hairbrush, the professional stylist's mainstay. Oh, go and get a fabric steamer. I can see you need it."

Faleen York sucked a tooth.

"Do you jog? Start jogging. I want to see you running, not in sweatpants, but in a snug-fitting black and fuchsia performance fabric. Do you patronize trend shops? Have you any investment clothing? I am not hearing you saying anything. I won't tolerate a blank stare—hollow beauty just does not do it for me."

She snatched up her right hand. "Christian Louboutin nail polish would work wonders for you. No cheap lacquers. In general, the higher priced bottles in the best shops contain a higher quality paint, which means they should last a few days longer than the cheaper alternatives. Do a fashion re-think. If you're used to switching up nail polish often, cheap is probably fine for workaday Winnies, but if you want your manicure to last longer, consider spending the extra cash." She seized Chosen's chin and began turning her face one way, then the other. "No *lumière*. I see I need to teach you how to contour with shading. If your face isn't your fortune, you're a fool. I recommend Erno Lasazlo detoxifying cleansing oil. Avoid setting foot in the sun. I am going to badger you for style. Seduction is the female form of power. And no wrist-watch, I notice. Coco seldom wore jewelry, although she owned scads of it. Pearl earrings, only."

"I don't wear jewelry," said Chosen.

"Jewelry is made as much to adorn you, as it is to make you look rich," said York, reprovingly. "Still, you don't seem the jewelry type to me anyway—you know, *flash flash*." Was this girl going to be trouble?

York stepped back. "Do I need again to tell you a model's rules? Keep in shape. Pay the price. Visit a gym before you come to work. Have one boyfriend, no more, if you must have any. You must retire good and early. No nonsense. You never see a great model in a nightclub late, never. Practice your face, your walk, your smile. Do not look down. Never. Let's see, what else?"

She put a finger to her nose. "I hate eyewear addicts.

Arabs despise fashion, but I loathe Arabs, so we're even. California outerwear belongs in *Tiger Beat*, OK? Sandals, baby tees, serial killer glasses—ugh. Only the best chocolates are welcome as gifts, thank you. Never send me chrysanthemums. I drink only Gonzalez Byass Sherry Palo Cortado Anada." Without pause, she offered an ice-cold handshake. "You can reach me—look, I live over the store, like the Goodmans did, above Bergdorf's, but you best have a damn good reason to do so."

On her way out, a pretty model took Chosen by the arm to whisper, "A recent *Consumer Reports* study found that the longest-lasting nail polish on the market is sold for just $2 a bottle. I am not kidding. Don't report me?"

"I won't."

"Say nothing, please. Whenever Faleen comes to work in the morning, she is ready to bite the tits off a bear. The bristlecone tree? I have been the object of her wrath, like, for-*ever!* If she has one more face-lift, she can wear her ass as a hat."

§

Chosen, grateful, got to work. She was called "Yarrow" now. She washed her hair in dead champagne. She tried out various looks, powdering her hair with cudbear, a purple made from lichen and working all sorts of lotions and unguents into her skin. She drank gallons of water. She avoided almost all food, nipping mainly on dry crackers and black olives. She sat for manicures. She went for auditions, sat for many sessions, and dutifully posed before the many photographers who began to solicit her, twirling, pouting, pirouetting, dancing about, and walking kicky walks.

Several years had passed. Yarrow got many bookings. Her career was launched with great success. She appeared on a *Vogue* cover wearing a Gobelin tapestry jacquard with a "velour" of cut parrots and lions; in *Glamour* modeling a sharp bolero, sleeveless jacket, and slim tuxedo pants; did another for *Mademoiselle* attired in a series of elegant strapless dresses, all midnight blue, in satin and organza flowers. Glossy magazines courted her. The photographers loved her. *Outfits* loved her. Sunray pleats on skirts, down jackets, backs, blouses of framing décolletage, in luscious hues of rose and jade and sand—she seemed suited to perfection, defining loveliness in a dress, with nothing else required. She went to France for photo shoots, Dubai for spreads. She was able to watch the sun set in mid-afternoon in Iceland, the deep color of farm-fresh egg yolk, and then saw it set in an avocado green stripe in Japan.

She was so pretty. She became the cynosure of all eyes. Hairdressers flirted with her. Waiters in restaurants treated her with extra favors and frequently a bottle of comped wine. Gentlemen would fall in step with her, walking in Manhattan, to ask her out. Taxi cabbies would shout out compliments. A guy in a two-tone blue Buick Electra 225 with mirrored rims and a horn that blared "La Cucaracha" once screeched up beside her and offered her a ride. That was nothing compared to the fealty of others, suitors and playboys whose lavish generosity was excessive. One admirer had delivered to her a classic futuristic-looking Citroën DS-19 to have for leisurely rides. (She immediately returned it.) Another millionaire bought, paid for, and kept open for her *in perpetuo* a suite at the posh Hotel Ruhl in Nice with a balcony that fronted on the *promenade des Anglais* and overlooked the beach beyond—rejected.

Treated like royalty, Chosen almost bewailed the extra consideration given her. The attention to her hair alone, trims, waves, and flips, was too much. One night, she had a dream that the angel who took up Habakkuk by the hair of his head by the force of his spirit carried him to her with the dinner he had prepared for the harvesters that the food might be given to her, and she had responded like the prophet Daniel, saying, "*Thou hast remembered me, O God, and thou hast not forsaken them that love thee.*" Good grief, she thought. Am I that vain about my hair?

Traveling everywhere was an education; she learned so much. She visited old churches, art galleries, museums, flea markets. There in the Louvre were her grays again—the color she so loved! She marveled at the elegance of Corot's "Young Girl at Her Toilet" in her gray blouse and gray blue skirt. She particularly loved that painter's work and sought out what of it she could. She found among his drawings his study "Nude Woman Lying on Her Left Side" and "Study of Trees at Civita Castellana." She remembered his exquisite pencil drawing on gray paper, "Young Beauty with Arms Crossed," that she had seen at the Beaux-Arts Museum in Lille, right near the border of Belgium, where during a shoot she wore wooden shoes and walked the old cobbled streets where handsome young men walking elegant malinoises flirted with her.

Corot's grays are famous, she learned, softly gleaming, and familiar, his many shaded pastels and variants of restraint and subtle beauty, understated and cloudy like a woman's emotions. Chosen favored the color in her soft sweaters and shirts. Why did she love gray so much?

She smiled one night in Casablanca. It was the numinous experience of looking high into the Arab sky, so enchanting to her soul with the magic of its curved black bounty: "Two things fill the mind with ever new and increasing admiration and awe, the more often and steadily we reflect upon them: the starry heaven above me and the moral law within me." She had read those words on Immanuel Kant's tombstone near the cathedral of Kaliningrad, the former Prussian city of Königsberg, stating as it did the famous passage from his *Critique of Practical Reason* in the original German. They spoke to her, and she had written them down.

Was it possible that the aesthetic, along with the understanding and the intellect—look how far and how, through fashion, she had come!—was an invaluable assistant of the moral faculty?

She sought some solitude, even anonymity, whenever and wherever she could and almost always traveled in sunglasses with an army jacket tossed nonchalantly over an orange silk blouse and black trousers. She was on the go, day in and day out. She called on an energy she often did not have. She also went to see a doctor who once week would shoot her up with some kind of speed cocktail.

Yarrow was photographed on the sands of Waialua wearing a Buccellati diamond in her hair. A one-shoulder stop-light-red Grès jersey she wore in a smoldering shot at the City of Dreams Casino in distant Macau literally became a fashion icon and sold copies—mostly knock-offs—all over the world. She held sway in front of a herd of black rhinos in Lesotho wearing a Miuccia Prada black velvet, white sashed, tight-sleeved, ankle-length gown and a huge smile. They stopped off for a shoot in Basel where she had a chance to see Holbein's grim *The Body of the Dead Christ in the Tomb* and was moved beyond words, the holy body so utterly human, mouth open, his hands and face bloody and vacated of sense and already black. It was snowing and cold there and suddenly she missed her white cat, Heiglot, and hoped he was warm.

They photographed her in Burkina Faso in the hot desert with the striking blue men and Touareg people, savagely lovely in their indigo-dyed skin, and in Marrakech she sat on a camel half-naked wearing a glass citron necklace from Gripoix, the Paris firm unrivaled for the luscious sheen of its *pâte de verre*. They did a spread on her in Bali for *Elle*, a butch *garçon manqué* look, with hair cropped short. It was a real working life by any normal definition. She rose at noon, swam some, and like all the other aristos, decadents ands hangers on, she was *aller-aller*, lounging by European pools and drinking Campari-and-sodas. Day began at tea time.

One of the most memorable shoots she did was in the Louvre in front of the tapestry of *The Miracle of Saint Quentin*, which portrays one of the *post-mortem* miracles performed by the Roman saint in eight beautifully woven scenes explained in quatrains written along the bottom of the work of art. They shot a series of her in front of Raphael's magnificent *Baldassare Castiglione* and another in front of La Madeleine, the great parish church of the Parisian elite, close by the Chanel's rue Cambon, where a passing thought crossed her mind: *maybe I'll be married here!*

Yarrow became a household word. She was photographed for the cover of both *British Vogue* and *Vogue Italia*. She was one of four covers of *FLAIR* magazine and on four separate covers of *Serena* magazine's 20-year special issue, and three times the cover of *Vogue Japan*, a country—anything new exploded there—where young girls once caused a near riot when she made an appearance.

She promoted perfumes, gloves, new cars, shoes, hats, even plush wedding gowns. She was shot in jungles and deserts, on big boats and trains, in castles and huts. She appeared in commercials sipping designer water. She loved France. At a special installation at Versailles, she saw a display of Madame de Pompadour's jades, ivories, girandoles and her panniered skirts of silk and brocade with high whale-boned corsages and collarettes of lace, patchboxes, all lavish beyond words—Yarrow was momentarily given pause at the opulence that seemed in a way almost pagan in its expense—and even her dress costume as Venus, described as *"corps et basques d'étoffe bleue en mosaïque garnie de réseau argent chenillé bleu, mante de taffétas bleu imprimé argent."* Yarrow also sported veils, wasp-waist jackets—*guepieres*—snoods, rare jewels, and once, wearing a St. John liquid satin blouse in that velvety gray known as *gorge de pigeon* and chic maroon trousers, was photographed on the steps of the Basilique du Sacre-Coeur in Montmartre patting a pet caracal. She was mocked by her crew for stopping in to say a prayer.

When abroad, especially in Europe, always in France, Chosen cooked at night. She enjoyed an austere dish, when she mashed tiny pieces of Caerphilly with a fork in a tablespoonful of beer, a sort of dieter's *gougère*, which she gently cooked until smooth and ate it with toast—and Champagne! She slept late, rose with joy, and, waking, loved to sit at fountains and eat croissants in the sun and read Simenon novels. *Comprendre et ne pas juger* was his motto, a good one. She took long walks and saw films like *La Nuit du Carrefour,* the one with the two lost reels, which Jean-Luc Godard, called "the only great French detective film ever made."

She was out in the ocean of life. A close-hauled ship gives way to one running free. The question was, which was she?

§

One week, completely exhausted from three days of overseas travel, Chosen was late for a downtown shoot. Learning of it, Faleen York virtually assaulted her, barking at her into a corner with that raw, honking, vowels-as-diphthong New York City accent of hers and raking her over the coals. "Do not talk to me—'*tawww-uhk*'—about being busy. I have no time—'*toyme*'—for it, you hear me? Can you not grasp that? Can you never quite *ghrasp* that? *Ghraasp that?*" Castigation was her strong suit, a very special skill. "Do you know how lucky you are to be here? That was a YSL account! I mean, brand value, like Dior, Burberry, Chanel? Their ads 'pull,' missy. You get paid well, not counting all the perks: four-star restaurants, five-star hotels, first-class travel, theater tickets, front-row seats, cars, personal drivers. And the best clothes—the latest Hermes, Armani, Garavani, Prada, Lauren, Nina Ricci, all complimentary."

"But when the—"

"No buts! I want my people to *motorboat*—factory-direct! Fully-loaded. Rocks gotta glow red, do you hear me? We are talking ducats! The job is to bring in the dividends, do you get it? Yield. Profit. Mazuma! Scratch. Am I making myself clear?" Faleen scowled. "I will squeeze your asses until they fart cash! I will meddle, interfere, infringe, entrench, and, let me tell you, usurp your fucking pretty little faces off until things begin to go my way!"

Money, thought Chosen. Never anything else. *Money.* The word itself was stupid. It rhymed with honey only to the kind of grasping souls she was coming to dislike. It was always the same old diatonic honk, the prevailing key with only the proper notes and without the slightest chromatic shift.

Chosen's became a soft crucified face. Pale, mute. The virgin dragged to the feet of the Inquisitor in insulting presentation to behold obscenities, take the abuse which silenced her dry and unspeaking lips. Faleen was ripping mad. "Be up to the job, sister, or be out of here. Be on time, or be gone. Can I say it any clearer? Be grateful, or beat it, bug off, and be off with you. And, by the way while we are on the subject, try staying at your target weight, which buyers, trend-setters, photographers, and especially the designers all *expect* of you! Miss another shoot, I swear to God, and I will replace you with a boy or a stick insect! Do you hear me? Otherwise, I am absolutely not shitting you, pal, have a nice day—someplace else."

A certain decadence prevailed in the clothes Chosen paraded, the lipsticks she wore, the lingerie, she felt, in which for beckoning photographers, with head back, laughing, she heedlessly twirled with spirit and élan. It was no longer green, yellow, or a touch of blue, but nature seemed twisted when the glossy pages of *Vogue* and *Harper's*, calling for shoots in leotards, jackets, bathing suits, hats, and knit dresses, somehow always featured them—often dubiously with two girl models together—in new and bizarre over-the-top hues, like sorrel and puce, perse and ochroleucus, nankeen and watchet, nacarat and cramoisy, smalt and jessamy, liard and eau-de-nil, badious and haematic, infuscate and lovat, tilleul and atrous! Such inanity.

The catwalks were a pain. Straight back, core tight,

shoulders back and down, but always held in a relaxed and never a forced way. Arms must swing slightly, hands relaxed, all to help you keep a strong pace. One's hips, of course, must stay straight, and never move too much. Movement should come from the legs. The drill was always the same. As you walk, place your feet on the floor with confidence and style. Select comfortable high heels to fit, and get used to walking in them. It helped to try it with flats in order to learn the pace, before later adding heels. A strong expression must be held, oh, and look straight ahead at all times—you know, pick a spot in front of you and focus on that as you proceed. If you happen to fall, pick yourself up with good humor! Do not sit there, like an idiot! The key is to laugh it off, to get up—and to carry on with the show! Chosen knew it backward and forward.

Sly and scheming York would wink at her and pass on the advice, "There is a certain way a girl can walk on the runway or a ramp that is provocative and works. It is the 'Arden Walk'—Donn Arden? The choreographer? Out of Las Vegas? The best in the business. Look him up, and learn something. The act of simply twisting the foot swings the pelvis forward, which is always suggestive and sensual. When crossing your feet, if you twist right and swing that torso, you get a revolve going on that is just right, the way no woman should walk, of course, unless she's a hooker. But then so who cares?"

It sounded like pure nonsense.

"You're selling the pelvis, remember."

"Selling *what?*"

"You heard me, sweetheart. Wake up, for heaven's sake. Straightforward, homespun, and the routine, forget."

Chosen found her advice more contemptible than worthless. It was not her way, at least as she heard it. She wanted to look as natural as possible, understated, not cheap or flashy, not a commercial puppet—cultivated and unfeigned in the way she walked, in style, in presentation, in clothes. She favored neutrals, soft pastels, sober blacks, creamy whites, duchess satin fabrics and chestnuts and caramels with touches of russet and auburns and umber, sober black mattes. Svelte, slender and tall, she walked with an elegance that somehow belonged in white, tasteful monochromes, a minimalist approach to clothes. "Never order the 'successes' of a collection," she would tell her fellow models, laughing. "Don't buy a lamp, be a lampshade!" The wolfish eye palettes that she was often asked to feature, garish and tarty, she rejected. She had far more in common with the gentle Madonna in Fra Lippo Lippi's *Mystical Nativity* than with the trivial and unthinking shadow tutorials in *Elle* or *Harper's Bazaar.*

The York Agency meanwhile, fattening on her earnings, was always careful to flatter, compliment, and gratify Chosen while she sank deeper and deeper into a lush life in which she saw nothing overly dissolute, simply because she gave none of it a single serious thought, just went along with it day to day. Still, she said short prayers every night with closed eyes before retiring. They were a necessary solace for her, in George Herbert's words, "the soul in paraphrase, the heart in pilgrimage."

§

Chosen was not *en couple* with anyone. She tried to keep a refined balance to her life. Her daily dress was always simple, a camisole, black trousers, clogs, a gold bracelet, and maybe a fresh lily pinned to a Johnstons of Elgin cashmere cardigan. On the other hand, she could be a bit wild when she traveled, feeling bored under lights, sitting immobile for endless *toiles* and mock-ups. She would sip martinis or pear brandy. Once or twice, she smoked a cheroot. She even tried skiing on opium, encouraged by a few audacious colleagues of hers, after she became celebrated, a scintillating bright star in the constellation of intercontinental *élégantes*. She was a free spirit. She sang into the wind and wrote poems in the air with her forefinger. She stood never aloof or hieratic. She was always pure of heart and body, with a thinking heart. On outdoor shoots she would dance and prance. She would never fail on a stolen minute, in the city, to duck into various chapels to say a prayer or two, St. Patrick's or St. Thomas's Episcopal Church on Fifth Avenue, society's preferred place of worship. She was no silk stocking but a gentle soul, moving about the world with anyone, everyone, joining in, loved by all.

In the middle of a shoot on a busy Manhattan sidewalk, although they would be cordoned off, with a police presence, her stylists—make-up artists, beauticians, cosmetologists—while delicately applying mascara would go so far as to separate each of her eyelashes with a safety-pin, just to get it right. The young artists were male and squeaked, "The dark cilia—put up with the regimen, Yarrow—are fabulous! You have searchlights even an ostrich would die for!"

"I am a beautifully wrapped bonbon—*une* Angélique de Niort, *une* Prasline de Montargis, *une* Caramel au Beurre Salé!—in a Paris confiserie," she told *Le Monde* in an exclusive article done on her, laughing at herself.

A *mannequin mondain*, Chosen was nevertheless an innocent frivol who, pretentious at times, like so many models, lest

she offend, often feigned to feel deeply and emotionally concerned when it was so easy to do so from the luxury and pamper-
ing of a model's languorous lifestyle. She became a champagne
bunny, happy as Peaseblossom, and threw out air kisses and big
outlandish insincere hugs. Squealingly she greeted other models. Still, deep down she was herself. She loved to read from an
anthology of English poetry as she sat having her hair combed or
getting made up. Photo shoots became athletic contests, dramas,
masques, plays.

Photographers goggled over her, mincing about with
sharp directions. "No, no, have those smoky eyes *say* something!"
"Be crisp, come on." "Simpering. Too weak a register there," one
would complain and, lowering his camera, stand back with disgust. "Give it a minute. OK, reframe a thought. Give. Go over
the rainbow for me." "*Hear* the pose you want to assume. Listen to
your image." "Close your eyes and see what's imbedded inside."
"Lose the organza shawl." "I like the gloves, but keep only one
on." "Better, but put some skin in it." "Smile. C'mon, big time.
That's not a smile. Light up the room!" "Again, we're going to
do the soft jacket with the passementière buttons and silk Zou-
ave pants." "Costume change. You're down for the sheath dress."
"Moggy that face, sexy like." "Too tight in the jaws."

"What is it now?"

"Lean back more. No, further. Give some recline! Come
on, baby. Pooch that abdomen. I love that little fat pocket."

They would break the shoot, often fussily with great
impatience, call in make-up, hair stylists would be jumping about
with combs, consulting the mood-board, dodging screens and
lighting umbrellas.

"But here, sweetheart, it's not right in that dress," one

photographer told her, setting up his lights. "The great painter Modigliani always said that the beautiful women artists seek are impaired by the clothing they put on. Wearing the right thing at the right moment can change your life. Wearing nothing can make your name! Come on, just this once. Get with it, just the top."

"No, no."

"Yarrow! Lose the shirt!"

She shook her head.

"Oh, please Don't be a priss."

She refused with a weak laugh.

Comprendre et ne pas juger, she thought. Understand and do not judge.

"Come on, oh come on, sweet Yarrow. For me? *Spogliati, Déshabille-toi.* It's for art. Sweet Jesus, are you a prude?"

He began fondling the ribbons by her waist.

"Women of beauty worthy of painting and sculpture seem heavily dressed in their clothes and offend the gods. Come on, get naked as night. Alone in your universe. *Clair de lune.*" He stood back, set aside the camera, and, lighting a cigarette, pleaded with her. "Do you know how Contessa Christina Paolozzi got famous in a shoot in 1962? That's how. By appearing bare-breasted in *Harper's Bazaar.*" He smiled, coaxing her, urging her on with, "Strip, come on, off with it, baby. Be the Venus de Milo for me?" Chosen thought better of it and refused.

"The answer is no," said Chosen. She stopped still, unmoving, stared, and grew momentarily serious. There was a sudden and distinct change of mood in the room, a transformation in the air itself.

Standing up, the photographer asked, "What is the matter?"

Chosen said, "Please, I am asking you politely, do not use the name of Our Lord's name in vain again."

Long pause.

"You're kidding me, right?"

"I have asked you this before. If you repeat it, I promise you, I am leaving." She stared a drill at him. "I mean it."

§

Deeply concerned for Chosen, her solicitous aunts took the train down from Boston to New York for the Christmas holidays, Loulouze having purchased for the girl a holiday basket of gifts and fruit from S.S. Pierce & Co., Importers and Grocers, Inc., Boston's legendary provisioners (Chosen would later bring the gifts to the poorhouse to share them with the unfortunate). They greeted each other with hugs at Grand Central Station. "'Character is formed by compression: emotions and experience that evaporate in expression, contribute little, my dear child,'" said Aphra, taking her arm, quoting Lady Scott Moncrieff. To which Amity, nodding in full agreement, added, "Any pain, or want, or sadness, or disappointment borne silently only strengthens the soul." These were the immutable laws of "Cold Roast Boston," time-honored rules which stood for abstinence, sobriety, and self-restraint. It was frivolity that brought one down. Moderation reinforced an already strong nature and disposition. For Chosen growing up, daily, it was porridge and lessons, recess for play and lessons, dinner and lessons.

Although her concerned aunts greatly feared that too austere a strictness could possibly instigate rebellion, they knew their Emerson and encouraged Chosen's prudence and declared, "Finish each day before you begin the next, and interpose a solid wall of sleep between the two. This you cannot do without temperance."

The warm and affectionate visit of her aunts, these two sisters of her grandfather, along with the ministering comfort of accompanying Loulouze, greatly lifting Chosen's dampened spirits, reinforced the need by way of the celebration of their love to empty the day of its sorrow, even if it was further to deplete her of her strength. New York City was so big, the buildings so tall, the traffic so crazy, the ringing commerce so alarming—wasn't Chosen in her ambitions far too daring? On the train ride home, Loulouze assured the anxious aunts as she covered them with warm blankets, *"Cabritt qui pas malin pas gras"* (The goat that is not rascally is not fat).

Chosen, revived, began living it up again. Her high spirits took hold. She danced and drank, smoked and caroused, traveled about and sought to experience all the things that she hoped were worthwhile. Didn't Mrs. Jack Gardner jump into life with both feet? There was no end of false merrifying with all the snobs, extraterrestrials, and world culture vultures with their fantasies. She needed only enter a room for men to fall at her feet. She took cocaine and smoked pot and, laughing, drank full of Mephisto's wine until it turned into fire. She ate virtually nothing most of the time. She fixed up her apartment, Moroccanized with drapes, throw pillows, bright prints, and for fun at home began accessorizing a mannequin with last century shawls and démodé hats stuck with partridge feathers and wonderful buttons.

It was a world of leisure, limousines and luxury. Dom Perignon, Imperial porcelain, Meissen bone china, Vermeil candelabras, Fornasetti Nuvola Mistero candles, Scalamandre Gilded Leaf wallpaper, Burberry scarves, and a touch of the fragrance Joy Baccarat on her lightbulbs.

When checking into a hotel, she would flounce into the biggest suite, turn on the television, drop a favorite book on the bed to read later, crank up the air-conditioning, draw the blackest drapes across the windows against the afternoon, maybe light a scented Diptyque candle, quickly run a hot bath into which she would drop a splash of Ambre Nuit to luxuriate, and then, no matter the time of day, stretch and climb into a pair of her gorgeous red-and-navy-striped soft Brora pajamas, and have a long nap.

A paycheck she received once was so big that she walked up to the roof of the St. Pierre where she was staying for a few days and, saluting a full moon, drank a toast to the future with a stone-cold white Martini.

There were endless parties with Chinese lanterns that seemed to last for days. It was all so new. What verve, such levity, perfect glee, unending mirth, jocularity, amusement, and glorious pleasure. She oxygenated the room wherever she was. She loved a St-Germain cocktail, the liqueur with Champagne and lemon. She delighted in naughtily sipping absinthe with its taste of tarragon, sage, and wormwood. Her favorite cocktail was the Manhattan, its rich whiskey, sweet vermouth, bitters, and always garnished with a cherry. Nights without number, Chosen would sit back and tipple one bright red drink after another, the invention of which has been credited to the striking, voluptuous Jenny Churchill, the dark-eyed beauty who was the American mother of Sir Winston Churchill and to whom the young model bore more than a passing resemblance. For wine she drank only rare prestige "cuvée" rosé Champagne, with its aroma of wild straw-berries.

She felt untamed. But wasn't that how life should be lived, going directly over the horns, as Ernest Hemingway advised in killing a bull? Still, Chosen was always looking at Yarrow, even if Yarrow too often tried to ignore Chosen in her wild and rampant charades.

A chic pop poster of Yarrow wearing a midnight-black Azzedine Alaia femme fatale with a 1990s vintage sexy leather cutout hip slash D-ring buckle pencil skirt meanwhile had became quickly famous and was in no time selling out in shops across the country, scarfed up by adolescents, devoted high school boys, big fans, to pin up and ogle in the privacy of their bedroom walls. One celebrated *filles photo*, with her smiling and arched backwards, featuring her in an aquamarine bolero jacket and black satin jacquard trousers wearing black Saint Laurent Cassandra studded stiletto heels, became famous country-wide. Another provocative photo of Yarrow that brightly appeared on the cover of *Cosmopolitan* in a wedding-white Lulu's Sway Away white crotchet lace dress elicited a spate of marriage propos-als, as did the smoky purple-red-hump-me Schifosso wrap dress with matching dolly-dagger-let's-get-it-on Manolo Blahnik disco shoes, with just as many of those proposals becoming proposi-tions.

She was nevertheless coming to see fashion as a meme, a replicator, a servile mode of an acquisitional round robin to sell to rapacious consumers for money to spend on even more mate-rial things to buy. Could her Aunt Aphra have been correct when she told her, "Fashion is not—and never was—art"?

§

One evening heading into a grand New York Fashion Week party, Faleen York noticed Chosen, halfway up the stairs, stop to return and quietly give a begging hobo in an old overcoat a twenty-dollar bill. York turned to her to say, "You went and shmeared that old crumb-bum with a twenty? I could *plotz!*" She grabbed Chosen's arm to squawk, "Charity—your besetting sin. My god! You have an infatuation with sacrifice. I saw it from the first. Look, leave dirty old shlumbergers in doorways like that to get rat bites, and keep on moving! You should know better. It's a loser's game." But Chosen was always a committed infracaninophile—a friend of the underdog. It disgusted her boss. Faleen had long felt that Chosen was throwing shade, claiming the foreground. "You're fasting, like a fairy. It is giving you a horrible lion's wrinkle on your forehead, look"—she tapped Chosen between the eyes—"a worry line. It spooks photographers, for fuck's sake! Slim I can take, but you are getting too cadaverous. Wonderful for drapery, but like a broom, what the French call '*sèche*,' too dried, far too *unappealing!* Call it what you want, meager, scant, *maigrelet*, emaciated, I don't give a care, just do something about it, and the trousers you're wearing? I loathe ostrich skin—especially when it is beginning to look exactly like your own." She snorted and butted on ahead. Like all bitchy magazine editors, she took her office *au grand serieux*, very much *au plus grand.*

"I have also heard that you made a *pro bono* catwalk appearance at a charity fashion show in D.C. *Why?* Washington, D.C, is a dowdy fashion wasteland and always has been. Why waste your time? In any case, I don't go for the freebies. We give nothing away. Do it again and you'll be sorry."

With Faleen and Chosen, it was gravity versus buoyancy, push competing with pull, with subsequent surface tension. One ineluctable force pulling down, the other trying to keep things afloat. As with a turgid sea, the buoyant force was proportional to the volume of fluid displaced. When an object floats, the buoyant force balances the force of gravity. When it sinks, gravity wins.

Faleen York always won simply because she refused ever to lose. That was the nature of the business. Her business.

Chosen stood chastised, only bewildered by the alternate charges of fat and thin, but she kept on with her schedules, not stopping for a minute, aided by hourly tumblers of vodka or scotch. It was a high life, indeed, but she often felt low. Hollow. A light would shine in her eyes and then flicker out. Her smile rarely reached her eyes anymore. It was frustrating simply because smiling was the one thing that she was most often required to do. Smiling falsely is frowning. She found herself now often constipated and got cold hands and feet, suffering, it turned out, from odd bouts of ischemia, a deficiency in blood supply to parts of her body. She gulped painkillers by the handful and drank ipecac syrup to stay thin but got diarrhea and croup. Her psyche began to fissure. Time passed. *Clack, clack, measure, measure, snip, snip, snip* went the three ancient Greek Fates—Clotho, Lachesis, and Atropos.

One day dressing in front of a mirror, she was alarmed at what she saw, and she pressed her nose closer to it and heard *You cannot see the mountain near.* Wasn't that what Emerson had said? She stepped back and took a good look at herself.

Was this what it was all about? So much of it felt so hollow.

She had learned much and what she read of the soullessness of high life seemed pointless. Coco Chanel? She never married, she was unable to bear children, she was notoriously shrewd, small-minded, petty, and jealous. The woman pulled apart clothes she'd made the previous day, then reworked them for the following day. She took a German Nazi officer as her lover and even cooperated with high-ranking Nazi officials, only to be exiled in Switzerland for nearly ten years because of it. She ended up bitter and alone.

Chosen stopped drinking alcohol and now began strictly limiting herself and as a hedge against *de corruption et d'abus* sipped only spicy limeade, kombucha, Agua de Jamaica, and root beer. Wanting to be alone for a while, she took a break that winter and, telling nobody, drove up to one of the old resort hotels on the coast of New England, up around Kennebunkport, a tall, rectangular, narrow hundred-room inn perched on a bluff overlooking the ocean and washed by cold light. Wrap-around porch, wide verandas, wicker furniture. No ostentatious luxury.

Chosen sat looking out at the crashing gray breakers. What exactly was she listening for? More importantly, what was she hearing beyond the crashing waves, the gray solitude, the pounding sea?

Fashion was all about compliance. But faith was about insurrection—a mutiny against the obliging acceptance of things. It lived in harmonious union with the spirit in revolt against its own time. That was what she wanted and what Isabella Stewart Gardner knew! We must never settle, surely, but become *disturbed*—a disruption of awakening! Wasn't it out of this conspiracy that one grew up? In contrast, conformity robbed one of vision. Only from an anguished protest can we emerge, she rea-

soned, never by calm consent. Whatever is placed in the service
of merely consoling us is really a curse, opposing the possibility
of personal dignity. She perceived that person alone has worth
who finds the mystery in what is ordinary and can transform a
solution into a *problem!* She had adapted and accepted and complied.

Her problem was she was *not* distraught!

She needed rebellion.

For now, she decided she would strive for more harmony
and perfection in her fashion preferences, learning what years
before Yves Saint Laurent in a knowing way tastefully referred
to as the "silence of clothes," seeking when she could to display
clothes that enhanced but did not overtake a person.

Personhood *mattered!*

§

One day out of the blue, astonishingly, her old teacher,
Mr. Warmouth, wearing a long bright yellow necktie, confidently appeared in the lobby at the Barbizon Hotel for Women,
inquiring for the celebrated fashion model Yarrow, the lovely
mononym, slim-sounding and elegantly exotic, that the young
woman had adopted as her professional name. She had also
changed her address and was now living high in a smart designer
suite at the St. Regis Hotel. Warmouth quickly hastened over to
East 5th Street. Waiting for his former pupil, he buttonholed the
surprised young woman just exiting a taxicab directly in front of
the hotel.

"Chosen! Lovely Chosen! At last, we meet again," he
hooted heartily upon seeing her and with goggling humor gave

her a huge bear hug. He dramatically stood back to surveil her. "Your eyes, limpid, so beautiful, gray pools from which the morning mist has lifted." She was stupefied. "I want you to appear in my plays," he explained. "I need you. You need me," he squawked loudly, stepping forward, then wheedling up to her with such an inordinate lack of decorum that it invited several people on the sidewalk to stop and stare. Feeling uneasy, she saw with sudden shock that something had been confirmed. She had unexpectedly received several letters from Warmouth in the past, disturbingly ardent ones. She suddenly felt ill, for he was just now literally standing there in front of her. While previously she had tried to face the problem by ignoring it, there was here all of a sudden a flooding of the bulkheads. "They are peddling you like suds," he said. "Only this afternoon I witnessed on the street a greasy Seventh Avenue garmento in a bespoke suit and slick nigger haircut holding up a photograph of you to a bunch of churls and making all sorts of lustful remarks."

Chosen, who had just finished a shoot, was wearing a sheer raw silk skin-tight pastel rose evening dress and never looked more beautiful. At first absolutely stunned, she was then horrified. "Were y-you *spying* on me?" she asked the man, almost breathless, standing there right on the public sidewalk.

"Listen," he said. "Look," he pleaded. "Please. Will you look at me? No, don't turn away," he said importunately, a demand that almost seemed in its angry insistence to be almost a comminatory threat. "I've been walking around in this crapulous city for almost a full day, bumping through ugly crowds. I have come to take you home." She had no idea what to do, stepping left and then right to get out of his way. She kept turning her hands over and over, rinsing them. "But here, my dear, let me look at you—let me give you some room and admire."

Mr. Warmouth, grinning, saw what he could own.

Stepping back off the curb, he was immediately walloped by a truck, bow-knifing into the air, and was instantly killed. Looking up, Chosen saw with shock that on the side of that New York crate-shaped delivery vehicle knocking the fat man ass-over-wattle was a full-scale perfume photo-advertisement color poster of herself wearing that black Azzedine Alaia femme fatale with a 1990s vintage sexy leather cut-out hip slash D-ring buckle pencil skirt! It was if preternaturally in that fatal event her eyes had finally opened to see how hollowly vain and pointless a life she was living, how in her world madness took such terrible precedence.

Racism? Drug addiction? Shootings in schools? The homeless sleeping on grates? The growing poor, the disenfranchised, the losers and the lost? Military escalation? Obscene movies? Thieving Wall Street brokers? Vanity in magazines? Corrupt politicians? Inane television shows? Biased cable news? Lack of privacy? Video porn? Saturation advertising? Buffoons on the radio? Churches locked? Library hours curtailed? Processed foods? Class warfare? Commercialized sporting events? Broken infrastructure? Street crime? Pollution everywhere, in the air, on land, in cities, even on the high seas? Christmas secularized? Decade-long wars?

This was not living, this was existing.

Suddenly, she fainted, falling like a trayful of crashing crystal. When she was brought to her feet, dazed, a policeman took her inside the hotel to comfort her. It was then that she heard a soft voice from somewhere calling to her, a gentle comforting voice. Was someone speaking directly to her? If so, who?

Concentrating on the sudden and overpowering manifestation she felt, she struggled to see, as if through a fog, how it signified. It all came to her in a sudden epiphany.

Striving is fakery. Fashion is artifice, she realized, all of it glitz, one level below flash. She suddenly recalled with regret the Pompadour displays she had seen at Versailles and sumptuous squandering and superfluousness of expense. Fashion is fakery, striving artifice. Now look where she was! She found herself inside some odd hotel, in a strange hallway, staggering, where she stood while shivering in a corner and feeling a terrible darkness. She now realized with a sudden intuition that without God she was never happy, never satisfied, never at peace, and, along with that, the brevity of life hit her—in thunderous shock—like an earthquake.

And like drifting mists that gather above a gliding river, Wordsworth's gentle words came to her as a reminder,

> "If Care with freezing years should come,
> And wandering seem but folly—
> Should we be loth to stir from home,
> And yet be melancholy;
> Should life be dull, and spirits low,
> 'Twill soothe us in our sorrow,
> That earth has something yet to show,
> The bonny holms of Yarrow!"

The selfishness of her vain pursuits came home to her, as immediately she thought of Isabella Stewart Gardner scrubbing the steps of the Church of the Advent. She saw again the purple martins on her wallpaper, the struggling clematis. "I had a dream. I made it out of a mouthful of air," she whispered to herself and thought this: *With whatever terrible darkness surrounds me, dear Lord, let me be content, only pray me into goodness that my ways become immaculate to God.*

§

At her wit's end, alone that night in the hotel, Chosen took up a Gideon Bible randomly, closed her eyes, pointed—arbitrarily—to Romans 2:4, it turned out, and she read: "Or do you despise the riches of His goodness, forbearance, and long-suffering, not knowing that the goodness of God leads you to repentance?" Suddenly Chosen began to tremble. She shook, sobbing, her hands shaking, trembling, her entire body shuddering now with an unquenchable thirst for closeness with the Lord and the comfort of his saving grace. From somewhere far like a distant echo, she heard her nanny Loulouze whispering over and over in her creole patois, "*A jounou pas ayen, ce priédie qui mait*" (Kneeling is nothing, praying is hard).

Immediately came to her as if out of the blue in the whispered words of her many mornings the echo of John Donne's words,

> "I wonder, by my troth, what thou and I
> Did till we loved? Were we not weaned till then?
> But sucked on country pleasures, childishly?
> Or snorted we in the Seven Sleepers' den?
> 'Twas so; but this, all pleasures fancies be.
> If ever any beauty I did see,
> Which I desired, and got, 'twas but a dream of thee."

In her wild confusion, Chosen prayed, "O God, I submit

my affection to thee, even my affectations, beseeching thee to save me from vanity and the follies that I have pursued. For my salvation take from me all particular objects of desire, for harmless they may be in themselves, they remain a distraction to my soul. Grant me a change of heart that I may refrain from what I was so hungrily, so greedily flying to. In your blessed mercy alone is my salvation. Preserve me from the extravagant infirmities into which I have fallen and please redeem me. Amen."

Chosen then disappeared. Nobody knew where she had gone or when. She could not be reached. There was not a trace of her to be found anywhere. For weeks it was as if she had vanished from the very world itself.

The York Agency, meanwhile, was furious. When the young model's absences and missed appointments mounted up, as the scandal of her disappearance fully broke, at the bright glaring cost of significant income, Faleen York unleashed a freshet of obscenities and, running to her cabinets, yanked out her personal file, which she shuffled to read in anger and then virtually bit in two. She sat down and began snapping pencil after pencil and hurling the bits into the air, raging over her fate, scratching at the nervous irritation on her wrists until the skin was raw. When she then learned of Chosen Locksley's specific whereabouts, being simultaneously advised by the formal request of Squinch and Pendentive, Attys, that the entire sum of that individual's money, along with any and all of her residuals, be forwarded to a convent somewhere in New England, York went ballistic—she leapt in the air—almost foaming at the mouth and herniating. "What? *What?* I knew it! The insubordinate snipe! The pretentious ungrateful rat! A lickspittle! A hustling *septième arrondissement* tart!"

Nobody could calm her down.

In her wrath like a snake with a broken spine, York bit herself and sank the venom of spite into her own vein.

"She was *worse* than the alder I suspected she was! Toxic in fruit and bark! She was a stinking box-elder—a filthy trash wood commonly used to turn small, disgusting inconsequential objects, hideous *tchotchkes*, junk and dross for wood-pulp, for charcoal, for chintzy fruit boxes, and monkey crates. She was vainer than Cassiopeia, all that fussing with her hair! I wish her *dooooom!* A lost revenue stream! I knew it!" howled Faleen York, madly hurling papers into the air and cranking her office windows open and bellowing scarlet, "*The little bitch went and swam the Tiber!*"

Where had Chosen Locksley gone?

She had taken a long train ride that very week on a rainy gray January day to go on retreat to a Trappistine Convent in Wrentham, Massachusetts, where she told Mother Abbess, "I have hearkened to a voice that was the softest I've ever heard."

"That was a call for you, dear child, from the counselor beside you. 'The comforter, which is the Holy Spirit, whom the Father will send in my name, and he shall teach you all things.' John 14:26. The Greek word is *paraclete*, and the literal translation would be 'one called alongside.' It is a word that appears nowhere in all of the New Testament, except in that discourse recorded by John."

"I am astonished to find myself here, to be where I am. I am undeserving of the sacredness of this holy place."

"Jesus himself could be astonished. So, why not you? The word 'to marvel' or 'to stand amazed'—*thaumazo*—is common in the Gospels. But it's almost always used in connection with the crowd's response to Jesus, for they are usually the ones amazed or marveling, not Our Lord. There are only two times in the New Testament where Jesus is said to marvel, in fact. One is in Mark 6:7 where Jesus marvels at the unbelief in Nazareth. The other occasion is in Luke 7:9 where Jesus marvels at the Roman centurion and his great faith. These are the only two times we have record of Jesus marveling. And why did he have to be consistent? He marveled both at the presence of faith, and at its absence."

Mother Abbess took her hand.

"Note that Jesus offers to go to the centurion's house in order to perform a healing for that man's servant who was ill, but the centurion—whose loving compassion extended even to a lowly subordinate—hesitates and suggests that Jesus's word of authority would be sufficient. We walk by faith, not by sight."

Chosen inquired of the Mother Abbess, "Was Jesus speaking to me in such an obliging way? What was his message?" She bluntly exclaimed, "I am such a failure. I have failed my aunts, I have failed myself, I have failed God. I have become so vain. Please tell me, what has become of me? Where can I find peace? How can I improve?" She wept softly into her hands, looking up as she interposed herself only to add, pleadingly, "Do I ask too many questions?" adding right away, mortified, "Look there is another one, correct? And yet another! I apologize from my heart, dear Mother." She would always remember that memorable day, for she heard the sisters singing "*Justus ut Palma florebit*" in a Mass for the feast of St. Lucy, Virgin Martyr.

"Be not afraid, my child," said the kind Mother Abbess. "In the Holy Gospels, Our Lord Jesus himself asks as many as 290 questions. What is seeking but aspiration? What speaks to the soul escapes the ability of our poor human measurement fully to know it. 'The lust for fame is the very last vice that wise men shake off.' That is the Roman historian Tacitus speaking, a writer who in his *Annals* actually provides a non-Christian confirmation of the crucifixion of Jesus." She embraced the young girl's hands. "Learn to be humble. Fashion always fades, sweet child."

"I know that. I have come to see that."

"Seek that which does not. St. Paul himself knew the bitter failure of following the world's way instead of God's," said Mother Abbess. "Shall I tell you how?"

To this, Chosen nodded.

§

"At the ancient city of Athens, St. Paul made exactly two converts, Dionysius and a woman named Damaris. No more. I have no doubt it was a shock to him," said Mother Abbess. "His talks with them proved to be a great failure there. Was it the view from the high hill that took his attention? The lofty laws discussed? The philosophers who had flattered him by their invitation? Their strong Stoic history? Their Epicurean wisdom? The intellectual sophistication of the Areopagus and legends of the place? We know that he left the city immediately after his address to the Athenians on the Hill of Ares—Acts 17:22–34—and walked all the way to Corinth. No man of faith in all of history was ever so undaunted. He never went back to Athens again, never wrote a letter to the Athenians, and there is no record that he established a church at Athens. Nothing has ever been written of the results of that ministry. Why did he fail? For he himself saw he failed in the matter of humility. How so? He had failed to mention to them the name of Christ and His Crucifix. It was the result of trying to appease them in the fashionable way *they* lived—by accommodation. Do you understand, my child?"

"I do, I do, Reverend Mother," said Chosen.

"He had joined them intellectually."

"I do not want to conform."

Mother Abbess earnestly continued. "St. Paul visited Corinth after leaving Athens—Acts 18:1—and he later wrote to remind them, significantly, how he had come to them preaching 'Christ crucified' and not as he had at Athens, mistakenly, speaking 'with lofty speech or wisdom,' quoting their philosophers and poets which at the time was all the fashion there. Forgive me, this is what is called *eisegesis*—reading into something—rather than exegesis. I only wanted to tell you that ever after, whenever he set out to preach, I am certain that St. Paul repeated to himself over and over, 'I am resolved never to make that mistake again.'"

"I understand."

"It is the heart that tells us what we are."

Came a long pause.

"Am I—am I an alder?" asked Chosen, timidly. She looked up; she had been weeping into her hands, hands she was squeezing imploringly as she reflected not only on St. Paul but on Isabella Stewart Gardner and her humility.

"Why *not* an alder? You are tall, stalwart-strong and brave. Half of the City of Venice is built on alder piles, did you know that?" replied Mother Abbess, kindly, gently caressing Chosen's shoulder with her compassionate hand. Chosen smiled. A flutter of purple martins, so long gathered there, flew out of her heart. She realized with joy that faith in Christ and repentance are inseparable. Faith in Christ burst her heart with joy. She had a rising insight now into the mystery of God's love, and, feeling purged of all her follies, now felt as white and wild as the withy wind.

"I want to look beyond, not behind. Is it possible?"

The older nun tapped the beauty's knee. "One day when the painter Corot was at his easel outdoors, a passerby stopped to scrutinize his picture, peering closely, saying he recognized the sky and the trees, but, shaking his head, saw that there was no lake on the canvas which appeared in the natural scene, so where was it? Without pausing, the painter replied tersely, 'It is behind me.'"

Corot, her gray painter! In Mother Abbess's habit, her cassock, she saw the very color she loved, the one most commonly worn by peasants and the poor, warm grays, receiving grays. Was that it, was that the secret of the color for her? It was the color of ashes, as well as a Biblical symbol for repentance, described as sackcloth and ashes. It was used during Lent and on special days of fasting and prayer. As the color of humility and modesty, gray was worn by friars, monks and priests in the east and the west in the sleeved grays, browns, and blacks of the outer robe. She recognized at last the life-long pull it seemed to have for her. Gray, the intimist's most spectacular triumph—*to achieve intimacy with the visible and the spiritual heavens.*

Mother Abbess then said to Chosen, "'The meaning of anything is to be found in its fruits, not its roots,' or so declared Professor William James of Harvard. It was he who also said that one can never truly know a person until one fully knows what gives that person joy. I feel such joy emanating from you. There can be no difference that does not *make* a difference. Do you see, dear child? But there is a permanence." She folded Chosen's hands into her own and said, "*Stat crux dum volvitur orbis*—the

Cross is steady while the world is turning."

The convent bells now rang for compline.

"Seek the interior. Be not vain. Failure is nothing; only sadly ceding to it is. Does that answer some of your questions?"

"Yes, Reverend Mother." Chosen swallowed nervously, hesitated. "I have only one further question. May I ask, please, when I may join the Order? I want to devote my life to Christ." So, it proved in the end, ironically, that the young woman was in the end still a tried-and-true daughter of New England, a Bostonian to the core, determined to opt for abstinence and, along with her spiritual vows of poverty, chastity, and obedience, to renounce self-indulgence. They both stood up. Mother Abbess said, "Come with me. Let us follow the bells."

Chosen elected to confide the good news, alone, to her great-aunts Aphra and Amity who made plans to travel by train to attend the ceremony—they who admired her bravery always hated anything that savored of compromise—but immediately, that very morning, they walked together to the Church of the Advent to offer their prayers and, with the vicar's assistance, sent a heartfelt telegram to Mother Abbess: "*Optimum partem elegi* Luke 10:42" (She has chosen the best part).

§

On the bright snowy morning of Candlemas Day, February 2nd, a day commemorating the Feast of the Purification of the Virgin Mary, under the protective nave of the small convent church, the beautiful young woman made her profession of vows in a holy ceremony of investiture for solemn admission into the Novitiate of the Cistercians of the Strict Observance. All in attendance got down *à genoux*, kneeling on the floor of hard stone, as a choir of shining-faced novices, filled with a spirit of grace, sang the blessed words to the lofty music of Palestrina's magnificent hymn,

Veni sponsa Christi, accipe coronam
quam tibi Dominus praeparavit in aeternum
pro cujus amore sanguinem tuum fudisti
et cum Angelis in paradisum introisti.
Veni, electa mea, et ponam in te thronum meum
quia concupivit Rex speciem tuam

(Come, bride of Christ, receive the crown
which the Lord has prepared for you for all eternity;
for whose love you have shed your blood.
And you will enter into the Paradise among the angels.
Come, O you my chosen one, and I will set my throne
    within you:
so shall the King have pleasure in your beauty.)